Thirty-Four
and a
Half Predicaments

A ROSE GARDNER MYSTERY

Books by Denise Grover Swank

Rose Gardner Mysteries
(Humorous Southern mysteries)
TWENTY-EIGHT AND A HALF WISHES
TWENTY-NINE AND A HALF REASONS
THIRTY AND A HALF EXCUSES
FALLING TO PIECES (novella)
THIRTY-ONE AND A HALF REGRETS
THIRTY-TWO AND A HALF COMPLICATIONS
PICKING UP THE PIECES (novella)
THIRTY-THREE AND A HALF SHENANIGANS
RIPPLE OF SECRETS (novella)
THIRTY-FOUR AND A HALF PREDICAMENTS

The Wedding Pact Series
(Romantic Comedy)
THE SUBSTITUTE
THE PLAYER (June 2015)
THE GAMBLER (September 2015)

Chosen Series
(Urban fantasy)
CHOSEN
HUNTED
SACRIFICE
REDEMPTION
CULLED (summer 2015)

On the Otherside Series
(Young adult science fiction/romance)
HERE
THERE

Curse Keepers
(Adult urban fantasy)
THE CURSE KEEPERS
THE CURSE BREAKERS
THE CURSE DEFIERS

New Adult Contemporary Romance
AFTER MATH
REDESIGNED
BUSINESS AS USUAL

Thirty-Four
and a
Half Predicaments

A ROSE GARDNER MYSTERY

Denise Grover Swank

This book is a work of fiction. References to real people, events, establishments, organizations, or locations are intended only to provide a sense of authenticity, and are used fictitiously. All other characters, and all incidents and dialogue, are drawn from the author's imagination and are not to be construed as real.

To my editor, Angela Polidoro
You're my safety net for this crazy tightrope walk.

Chapter One

Cold late January rain beat against the windows of the RBW Landscaping office on a Tuesday morning, and I shoved my hands deeper into my sweater. This weather had to let up soon—I wasn't sure how much more of it I could take. Especially since so many other things in my life were such a mess.

"Aren't you the cutest little thing?" Bruce Wayne, my friend and business partner, asked, looking down at my dog. Muffy jumped up and rested her paws on his knees, convincing him to give her a piece of his biscuit. He complied, of course. "How could I refuse that face?"

I loved my dog more than nearly anything else in the world, but I wouldn't necessarily call her a cute little thing at the moment. At Violet's suggestion, I'd taken her to the groomer's, and the woman had tsked the moment I handed her over. Not that I was surprised. With her big ears and pointy nose, her gray and brown wiry hair, Muffy was never going to win any "cutest dog" awards. The groomer had attempted to beautify her anyway. When I stopped to pick her up before coming into the office, Muffy had emerged from the back with pink bows on her ears and a white lace elasticized collar that made her look like she belonged in a clown act at the circus. But every time I tried to remove them, she would release a low growl and run away. "Don't encourage her, Bruce Wayne."

"She's cute." Bruce Wayne was probably the only other person alive who appreciated Muffy's special charm. He gave her the last of his biscuit and looked up at me. "Is Neely Kate coming in today?"

"I don't know," I sighed. "The doctor's cleared her to drive, but she only leaves the house if someone forces her. All she does is sit on her sofa and watch TV."

"She ain't worked here long, but I miss 'er."

"Me too." I looked at my computer screen and the landscape design I'd come up with using our new design software. There wasn't much call for landscaping in January, even in southern Arkansas, so Bruce Wayne and I were taking advantage of the down time.

The door opened and cold air seeped in as Jonah Pruitt, Henryetta's own televangelist, walked in.

"Jonah," I said in surprise, jumping out of my seat. "What are you doing here?"

He walked toward me with a grim expression. "I've just come back from visiting Neely Kate." He unbuttoned his coat. "Ronnie asked me to stop by and talk to her." He glanced at the other side of the room. "Hey, Bruce Wayne." Then Muffy ran out from under Bruce Wayne's desk and Jonah's eyes widened to the size of plums. "What on earth…"

Muffy stopped in front of Jonah and stood on her back legs.

I put my hands on my hips and laughed at my little dog's antics. "Apparently, Muffy thinks she's joining the circus."

Then, as the finale to her performance, she let out a plume of gas that made my eyes water. "Muffy!"

Jonah began to cough and wave his hand frantically in front of his face. "Oh, Sweet Baby Jesus."

I stalked over to the front door and started to swing it back and forth, trying to dispel the fumes. "Bruce Wayne! Stop feeding her biscuits!"

He laughed and grabbed his coat. "How about I take her out back and see if she has to go."

Like that was going to help. Every time I tried a new dog food or routine, her flatulence problem only seemed grow worse. At this rate, I was going to have to hand out gas masks to anyone who visited the office.

Muffy began to dance in circles when she saw Bruce Wayne grab her leash off my desk. As they went out the back door, I shut the front and returned my attention to Jonah.

"How'd it go with Neely Kate? Did she talk to *you?*"

"Other than the pleasantries of playing hostess, no."

I pressed my knuckle to my teeth. "I'm worried about her, Jonah. Really worried."

"So am I."

I ushered him over to the overstuffed chairs in front of the window and sank into the nearest one. "What can we do?"

"She needs to talk about losing her babies. She's keeping it all bottled up and it's festering inside her." He paused. "But mostly she needs time. Time to deal with her loss and to find a way to accept it."

I shook my head, tears filling my eyes. "*I* can barely accept what happened, so how on earth can she?"

"She'll find her own way."

I wasn't so sure. My best friend, who was always so boisterous and loud and fun-loving, seemed deflated, like a balloon after all the air had been let out.

"In the meantime, don't let her push you away. Keep going over and spending time with her. Try to get her out of the house." He glanced over his shoulder out the window. "Although today's not the best day to be out and about."

"There has to be something more we can do, Jonah."

He shook his head. "Neely Kate needs lots of time and lots of love."

I nodded. I wasn't the most patient person, but I loved that girl like she was my own sister. The loving part wouldn't be hard. "I'm goin' to see her this afternoon after I talk to Violet about her interviews for help at the nursery."

He smiled. "Good. She'll be glad to see you, even if she doesn't act like it." He cast a glance toward the back door, making sure Bruce Wayne was still outside. "You and I haven't had a meeting in over a month," he asked in an undertone. "How are *you* doing?"

I tucked my feet underneath me. "I'm sure this isn't what you're askin', but I'm perpetually cold. I'm dealing with two furnaces that can barely keep up—both here and at home. The landlord keeps doin' patch jobs on this one rather than getting us a new unit, and I can't afford to replace the one at the farmhouse."

Jonah gave me a pointed look and started to say something, but I held up my hand.

"No, I won't let Mason pay for it. And yes, he's offered a half dozen times."

"Rose…"

I leaned closer, lowering my voice. "He's paying for all our living expenses. Shoot, I'm so broke he had to give me money for gas this morning."

Worry filled his eyes. "Maybe you shouldn't hire someone to help out at the nursery."

I shook my head. "No, the nursery is actually bringing in money. Thankfully, the town's overlooked Violet and Brody MacIntosh's affair, and they're flocking to it, even in January. Violet's carrying more home décor items, and now she's offering home decorating services. We need someone to cover for her when she's gone." This new part of the business had been a lucky accident—much like how the landscaping portion of our business had fallen into our laps months ago. One of Violet's friends had asked her opinion on which of several items would look better in her house, and by the end of the week, Violet had three appointments to go to homes for consultations.

"And you can't cover the shop?"

I squirmed in my seat. "Yes…but it's busy enough that we can justify hiring someone. We figured we'd be able to train the new person before RBW Landscaping gets busy in the spring and I won't be able to help at all."

He pressed his lips together but didn't say anything.

I scowled. "I know that look, Jonah Pruitt, and no, this is not an instance of me avoiding my sister. I've already filled in several times."

A grin tugged at the corners of his lips. "I didn't say a word."

"You didn't have to."

"But isn't the fact that it was the first thing to jump into your mind a telling sign?"

I groaned and gripped the arm of my chair.

He leaned forward and patted my hand. "Rose, you've made tremendous progress. Sometimes you just have to deal with the issues as they come."

My head began to tingle and my peripheral vision faded. I very well knew what that meant. Ever since I was a little girl, I've had visions. They always show me a moment from the future of the person next to me, seen through their eyes.

This time, I found myself in Jonah's office, sitting in his chair. A man I'd never seen sat in a chair in front of Jonah's desk. He was middle-aged with a slight pouch on his belly. His hair was light brown and his cheeks were as rosy as Santa Claus's.

The man leaned forward, his fingers drumming nervously on the arm of his chair, and stared at me with eyes full of desperation. "Do you take confessions?"

My mouth dropped open. "Well, I'm not a Catholic priest who can give you absolution."

He shook his head and stood. "This was a bad idea. I'm tellin' ya, there's trouble afoot in this town and it's about to get worse."

The vision faded and I blurted out, "There's trouble afoot and it's gettin' worse." Just another side effect to my "gift"—I always blurted out part of what I saw. Sometimes it got me in trouble, but Jonah was one of the handful of people who knew about my visions.

"There's always trouble afoot in your life," he said with a smile, "but judging from the vacant look you just had, I suspect you had a vision. Of me."

"Yes." I told him what I'd seen, including a description of the man. "Do you know who he is? I didn't recognize him."

"No, but the description is generic enough it could fit a lot of men. I suspect the important part is the message he gave me. Do you know of any trouble?"

"Hilary's pregnant with Joe's baby and he won't marry her; Neely Kate lost her own babies; someone tried to kill Mason; I'm broke and my furnaces are about to die. There's all kinds of trouble afoot."

He laughed. "Yes, but I doubt any of those examples explain the mystery gentleman in my office."

"True." I doubted we were going to find an answer right now, so I forced a grin. "Enough about that. I want to hear about your new girlfriend. How's it going with you and Jessica?"

A blush rose on his cheeks. "It's the same as the last time you asked, thank you. And I can recognize a deflection when I see one."

I laughed. "Can't blame a girl for tryin'."

"Have you talked to Joe lately?"

My smile fell. I hadn't talked to Joe since that awful day in the hospital—two weeks ago now. I'd stayed away on purpose. It unsettled me, but when I thought of the man who'd been so strong and supportive and gentle that day, I saw Joe McAllister, the man I'd fallen in love with, not Joe Simmons. "No. Did you know his sister has been spending time in Henryetta?"

"Joe has a sister?"

"Kate. I'm sure you'd remember her if you saw her. She has a short dark bob with blue streaks."

And suddenly I had an idea how to cheer Neely Kate up. I pulled my cell phone out of my pocket.

"No. I haven't seen her around. Is she staying with Joe or Hilary?"

"No. She doesn't get along with Hilary and Joe's only just moved out to the farm south of me."

"Strange."

"I know," I mumbled, but my attention was elsewhere. I pulled up the number for the Nip and Clip Salon.

"Just a minute," I told Jonah before putting the call through.

"Hello, Beulah?" I said when the owner answered. "I'd like to make an appointment for Neely Kate Colson this afternoon to get colored streaks in her hair."

"That poor girl," Beulah said, then tsked. "How's she doin'?"

"She's hangin' in there. Do you have an opening this afternoon?"

"I can squeeze her in at two. Will that work?"

"We'll be there." I hung up and looked up the shocked minister, which I found ironic since he obviously had regular appointments to get his own highlights touched up. "What? She's mentioned several times that she wants them and I've done my best to talk her out of them. But why not? If Neely Kate wants to dye her hair purple with yellow polka dots, I'm gonna be there to help her pick out the right shade."

He smiled. "Neely Kate's lucky to have you as a friend."

I wasn't so sure about that. The last two weeks I felt like I'd failed her miserably.

But that was about to change.

Chapter Two

A fter my chat with Jonah, I couldn't concentrate on the design program, so I left Muffy with Bruce Wayne and headed over to the nursery.

Violet was talking to a customer when I walked in the store, but she pointed me toward a card table she'd set up in the back. I stopped short of it, my stomach a bundle of nerves. The folding chair reminded me too much of the day after Thanksgiving when Violet and Joe had ganged up on me to tell me Joe had saved our business. Violet had mismanaged our nursery so badly that we were about to lose it all, especially after a big bank deposit had been stolen from me in a bank robbery. I'd gotten the money back in time—although in the process I'd dug the first shovelful of a very deep pit I was now in with Skeeter Malcolm, king of the Fenton County crime world, in my attempts to get it back. But it had been all for naught. Joe had helped Violet and me prepare the nursery for its first opening, and Violet had played on Joe's previous involvement with the business, not to mention his hopes to win me back, to secure his help. Joe had paid off our entire bank loan and there was no way to pay him back. I was stuck with my ex-boyfriend as my business partner.

That very same day Hilary Wilder, Joe's ex-girlfriend many times over, had waltzed in to announce she was pregnant with Joe's baby. Nearly two months later, I'd gotten over the fact that Joe had put money into our business without my permission, but I still hadn't gotten over Hilary's bombshell. Maybe it was because when we were together he'd sworn to me time and time again he was done with her…yet he'd run right out my door and into her arms. I knew that wasn't entirely true—he'd waited several weeks—but it made me question everything we'd shared.

It didn't matter anyway. Now I was with Mason. And what Joe needed most now was love and support from friends. I shook off the old memories and hurts.

The bell on the door dinged as the customer left.

"How many people did you interview?" I asked, looking over the folders on the table.

Violet walked over to me. "Three. All were great applicants on paper, but the interviews really helped."

I watched Violet closely, looking for any sign that she resented my insistence on providing my input. Thankfully, I found none. "Do you have a favorite?"

She opened one of the folders. "I do, actually. Anna Miller. She's in her early thirties and she just moved to Henryetta. She has retail experience."

I looked at her work history on her application. "She moved to Henryetta? This town is like Alcatraz—everyone one wants out, not in, and it's pretty much inescapable." I shook my head. "Does she have family here?"

"No, and when I asked her why she'd moved here, she was evasive."

I glanced up at my sister. "Maybe she's just a private person."

"Could be…"

"You think there's more there?"

"I don't know, but I'd still like to hire her. She's a sweet girl and I like her enthusiasm. The other two applicants didn't seem to want it as much."

I slid the folder back to her. "And she knows it's only part-time to start?"

"Yeah, although she's hoping to work full-time soon."

"If you like her, then you should hire her. She'll probably be great."

Violet gathered the folders together. "That was easy. I thought you'd ask a lot more questions."

"I'm not trying to make things difficult for you. I just think it's best if I'm a little more hands-on for now."

She stood and headed to the counter. "I understand." But her tone suggested otherwise.

My head tingled again, and though the last thing I wanted right now was to be sucked into a vision, I tried not to resist it. I'd learned from experience it was pointless.

I was in the shop, humming.

A pretty African-American woman emerged from the back room, a soft smile warming up her deep brown eyes. She wore a Gardner Sisters Nursery apron over a burgundy shirt and jeans. "I think we're all ready for Valentine's Day."

"You're a natural, Anna," I said in Violet's voice. "You're a blessing sent from heaven. It's like you literally just dropped out of nowhere."

The vision ended and I said, "Anna's a blessing sent from heaven."

Violet's eyes widened. "What?"

Though I could have explained the vision to her, there was no real point. It hadn't told me anything important or pressing. I sighed and followed her. "I think Anna will be great. When do you want her to start?"

"Don't you think we should discuss it with Joe first?"

"I thought you said Joe doesn't care."

"He *is* part owner."

"I don't want to discuss it with Joe. I'm majority owner and I say it's fine. But if you feel the need, go ahead and run it by him."

She gave me a pointed glance. "You have to talk to him, Rose. You're acting childish." She was quiet for a moment. "You haven't spoken to him since the day Neely Kate lost her babies, have you?"

I didn't answer. What did it matter to her?

"How's Neely Kate doin'?"

"Not so great, but I have a special surprise planned for her this afternoon."

"That's good. Just give her lots of love." Tears filled her eyes. "Your love was the best medicine when it happened to me."

I pulled my sister into a hug. "Sometimes I forget you lost a baby right after you and Mike were married. How'd you survive it?" After my own baby scare and the surprising disappointment I'd felt after finding out I wasn't pregnant, I couldn't imagine losing a baby I'd planned for and wanted from before its conception.

She gave me a soft smile. "It helped knowing I was loved."

"Is it hard to think about how happy you once were after everything that's happened?"

Her eyes filled with sadness. "I have to believe everything will work out for the best." She forced a smile. "Besides, I have Ashley and Mikey now. Neely Kate will have other babies." She grabbed my hand, worry wrinkling her forehead. "But don't be telling her that. Too many well-meaning people say things like that and it hurts more than it helps."

I shook my head. "I won't."

"Just be yourself. That's the best you can offer her."

"Thanks." I headed out to my truck and glanced at my phone, seeing I had a missed call and a text from Mason.

Sorry I couldn't get away to meet you for lunch, but I can spend a few minutes with you this afternoon if you get a chance. I smiled and texted: *Lucky you. I have about fifteen minutes to spare.*

I drove back downtown and parked halfway between the courthouse and Dena's Bakery, the new competition to Ima Jean's Bakery. Ima Jean's was a Henryetta institution. Rumor had it her bakery had been open since the town's incorporation in 1865. I wasn't so sure about that, but her baked goods certainly tasted old enough to have been prepared for the grand opening. Dena, on the other hand, had a knack for creating delicious treats. I knew for a fact that Neely Kate loved her strawberry cupcakes, and since Mason had a weakness for pie, I figured I could kill two birds with one stone.

Dena greeted me as soon as I walked into the bakery, glancing up with a smile as she packaged a cupcake for the man at her counter. He had thinning gray hair and wore dress pants and a white dress shirt. I was pretty sure I'd seen him at the courthouse before while visiting Mason or Neely Kate, back when she still worked there. He cast a baleful glance at me as I let the chilly January air inside, then turned back to the case.

Another customer was waiting at the counter. She wore a heavy cable knit sweater over a shirt stretched over her middle-aged spread. Dark circles under her eyes suggested she was exhausted. Dena took two boxes to the register and let out a big sigh. "Thanks for waiting, Marta. If I stay this busy, I'm gonna have to hire some help."

"That's a good problem to have, isn't it?" the woman asked, but she didn't sound happy about it.

"That it is." Dena rang up both of the customers. The woman took her box to one of the few small tables in the back, and the man bustled out of the shop so fast, I was surprised the door didn't hit him on his rear.

"Rose! How're you doin'?" Dena asked as I walked up to the counter, occupying the space they had just left.

I perused the glass case. "If you have any of your strawberry cupcakes left, I'll be great."

"It's your lucky day. There are two of 'em."

"I want them both. And a chocolate caramel one too. And a piece of apple pie."

Dena laughed. "I hope you're not eating all this yourself, or you're gonna have to do some serious workouts."

I grinned. "The cupcakes are for Neely Kate and the pie's for Mason. So if you could box them up separately…"

"Not a problem," she said, grabbing a box for the cupcakes.

"So, business is good, huh?" I asked. "Every time I come in, you just get busier." It wasn't hard to figure out why. In addition to selling food that was actually good, Dena's bakery had a cozy atmosphere. While it was small, it had lots of charm—from the soft pastel swirls painted on the white walls like decorator frosting to the kitschy ceramic cookie jars lined up on the shelf behind the counter. The interior of Ima Jean's shop looked about as ancient as her baked goods tasted.

"Most of my customers are under the age of forty-five." She shrugged. "Everyone over that age still goes to Ima Jean's. I think they're afraid not to. I've had a couple of people tell me they came here the first time because she was so rude to them, but they keep coming back because the food's better than hers."

"I'm not surprised about either part of that statement." I'd had more than my share of tongue-lashings from Ima Jean both in the bakery and out. Most of the town had tolerated her rudeness because they didn't have a choice, and I suspected the ones who continued to go to her shop only did so because they hated change. That, or they were afraid of her.

Dena folded the lid of the cupcake box and tucked it in. "Momma says she wasn't always like this. She used to be the sweetest woman in town."

"Really?" I tried to hide my surprise. I'd always suspected some of her crankiness came from being older, kind of like Miss Mildred, my former neighbor. Even though she owned a bakery, I never once suspected she'd ever been sweet.

"My momma says she changed after her husband's business went under about twenty-five years ago."

"I thought her husband died about twenty-five years ago."

She leaned over the top of the case. "Rumor has it he committed suicide after losing the business."

"Oh dear." That was bound to make someone cranky, and I felt a little bad for thinking ill of Ima Jean.

Dena started to box up Mason's pie. "Momma says it was a huge scandal. He was caught havin' an affair, then there was a mysterious fire at his warehouse. For some reason, he announced he wasn't gonna rebuild and a week or so later he hung himself in his basement."

I gasped, my hand resting at the base of my throat. "Oh, my goodness! That's horrible."

She shook her head, a knowing look in her eyes. "Momma says she was never the same."

I couldn't say I blamed her. I couldn't even imagine living through something like that.

Dena looked behind me and I glanced over my shoulder to see Marta shooting me a glare, although for the life of me, I couldn't figure out why. Maybe she didn't like that we were gossiping. I noticed there was another, younger girl in the seating area too, but she seemed to be much more focused on her cell phone than our conversation.

As soon as she finished fussing with the boxes, Dena rang up my order. I dug the spare change out of my purse and handed it over to her, suddenly wondering how I was going to pay for Neely Kate's hair appointment. I'd never been this broke before, and though I knew it was temporary, it scared the bejiggers out of me. I wondered if I should get my own part-time job to help fill my pockets for the next month or two.

"Thanks, Dena," I said as I headed for the door.

"Come back soon, Rose."

I held up the bag. "No worries there!"

It took no more than a couple of minutes for me to walk to the courthouse. The security guard on duty was an elderly man who loved to tease me whenever I came to visit Mason.

"You brought me a piece of pie, Rose?"

I laughed. "You know darn good and well whose pie that is."

He chuckled. "I bet Mr. Deveraux didn't know he was gonna get fed so well when he started dating you."

"I've got to think of some way to convince him to keep me around," I teased as I walked through the security sensor.

He shook his head, his eyes dancing with merriment. "I'm certain he doesn't need much convincin'."

When I walked into Mason's office, his secretary, Kaylee, glanced up and a smile spread across her face. "Rose. Mr. Deveraux is expecting you, but he got called away for a few minutes. He said to tell you to go on into his office."

"Thanks."

Multiple files were scattered across his desk, making it look messier than usual. I didn't want to put his pie on any of the folders, and I certainly didn't want to move anything, so I set the bag on the window ledge and took in the view of the square. Thankfully the rain had let up and the sun was peeking through the clouds, which surely had to be good for Neely Kate's disposition.

I was going to have to ask Mason to loan me money and that burned my gut like I'd been stabbed with a white-hot poker. I knew he wouldn't mind. In fact, he'd be more than willing to help. But I hated to think I was about to be *that* girlfriend.

I moved back over to his desk and sat in his chair. My gaze drifted over the folders again, and a name on one of the tabs caught my eye. I leaned forward and gasped.

Dora Middleton.

Mason had a file on my birth mother.

Chapter Three

Mason was keeping secrets from me. A surge of anger rose in my chest, but I quickly stomped it down. This was an official file. Mason kept a file on J.R. locked in the desk drawer at home. That case was private. This file was mixed in with all his others, which meant it was probably official business in some way. He'd made it clear to me that he couldn't share confidential information with me, which I understood well enough. The question was why did he have a file on my birth mother? Was it about the car accident that had killed her?

I cast a quick glance toward the door. Kaylee was sitting at her desk, her back to me. I knew what I was about to do was wrong. It was a breach of trust between Mason and me. But a file with information about Dora was *right there* in front of me. What was I supposed to do? Just let it sit there?

I quickly slid the manila folder off the desk and spun Mason's chair around so I had my back to the door, hoping it would keep Kaylee from realizing what I was doing. Holding my breath, I opened the file, but I instantly realized there was very little information inside. He'd found a photo of her somewhere—it looked like an employee ID photo—and paper-clipped it to the front flap of the folder. She was staring at the camera with a serious expression on her face. I had no idea when the photo had been taken, but her hairstyle and youthful appearance led me to believe it had been taken a few years before my birth.

A yellow legal pad sheet was in the folder, covered in Mason's neat handwriting. That surprised me. He kept most of his case notes in files on his computer. And anything he needed a hard copy of was printed out. This didn't look like an official file after all, which helped me feel less guilty when I picked up the paper and started to read.

Dora Colleen Middleton, died December 10, 1986

Born in Shreveport, LA on March 13, 1960. Parents Ned and Barbara Middleton, Shreveport. Parents died when she was five. Raised by maternal grandparents John and Rose Forester, Fenton County.

Attended Eastern Fenton County High School

Fenton County Community College 1978-1981

Moved to Shreveport 1981-1983 employment unknown

Employed by Atchison Manufacturing February 1983-September 1986

Employed by Pierce Construction September 1986-December 1986 (death)

Small life insurance policy ($25,000)

Farm and small inheritance from grandparents went to Rose (approximate worth $200,000 at time of death)

Seeing Harrison Gardner from ??? until death

One known child, Rose Anne Gardner November 8, 1986

No known living relatives

Part of possible extortion scheme in the summer of 1986

I gasped. Extortion? What did that mean? Had she been extorted or had she been the one doing the extorting?

Mason's secretary's voice shook me out of my stupor. "Hi, Mr. Deveraux. Rose is waiting in your office for you."

"Thanks, Kaylee."

My head was still whirling from shock, but I gathered my senses enough to slap the folder shut. I spun around in the chair and slipped the file under another one. It looked innocuous enough, but fear made my heart stutter as Mason's broad shoulders filled the doorway. Had he seen me?

A smile spread across his face, mischievousness filling his eyes. "You look like you belong in that chair, Ms. Gardner."

I laughed nervously, thankful my covert actions appeared to have gone undetected. "I won't be fightin' you for it, if that's what you're worried about." I gave him a mischievous grin of my own. "I have something for you."

"Kaylee, hold my calls," he said as he shut the door and moved toward me.

A warm flutter replaced my nervousness. Mason Deveraux was a strikingly handsome man. Before I snatched him off the market, he was considered the second most eligible bachelor in Fenton County, after Brody MacIntosh, the Henryetta mayor. Staring into his hazel eyes and his gorgeous face framed by dark blond hair, which was currently in need of a trim, I had to wonder why they hadn't pegged him as first. Even now, months into our relationship, he still took my breath away, reminding me that I trusted this man. It took away some of the sting that he was so obviously withholding information about Dora from me. "From the look in your eyes, I suspect you're going to be disappointed."

He placed his hands on the arms of his chair and leaned over, his face inches from mine. "If it's from you, never."

I gave him a soft kiss, then murmured against his lips, "This isn't it."

He kissed me again before he lifted his head. "I suspected as much. But it's a good substitute for now."

I pushed on his chest and he captured one of my hands in his, pulling me up with him. "So what's this surprise you brought me?"

I walked over to the window. The partially obscured file on Mason's desk caught my eye and I considered pulling it out and confronting him now, but I still felt caught off-guard. It would be wiser to sit on the information for a spell so I could think of the best way to broach the topic. I picked up the pastry bag instead.

"Do I see Dena's Bakery on that bag?"

I laughed. "Nothing gets by you, Mr. Assistant DA." I pulled out the cardboard box and a plastic fork. "Not even apple crisp pie."

"You sure know how to spoil me, Rose," he murmured as he took the pie from me and sat down at his desk. He opened the box and grinned.

I carefully sat on the edge of his desk, trying not to disturb his papers. "Actually, I'm trying to butter you up."

Something in my tone caught his attention and he looked up, worry in his eyes. "Why?"

I glanced down at my lap. Oh, crappy doodles, this was hard. It would have been hard to ask him for money at any time, and it was even more so now. Why hadn't he told me he was investigating Dora? But I wasn't ready to let him know what I'd seen, so I forced myself to focus on my original task. I took a deep breath and looked up into his face. "I just gave Violet approval to hire someone to help her at the shop. I think she'll start soon."

His eyebrows lifted in a hopeful expression. "That's a good thing, right? The shop's busy enough to warrant hiring her."

"Yes, of course." I glanced down at his desk again. *Out with it.* Squaring my shoulders, I faced him again. "But the shop is the only thing making money right now, and I'm sinking it all back into the business. I'm currently *losing* money with the landscaping business." I shook my head slowly. "Maybe I was too hasty decidin' to open it this soon."

He put his container on his desk and leaned forward, snagging my hands in his. "Rose. You knew it wouldn't make money at first. Especially in the winter. But come spring, I'm sure you'll have more than enough business to keep you busy *and* afloat. Where's this coming from?"

Tears burned my eyes. "I'm broke, Mason. The truth is, I scraped together the last of my money to buy you that pie and Neely Kate a few cupcakes. I'm twenty-five years old and I don't have a penny to my name."

He stood and pulled me into his arms, my cheek resting against his chest. "Sweetheart, you're far from broke. You're currently cash poor with no easily accessible liquid assets. There's a difference."

"It doesn't feel like it at the moment. I can finally shop at the Piggly Wiggly now, but I can't even go in there and buy something to make dinner."

"Of course you can. I've been chipping in with grocery money."

I pulled back and looked into his face. "No, you've been outright payin' for the groceries."

A soft smile lit up his face. "And I've been eating them too. Hell, I eat way more than you do. Why shouldn't I be paying?"

I closed my eyes and shook my head. "I know. It's just…"

His hand cupped my cheek and tilted my head up to look into his eyes. "I know how important it is for you to feel independent. Even though we're together. And trust me, I love that you're not a clinging, helpless woman." He leaned closer, his voice dropping. "I've made no secret of the fact I want to marry you someday. I'm as sure of that as I am that Miss Mildred will be calling in a new neighborhood watch complaint on some pour soul within the next couple of days." He grinned. "When we're married, I hope you won't insist on keeping our money separate."

"No, of course not." Honestly, I hadn't considered it, but as soon as he said it I knew I would want to share everything with him, including money.

He paused, seeming to think through his next words before saying them. "You love me, right?"

"How can you even ask that? You know I do."

"Do you plan on breaking up with me in the near future?"

I was about to lambast him, but I saw the teasing gleam in his eyes. I gave him an ornery grin and tilted my head. "I'm still weighing my options."

He laughed. "Then I guess I need to step up my game." He pressed his lips to mine, his kiss full of passion and fire, leaving me breathless and wanting. "Does that help sway you?"

"I forgot the question." He laughed again, a rich, warm sound that filled me with happiness and contentment. "No, Mason. I have no *current* plans to break up with you."

His grin lit up his eyes. "Keeping me on my toes. I always knew you were a smart woman." But then his expression turned more serious. "I have no plans of going anywhere, and we both see marriage in our future. Why don't we take a test drive, so to speak?"

My playfulness slipped away. "What does that mean?"

His arms tightened around me. "I'd like to open a joint bank account."

"Why?"

"Then it's *our* money. Not yours and mine."

"But I don't have any money to put in it."

"You don't right now. But you will this spring." He sensed my hesitation and pushed on. "We can keep our separate checking accounts, but agree to put in, say…two thousand a month. Enough to pay the utilities, the groceries, eating out, and so on."

I tried to pull loose from him, but he held me close. "I don't know."

"That's all money we spend on *us*, right?" he asked.

"Well, yeah..."

"So we fund it every month. We'll make the contributions based on percentages of the previous month's gross income."

"That means you'll be funding it all."

His eyes lit up. "This month. And probably for another month or so." His grin turned wicked. "But soon the nursery and the landscaping company will be busting at the seams with business and you'll be making twice as much as me. Then you'll be the majority funder."

I patted his chest and laughed. "So this is all part of some devious long-range scheme for *you* to live off *me*."

"Dammit, you caught me."

I knew he was teasing, and I also recognized this for what it was: his attempt to give me money without making me feel bad about it. It only made me love him more. "Okay."

"Okay? *Really?*"

I tilted my head. "You're very convincing. I can see why you placed third at state in debate in high school."

A mock-serious look filled his eyes. "It was second."

I wrapped my arms around his neck and kissed him. Sweet moments like this one made me believe that everything would work out. That J.R. Simmons would destroy his false blackmail charges against me. That Skeeter Malcolm would drop his claim on me as the Lady in Black. That Mason would never find out about my secret life and we'd get married and have kids and live at the farmhouse until we were ninety-five, spending our days on the front porch watching our great-grandkids play while we drank iced tea.

His hold on me tightened and one of his hands slid down to my butt. "You do get me stirred up." He groaned as he moved his hand back up to my waist and leaned down to kiss me softly. "In a couple of months, we need a vacation. Just you and me. Alone."

"I like the sound of that."

He kissed me again. "Or if you feel like roughing it a little, we could borrow my uncle's cabin up in the Ozarks and bring Muffy with us so you won't miss her so much."

I leaned back. "You would do that?"

"Of course. She's special to you. And I've grown pretty fond of her myself."

Mason always knew just what to say to grow my heart two sizes. "I love you."

He gave me another gentle kiss before dropping his hold. "I love you too. Now help me eat this pie."

"I can't. I need to get goin'. I made an appointment at the Nip and Clip for Neely Kate to get her hair colored with streaks."

His eyes widened. "Do I want to know?"

I smiled. "She'd been talkin' about it for weeks and I kept telling her it was a bad idea." I shook my head. "Why was I so judgmental? That's not like me." Then a new fear hit me. "Is it?"

He sighed and rubbed my arm. "Of course not. You're one of the most accepting people I know. But we both know Neely Kate can be impulsive. You were being a good friend by encouraging her to think it through."

No, I'd flat out told her not to do it. There was a difference, but pointing it out wouldn't help anything. "Well, I made the appointment, but she doesn't know yet. I'm gonna surprise her and hope it cheers her up a little bit."

"I think it's great idea. And even if she doesn't get excited in her usual manner, I'm sure she'll appreciate it. When I talked to Ronnie this morning, he said she's just as desolate as she was the day they came home from the hospital two weeks ago."

"You talked to Ronnie?" I asked in surprise.

"Yeah..." He paused. "We're friends, and I'm as worried about him as I am about Neely Kate. Ronnie's beside himself."

"Oh." Now I really felt awful. I'd never even considered how Ronnie was handling it all. "How's he doin'?"

"He's upset about losing the babies, of course. But he's more worried about his wife."

"Oh. Poor Ronnie."

"Maybe you could take Neely Kate on another girls' trip."

I lifted my eyebrows and said in a mocking tone, "Because the last one went so well."

"Neely Kate loved every minute of it. Maybe she needs an adventure."

"Maybe." I felt so inadequate to help her, but it didn't mean I was about to stop trying. "I'll try to talk her into it."

"Good."

I gave him a sly grin. "You seem a little too eager to get rid of me."

"I'll miss you every second you're gone, so my suggestion only proves how much I care about Neely Kate."

I rested my hands on his chest and reached up to kiss him. "You're an amazing man, Mason Deveraux."

He grinned. "I know. I keep telling you that."

I laughed. "You're awful."

"I'm amazing *and* awful. I'm glad you love me anyway."

I lifted my eyebrows. "Good thing for you," I stepped away from him and picked up the bakery bag, "I need to head over to Neely Kate's. Her appointment is at two, and she probably needs to get dressed."

Mason reached into his pocket and pulled out his wallet. "Here, take this with you." He handed me several twenties and his credit card.

I reluctantly reached for it, my face burning with shame.

"Rose."

I looked up into his face.

He placed the money and the card in my hand and curled his fingers around mine. "I know how hard this is for you. But you know I'd do anything for you. And if it helps, consider it this way: this is my gift to Neely Kate." Then he handed me his car keys. "Why don't you take my car? It will be easier for Neely Kate to get in and out of it than your truck would be."

"Thank you."

"You're welcome. Now go try to cheer up our friend."

Chapter Four

As I knocked on Neely Kate's front door, I suddenly felt unsure about my plan. What if she hated it?

She answered the door wearing a pair of gray yoga pants, a stained white T-shirt, and a pair of white socks. Her face was clean of makeup and her hair was flat and lifeless. She looked like a shadow of her normal self and my heart broke all over again. I forced myself to sound cheerful even though I wanted to cry for her.

"Hey, Neely Kate. What are you up to?"

"Nothin'."

"I have a couple of surprises for you." I held up the bakery bag.

She looked down at my feet. "Thanks. I'm not really hungry."

"Can I come in anyway?"

For a second I thought she might actually refuse me, but she took a step back and let me in.

A soap opera was playing on her television when I followed her into the living room. She sat on her sofa and pulled a red knit afghan over her legs.

"How are you feeling today?" I asked as I sat in the chair next to her, even though the answer was obvious.

"Fine."

"Have you driven yet?"

"No. I've got nowhere to go."

"Well, you know Bruce Wayne and I are eager for you to come back to work when you feel up to it."

She remained silent.

"Violet's hiring a new girl to help her—Anna. Violet says she has a mysterious past."

It was an exaggeration, but she loved hearing gossip, so I'd hoped to get some reaction out of her. Instead, she remained stoic. "That's nice."

Neely Kate had known exactly how to comfort me after my breakup with Joe. She'd come over with the first season of *Grey's Anatomy* on DVD and two containers of Ben and Jerry's. But breaking up with a boyfriend, no matter how earth-shattering it felt, couldn't begin to compare with a miscarriage. I felt helpless and hopeless. I was failing my friend.

I moved onto the couch next to her and leaned my head on her shoulder, taking her hand in mine. "I love you, Neely Kate. I'll do anything I can to help you. What do you need me to do?"

Her shoulders began to shake and soon she was crying. I turned and wrapped my arms around her back, tears burning in my own eyes. She rested her cheek against my hair, sobs wracking her body. I hadn't seen her cry, *really* cry since coming out of surgery two weeks ago. And even though it killed me to see her like this, I just held her close and let her cry it out. I wanted to tell her it would be okay, but I wasn't sure it was true. The only thing I knew to do was hug her and let her know I was here. Through thick and thin.

But a part of me was filled with guilt. Could I have spared my best friend some of her pain? Neely Kate's grandmother's tea leaves had told her that she was having twins, but the ultrasound had only revealed one baby. The tech had missed her ectopic pregnancy. And that wasn't the only premonition her grandmother had made—she'd also foreseen Neely Kate losing her babies. Though she was notoriously wrong in her premonitions, my friend had begged me to have a vision to see if it was true. I'd dug in my feet, afraid to tell her if I really saw it happen. But what if I *had* foreseen it? Maybe I could have saved one of Neely Kate's babies. What if Neely Kate blamed me for her miscarriage?

She cried until I was sure she had to be dehydrated. After a time, her sobs softened and she sucked in deep breaths as I stroked her hair. Finally she sat up and looked at me with bloodshot eyes. "I killed my babies."

My mouth flopped open as if it were on a hinge. "What on earth would make you say that?"

"I got in that fight with Tabitha last month. And when we were in New Orleans I forgot to bring my prenatal vitamins."

"Neely Kate." I gently cupped her wet cheeks. "The doctor said there wasn't a doggone thing you could have done to change things. Nothin' you did could have caused an ectopic pregnancy."

She started to cry again. "But if I'd gone to the doctor sooner, I might have saved my other baby."

"The only pain you felt was that backache. And you were having terrible morning sickness, so of course you wouldn't have taken notice of any nausea." I fought back my own tears. "Oh, honey. You did everything right. You know that deep in your heart. It's downright awful not to have something to blame, but you didn't do one thing wrong."

"I have to blame something."

I offered her a weak smile. "Then we'll find you something to blame, just so long as it's not you."

The corners of her mouth lifted a twinge, but I'd take it as the first smile I'd seen since the morning of the nursery's open house. The day she'd lost her babies.

I wiped her tears off her cheeks. "I know you said you're not hungry, but the cupcakes aren't the only surprise I have for you."

"What is it?"

"It's not here. I have to take you to it."

"What is it?" she repeated.

The touch of curiosity in her voice gave me hope. "It wouldn't be a surprise if I told you, now would it? It's gonna be fun. But you're gonna see people, so if you want to change, you have some time to do that before we need to go."

She sighed. "I don't know if I feel like goin' out."

"I'm not takin' no for answer on this one. At least not until I take you there and you find out what it is."

A tiny bit of fire filled her eyes. "You're not gonna let this go until I give in, are you?"

"No."

"Fine," she heaved out as she slowly stood. "But I'm not changin'."

"That's fine. You wear whatever you want." I stood next to her, wanting to offer assistance but not wanting to upset her. "Do you still have pain from your incision?"

"Only if I move too fast."

"Then we'll go slow. Where's your purse?"

She shook her head. "I can leave it."

She was leaving her purse? Things were really bad. Neely Kate always had her purse with her, even when she went to check the mail. I worried walking around without it might throw off her balance, especially since it usually weighed a good ten pounds. "Then let's head into town."

I grabbed her keychain off the entry table and locked her front door while she climbed into Mason's car. I knew she wasn't herself when she didn't ask why we weren't taking my truck. As I drove us into town, I glanced over at her. "I brought the cupcakes in case you change your mind." I patted the bakery bag on the console between us. "They're Dena's. I got your favorites."

She grinned. "Are you tryin' to get me fat?"

"Yes. As big as a house."

She laughed. It was a small one, but I'd take it.

"So Violet's hiring someone?" she asked.

I told her what little I knew about Anna, and how I'd worried Violet would be irritated with me for taking a role in the hiring process.

She waved an unmanicured hand. "She's lucky you're lettin' her work there at all after the stunt she pulled."

"I know, but it's complicated."

"What's so complicated about misappropriatin' money?"

It was hard to argue with my bookkeeper.

She fell back into silence the rest of the way into town. I pulled into the closest open parking space near the Nip and Clip, but it was next to the landscaping office.

"Are you trickin' me into goin' to work?"

"Shoot, no. I promised you a fun afternoon. Although you do love workin' with that accounting program."

"Then where are we goin'? Because you have Dena's cupcakes sittin' right next to me, and I'm not feelin' inclined to go anywhere without them."

"Let's take them with us. I'll explain where we're goin' while we walk."

"Okay..." She sounded unsure, but she still got out of the car. I looped my arm through hers and we started walking slowly down the sidewalk.

"It's warmed up a little and the sun's come out," I said.

Neely Kate stopped and turned toward me. "Is this what we've resorted to? Talkin' about the *weather?*"

"I don't know what to say, Neely Kate," I said in a quiet voice. Every word I thought of seemed inadequate.

She sighed. "Just treat me like normal. Even if I'm anything but."

I cracked a grin. "You've *never* been normal. That's what I love about you."

A real smile spread across her face. "Then treat me like you always did."

"That's easy enough. And that means you should love my surprise." I led her to the beauty salon and stopped outside the door. "This is it."

She lifted her eyebrows and turned to me with a questioning look.

"I made an appointment with Beulah to get colored stripes in your hair."

"*What?*"

Oh dear. Maybe this had been a terrible idea after all. "You've been saying you wanted them—"

She threw her arms around my shoulders. "Thank you."

I hugged her back, careful not to crush the cupcakes. "I'm sorry I've been such a Negative Nelly about you getting them. If anyone can pull off this look, it's you. You're gonna be even more beautiful."

We walked into the shop and Beulah fawned all over Neely Kate, as did the other hairstylists, never once mentioning the miscarriage. Neely Kate decided on pink and purple for her colors, and I sat in the empty chair next to her. We ate her cupcakes while her hair sat in its foils. She was still quiet but she gave me a ghost of a smile when I teased her about looking like something out of a science fiction movie. A little over an hour later she sat in the hairdresser's chair, smiling at her reflection. Beulah had curled her long blond hair, and even though Neely Kate wasn't wearing makeup, she was beautiful.

I stood behind her, beaming. "I'm sorry for trying to talk you out of this. You look like a model."

Her smile was genuine, but it disappeared as soon as she glanced at her reflection.

I wrapped my arm around her shoulder, and looked into her eyes in the mirror, whispering, "Don't you feel one bit guilty for bein' happy, Neely Kate. You deserve it."

Tears filled her eyes and she forced a smile. "Thank you, Rose."

I gave her another squeeze and stood. "Come on. We're gonna show your new hair off all around town."

I followed Beulah to the register and gave her Mason's credit card. She ran it through without comment, but as I signed the slip, she glanced at the name and raised her eyebrows. "Is there something you're keeping from me?"

My heart leapt into my throat. What did she mean? Did she suspect I'd stolen Mason's card? Or maybe that I was taking advantage of him? But a smile spread across her face. "Girl, are you marrying Mason Deveraux?"

Neely Kate's head whipped around to look at me, her eyes wide with surprise.

I shook my head. "No. Nothing like that. At least not yet."

"But this…" Beulah waved the card at me, and my face burned with embarrassment.

"I think you two make a lovely couple." The voice behind me sent ice water through my veins.

I spun around and faced my least favorite redhead, although it was a very tight race with Deputy Abbie Lee Hoffstetter. "Hilary. I'm surprised to see you *here*."

She glanced around, then smiled at the stylist. "Why, everyone knows Beulah is a miracle worker. In fact, I've bragged about her so much, I have friends from Little Rock and El Dorado who come here to have Beulah her work her magic."

I stared at her in shock. While she'd moved to Henryetta to try to convince Joe to resume their volatile relationship, she'd made it perfectly clear that she considered the town equivalent to a third-world country. The fact that she would not only slum it by going to a Henryetta hair salon, but she'd tell her friends about it, was jaw-dropping. Although I had serious doubts she was capable of having friends.

"So are you and Mason Deveraux secretly engaged?" She grabbed my left hand. "Tell him to get you something simple. Probably a round solitaire, nothing too fancy—that wouldn't fit you at all. A third of a carat would be good."

Neely Kate put a hand on her hip as I jerked away from Hilary. "I don't think that's a good idea, considering *Joe* gave her a ring that looks exactly like that. Last I heard it's in her underwear drawer, just waiting for her to change her mind."

Hilary was still holding a fake smile in place, but it looked like the effort of holding it would give her a headache.

Neely Kate leaned closer. "Because we both know that Joe Simmons would marry her in a heartbeat. All she has to do is snap her fingers—" Neely Kate snapped hers, waving her arm with more sass than I'd seen her use in weeks, "—and he'd take her to the courthouse as soon as he could get her there. But then look at you, wearing an engagement ring you had to buy yourself because he'd rather set himself on fire than marry you."

Every woman in the salon was watching our exchange with open mouths. Beulah could have sold tickets at twenty dollars a pop and she would have sold out in thirty seconds flat. But as Neely Kate had pointed out when we were looking for her missing cousin a month ago, the hair salon was the absolute best place to get caught up with the town's gossip. And we sure were putting on a show.

Suddenly I realized something—rumors that I was playing both Joe and Mason were going to spread like wildfire. I grabbed my best friend's arm and tugged her back. "Neely Kate."

Hilary turned toward me, the look in her eyes saying she wanted nothing more than to stab me with a pair of hair scissors. "Were you engaged to Joe?"

I took a step back, the room closing in on me. No, it was the fifteen sets of eyes that were glued to me. "Not technically."

The women began to murmur.

"Not *technically?*"

"He proposed, but I never said yes."

I heard the bell on the door ring, signaling the arrival of yet another gawker.

"When?" Hilary forced out through gritted teeth. "When did Joe propose and give you the ring?"

"What does it matter, Hil-monster?" another familiar voice asked. "She's the one he wants to marry, not you. That's all you really need to know."

Hilary stepped back and shot a glare at Joe's sister, Kate, who grinned back like the Cheshire cat.

She'd shown up in town right after Christmas. Rumor had it she was taking up residence at the nicest motel Henryetta had to offer. I had no idea why, other than she seemed to be snooping around about anything that had to do with Joe. Violet, who had more contact with Joe than I did, said he was aggravated by his sister's sudden appearance and had very little to do with her. She'd been in the nursery when Neely Kate collapsed. And although she'd been antagonistic before the trauma, she'd insisted on riding to the hospital with us in Joe's sheriff's car. She'd even stuck around to try and make me feel better in the waiting room. I hadn't seen her since, but I'd heard she was still around.

Now Kate's gaze was locked on my face. "Do you still have Joe's ring?"

I started to answer, still in shock that this was happening, but then I came to my senses. What was Mason gonna think if he heard about this? "Neely Kate, we need to go." I pulled on her arm, but she refused to budge.

Kate turned to my friend and picked up several strands of her newly colored hair. "Looks good on you, N.K. I could never pull off pink."

Hilary put her hands on her hips, finally gathering herself enough to make a rebuttal. "What are you doing here, Kate? Are you following me again?"

Kate shrugged. "It's a small town. I can't help it if I keep running into you. This place is like a pinball machine."

Hilary lifted her chin with a haughty air. "If you continue to harass me, I'll be forced to file a restraining order against you."

Kate smirked. "That shouldn't be too hard, considering how friendly you used to be with the current Fenton County assistant district attorney."

"What?" I gasped in horror.

Kate crossed her arms, a satisfied gleam in her eyes. "You don't know about Hil's history with your current boyfriend?"

I shook my head, finding no words, but Neely Kate had no such trouble. "What in Sam Hill are you talkin' about?"

Kate tilted her head toward Hilary. "You should ask Hilary for the details. Everything I know is hearsay."

Hilary's mouth pinched into a tight line, making it clear she didn't intend to say one word. I was grateful for her uncharacteristic silence; I had no desire to hear anything about Mason from her.

I took a deep breath and turned to face the gathered stylists and their clients, who were still very much watching us with bug eyes, not even pretending to do otherwise. "I'm very happy with Mason, and while I love him very much, we are not yet engaged—secretly or otherwise." I grabbed Neely Kate's arm and tugged. "Let's go." I didn't so much as look back at Hilary or Kate.

She followed me this time, both of us silent until we were about ten feet away from the door.

"I'm sorry, Rose," she gushed. "I don't know what overcame me. It's like all this fire has been building inside me for so long, and it just burst right on out. It was all I could do to not scratch her eyes out." Tears filled her eyes again.

"Oh, honey, it's okay."

"No." Her voice was hard, but it cracked with emotion as she pointed toward the beauty shop. "No it's not. That horrible excuse of a human being is pregnant with a baby she's only using as tool, while I lost..." Her words broke off and she started to cry. "It's not fair, Rose."

My throat burned as my chin quivered. "I know, honey. It's not fair and I'd do anything to make it right."

She sucked in a deep breath and pulled back her shoulders. "I'm done taking her crap, and I'm gonna do everything in my power to bring her down."

The look in her eyes scared me a little. "What does that mean?"

She shook her head. "I'm still working on it, but I'll let you know when I have a plan."

I wasn't sure revenge was a good alternative to despondency, but at least she had some fire in her. Then Kate's implication hit me full force.

I turned toward the courthouse. "I have to talk to Mason."

"No." She looped her arm through mine. "I don't trust Kate one bit more than I trust Hilary. She *wants* you to run to Mason. She *wants* you to question your trust in him." She turned to me. "I'm craving a hamburger from Merilee's."

Her abrupt change in mood worried me, but I let her lead me across the street and into the café. We sat at a table and she ordered a hamburger while I sat in silence, reliving the nightmare at the Nip and Clip over and over again.

"She's lyin'," Neely Kate said as the waitress walked away.

"I'm not so sure."

She leaned her elbows on the table. "Okay, so let's say she's tellin' the truth. I can't see Mason dating Hilary. She's not his type."

"She could be, for all I know. He's barely told me anything about his old girlfriends."

"It's a good bet that his type ain't crazy-ass witches."

True, but the thought of Mason possibly dating Hilary—or even befriending her—made me sicker than the time Muffy ate a dead possum she'd found in the back yard.

"Look, you said Mason and Joe had history even before Savannah because they worked in the same sphere. Hilary was with the state police just like Joe was. If Mason knew her before coming to Henryetta, that's probably how."

"Yeah, you're probably right."

The waitress brought Neely Kate her burger and I decided to tell her about my discovery. Though I'd been trying not to think about it, the memory kept resurfacing in my mind. "I stopped by Mason's office before I came to see you. He wasn't in his office, but Kaylee sent me in and I saw a file on his desk. One I wasn't expecting."

She stopped mid-bite. "What was it?"

"A file on Dora."

She plopped the burger back down on the plate. "He's working on her case? And he didn't tell you?"

"No. And I looked inside it." I cringed.

"Of course you did." But there was no recrimination in her voice, only pride. "I'd expect nothing less."

"I don't think it's an official file. He has handwritten notes in her folder, and he usually keeps his notes in documents on his laptop."

"Do you think it's because he might get in trouble with his boss for working on a case that's so old?"

"No…" I looked up at her. "I think it's because she might have been doin' something bad."

"Why would you say that?"

"His notes said she might have been part of a possible extortion scheme."

"What did he say when you asked him about it?"

"I didn't. I panicked and I stuck the file back on his desk when he came back. Then I figured it would be too obvious if I asked about her. I didn't want him thinking I was snoopin'. Even if I was."

"So what are you gonna do?"

I'd been asking myself that very question since leaving Mason's office, and I'd finally reached a decision while sitting in the salon. "I'm gonna ask him about it tonight. Along with if he knew Hilary before he came to Henryetta."

"Good idea."

My phone vibrated in my pocket and I pulled it out, my stomach tumbling to the floor when I read the name: SM

Skeeter Malcolm.

Chapter Five

I hid my phone under the table as I sent the call to voice mail, but Neely Kate didn't seem to notice. "I need to go to the restroom."

Neely Kate gave me a strange look, my tone probably throwing her off. "Okay."

"I'll be right back." I hurried to the one-stall bathroom and locked the door before hitting redial.

Skeeter answered on the first ring. "Lady. I thought you were avoiding me."

"I couldn't very well answer while I was sitting with Neely Kate in the middle of Merilee's Café."

"Good point. Long time, no see."

Actually, longer than I'd expected. The last time I'd seen or talked to him was a month ago, the night he'd agreed to save Mason in exchange for my willing participation as the Lady in Black for six months. I'd worried Skeeter would utilize every moment of those six months. Then a new thought hit me—maybe he thought my indentured service would start at the time of his choosing. I planned to nip that idea in the bud right away. "I'm surprised you let a month of our six-month contract slip by."

"If I didn't know any better, I'd say you missed me." I heard the grin in his voice.

"Hardly."

"I need to see you soon."

That's what I was afraid of. "How soon?"

"Tomorrow night."

My mind started to race over my schedule. "That's more notice than you usually give."

"Give and take, Lady. Give and take. Plus, I have more notice this time."

Butterflies fluttered in my stomach. "What do I need to do?"

"Sit in on a simple meeting with a few associates. Jed will pick you up at eight tomorrow night. Behind the Sinclair station."

"Okay."

"No worries, Lady. You'll do great."

"There's a lot more to worry about than that, Skeeter."

"But it's the only thing that matters to me." Then he hung up.

Butthead.

I went back to our table and stopped as I rounded the corner. This day was worse than a drunk stuck on a tilt-a-whirl ride.

Kate was sitting at our table.

She glanced up at me with a sardonic smile. "Don't be shy, Rose. Come join us."

I looked over at Neely Kate, who dipped a French fry in ketchup and shrugged. *Great.* Reluctantly, I took my seat.

"You don't look very happy to see me," Kate said. "I thought we'd bonded in the waiting room."

The mention of Neely Kate's hospital stay made my friend freeze, French fry mid-air. She set it down on her plate.

Now I was pissed. "What do you want, Kate?"

"And here I was trying to be helpful and return this to you." She slid Mason's credit card across the table.

I stopped myself from cringing. Mason had only given it to me a couple of hours ago, and I'd already almost lost it. Just great. "Thank you." I grabbed the card and picked up my purse.

"Were you and Joe really engaged?" she asked.

I put the credit card into my wallet. "Why don't you ask Joe?"

"Because I'm asking you."

I looked up into her face. "I'm not sure why you even care. Joe and I broke up. I'm with Mason and I'm happy. Joe is moving on."

She laughed, but it was a harsh sound. "You really believe that?"

"It doesn't matter if I believe it or not. Joe is no longer my problem."

Kate studied me for a moment. "No. You can claim you don't care all you want, but I don't believe it for a minute."

I leaned forward. "Why do *you* even care?"

"Joe's my brother. I want him to be happy."

I shook my head. "Then where have you been these last two years? He's been through hell. He needed you then."

Her smile fell. "He had you."

"No. Not when it mattered. He was all alone." I turned to Neely Kate. Her face was pale and she looked like she was about to cry again. "Are you ready to go?"

She nodded and stood.

I got out of my seat and handed her some cash. "Neely Kate, why don't you go pay. I need to talk to Joe's sister for a moment."

Neely Kate glanced between the two of us, but when I nodded to show her I was okay, she walked to the register.

As soon as she was out of earshot, I turned my wrath on Kate. "She's been miserable for two weeks, but she finally found a tiny bit of happiness today. But you and Hilary Wilder just keep snatching it from her—you with your careless tongue and Hilary parading around with a pregnancy nobody wants but her, and even then only for selfish reasons."

Her eyebrows shot up in bewilderment. "What did I do?"

I lowered my voice. "I have no idea what kind of game you're playing, but I'm not part of it. Leave me and Neely Kate alone."

Neely Kate had finished paying, so we left the restaurant, leaving Kate still sitting at the table.

As soon as the door closed, I turned to her. "Neely Kate, I'm so sorry. I just wanted you to have a nice afternoon, but Joe's sister and his witch of an ex-girlfriend went and ruined it."

"Oh, Rose. This is the best I've felt since losing the babies."

"But Kate…"

"One good afternoon isn't gonna make me instantly better. You know that after your breakup with Joe."

"I know. But I wanted it to last as long for as long as possible."

She lifted her hand to her pink and purple streaks. "I love my hair, although you still haven't explained why you had Mason's credit card."

I cringed. "I think you can figure it out if you think about the business's cash flow."

"That bad, huh?"

"Only temporarily, as Mason pointed out. Plus he made a suggestion that makes me feel better about letting him help me out."

"Good, because that man loves you somethin' fierce."

"I know."

"Don't back down from talking to him about Dora and Hilary tonight. I'm sure there's a logical explanation for everything, and you'll feel better knowing."

I sure hoped she was right.

I unlocked the car so she could climb inside, then walked over to the office to pick up Muffy. Bruce Wayne had already left, so Muffy was happy to see me, and even happier to see Neely Kate once I let her into the car. My little dog covered her with licks until she started laughing. "Okay, girl. That's enough lovin'."

After I dropped Neely Kate off at her house, I stopped at the Piggly Wiggly on the way home, leaving Muffy in Mason's car. I hadn't been in the grocery store since an unfortunate incident right before Thanksgiving involving a shopping cart and a can display had resulted in my equally unfortunate arrest. I halfway expected alarms to go off and security guards to tackle me, but the only one who seemed to notice was Bennie, the guy who'd replaced Bruce Wayne's best friend as a bagger.

I knew Bennie from Jonah's church. He was in his twenties and had Down syndrome. He'd asked me to come see him while he was working, so he was excited when I walked through the door. He waved, his face breaking out into a huge grin. "Hi, Miss Rose! You came to see me!"

I gave him a quick wave. "Of course!"

"You're gonna let me bag your groceries, aren't you, Miss Rose?"

I gave him a warm smile. "I wouldn't let anyone else do it."

The cashier turned and gave me a glare.

I sighed as I pushed my cart toward the produce aisle. I should have expected some animosity from the staff. Even if the incident hadn't been my fault.

Since Muffy was in the car and I didn't want to leave her for very long, I only grabbed what we needed for the next few days, but the pile was bigger than I'd expected. I made it to the checkout lane and had put most of my items on the conveyor belt when Miss Mildred's voice grated out from behind me.

"I thought you'd been banned from the Piggly Wiggly."

I turned around to see my former neighbor standing in line behind me. The octogenarian looked the same as ever— *cranky*—only there were some new faint blue streaks in her white hair.

I lifted my chin. "I guess that's just proof you can't believe everything you hear." I pulled a bag of pasta out of the cart. "I like what you've done with your hair."

She patted the top of my head. "What happened to my hair is none of your business."

Fair enough. I turned my back to her.

"Are you still living in sin with the assistant DA?"

"I could argue that the answer to that question is none of your business, but I have nothin' to hide. So if you're asking if Mason and I are still living together, the answer is yes." I set a container of strawberries on the conveyor belt. "What have you been up to, Miss Mildred? Have you stalked any other neighbors lately?"

"The neighborhood has been remarkably quiet since you left. Murder and mayhem are at an all-time low."

"You can't blame Miss Dorothy's death on me. That was Jonah Pruitt's mother."

"And then there was the bank robbery."

"I was an innocent bystander. Besides, you weren't even there."

She pointed her finger at me. "I heard about your job at that stripper club. God rest your poor momma's soul."

"I never stripped! I never even took my clothes off!" I protested louder than I'd intended. She didn't need to know Neely Kate had taken a disastrous turn on the stripper pole.

A mother with two small children was rounding a corner just then, about to head down another aisle. Her mouth dropped open and she gave me the stinkeye as she shoved her poor preschool-aged boy on the other side of her, away from me, as though my presence might somehow infect him. Only she pushed him a little too hard and he crashed into a cereal box display on the endcap. An avalanche of boxes came crashing down on him and his mother.

"Look what you did!" Miss Mildred shouted, louder than any loudspeaker could hope to be. Every person in the front of the store turned their attention to her.

"Oh, for heaven's sake!" I shouted. "I wasn't anywhere near that display!"

The store manager walked toward the cash register as Bennie—who was sacking my groceries—stared, taking everything in.

Miss Mildred narrowed her eyes and pointed her finger at me. "You are a menace to society. I'm gonna start a petition to have you kicked out of town."

"You can do that?" If so, maybe I could somehow get Hilary kicked out on her rear. But my excitement over possibly evicting her was short-lived. I quickly remembered Joe saying if he had the authority to force her out of town, he would have done it by now. "Well, I guess that'll give you some excitement to take your mind off how boring the neighborhood's become without me."

That wasn't the reaction she'd wanted, but she clamped her mouth shut.

The mother of the boy was trying to dig him out from under a pile of boxes while her little girl started sobbing. "I lost my brother!"

The store manager had rushed over to help, but he kept throwing glances my way that clearly said he was trying his best to figure out how to blame me for the latest mishap.

Thankfully, the cashier said, "That will be one hundred and thirty-six dollars and fifty-nine cents." Her tone let me know she was just as eager to be done with me as her boss was.

Bennie was bagging the last of my items. "Look, Miss Rose. I was careful with your eggs."

"You did a great job, Bennie," I said as I dug through the cash in my wallet. The girl was crying louder and her brother had joined in the chorus, although not because he was hurt—he was upset his mother had dug him out of his new fort. The afternoon had gone from bad to worse and I just wanted to go home. When I realized I didn't have enough cash, I handed the cashier Mason's credit card.

She glanced at it and turned it over. "This isn't your card."

I rested my hands on the small shelf near the conveyer belt, wondering why I hadn't just slid the card through the card reader. "It's okay. It's my boyfriend's."

"But it's not *yours*."

"Well, no. But he gave it to me to use."

She looked over her register toward the fracas behind me. "Ed."

But Ed was too busy tripping over boxes and dealing with the irate mother to hear her.

"Ed!" she shouted, and when she got his attention, she continued. "We got a case of identity theft at register four."

"*What?*" I gasped.

The mother looked up at me like I was one of the horsemen of the apocalypse.

Bennie's eyes widened like saucers. "You're a thief, Miss Rose?"

"What? No!" I turned to the cashier. "I didn't steal his identity. If you'll just call Mason, he'll tell you it's okay."

Miss Mildred gave me a smug grin. "I knew you were wicked since you were little. It was only a matter of time before you were put away in prison."

"I didn't steal Mason's identity!"

The cashier's frown deepened and it was a wonder she hadn't set permanent lines in her face. "You can tell it to the Henryetta Police."

Crappy doodles.

Chapter Six

By employing a few evasive tactics, I managed to text Mason to tell him I'd used his card at the Piggly Wiggly and was in a heap of trouble.

The store manager, the cashier, poor confused Bennie, and Miss Mildred had formed a loose circle around me, as if corralling a dangerous criminal, by the time Officer Ernie arrived. The police officer slid through the automatic door as it was opening, only the door moved too slow and his shoulder got caught in the edge. He lowered his sunglasses and glared at the door as though it were a punk kid who'd pulled a prank on him. Then he turned, settled his sunglasses back onto the bridge of his nose, and strutted toward us.

Somebody had watched too many cop shows.

He stopped several feet away from me, his thumbs hooked on his belt, a cocky grin on his face. He was Henryetta's own version of Barney Fife and he played it to the hilt, whether he realized it or not. "Well, well, well. Look who's causing trouble again."

I put my hands on my hips and said, for what had to be the hundredth time, "I didn't do anything wrong. If you would just call Mason, we could get this all sorted out."

Officer Ernie gave me a satisfied smirk. "We'll sort it out down at the station."

Miss Mildred was fit to be tied since I was still blocking the checkout lane. "Some of us don't have all day to deal with your shenanigans. Just haul her off to jail and be done with it."

I turned to face her, my anger nearing the boiling point. "Then why didn't you move over to lane four like the manager told you to do?"

She shot me a scowl. "My stuff's already on the belt."

I was about to scoop her three bottles of Metamucil into her cart when everyone turned toward the doors. I whipped around to see Mason walk through them, already giving Officer Ernie an irritated look. "What in Sam Hill is goin' on here?" His annoyance came through loud and clear.

The policeman gave him a haughty look. "Rose Gardner has committed identity theft."

"And whose identity did she allegedly steal?" Mason asked in disbelief.

Ernie looked stymied by the request, so he turned toward the cashier and store manager. The cashier picked up the confiscated card. "Mason Deveraux."

"And do you have any idea who Mason Deveraux is?" my irritated boyfriend asked.

Some of the manager's arrogance faded. "Why you, of course. The assistant district attorney."

"That's right," he said. "And given the uncanny efficiency of the Henryetta gossip mill, everyone in town knows I'm living with Rose. Hell, Ed," he said to the manager, his voice getting tighter. "I've been trying to convince you to lift her ban from the store for the past month. I've made it no secret that she's my girlfriend."

"Yes, but..." the manager stuttered. "She was using a card that wasn't hers."

"She was using *my* card!" he boomed. He paused for a second, taking a deep breath. When he spoke again, his voice was calmer. "I am a very busy man. I don't have time to run down to the damn grocery store for such nonsense. Next time I'd appreciate it if you'd call me rather than interrupt my schedule." He took my hand. "On second thought, never mind. We won't be shopping here anymore."

I looked back at a shocked Miss Mildred as Mason pulled me out of the store. Bennie was watching me with disappointment in his eyes. Did he think I'd actually stolen the card? Somehow that was the worst part of this whole ridiculous situation.

Mason marched out of the store, his hand wrapped around mine, and I trailed behind. He didn't stop or release my hand until he reached his car.

I hated to ask, but it needed to be said. "What about the groceries?"

"Leave them," he barked.

I felt flabbergasted. What he'd said inside was right. He was too busy to be dealing with nonsense, and I was usually the cause of all his predicaments. "Mason, I'm so sorry."

He released a breath, the anger in his eyes softening. "Don't be sorry. This is my fault."

"How is it *your* fault?"

He rubbed the back of his neck. "I should have given you more cash, but honestly, I never thought you'd have any trouble."

"I should have just run it through the stupid card reader, but Miss Mildred was harassing me and the boy knocked over the cereal boxes because his mother thought I was a stripper..."

"*What?*" Then he shook his head, looking aggravated again. "Never mind." He pushed out a breath. "Rose. It's okay. It's this stupid town. Everyone in it seems to be ass-backwards." And if that didn't cut me to the quick. He was right, and there was only one reason he was mired here.

"I'm sorry."

"Why are you saying sorry now?" He sounded exasperated.

"You're stuck here because of me."

He closed his eyes and looked up. When his gaze finally lowered, his face softened. "Sweetheart, I'd follow you to the Arctic tundra if you wanted to live there, but I'd probably still complain about the cold. This is no different. But mostly I hate that so many people in this town treat you so poorly."

"It's okay. I'm used to it."

"That's just it, Rose. It's *not* okay."

"It's better than it used to be, I promise."

He looked like he wanted to argue. Instead he groaned and grabbed his phone out of his pocket. "I have to take this. I left in the middle of something important and I need to get back."

"I'm sorry."

He shook his head. "Stop saying you're sorry. I'll be home as soon as I can, but I suspect I'll be late." He glanced at his car and saw Muffy inside. "Do you mind if I drive your truck so I can get back to work sooner?"

"Sure. Of course."

He gave me a quick kiss and answered his phone as he rushed over to the truck.

I was about to climb into the car when I noticed a folded piece of paper under the windshield wiper. After tugging it out and opening it, I read the tight cursive script:

Stay out of things that don't concern you.

I read it again in confusion. Not only did I not know who wrote it, I didn't even know what it was talking about. I hadn't been mixed up in anyone else's business since Neely Kate and I had gone looking for her cousin a month ago.

Then it hit me. The note was meant for Mason.

I looked over my shoulder, but Mason was already pulling out of the parking lot. I wasn't sure what to do. He needed to get back to work. I considered calling Joe, but then I decided to just go home and tell Mason later, and let him decide what to do.

Muffy had seen me and was barking like mad. I opened the door and rubbed her head. "Did you see who put that note on Mason's car?"

She answered by jumping up on her back legs and licking my nose.

"So you don't want to tell me. Be that way."

Of course, I couldn't discount the possibility the note was for me. The handwriting looked like a woman's, and for all I knew, Miss Mildred might have put it on the windshield on her way into the store, as unlikely as it seemed. Whenever she'd had something to say to me before, she'd had no compunction about flat out telling me to my face. But as Mason had pointed out only moments before, there were plenty of people in town who didn't like me. My own momma—or the woman I'd thought to be my mother—had made no secret of her contempt for me as well as her belief that my "gift" was proof I was possessed by a demon. She'd been only too happy to spread the rumors of my strangeness. And there were plenty of other reasons someone might think I was sticking my nose in their business. We'd just reopened the nursery. I was opening the landscaping business with Bruce Wayne. Shoot, for all I knew, the note could be from Ima Jean. She'd made no secret that she was upset that I'd bought the cake for the store's reopening from Dena's.

But the most logical conclusion was Mason had ticked off some citizen and she was letting him know. Which meant he really couldn't let his guard down, despite the fact that Joe and Mason both kept insisting he was safe now.

I stuffed the note into my purse and considered heading to the Peach Orchard grocery store, but rumor had it that the meat department had failed yet another inspection. I could stick to canned goods, but after my recent experience, I wasn't up for shopping. I was still too upset that I'd once again disturbed Mason at work. I knew he didn't blame me, but it was ultimately my fault. If only I'd been carrying more cash. If only I hadn't let Mildred distract me...

If only I could stay out of trouble. Try though I might, trouble seemed to have a knack for following me.

I gave up the shopping idea and drove home, figuring I'd scrounge a meal together from the ingredients we already had. I was lost in thought when a dark sedan approached quickly from behind me, riding close to my bumper. A car whizzed by, going the opposite way on the two-lane road, and as soon as it was a short distance away, the sedan behind me swung around to pass. It didn't alarm me much—there were plenty of reckless drivers in Henryetta—but as soon as it was next to me, it swerved toward me.

I whipped the wheel to get out of the way, turning sharply toward the shoulder of the road. Gravel flew up all around Mason's car as I tried to slow down, and then my tire got stuck in a rut, jerking the car further off the road and toward several trees. I swerved just in time to miss the trees, but the car slid through the mud in the grass before coming to a stop.

The brake lights of the car that had passed me glowed about fifty feet ahead, pausing for a moment, but then the car sped off.

The numb sense of shock started to wear off and my heart leaped into my throat as I looked around the car for Muffy. I found her huddled and shaking on the floorboards on the passenger side. "Muffy!"

She jumped up on the seat and launched herself into my arms.

"Are you okay?" I asked, looking her over as I felt her legs and body. Satisfied she wasn't hurt when she didn't whimper, I checked out the state of Mason's car. I hadn't hit anything, only skidded off the road. But when I tried to drive, the tires spun uselessly in the mud.

Great.

Calling Mason was out. He'd drop everything to come help me, but I knew he was busy and I'd already bothered him. I was about to call Bruce Wayne when I noticed a sheriff's car pulling up on the shoulder behind me. I wasn't sure whether or not to hope it was Joe.

Thankfully, I didn't have to decide because it was Deputy Miller, who'd helped me out of more than one jam. I opened the door, stepped out of the car, and promptly sank into the mud.

"Rose," he said, moving toward me and reaching out his hand. "I thought I recognized Mr. Deveraux's car. Is he with you?"

"No. We traded cars."

Muffy saw the deputy and broke out into excited barking. I turned back and scooped her up in my arms, grabbed my purse, then schlepped toward Deputy Miller.

"What happened?" he asked as he grabbed my hand and pulled me out of the mud.

"Some car was passing me when it swerved toward me and ran me off the road."

He looked back at my skid marks, both on the pavement and off. "You're lucky you missed the trees," he said with a furrowed brow. "You and Muffy could have been seriously hurt. Can you give me a description of the car?"

I took a deep breath, and was surprised to realize I was shaking. "It was a black car—new and shiny. It had dark windows, so I didn't see who was inside. And I didn't catch the license plate either."

"I'm gonna call it in and have the deputies keep an eye out for it."

A new thought hit me. "I don't think this was an accident."

His eyes widened. "You think they purposely tried to run you off the road?"

I shook my head. "No. I think they tried to run *Mason* off the road. I'm driving his car and I just found this note on his windshield when I was parked in the Piggly Wiggly parking lot." I reached into my purse and pulled out the paper.

He quickly glanced it over and became more alert, glancing around as though looking for lurking danger. "I need to call this in."

He walked back to his car, but I stayed close to Mason's car. I was never going to drive it out of this quagmire. It would have to be towed, and I didn't have the money to pay for that nonsense. But Bruce Wayne had bought a front-end loader and a couple of other pieces of large equipment for our landscaping jobs. I would have bet ten cents to the dollar he could pull me out.

I pulled out my cell phone and called him, then breathed a sigh of relief when he promised to get the equipment at my farm and return to pull me out.

Deputy Miller got out of his car and walked back toward me. "I called it in, but I'll have to file a report and take your statement." He paused. "I called Chief Deputy Simmons to let him know."

I groaned. Joe was going to read me the riot act and this wasn't even my fault. "Is he on his way?"

"No, he wanted to come, but he's tied up with something else right now."

Relief washed over me. After the day I'd had, I wasn't up to dealing with Joe.

He glanced over at the car. "Do you want me call a tow truck or take you and Muffy home? We can fill out the report there."

"Nah. Bruce Wayne is gonna come get me in our tractor."

"Then why don't we go sit in my car and I'll start filling out the paperwork."

"But my feet are all muddy," I said, gesturing to my legs. It looked like I'd gone swimming in a swamp. He waved me off and insisted I get in the car anyway. I sat in the passenger seat and set Muffy on my lap. "So what have you been up to, Deputy Miller?"

"Oh, keepin' busy." He pulled out a clipboard with papers and began to write. "Chief Deputy Simmons has been givin' me more responsibility."

"Well, that's good news, isn't it?" I chuckled. "You know, it's funny, I could have sworn I saw you out at the farm last week."

His hand tightened around his pen. "What makes you say that?"

"I couldn't sleep one night, so I went to the kitchen to make some hot tea and I thought I saw you out by the barn."

"Are you accusing me of trespassin'?" he asked, sounding offended.

"No. Of course not. I know you weren't really there. I must have been half asleep."

The scratch of his pen was the only sound for about thirty seconds. Then he looked up at me, worry in his eyes. "Have you seen any other people lurking around on the farm?"

"*Other* people?"

He swallowed. "You know what I meant." He turned to me. "Have you seen anyone lurking around?"

The way he posed the question scared me. "No."

"If you do, will you tell me?"

"Do you *think* someone's lurkin' around on my farm?"

"No. Remember when I told you that most police work is boring? Consider this my pathetic attempt to try to liven it up."

He wasn't telling me the truth, but I wasn't sure calling him a liar was going to help matters. "If I see someone lurkin' at my farm, I'll call you straight away." Especially given the mounting evidence that someone was still intent on hurting Mason.

"Good."

He finished filling out the paperwork and Bruce Wayne pulled up with the tractor a few minutes later. Deputy Miller helped Bruce Wayne pull Mason's car out of the muck and onto the shoulder, and soon Muffy and I were back in the front seat of the car where we'd started. I said goodbye to Deputy Miller and arranged to meet Bruce Wayne back at the farm.

Thankfully I'd gone off the road only a few miles from the farm, but I still beat Bruce Wayne by a good five minutes. I met him out at the barn and helped him get the tractor put away. He was quieter than usual and it worried me. We shut the barn doors and started down the small incline to the house. "Why don't you come inside for a few minutes? Maeve sent home half a carrot cake yesterday, and Mason and I can't possibly eat it all ourselves."

He shrugged. "I wouldn't want to put you out."

"Put me out? You just went out of your way to help pull Mason's car out of the mud. It's the least I can do."

He gave me a sheepish grin. "Well, when you put it that way."

"Good. It's settled."

We walked in silence for a few seconds, Muffy romping around like a crazy dog, before Bruce Wayne asked, "What were you doin' driving Mason's car?"

I shrugged. "I took Neely Kate to get colored streaks in her hair. Mason thought it would be easier for her to get in and out."

"So how'd you end up off the road, anyway?"

I told him everything, including my suspicion that someone had thought I was Mason.

"He's not gonna like that you didn't call him," he said as he followed me into the house through the back kitchen door.

"I know. I'll deal with it when I have to." I kicked off my muddy shoes, then slipped off my coat and put it over a chair. "Coffee or hot tea?"

"Coffee if you have it."

"Sit on down," I said, gesturing toward the kitchen table as I headed for the coffee maker. "You're not wrong, but I hate makin' him worry. He had to come bail me out at the Piggly Wiggly this afternoon and I interrupted him from doing something important. He gets upset if I don't call him, but I hate draggin' him away from work." I held the coffee pot under running water and turned to look at him.

He chuckled. "He's gonna see that mud plastered all over his car. Better to tell him straight away and not look like you're hiding anything."

I grinned. "You're a pretty smart guy, Bruce Wayne."

His cheeks reddened. "I ain't never been accused of that before."

"Well then that just makes everyone else fools, doesn't it?" I asked, pouring the water into the coffee maker and scooping coffee grounds into the filter. After I turned on the machine, I grabbed up a couple of plates and forks and took them to the table.

He laughed. "Ain't you ruinin' your dinner eating a piece of cake at nearly six o'clock?"

"Seeing as how I don't have much else to cook, why not?" I cut a generous slice and put it on his plate. "Besides, there's carrots in this cake. That means it's practically a vegetable."

He laughed.

"And I could say the same to you. What about *your* dinner?" I asked, cutting my own slice and putting it on my plate.

"Well, Maeve's carrot cake beats canned soup any day."

I sat down across from him and picked up my fork for a big bite of cake. "Now you sound like me after Momma died. I thought David did most of the cooking." Bruce Wayne was living with his long-time best friend, David Moore, but David was about as reliable as a drunk surgeon.

"He hasn't been around much."

I lifted my gaze, suddenly worried. "Where's he been?"

"He spends most of his time with that new girlfriend of his."

"They're still *together?*" According to Bruce Wayne, David had never had a girlfriend for longer than a month.

"Yeah..." He looked down at his cake and took a bite.

I got up and grabbed the coffee pot and a couple of mugs before returning to my seat. "Is he still livin' with you?"

"His stuff's still there and he's payin' his share of the rent and utilities, but it's like I said—he's not around much."

"So his new job at the convenience store is workin' out?"

"Yeah. He works the evening shift, so I hardly see him now," he said, his voice quiet.

Bruce Wayne was lonely. I'd suspected, but this confirmed it. At least David was still helping with the bills. I wasn't sure I could handle another financial crisis, even if it wasn't my own. I poured our coffee and took another bite of my cake.

"Rose?" Mason's voice called from the other room.

"In the kitchen."

He came through the doorway and smiled when he saw who was with me. "Hi, Bruce Wayne. I saw your car out front." He bent over and gave me a kiss. "Are we having cake for dinner?"

"It's the appetizer," I teased. "The main course is ice cream."

"Then count me in." He pulled a plate out of the cabinet and sat beside us.

It was unusual for Bruce Wayne to visit the farm at all, let alone at this time of day. I decided to take the offensive on the whole running-off-the-road incident. "Cake is Bruce Wayne's payment for helping me get unstuck."

"Unstuck?" Mason turned to me. "Is that why the car is all coated in mud?"

"Yeah."

He stiffened as he put things together. "Are those tire ruts a couple miles back from you?"

My eyebrows rose. "It wasn't as bad as it looked, Mason. I promise your car's okay."

"I don't care about the car, sweetheart. I care about *you*. You damn near hit the trees. You could have been killed, Rose."

"But I wasn't." I patted his arm in dismissal. "Muffy and I are just fine."

"What happened?"

I took a breath, casting a glance to Bruce Wayne before I gave my attention to Mason. "I was on my way home when a car came up behind me goin' too fast and passed me. But it was too close and I veered toward the shoulder. You saw the rest."

Anger and worry filled his eyes. "Someone tried to run you off the road?"

I had to handle this just right or I'd freak him out. "No," I said. "I think they were tryin' to run *you* off the road."

"What? Why?"

I told him about the note and his entire body tensed. "Why didn't you call me?"

"I hardly had time to do anything before Deputy Miller happened to pull up. He called it in so the deputies could be on the lookout for the car. And then he filed a report."

"Why didn't you call me?" he asked again, sounding hurt and a tad bit angry.

"Because of how you're reacting right now." I waved at him. "Mason, I can't call you about every little incident that happens. There's just too doggone many of them, and I keep interrupting your work."

"Someone tried to kill you! You're more important than my damn job."

"For all we know, it was an accident and the note was entirely unrelated." I took a breath. "I filed a report. The deputies are looking for the car. There wasn't anything you could do. Besides, if my hunch is right, *you're* the one in danger. Not me. *You're* the one who needs to take precautions." When he scowled, I leaned over and gave him a quick kiss. "I promise to call if I'm ever in real trouble. Like almost getting arrested," I teased, trying to ease my own fear for *his* safety, but his arm was still tense. "Look, I'm a grown woman, Mason. And if I can handle a situation without you, I'm gonna do it and tell you about it later."

His anger faded, fear creeping in behind it. "Do you realize how close you came to hitting those trees, Rose?"

"Seeing as how I was the one driving the car, I do."

"I don't want to lose you."

"I'm not goin' anywhere. I'm fine."

Bruce Wayne's chair scraped against the floor. "I think I need to get goin'." They were the first words he'd said since Mason got home, and I suddenly realized we were making him feel awkward.

I turned toward him. Bruce Wayne was lonely and I wasn't about to send him home to his empty house with only cake in his belly. "You keep your booty in that chair. Like I told Mason, this cake is the appetizer, and it would be rude of you to leave in the middle of dinner."

Bruce Wayne cast a glance at Mason.

Mason grinned, but I could see the anxiety in his eyes. "You heard her. You and I both know there's no arguing with her once she's set her mind on something."

I stood, nodding my head. "Good. That's settled. Now I'm gonna figure out what the main course is."

I made buttered noodles and frozen broccoli while Mason disappeared into his office to call Joe. When he returned about ten minutes later, he and Bruce Wayne talked about our plans and preparations for RBW Landscaping. I was dying to know what he'd found out, but the worry lines around Mason's eyes kept me from asking. Bruce Wayne seemed to sense the tension, so he left as soon as dinner was over, but he seemed to be in better spirits.

As soon as I shut the door, I spun around to confront Mason. "What did Joe say?"

"Not much. While the accident seems suspicious and the note is threatening, there's not a whole lot he can do."

I put my hands on my hips. "So he's gonna do *nothing?*"

"No. They're looking for the car and he's going to question the driver. He's determined to get to the bottom of it."

I nodded. Joe and Mason might be adversaries, but I had to trust that Joe would keep Mason safe. I gave him a hug and then headed into the kitchen, Mason on my heels.

"How was your afternoon with Neely Kate?" Mason asked while we started to clean up the kitchen.

I decided there was no better time than the present to bring up one of my two pressing issues. And while I really wanted to know what he was doing with that file on Dora, the Hilary issue burned my gut more. I just needed him to verify it was nonsense before turning the conversation to Dora.

"It was interesting…"

"Why do I think there's a lot more to that *interesting?*"

I grinned and pressed my chest to his, a dishtowel still in my hand. "Because you, Mason Deveraux, are a very smart man."

"Why am I suddenly worried?"

"I'm sure there's nothing for you to worry about. I just need you to clear something up."

"What is it?"

"Neely Kate got her streaks, but as I was paying at the register, Hilary Wilder showed up."

"Uh-oh. How'd that go?"

"She was her usual self, but her behavior inspired Neely Kate to act more like her usual self. Which is how she ended up telling Hilary off in front of the whole beauty shop."

He chuckled. "So the outing really was good for Neely Kate."

"It got more interesting from there."

My tone lost some of its lightheartedness and Mason picked up on the change. "What happened?"

"Joe's sister showed up." I turned to face him. "She has an agenda and I don't trust her at all, even though she keeps insinuating she wants to be friends."

"You've got great intuition, so I think you should listen to it."

"She said something about Hilary that caught me by surprise."

He dried the pot I'd used to boil the noodles, seemingly unconcerned. "And what was that?"

I watched him closely as I said, "She said you and Hilary had history."

His hand stopped mid-wipe. "*Kate* said that?"

"Do you?"

"How would Kate know if we had history or not? Hasn't she been gone for over two years?"

It didn't escape my notice that he'd evaded the question. "I don't know how she came by the information, and frankly I don't care about that part, Mason. I want to know if it's true."

He set the pot on the stove and studied me with guarded eyes. "What did Hilary say?"

Fear wormed its way into my stomach. "I'm asking *you*."

He rubbed the back of his neck and glanced out the kitchen window before turning back to me. "I do, but probably not how you think."

"Was it work-related?"

"No."

Oh, God. I took a breath and forced myself to voice my greatest fear. "Did you *date?*"

"What? No!" He moved toward me and placed his hands on my shoulders. "I knew her socially."

"What's that mean?"

He sighed and took my hand. "I saw her at parties, fundraisers. It was while Savannah was seeing Joe. I had no idea she was Joe's old girlfriend."

"*So you went to parties together?*"

"Rose, no. It was nothing like that. When I was at events, I'd see her there. She always approached me, though, and she'd stay by my side for most of the night."

I swallowed. "She's a beautiful woman. You weren't interested in her?"

"No."

"Why not? Were you seeing someone else?"

"*Rose.*" He dropped my hand. "Even if I *had* dated her, I wouldn't have been doing anything wrong. I was single at the time and had no idea about the nature of her connection with Joe. If I *had* known the whole story, I wouldn't have given her the time of day."

I put my hand on my hip. "So you *did* give her the time of day."

His eyes hardened. "What exactly are you accusing me of?"

"I'm not accusing you of anything. I just want to know the truth."

"This is starting to feel an awful lot like an interrogation."

"Maybe if you'd told me the truth from the start, I wouldn't be interrogating you."

Exasperation filled his eyes, and he took several steps away before turning to face me. "I was an ADA in Little Rock, Rose. I knew a lot of people. Am I expected to give you a list of their names?"

"That's not fair, Mason."

"And your accusations aren't fair, Rose. Have I ever given you any cause to not trust me?"

I clenched my fists at my sides. "You should have told me you knew Hilary Wilder."

"What did you want me to say?" He flung his hand toward me. "'Hey, Rose. I met Hilary Wilder in Little Rock at a fundraiser and some other events'?"

"Yes!" I shouted. "It would have been a hell of a lot better than finding out from Joe's sister in the middle of a beauty salon."

"She was just pumping me for information on my sister, Rose! And I goddamned gave it to her. I gave her every piece of information she needed to break up Joe and Savannah and keep them apart. Forgive me for not telling you about something I'm deeply ashamed of."

Some of my fight faded. "Mason."

"You want details? Fine." He sucked in a breath, then pushed it out. "The first time I met her, she approached me at a fundraiser. Joe was there with Savannah. Joe's father was there

73

too. I was trying to stay as far from them as possible when Hilary walked up and handed me a drink. She made small talk and fed me a couple more drinks. She saw me looking at Joe and Savannah, which is when she told me that Joe had screwed her over. When I told her my sister was dating him, she said she was worried for her, but she left it at that and changed the subject. Like I said, I saw her several more times. She would always approach me, make small talk, and then get in some jab at Joe. Then I saw her in the lobby at a play. Savannah was supposed to go with me, but she'd cancelled at the last minute to be with Joe. Hilary told me her date had stood her up, and her tickets were better than mine, so she invited me to sit with her. We went out for drinks afterward, and about a half hour into drinks, she asked about Savannah. How she was doing. If Joe was being good to her. I didn't suspect anything. It was just conversation, and we'd just spent a few hours together as friends, so I told her about my concerns." He walked over to the kitchen table and stood there, looking out the back window. "I was damned clueless about what she was doing."

"You sat with her at a play and went out for drinks, and you don't call that a date?"

He slowly spun to face me, bewilderment on his face. "I'm telling you that conniving bitch played me to get information that played a part in my sister's murder *and you want to know why I'm not calling it a date?*" When I didn't answer, he said, "No. Rose. It was *not* a date. We talked about my job and hers and a project the state police had been working on in conjunction with my department."

Horror at my own behavior rushed through me like wildfire. My jealousy had hurt him and I wasn't even sure why I was so jealous. I knew logically that Mason didn't want to be with Hilary, but it still hurt to think about them being near each other.

"You were with Joe for *months* before we started dating, and I don't begrudge you one single minute of that. But you think I had one or two dates with Hilary Wilder—when you and I didn't even know each other existed—and you hold it over my head. I saw Hilary three more times after Savannah's death, and she never even *once* acknowledged she knew me. And frankly, I prefer to keep it that way. The only thing I'm guilty of is being a damn idiot. So forgive me if I didn't rush to give you the details."

"Mason," I said through the lump in my throat. "I'm sorry."

He stomped toward the living room. "I need some air."

I trailed behind him, unsure of what to say to make this better.

He grabbed his coat off the hook on the wall and a flashlight off the entry table, then opened the front door. "Come on, Muffy."

My startled little dog followed him without a backward glance at me, as if to tell me what a witch I'd been. They were still in my line of vision when my head started to tingle. I heard the front door slam shut as I was plunged into a vision as abruptly as if I'd been tossed into a frigid lake.

I stood in the courthouse hall, looking into the serious face of Carter Hale, a defense attorney Neely Kate and I had met a month before.

"Do you think you can help?" I asked in Mason's voice, which sounded strained.

"I'm still not sure why you asked me. You've made no secret of the fact that you can't stand me."

Anger made Mason shake and he clenched his fists. "Because you're the only person in this whole goddamned county who doesn't have his hand in someone's pockets."

"You're gonna ask Carter Hale for help," I mumbled. And just like that, I was back in the living room, overcome by a wave of nausea and a dull ache at the back of my head. The vision wasn't all that odd in and of itself. I was sure it had something to do with Mason's county business. But why did I feel so awful? This had been happening more often lately. Was it because I was forcing too many visions?

But before I could give more thought to the vision, the memory of the horrible fight I'd had with Mason hit me full force. What had I been thinking? I felt so awful, I grabbed my phone and sat on the couch to call Neely Kate, but I stopped before pressing the call button. She had her own issues. The last thing she needed to be saddled with was a problem of my own making. Instead, I called Violet.

"Hey, Rose," she answered, sounding guarded.

"Violet, I've done something awful…and I don't know how to fix it," I said as I started to cry.

Her voice softened. "I can't believe you're capable of doing something *that* bad. Tell me what happened."

I told her everything and when I finished, she was silent for a few seconds. "He was wrong to keep that from you, Rose."

"I don't know," I said. "I can see why he did. I'm not sure I'd confess to something I felt so guilty about."

"Yes, you would."

But she didn't know about the Lady in Black. I had the sudden urge to tell Mason everything when he came back inside, but while it might appease my own guilt, there were other considerations. For one thing, it might potentially destroy Mason's career. I had no idea what he'd do to Skeeter if he knew I was the Lady in Black, and I couldn't take the risk. But it made me a whole lot more understanding of his reasons for choosing not to tell me about Hilary. "What's done is done. He kept it from me and now the truth is out. I was jealous, Violet, and nothin' good ever comes from that. I hurt Mason and I need to figure out how to make it up to him."

"I think you need to ask yourself why you were jealous."

I pushed her question away. "Because Hilary Wilder destroys everything she touches and I couldn't stand the thought of her tainting Mason."

"Hmm…"

"What does that mean?"

She sighed. "Mason loves you. He'll get over it. And if he doesn't, then maybe you two aren't meant to be."

I heard stomping on the front porch and a bark from Muffy. "He's back. Thanks for listening, Vi."

"That's what sisters are for. Thanks for trusting me enough to call me."

I hung up and set the phone on the coffee table, standing as the door opened. Mason walked through the opening, Muffy at his heels. He closed the door behind him and stood by it, his face emotionless.

I studied him for a moment, wondering if he was still as upset as he'd been when he left. "Oh, Mason. I—"

His eyes softened. "Sweetheart—"

That was all I needed before I ran to him and threw my arms around his neck. "I'm so sorry."

I sighed in relief when his arms encircled my back, pulling me close. "No, you were right. I should have told you." His voice was husky in my ear.

"I handled it so badly. I'm so upset that I hurt you."

He held me tighter. "Rose, it's okay. Given the circumstances, I understand."

I clung to him, thankful that he wasn't the type of man to hold a grudge.

He pulled back and looked down into my face. "On my walk with Muffy, I decided I should be flattered you were jealous enough to get that upset over it."

I sighed, feeling foolish about my overreaction. "I figured you knew her through the state police... I just couldn't let my mind wander to you two bein' together. So when you said you'd spent time with her socially, my imagination ran wild." I gave him an apologetic smile. "I know you have a past with other women, but the thought of you with *her*—"

"And now you can banish the thought because it *never* happened."

I wrapped my arms around his neck again, clinging to him. "I had a vision."

"Of me?"

"As you walked out the door."

"The way you're holding on for dear life has me worried."

"The vision wasn't bad, but it was the way I felt afterward that had me worried." I looked up at him. "You were talking to Carter Hale in the courthouse, asking him if he'd help you with something, and he seemed surprised you'd ask him."

His mouth quirked to the side as he pondered it. "There's an upcoming case that Hale wants me to be more lenient on with a plea bargain. Maybe that's it. But I'm more worried about how you felt afterward."

"I felt sick to my stomach and had a headache, but I've started feeling bad with some of my visions lately."

Worry filled his eyes.

"I feel fine now. It's probably nothing."

He started to say something but stopped short when his phone rang. He drew it out and gave me an apologetic grimace before answering. "What do you have, Deputy Miller?"

That got my full attention. I hoped the deputy would have more information about the car that had nearly run me off the road.

"Okay." Mason sounded disappointed. "Well, let me know if something turns up." He hung up and looked into my face. "I called Miller while I was on my walk with Muffy to see if they'd found the car that passed you on the highway."

"I take it they didn't?"

"No." Worry wrinkled his forehead.

"Mason, no one's after me. I'm more worried about you."

He sighed and wrapped his arms around me. "I'm fine. But I promise to be hyper-vigilant until all of this is sorted out. We have the alarm system I installed here and everyone going in and out of the courthouse goes through security. I think I'm pretty protected." He leaned down and kissed me, making my toes curl. "But who's going to protect me from you in our bed? Because right now I intend to take full advantage of the make-up sex clause."

I gave him a half-hearted grin. "That's the only good part of fighting."

Later, as I snuggled against him in the dark, drifting off to sleep, I realized I'd never asked him about Dora.

Maybe it was better that way. I wasn't sure I could handle another fight right now.

Chapter Seven

Soft gray sunlight filtered through the bedroom curtains when I woke up the next morning. I was surprised Mason was still sleep, but he had gotten up multiple times in the night, so he had to be exhausted. As I snuggled closer to him, the events of the previous day flooded my head, ending with the car that had run me off the road. In the cold light of a new day, I felt certain it hadn't been an accident. Which meant Mason really was in danger.

Was this what life was like as the significant other of an ADA? Would our lives constantly be threatened? While the thought was sobering, it wasn't exactly surprising.

The question was, did I want to live *my* life this way?

I stared at his sleeping face and lightly traced my thumb over the worry lines at the corner of his eye. Mason truly believed in justice. He believed in punishing the perpetrators of violent crimes to the full extent of the law to protect innocent people, but he also advocated for leniency and second chances for those who had made foolish choices. He was a just man who poured himself into his work, always keeping the safety of other citizens in mind. How could I fault him for that? Those very tendencies were part of what made me love him so much. Besides, it wasn't like my own secret life didn't come with its parcel of trouble.

My hand slid across his chest, his T-shirt rubbing against my fingertips, before I even thought about what I was doing. Touching Mason had become as natural as breathing.

And that right there was my answer. Not the sex—although I definitely had no complaints there—but the fact that he had become a part of me. I couldn't bear to think about what my life would be like without him in my bed, in my world, as my confidant and partner. He was devoted and loyal, kind and patient, supportive and encouraging, like no other person had ever been to me. Some days he believed in me more than I did in myself, and I had grown in leaps and bounds since he'd wormed his way into my heart. I was with him until the end, whatever that might be, come what may.

While I'd been musing over him, my hand had found its way under the covers and I discovered that he was already stirred up. After only a few strokes, he released a low groan and rolled toward me, capturing my mouth as he began to fondle my body.

Within seconds, I was stirred up myself, but I felt more serious than playful. Mason lifted his face to look at me, and I cupped his cheek so I could stare into his eyes.

His smile faded when he saw my expression. "Rose, are you okay?"

I didn't answer as I tugged his T-shirt over his head, then pushed him onto his back and straddled him, slowly sliding down on top of him, but not moving.

He watched me as he lifted my nightgown over my head and tossed it onto the floor. His hands skimmed up my waist, then cupped my breasts. I gasped and leaned my head back as his thumbs brushed my nipples.

A fire ignited in me and I began to move, closing my eyes and reveling in the moment. Within minutes we were both panting. Mason rolled me onto my back and took over. I locked my ankles around his back as his mouth claimed mine. I lifted up to him and cried out his name as I found release, which pushed him over the edge. He groaned and rested on top of me for several seconds before gathering me gently into his arms and rolling us to our sides, chest to chest.

His fingertips stroked my arm and he searched my face. "I love you."

"I love you too," I said through the lump in my throat.

"Have I done something to upset you?" he asked softly with a worried look in his eyes.

I shook my head. "No. I was just thinkin' about how much I need you."

A soft smile lit up his face. "And the thought is so devastating that it's made you cry?"

"I'm not cryin'," I protested as a single tear escaped the corner of my eye.

His thumb swiped away the traitor. "I can see that."

"Someone wants to hurt you. I'm scared I'm going to lose you."

His eyes filled with adoration. "I'm not going anywhere. I promise."

"You can't promise such a thing."

He grinned. "Rose, I'm not sure if you've noticed this, but I can be a stubborn son-of-a-bitch. I'm not leaving you, by my own free will or someone else's attempt to get rid of me."

He gave me a slow, lingering kiss that had me stirred up again. "I think we need some time away from Henryetta and all our current problems sooner rather than later," he said. "My uncle's cabin is sounding better and better."

"Let's do it," I said. "Obviously I can get away from work now. The question is if *you* can get away."

He looked down at me, a war waging in his eyes. Finally he said, "Let me check my schedule and call my uncle. Maybe we can go away this weekend. It's not as good as having a full week, but I'd rather get you all alone sooner rather than later."

"That sounds wonderful." I kissed him and ran my hands down his back and to his butt.

He groaned against my lips. "You make it very difficult for me to get out of bed."

"Then I'm doing my job."

He laughed. "Speaking of jobs, I need to start getting ready for work. Otherwise we'll be able to live at my uncle's cabin since I'll be unemployed."

"My previous job offer still stands."

He slid out of bed and tugged me with him to the bathroom. "Last I heard, your job offer involved me digging up plants while shirtless. If I'm thinking of applying, I'd better start working out." He winked as he turned on the shower water.

I placed my hands on his chest, taking in the sight of his naked body. "You don't need to do a thing. You're absolutely perfect."

He grinned and gave me another long, slow kiss. "Your job offer's sounding better and better."

I laughed and he pulled me into the water with him.

After we got out of the shower, I got dressed while Mason stood in front of the mirror, shaving.

"What do you have planned for the day?" he asked.

"I have two appointments set up for landscaping consultations. I'm thinkin' about calling Neely Kate to see if she'll come with me."

"That's a good idea. But after yesterday's event, I think I should take my own car. Do you think she'll have any trouble climbing into your truck?"

"We'll manage. But I'm worried about *you* driving your car."

"I'm going to talk to Joe again later, but you better be sure to *call me* if you have any trouble."

I didn't answer and hoped he didn't notice. Instead, I pulled Dora's journal out of my underwear drawer, fingering the worn edges of the leather cover.

Mason walked into the bedroom and pulled a shirt out of the closet. He glanced over his shoulder as he slipped it on. He saw the book in my hand and gave me a questioning glance.

I smiled. "Neely Kate is dying to know more about Dora, so I thought I'd take it with me and we could look at it together. It might give her something else to dwell on besides her miscarriage."

His gaze was troubled when his eyes met mine. "Rose, I know you want to know more about your birth mother, but be careful how deep you dig."

I stiffened. "What makes you say that?"

He walked over to me and set his hands on my shoulders. "I know the woman who raised you was a sadistic witch, so it's only natural that you see your birth mother as the perfect mother who was stolen from you. All I'm saying is that no matter what you find, it might not match up to the fantasy you've created." He pulled back and held my gaze. "You've had enough disappointment and pain in your life. I don't want you to endure any more. So just be careful, okay?"

What did Mason know that he wasn't telling me? I decided now was the time to press him. "You said you'd reopen her case when you had time. Have you done it yet?"

He hesitated. "Yes, but barely." He held up his hands in surrender. "And before you lambast me for not telling you, I'd like to state my defense."

"Okay."

He looked surprised by the lack of anger in my voice, but he forged on. "I know how important it is to you, but I can only justify working on it in my spare moments, which we both know are few and far between. I didn't want to get your hopes up before finding some real information, and sadly I only have the basics at this point. Mostly her employment history and not much else."

"It's okay."

"Really?" he asked in surprise.

"Yeah." I rubbed his chest with my fingertips. "I know how relentless I can be when I want something."

A grin lit up his eyes. "Like a bulldog."

I twisted my lips and gave him a dirty look. "All I ask is that you tell me the truth about what you find, okay? Even if you think it's not what I want to hear."

He studied me for a moment and said softly, "Deal." He glanced down at the book, then back at me. "When things settle down, would you let me go through her journal to see if there's anything I can use?"

"Of course."

He finished getting dressed, then checked the time on his phone. "No time for breakfast with you today, sweetheart. I'll be lucky if I'm not late for a meeting as it is."

"That's okay. I need to head to town soon too."

I followed him downstairs and grabbed my coat to take Muffy out so I could walk Mason to his car. She trailed after us, taking off barking to chase a squirrel up a tree.

I cast a quick glance at her as I debated bringing her with me today, but I hated to leave her in the truck while I was talking to potential clients. Her barking was distracting for one thing, but more importantly, I hated leaving her cooped up. The temperature was supposed to be in the upper forties, so she'd be perfectly safe, but I always felt bad when she watched me through the window with that universal dog look that said *how could you leave me in here?*

Mason opened his car door. "I'm not sure when I can get away to open our joint bank account."

"Oh." After all the fuss last night, I'd forgotten about the whole credit card fiasco. "Okay."

He rested his arm across the top of the door. "Do you want to go by this afternoon and start setting it up?"

I was pretty sure this afternoon wouldn't be an issue; after all, I wasn't supposed to meet Skeeter until later that night. I still hadn't figured out how to get away for our meeting, but I'd deal with one problem at a time. And the current one made me slightly less anxious. "Seein' how you're the one funding the account, I'd rather wait and go with you."

"I understand." He pulled out his wallet and handed me his debit card. "Here. If you need money, you should be safe enough getting cash from an ATM."

"Thank you." I took it from him, then pressed my hand to his chest. I stared into his eyes for a long moment before giving him a kiss, overcome with the knowledge of how very lucky I was. The idea of the checking account still made me uncomfortable, but I told myself I wasn't taking advantage of him, and if our roles were reversed, I'd do the same for him. As he drove away, I pushed aside my guilt and embarrassment and pulled out my phone, hoping Neely Kate would pick up. She'd been screening her calls a lot lately.

I was happy when she answered, but her tone was dull and lifeless again. "Hey, Rose."

"Hey, Neely Kate. What did Ronnie say about your hair?"

"He liked it."

"Well that's good, right?" When she didn't answer, I pushed on. "I have a couple of landscaping consultations today, and I thought you might want to come with me."

"I don't know…"

"It would be really helpful if you could help with some of the consultations I have this spring and summer. Bruce Wayne flat out refuses and I'm not sure I'll be able to handle them all myself." Perhaps it was underhanded of me to take the guilt trip route, but I was sure what Neely Kate needed right now was fresh air and interaction with other people. She thrived off social situations, so being locked up alone in her house had to be hurting rather than helping.

"I guess I could come. But I have a doctor's appointment at three."

Relief washed through me. "We can make that work. I won't be there for another hour to pick you up. Is that enough time for you to get ready?" If Neely Kate had to wash her hair, I knew it would take her a minimum of an hour to wash, dry, and style it.

"Yeah."

She hung up, not sounding too excited by the proposition. I swallowed my disappointment. But she'd agreed to go with me, so I told myself to find happiness in that small victory. This was probably going to be a long battle.

Muffy was taking her sweet time, so I called Bruce Wayne to check on him and remind him about my appointments.

"I'm taking Neely Kate with me," I added.

"And she agreed to go?"

"Reluctantly."

"I hate seeing her so sad," Bruce Wayne said. "I sure wish we could make her feel better."

"It's just gonna take some time. Probably lots of it."

Muffy finished her business—which included sniffing the ground like she was a bloodhound, especially around the front bushes—and we went inside to get to work.

After I poured a cup of coffee, I sat at the table with the journal and a pad of paper and a pen. There were probably answers in these pages, answers to questions I had avoided asking for too long. But now I was ready for the truth, as hard as it might be to face. Running away from the possibility of something ugly in my birth mother's past wouldn't make it any less true.

I started at the beginning.

I'd already read about how she started the journal as a high school project. She wrote about school, boyfriends and friends, usually referring to people by their initials rather than their full names. Her best friend was H, but they also hung out with BM (unfortunate girl) and A. After flipping through the journal for a minute, I got to Dora's time at community college. She had several boyfriends—all disastrous relationships—who occupied her time. But her world fell apart when her grandmother died. She had already lost her parents when she was five and her grandfather when she was fourteen. She had no siblings or extended family. Her greatest fear was being alone.

I've prepared myself for this day for practically my entire life, but now that it's happened, I can barely breathe. I go into Grandma's room and lie down on her bed, trying to breathe in what's left of her lavender perfume. Because as long as I can still smell her, I can pretend she's here with me. When it's finally gone, I'll truly be alone.

She then wrote about her money troubles. Her grandmother had a Social Security income that ended at her death, leaving Dora destitute. She sold off her beloved horses to make ends meet and took off for Shreveport for a few years until she moved back to the farm, heartbroken after her latest breakup. Her friend BM told her about a job at Atchison Manufacturing.

She didn't write much about the job except to say her boss was a kind man who sensed how alone she felt in the world. She had stopped dating, despite her loneliness, because she'd fallen into a deep depression.

In December of 1985 she talked about a man she only referred to as 'he' and 'him.' He was married and older than she was, and she made vague references to seeing him at work and avoiding each other as much as possible to avoid suspicion. They had a brief, heated fling. She knew it was wrong, but she felt like she finally had a purpose for living.

That passage caught my breath. As far as I knew, Daddy had always worked for the lumberyard. Did that mean he wasn't the man she had an affair with? Did that mean he wasn't my father?

I sucked in a breath and pushed on. In January she wrote:

He noticed how upset I was and one thing led to another. I'm horrified. I knew how he felt and I took advantage of that. Now what will I do?

She wrote a single entry in February.

How can something so wonderful be so terrifying at the same time? It's so wrong, yet I've never wanted something so much. Finally, I'll have someone to love, someone who will never leave me. Finally, I will have the family I've always dreamed of with my own precious baby.

Her entries were sporadic after that, with no mention of my father other than her desperation to keep her pregnancy a secret from everyone for fear the baby's father would find out and try to convince her to abort.

In April she wrote an entry that confused me.

He's shown more interest than I expected, and I'm finding him difficult to manage. He's a man I can't deny and it scares me.

Who was she talking about? Daddy? I'd never seen him be forceful with anyone. It was also hard to tell whether the man she wrote about scared her, or if her feelings for him were what frightened her.

In June she wrote about trouble at work.

I find myself caught in the middle of something that has accidently landed in my lap. I can choose to look away or I can do the right thing, but what is the right thing? I only know I must protect my baby.

How had I missed these entries before?

There were more entries about the farm and her pregnancy; then in July she mentioned Daddy.

H has found out about the mess I'm in and has offered to help me find a way out. While I'm grateful, I can't screw up his life any more than I already have. What am I to do?

What did that mean? Was Daddy her lover from the previous winter? Or could she have been referring to something else?

In the beginning of August, I found the first entry that explicitly mentioned her boss's name.

Henry is obstinate in his belief that all is well, but the books continue to prove otherwise. Money is disappearing. He's cold and evasive when I press the matter. He's told me that he's doing this for me just as much as he is for himself.

Why would her boss be doing something for them both that involved missing money? I told myself not to think the worst. The rest of the entries in August were about getting ready for my birth and Daddy.

I've told H that he must think things through carefully. There is his toddler to think about, as well as his wife. He says that he loves me, but things are complicated.

Then a week later, Dora wrote:

A girl. I'm having a precious baby girl. I've decided to name her Rose after my grandmother. How I wish my grandmother were with me now to help me with the decisions I face. I think she'd welcome my baby—despite the circumstances of her conception.

Dora began to write about Gloria and how mean she and the other office girl had become.

I know they think the worst of me, but they are small minded and petty. I don't expect them to understand what Henry and I share.

Then in middle of September she wrote:

Bill is worried and thinks things are about to go bad. I can't deal with this any more. I have to think about Rose.

Bill? That was a new person, and she'd actually shared his full first name. But without a last name to go with it, it wasn't enough to help me.

I can't continue down this path. Henry refuses to change his mind and Harrison has helped me realize what I need to do. As long as I can placate Dirk, I should be fine.

I hope.

Another new name, although it was just as unhelpful at the last.

She wrote about quitting her job and how thankful she had been to get a new one even though it entailed a salary cut. But by then an attorney had contacted her to let her know her grandparents had possessed oil stock, which should have been transferred to Dora. Soon Daddy moved in with her, so she decided to save the stock in case she needed it after the baby was born. She wrote about how happy she was in spite of her continued fears that she was going to get caught, although she never said what she had done.

Then, weeks after my birth, she wrote her last entry:

He came to my house, with Rose sleeping in the next room. In the middle of the day! He told me that if word gets out, he'll make me pay. I don't know what to do. I wish I'd never met him.

I went to Henry because if I tell Harrison he'll take matters into his own hands. Henry's the only one who can stop this madness, but he told me I'm overreacting. That man threatens my baby and he says I'm overreacting.

Something bad is going to happen. I can feel it.

Who had threatened her? Could the same person have also played a part in the fire and Dora's accident?

I looked at my pages of scribbled notes and only one thing came to mind.

What on earth had Dora mixed herself up in?

Chapter Eight

A little over an hour after I called Neely Kate, I pulled up to her house, half-expecting her to tell me she was still getting ready. But she met me at the door wearing a pair of jeans, one of Ronnie's flannel shirts, and a pair of boots. She wasn't wearing any makeup, but her hair still looked pretty from the day before.

"Are you ready?" I asked, refraining from making a comment on her appearance.

"Let me get my coat." She disappeared behind the door and came back a few moments later wearing what looked like one of her cousin's canvas work coats. It was so anti-Neely Kate, I had to keep from gasping.

I forced a smile. "Well, let's get goin'."

She paused and studied the truck for a moment before climbing in. When I got behind the wheel, she asked, "I heard you ran off the road yesterday, but your truck looks none the worse for wear. Were you still in Mason's car?"

The realization that she'd been tuned in to the Fenton County gossip washed over me, leaving a feeling of relief. She was becoming more engaged in the world again. "It's a long story."

"What happened?"

I filled her in, telling her about the note and the accident.

Neely Kate paid attention to the entire story, more interested than I'd seen her in weeks. "Did the deputies find the car?"

"No. Mason called Deputy Miller last night. Apparently nothing's turned up. I bet they're long gone."

"Thank goodness, I guess."

I leaned over the back of the seat. "I got you a surprise."

Her eyebrows lifted in expectation and she gave me a grin when I produced a donut box. "So you really are trying to get me fat."

"Hey," I said as I backed out of the driveway. "Sometimes a girl needs a donut." I pointed to the cup holders. "And I got you coffee too."

I was encouraged when, instead of arguing with me, she opened the lid to the box, grabbed a powdered sugar donut, and took a bite.

"So what's our plan?" she asked, her mouth still full.

"We're goin' to the Nestons' place first. It's an older bungalow in the Forest Ridge neighborhood."

"Hey," she said, turning toward me. "Isn't that where poor Mr. Mitchell lived? The guy Bruce Wayne was accused of killing?"

I cringed. "Yeah, but it's not his house." It wasn't Bruce Wayne's parents' house either. They lived across the street from the man he'd been accused of murdering. Considering the way they'd written him off after his arrest, I sure as Pete wouldn't have accepted a consultation request from them.

"Did you ask Mason about his investigation on Dora last night?"

I sucked in a breath. "No. I asked him about Hilary first and we had a huge fight."

"Wait. Was it *that bad?*"

I shook my head. "No. He had a perfectly logical explanation. But I completely overreacted and got angry with him for not tellin' me in the first place."

"That's not like you."

"I know, but that woman drives me crazy." Truth be told, she'd driven me crazy since before Joe and I even dated. I told Neely Kate Mason's side of the story and she listened in silence until I was done.

"I understand why you were upset," she said slowly, as though thinking through her words. "But I can also see why he wouldn't want to dredge up all those bad memories. When Hilary chose to ignore him, it must have been easy for him to pretend he'd never met her."

"Yeah."

"But Rose." She paused. "That doesn't sound like Mason. He doesn't ignore things. He takes them head on."

"I know. We both know there are things he's not telling me. He's investigating J.R. and he won't share all the details."

"J.R.?" she asked in confusion. "*J.R. Simmons?*"

Crap. Crap. Crap.

I'd majorly screwed up. She didn't know anything about J.R. and his blackmail against me. How was I gonna get out of this one? I didn't want to lie to her, but I couldn't tell her the truth either. Not now that Mason was risking his neck and his career to go head to head with the most powerful man in Arkansas. He'd told me that his trip to Little Rock had uncovered a lead on a possible bribery case up in Columbia County. With any luck, it might be the first in a series of dominoes that would topple J.R. Simmons. I knew he'd taken at least two afternoons to drive up to Magnolia to do a little more digging.

I had to keep what I knew to myself to protect Mason. But I had to tell her something. I scrambled to come up with a reasonable explanation, almost crying with relief when I landed on something she'd buy. "Yeah. Joe's dad."

"Why?" She was definitely suspicious.

"J.R. was behind the small business grant we got from the Arkansas SBA. Anything to do with the Simmons family makes Mason suspicious, so he's checking it out to make sure it's legit." Between Mason and Neely Kate, I was weaving so many lies and half-truths, I was making one ginormous spider's web of deceit. How in the world had I gotten here?

"Huh."

"But like I said, we had a huge fight. He took Muffy for a walk to cool down, and when he came back he apologized for not telling me and I apologized for getting so mad at him. It didn't seem like a good time to bring up Dora."

"So are you gonna ask him tonight?"

I'd actually spent part of the morning thinking about it. "If Mason has a file on her, you and I both know he's probably not gonna tell me what's in it. Besides, he saw me take Dora's journal out of my drawer and confessed that he was trying to gather information in his spare time, which is pretty nonexistent."

"Did he give you any details?" When I shook my head, she pursed her lips. "That hardly seems fair. She's your birth mother."

"But Mason has certain responsibilities associated with his job and it's not fair for me to ask him to break the rules to tell me." I was already putting his job at risk, both with his off-the-clock J.R. investigation and my own moonlighting as the Lady in Black that I couldn't ask him to break more rules. "Besides, the more I think about it, he would have put what he knew on his sheet of information." I turned toward her for a second before looking out the windshield. "I suspect that's the extent of what he knows."

"So you're really gonna just sit around and wait for him to tell you what's goin' on with his investigation and what he may or may not know?"

"Shoot, no." He'd always told me that Dora's cold case had to take a backseat to more current cases. But as far as I was concerned, that didn't mean the investigation had to stop. It just needed new investigators.

I cast a side-long glance to my friend. Neely Kate needed something to pull her out of her doldrums and she was always cajoling me into snooping. She was usually the one who had to push me. I suddenly had the perfect solution to two problems. It wouldn't make everything—or, heck, anything—better, but it was bound to give her something else to think about.

I turned to look at Neely Kate and lifted my eyebrows. "I want you to help me investigate."

To my surprise, she merely gaped at me instead of responding. I pressed on. "I told you that he didn't have much information in his file, and I can remember most of it. Plus, I have a resource full of juicy tidbits that I know he hasn't used to help us with clues."

"What?"

"Dora's diary."

There was still no response from Neely Kate and my heart sank a little. I'd really thought she'd go for my idea. She was always pressing me to use my visions to solve mysteries, and this was a mystery I'd been dying to untangle. And it had to be pretty safe. My birth mother had died twenty-five years ago. It wasn't like it was a current investigation. Besides, part of me suspected the woman who'd raised me had killed Dora, and she wasn't likely to hurt us from beyond that grave.

"You want the two of us to investigate your birth mother's death?" she finally said.

"And if she was part of some extortion scheme."

She shook her head. "You realize we've totally reversed roles, right? I'm always the one tryin' to coerce you into solvin' some mystery and you're the one tellin' me it's a crazy idea."

"So you're telling me this is a crazy idea?"

A slow grin spread across her face. "All our ideas are crazy ideas, but when did that ever stop us? You're sure you want to do this? I'm not sure Mason would approve since he's obviously keeping things from you, and you know Joe won't."

I waved my hand. "Joe's not an issue. And Mason... This isn't dangerous, so I don't see what the problem is."

"But you're still not gonna tell him?"

"I haven't decided yet." Probably not, given that he had bigger things to worry about. "But we've solved two cases. We're good at this, right?"

"Heck yeah, we are." I was happy to hear the excitement in her voice. "But you've solved more than that. You've got at least five cases under your belt. That's probably more than the HPD has solved in two years. The Henryetta police should have hired you instead of that incompetent Officer Sprout."

I snorted. There wasn't enough money in the world to entice me to work for the Henryetta police. "Well, we can discuss this more later," I said as I parked in front of the Nestons' house. It took Neely Kate a minute to climb out of the truck, and I reminded myself not to push her too much. She didn't have a huge incision, but she'd had surgery two and a half weeks ago, not to mention the trauma of almost dying and losing her babies.

We walked around the outside with the homeowner, an elderly woman who was moving to Florida and wanted to get her house ready for market. I had Neely Kate sit on the front porch while I took measurements and made notes. When I finished, I helped her up and we walked slowly to the truck.

Once we were inside, I turned to her, worried. "Maybe you're overdoin' it."

She sighed and leaned her head back on the seat. "I'm tired, but I'm not ready to go home yet. Besides, we need to come up with a plan for starting our investigation."

"How about we go do the consultation at the next house, and then I'll take you to lunch and we can figure out what to do first."

"Deal."

While we drove to the next house, which was in Violet's old neighborhood, I explained what I planned to do at Mrs. Neston's house and why. Neely Kate caught on quick, and although she didn't have the experience I did, I hoped to send her out on home visits when I was too busy. I could come up with designs from her photos and drawings.

The next stop was quick, and even though she stayed in the truck, she looked pale.

"Would you like me to take you home?" I asked, worried.

She sat up and shook her head. "No. I know I'm terrible company but I'm not ready to go home yet."

"Don't worry about what kind of company you are. I just want to be with you. How about we get some lunch?"

"Sounds good." Her voice was so soft and unlike her usual self it scared me, but I reminded myself that she just needed time and love.

We decided to eat at Blue Plate Diner outside of town. We had just ordered our food when my phone rang. I looked down at the number and grimaced.

Joe.

Great.

Chapter Nine

I shot Neely Kate a grimace, then answered. "Hey, Joe."

"I heard about what happened yesterday afternoon." He didn't sound one bit happy about it.

I should have known he'd have a fit about the accident. Why I hadn't prepared for this call was beyond me. But I'd had a lot of things happen the day before. For all I knew, he'd heard about the Piggly Wiggly incident.

"I've given them both a good talking to."

Oh, mercy, he *had* heard. "I didn't mean to stir up trouble. I promise."

He paused. "How could this be your fault? The way I heard it, you were there minding your own business."

I shook my head in confusion. There's no way he would have heard that at the Piggly Wiggly. Even if it *was* true. "What on earth are you talking about?"

"I heard about your run-in with Hilary and my sister."

"Oh. *That.* I thought you were calling about the accident or the...." My voice trailed off.

"What else happened yesterday afternoon?" He sounded exasperated.

"Nothing. I was about to say the note on Mason's car." Hopefully the Piggly Wiggly incident would stay under wraps, but seeing as how Miss Mildred was involved, I doubted that was likely. One problem at a time.

His tone turned angry. "You should have called me yesterday, Rose."

Whether I should have called him or not was debatable, and I didn't feel like getting into it at the moment. I sighed. "Joe, Deputy Miller took care of everything. How about we get back to the real reason you called."

He paused and his voice softened. "I want to apologize about Hilary and Kate. They've been at odds since they were in diapers. My sister has always seen it as a personal challenge to best Hilary. Kate has gotten it into her head that Hilary's the reason we broke up. She also knows that Hilary wants to marry me, so I think Kate's doin' everything in her power to get you and me back together."

My mouth dropped, leaving me speechless.

"I need you to know I do not approve of this. Contrary to my actions in the recent past, I'm no part of it."

Two months ago, I would have doubted his assertion. Now I actually believed him. "I know."

"Thank you." He sounded surprised, but he recovered quickly. "I've told Kate to back off, but she's never been good at listening. I'm doing my best to make her leave you alone, but short of arresting her for harassment, I'm not sure what else I can do."

"You would arrest your own sister for harassment?"

"If she keeps pestering you mercilessly? Yes, I would." I could tell he meant it.

"I don't know what to say, Joe."

"We're friends now, right?" he asked. "Kate might be my sister, but she ran off without a backward glance two years ago, worrying me to death. Now she has her own agenda and she doesn't care who she hurts in the process." He paused. "It's the Simmons way."

"You're not like that anymore," I said softly.

"I'm still workin' on it." We were both silent for a moment. "If she contacts you again, will you please let me know?"

I wasn't sure what good it would do, but if our roles had been reversed, I'd want to know too. "Of course."

"Thanks. Now tell me about the details of your accident yesterday afternoon."

"Joe," I groaned. "I already told Deputy Miller everything."

"Maybe you missed something."

"I didn't. There wasn't much to tell."

He paused. "Fine. I'll read the report, but I may call you with some follow-up questions. And if you feel unsafe at all, promise me you'll tell me."

"Joe."

"Promise."

Something in his voice caught my attention. "Do you think I'm unsafe?"

He chuckled, but it sounded forced. "You're always unsafe." This sounded like more than his general *you're always in trouble* attitude. What did he know or suspect that had him worried about me, but not worried enough to lock me away in witness protection? My breath caught.

Mason.

It only confirmed the fears I'd had since December. No matter how much Joe and Mason protested the danger was over, I wasn't so sure. Someone was still after my boyfriend. At least they were taking my claims seriously now.

"If I feel unsafe, you'll be one of the first people to know." And I meant it.

I hung up and looked into Neely Kate's questioning gaze. "I think you figured out the gist of that conversation."

She didn't say anything.

"He says Kate has her own agenda: one-upping Hilary. Her goal is to get me and Joe back together."

"Oh, my stars and garters."

"He's trying to get her to leave me alone. But he says she's determined."

She lifted her chin, a spark filling her eyes. "Then it's a good thing we're even more determined."

I grinned. "Yeah, I guess so."

The waitress brought out our food, a club sandwich for Neely Kate and a house salad with dressing on the side for me.

Neely Kate cast me a curious glance. "Since when do you get dressing on the side?"

I didn't answer for a moment, but when her gaze turned to a glare, I caved. "Since I've started wearing certain dresses."

Her eyes widened.

"They're tighter than anything I usually wear. They show my fat rolls."

Her head jutted back in disbelief. "What fat rolls?"

I sighed. "Neely Kate, I'm self-conscious enough about wearing skin-tight dresses, I at least want to look good in them."

She leaned forward and hissed, "No one even knows who you are!"

I set down my fork. "I know who I am."

"And so does Skeeter," she whispered.

"What does *that* mean?"

"Are you trying to impress him?"

My anger billowed. "No. I can *not* believe you just insinuated that!"

"Then why are you still going along with this madness?"

I scowled. "You know darn good and well. A deal's a deal. And besides, I've got one month down without incident. Only five to go."

"He's gonna call you again. Don't be thinkin' he won't."

I picked up my fork. "He already did." I kept my gaze on my bowl. "I have to meet him tonight."

"Rose!" When I didn't respond, she lowered her voice. "What do you have to do?"

"I'm meeting Jed at eight to go to a business meeting." I lifted my eyebrows. "And before you ask, no, I don't know what I'm doin' there. He said it was with a few associates, so I suspect I'll be lookin' for traitors."

She rolled her eyes and waved her hand in an exaggerated swoop. "Just the same ol', same ol'."

I groaned. "What would you have me do, Neely Kate? Tell Mason? It's eatin' away at me, but can you even begin to imagine what he'd do if he found out?"

Some of her irritation faded. "It wouldn't be pretty."

"No. It wouldn't." I stabbed my lettuce with more force than necessary. "I wish I wasn't in this situation, but if I could live that night at Gems over again and I was forced to either let Mason die or coerce Skeeter into helping me, I would do the exact same thing." I looked into her eyes. "I love him, Neely Kate, and I don't want to lose him. Please stop fightin' me on this and help me."

She closed her eyes, then pushed out a breath before opening them and grabbing my hand. "You're right. If I had to make the choice between letting Ronnie burn up in a fire or six months of indentured servitude with the Fenton County crime boss, I'd pick working with Skeeter." She squeezed my hand. "I'll help you."

"Thank you."

"But we only have another couple of hours until I have to get home for my doctor's appointment, so right now we're gonna work on figurin' out who killed Dora."

I pulled my notebook out of my purse. "I'm gonna list everything I've found out from Mason's file and Dora's journal."

"Good idea."

"Mostly Mason had a bunch of facts in his file. Dora was born in Shreveport. I already knew her parents died when she five and she moved to the farm to live with her grandparents." I scribbled down notes as I spoke. "After high school, she went to technical school and moved to Shreveport for a couple of years before returning to Fenton County and getting a job at Atchison Manufacturing." I looked up at Neely Kate. "In her journal she said she was worried about getting caught, which plays along with Mason's note about the extortion scheme. It also explains why she was eager enough to leave Atchinson Manufacturing that she quit and found another job two months before I was born. The question is whether or not she played a direct part in the extortion."

"It must have had something to do with her job."

"Her journal entries lend themselves to that. Her boss knew about it. And so did Daddy and two other men. Bill and Dirk. But there's no information about what they were doin'. There was someone who scared her, and I don't think it was any of those four men." I tapped the pen on the table, trying to dismiss the growing realization that there was a good chance my birth mother had been a criminal. "Do you know anything about Atchison Manufacturing?"

"I think my uncle used to work there after he graduated high school. There was a fire and the owner didn't reopen."

"Wait. I've heard this before," I said with a gasp. "Dena told me about it when I picked up your cupcakes yesterday. She said Ima Jean from Ima Jean's Bakery used to be nice. But her husband had an affair and his factory burned down. He killed himself."

She covered her mouth with her hand. "That's terrible."

"I bet it's the same place."

"But Ima Jean's last name isn't Atchison. It's Buchanan."

"Can we talk to your uncle?"

She shook her head. "Not if we want answers right away. He's up in Alaska on a hunting trip. My Aunt Thelma is paying him to hunt down new meat for her jerky business."

"Alaska? In the middle of winter?"

She shrugged. "He's always liked the cold. It doesn't bother him. In fact, he's camping."

I blinked. And I had thought Neely Kate's family was no longer capable of surprising me. "You can't call him?"

"Granny tried just last week, but there's no cell phone service in the tundra. She was gonna ask him to hunt her down a polar bear so she could make a fur coat. But my cousin Dolly Parton told her that that was ridiculous. She can't have a polar bear coat."

"No kidding."

"The winters here in Arkansas aren't near cold enough."

"That too…" I regrouped and asked, "How long's he gonna be gone?"

"Another couple months. He's stayin' up there until the day before the Ides of March."

"Why the Ides of March?"

"One of his sled dogs is named Brutus. He's worried he'll turn on him."

"Your uncle reads Shakespeare?"

She shrugged. "He saw the movie."

"Okay…so your uncle's out as a potential source." I took a bite of my salad. "We need to find someone else who'll remember what happened."

Neely Kate cringed. "There's no way Ima Jean's gonna talk to us, let alone give us any leads."

"No. Not Ima Jean. Someone who makes it her business to know everyone else's doings and has been around since the beginning of time."

Neely Kate let out a low whistle. "I only know of one person who fits that criteria and there's no way she's gonna talk to you either."

"She will if I bring some kind of peace offering."

"I think you must have whacked your head on the dashboard when you ran off the road. You could bring her gold bullion and she still wouldn't talk to you."

I gave her an ornery grin. "We'll just see about that."

Chapter Ten

I spent a good ten minutes trying to figure out what peace offering might soften Miss Mildred. Ultimately, I drove downtown to Ima Jean's Bakery.

Neely Kate had a royal fit when I told her to wait in the truck, but the square was crowded and I had to park in front of the florist, which was a good two blocks from the bakery. I was worried she'd overdone it, and I didn't want her to walk that far.

"Look, Neely Kate, you know I'm not gonna get a flippin' word out of her. In fact, I'm not sure I'm even gonna try. I'm only getting some kind of baked good to take as my peace offering, and you know Miss Mildred would scoff at anything from Dena's." I ignored her glare. "What do you think she likes?"

"Blood pudding, made from the sacrifice of heathen sinners." Her eyebrows lifted. "Did she ever try to sneak in your house and take your blood while you were sleepin'?"

"She was one of the few people who didn't try to break into my house when I lived there. Not to mention the fact that she's not a vampire."

"But it would explain so much."

I sighed. "I'll figure out what to get her. Or maybe ask Ima Jean."

She snorted. "Good luck with *that.*"

Ignoring her uncharacteristic pessimism, I left her in the still-running truck and headed toward the bakery. It was after lunchtime, but Ima Jean's shop was dead to the world. In fact, the shades were half-pulled, and given the northern exposure, I couldn't help but wonder if Ima Jean was the vampire.

"Can I help you?" a woman's voice called out when I walked inside.

I searched the shop and found her behind the counter, sitting on a stool and doing a crossword puzzle. She was a good twenty years younger than Ima Jean and a whole lot prettier, but in a rough living kind of way. She had bright red hair, which, judging from her dark roots, was obviously colored. "Uh…yeah. I need to get something for my neighbor. She's elderly—in her eighties—but I'm not sure what she'd like. Any suggestions?"

Without budging from her stool or putting down her pencil, the woman gave me a blank stare. "You're asking *me?*"

I shrugged. "Well, yeah."

She hopped up and strode over to the case. "What makes you think I'd know?"

"I…"

Her eyebrows lifted in mock surprise. "Because all the old people shop here now?"

"That's not what I meant. I—"

She laughed. "I'm just shittin' ya." When she stopped guffawing, she said, "Who're you shoppin' for? Maybe I know their favorite."

She seemed mighty jovial considering she was liable to be out of a job if Ima Jean heard her talking that way. "Mildred Winkleman. I'm hopin' to butter her up."

She burst out laughing again. "*Mildred?* Why, there ain't enough sugar in this whole shop to sweeten that woman up, let alone butter her to boot."

"So, she doesn't come in here?"

"Oh, she comes in here all right. She tries to tell me that our cakes are too dry and our pie crust is too tough. Why just last week, I told 'er she was more than welcome to show me how it ought to be done, but she stomped off, sniveling about the ungrateful younger generation."

I supposed the woman was young enough for Mildred to refer to her as a part of a younger generation. "There's nothing she likes?"

"I don't know if she likes them or not, but she always gets the double chocolate brownies. She claims she uses them as a laxative. Comes in every week like clockwork to get her week's supply."

I wasn't sure what to make of that.

"You want me to package some up for ya? I can put 'em in a box with a ribbon."

"Uh…" Was giving a gift that was the equivalent of Ex Lax, only tied up with a bow, a good idea? "Yeah. That would be great."

"Sure thing." She scooped out a couple of brownies and put them in a small green bag, then wrapped red ribbon all around it and tied it off. It looked like it had been wrapped by a drunken elf after he'd broken his hand in a tussle with a reindeer.

She slapped the bag on the counter and I fought a cringe. Between the smack and how tightly wrapped the bag was, the brownies had to be crushed.

"That'll be ten dollars."

My mouth dropped. "For two brownies?"

She shrugged. "What are ya gonna do? Inflation and all that jazz. Plus, we raised the prices to make more money since we only have a quarter of the customers we used to have before Dena's Bakery opened."

I wanted to tell her that raising prices in response to declining business was a terrible idea, but I figured that was the least of her worries.

"Have you been there?" she asked as I handed her the money.

"Where?"

"Dena's. Her marble cake is to die for."

"You've shopped there?" I asked in surprise.

"Of course," she said, acting as if I were a fool. "You think I'd eat this garbage?"

I picked up the bag and my head began to tingle. The next moment, I was in a bar, dancing with a man with thinning hair who smelled like peas. His paunchy gut bumped into mine.

I swayed on my feet, the room spinning around me, but the man held me upright. It was obvious I'd had too much to drink.

"So when you gonna get this fortune you claim is comin'?" her date asked, sounding skeptical.

"Sooner than I'd dreamed. The answer just dropped out of heaven."

The vision faded and I was staring into the face of the woman behind the counter, while a tidal wave of pain crashed through my head. "Your fortune's comin' soon."

She laughed. "If that ain't so? My fortune, you say? I gave up hope of my fortune ever comin' a long time ago. What are you doin' going around talkin' about fortunes?"

I forced a smile, eager to get out of there and take an ibuprofen. "It's almost Chinese New Year. It's something they say. Like Happy New Year."

"You don't say?" she said in surprise. "Your fortune's comin' soon." She grinned and shimmied her shoulders. "You learn something new every day. Now I feel all cosmopolitan."

"Thanks." I stuffed the bag into my purse and hurried out the door. I wasn't sure what to make of her vision, and although most visions usually had nothing to do with me, this one concerned me since it made me ill. Did her fortune have anything to do with Mason?

The cold air hit me the instant I walked outside and my hair blew into my face, obscuring my vision. I turned in the direction of the truck and ran right into someone. Brushing the hair out of my face, I was frustrated to see I'd stumbled into Kate Simmons.

Crappy doodles.

I took a couple of steps backward as I recovered my balance.

She put her hands on her hips and tilted her head. "Well, if it isn't little Rose Gardner."

I considered trying to make some kind of small talk, but Joe didn't trust her, which was a good enough reason for me not to trust her either. "Sorry, I wasn't lookin' where I was going."

I tried to step around her, but she blocked my path. "I was hoping I'd run into you in town, although not quite so literally." She laughed, but a determined look in her eyes told me I wasn't going anywhere until she deemed our conversation done.

I steeled myself. "Well, here I am. What can I do for you?"

"I think we can be friends," she said. "I'd like to be friends."

"Oh." I wasn't expecting that. "Well…"

"I know I haven't put my best foot forward, but I was hoping we could start over. Maybe we could meet for…" She glanced around the square. "What do you all do around here? Meet for moonshine?"

"Or coffee." She'd just confirmed why this was a terrible idea. "Look, Kate. I'm not sure why you're here in Henryetta, but if you're trying to get Joe and me back together, it's a wasted effort. We are over. I'm with Mason and I love him. I have no plans of leaving him. In fact, we plan on getting married."

All expression left her face. "So you really *are* engaged."

I wasn't sure why I'd added that last part, other than to drive home that she'd hopped onto the wrong bandwagon, but something told me it might not have been the best tactic if I wanted to encourage her to back down. "Not officially. But we're living together." What was I doing spilling my personal life to her? "Honestly, Kate. It's none of your business."

"Did you talk to Mason about Hilary?"

"And why would I do that?"

She grinned. "You did. You asked him because you had to know. What did he tell you?"

Now I was getting angry. "I know what you're doing. You're trying to cause strife between Mason and me, but it's not gonna work. I know all about Hilary and Mason in Little Rock."

"So you know that Hilary wanted Mason Deveraux instead of Joe?"

I shook my head. "I have no idea where you got such ridiculous information, but it's not true. Besides, you weren't even around. How would you even know? You were in California."

Her eyes widened and a wicked smirk spread across her face. "*Was* I?"

"What the Sam Hill are you doin'?" I shook my head in disbelief. "I'm done with all this double talk nonsense." I pushed past her, my anger spurring me forward, and she didn't try to stop me this time.

I'd taken several steps when she called after me. "I know things you need to know."

Against my better judgment, I spun around to face her. "About Mason?" Did she know something about who was trying to kill him?

"Think bigger, baby girl."

My breath caught. "About your father?"

She waggled her eyebrows. "Maybe. Maybe not."

"So you're not going to tell me?"

Her eyes twinkled with mischievousness. "Not yet."

I had no idea what she was talking about and I was done with this game. "Go home, Kate, wherever that really is. Go home and leave me alone."

She grinned. "I'm not going anywhere yet. When you're ready—and you'll know when that is—I'll fill you in."

I spun around and hurried away, suddenly wondering whose side Kate was really on.

Obviously not mine.

Chapter Eleven

Neely Kate didn't look too happy when I got back into the truck.

"Did I see you talkin' to Kate Simmons?"

"Yes," I groaned as I tossed my purse on the seat, remembering too late about the brownies.

"I thought you were getting Miss Mildred something from Ima Jean's."

"I did. It's in my purse."

She pulled it out, holding it between her thumb and index finger. "What in tarnation is this?"

"Miss Mildred's laxatives."

She dropped the bag with a screech. "*What?*"

"It's a long story."

"Lately it seems like everything with you is a long story."

I sure as Pete couldn't argue with that.

I pulled my truck up in front of Violet's house, the house I'd grown up in, then cast a glance at the tiny house next door. Joe no longer lived there, though, having moved into the farmhouse that bordered the southern edge of my property.

Right now, it was the house across the street that had my interest. Miss Mildred's house. I decided to approach her with hat in hand—or, more literally, crushed baked goods in hand—and go from there.

"I still think you're crazy," Neely Kate grumbled as we walked up to her door. "She's never gonna tell us anything."

"Maybe she won't. Or maybe she'll give us a lead, unwilling or not, that will point us in the right direction."

"Or maybe monkeys are gonna start flying out of my butt."

I put my hands on my hips. "I have to at least try."

She smirked. "Oh, I'm not trying to stop you. This should be fun to watch." She held up her phone. "Heck, I plan on recording it." She grinned. "I'm just tellin' you how it's liable to turn out."

I rolled my eyes. I wanted to protest, but I suspected she was right. I pointed at her hand. "You better not use that phone unless it's to call 911. One of us might need medical attention after this."

I knocked on the front door and stepped back. Neely Kate was standing right by the steps to the porch, as if she were ready to take off running if we needed to escape.

Miss Mildred opened the door leaning on a cane, surprise then suspicion flitting through her eyes as she stood in the frame.

"Good afternoon, Miss Mildred," I said as sweetly as I could muster. I held up the bag, suddenly questioning the wisdom of giving it to her. "I brought you a gift."

I cast a glance at Neely Kate for support, but she looked down, her shoulders trembling.

She was laughing. Great. But I told myself it was good she was happy for a few seconds, even if it was at my expense.

Miss Mildred was less amused and pointed her cane in my face. "You've got three seconds to get off my porch or I'm calling Officer Ernie."

I held up my hands in a defensive gesture, the crumpled bag hanging from my fingertips. "I'm here in peace." When she still didn't take the gift, I set it on the porch railing.

The elderly woman snorted. "What sort of devil's witchcraft are you up to now?"

I decided a direct approach was the only way I was going to get anywhere. "I'm here because I need some information about a factory that burned down in 1986. I know how diligent you are about keeping an eye on local issues, so I thought you might remember it."

Neely Kate covered her mouth with her hand, her shoulders outright shaking now. I shot her a glare. She had her phone in her hand at waist level, trying—not very well—to hide the fact that she was recording our conversation. I should have left her behind in the truck.

Miss Mildred gave me her own glare. "Why would I tell you anything?"

Crappy doodles, why would she? My peace offering plan was crashing and burning. Then it hit me. Miss Mildred had encouraged me to prove that Miss Dorothy had been murdered. I cocked my head and lifted my eyebrows. "Because I'm solving a mystery."

She leaned on her cane and shifted her weight. "And why would I care?"

"Because..." I forged on. "Because I think you secretly want to solve one too. That's why you're so good as president of the busybody club, uh, I mean the neighborhood watch."

She hesitated. "What kind of mystery?"

"I think someone was responsible for that fire. I'm trying to figure out who and why."

"And why would you be trying to figure out a twenty-five-year-old mystery?"

Neely Kate stepped forward. "The reward."

I looked back at her, my eyes wide.

"What reward?" Miss Mildred asked, her interest unmistakable.

I could see where this was going. My former neighbor was gonna refuse to tell us anything unless we split the nonexistent reward with her, which would certainly put me in a pickle owing to my distinct lack of cash money. "It's not a monetary reward," I said, my brain scrambling fast. "It's like a club… a competition. We get the reward of figuring it out before everyone else does." Then I hastily added, "And a certificate."

Her suspicion returned. "I may be old, but I ain't no fool. I've never heard of such a thing."

"It's fairly new. It's all because of those cold case TV shows," Neely Kate said. "It's inspired people to start solving their own cases."

She squinted at Neely Kate. "What's the name of this club?"

"The Fenton County Unsolved Mystery Club," she said without missing a beat.

"Huh."

I had no idea if this crazy story was gonna work, but there was no turning back now. Especially since she hadn't slammed the door in our faces. "So will you help us?"

She studied me, her eyes narrowing into such tiny slits it was a wonder she could still see me.

"Are you thinking about helping, or are you plotting how to kill Rose and dispose of the body?" Neely Kate asked.

"Neely Kate!" I gasped, spinning around to face her.

"I'll do it," Miss Mildred said, banging her cane on the porch railing.

I jumped and spun back around so fast I made myself dizzy. "Which one? Help us or murder me?"

Her lips curled. "I'd prefer to do both, but seein' as how yer boyfriend would probably have me tossed in jail, I'll stick with helping. But I have conditions."

"*Conditions?*"

"Okay," Neely Kate said. "What are they?"

She pointed her cane at me. "At no time will you be drivin' my car."

"*What?*" Why would I drive her car? Then I remembered that I'd once borrowed it to save Joe. "That was *one* time."

"And my name goes first on the paper."

"What paper?" I asked. "*The newspaper?*"

Neely Kate stepped up behind me and lowered her voice. "The certificate. For the competition, of course."

Miss Mildred's disdain returned. "For someone who's supposedly solved so many mysteries, you're awfully dense. All those bad guys must have turned themselves into you and brought their own handcuffs."

My hands clenched into fists at my sides.

For once, my best friend skipped over defending me. "I think you've misunderstood, Miss Mildred," Neely Kate said, fighting the grin that tugged at her lips. "We don't need you for our team. We just want to interview you."

The elderly woman shook her head. "Nope. I either help you solve the case or I don't help at all."

Neely Kate nodded. "Fine."

I grabbed her arm and carefully tugged her off the porch. "Miss Mildred, I need a moment to talk with my *partner*." When we were out of earshot, I leaned toward her and whispered. "What are you doin'?"

"She's one of the few people who was actually around when the factory burned down. We need her."

"No we don't. Half the town is over the age of sixty. *Everyone* probably remembers the fire." I pointed to the house next door. "If Miss Mildred won't help us out, we can just march over to Miss Opal's and ask her."

"Think about it, Rose. You were onto something when you said all that neighborhood watch business is her attempt to solve a mystery. You and I both know she's always filing away details."

"Not all of them are right," I pointed out. "She gets all kinds of things wrong."

"She only seems to skew them when *you're* involved. And you weren't even born when this happened, so I think you're off the hook. Besides, she was your momma's best friend and you think your momma might have killed Dora. All the more reason to keep Mildred around—you can pump her for information about Dora and your momma."

"She's not gonna willingly give us information that proves Momma killed Dora."

"Don't you think Miss Mildred would have built a wood pile in your front yard and burned your momma at the stake if she truly thought your momma was a murderer? I've never met a woman more judgmental of what she considers wrong-doin'."

She had a point. My jaw clenched. "Maybe so, but I refuse to traipse around town with *Miss Mildred*."

"Who said we have to take her with us? Let's tell her she's the home base and we're gonna do the leg work."

I groaned. This would be an absolutely terrible idea if it weren't such a good one.

"Ha!" Neely Kate said, her voice filled with excitement. "You know I'm right."

I couldn't outright admit it was a good idea. I still wasn't sure I wanted to involve nosy Miss Mildred by doing more than interviewing her, but I could see some of Neely Kate's points. "Fine."

Before I could change my mind, Neely Kate hurried back to the porch, leaving me to reluctantly follow behind.

"Okay, Miss Mildred," Neely Kate said, holding out her hand to shake. "You've got yourself a deal."

She gave Neely Kate's hand a brisk shake and proceeded to drop it as though it were on fire.

"So here's how this is gonna work," Neely Kate said. "You're gonna be home base. You'll stay here and be in charge—"

"In charge?" I blurted out, but Neely Kate ignored me.

"And we'll report back to you. You'll be like Bobbie on *Supernatural*."

Miss Mildred's face puckered like a prune. "What's *Supernatural?*"

Neely Kate blinked, her mouth parting open, and her full body seemed to shudder. "I'm gonna pretend you didn't say that." I felt an unexpected stab of sympathy for my former neighbor. Four months ago I'd been in her shoes. *Supernatural* was one of Neely Kate's favorite TV shows. She'd shamed me into watching it too.

Miss Mildred waved aside her comments about the show with much more bravery than I'd possessed. "If I'm hangin' around here, how am I gonna help solve the mystery?

"We'll bring back clues, and you can help us figure out where to go from there."

"Huh." She was actually considering this.

"We can get walkie-talkies," Neely Kate added. "So we can keep track of each other."

Miss Mildred nodded. "And we'll have code names."

This was getting out of hand.

"Miss Mildred," I groaned. "This is—"

"It was Atchison Manufacturing," Miss Mildred said, her eyes bright. "Henry Buchanan owned it. He never reopened it after it burned down in the fire right after Thanksgiving, and he hung himself in his basement a few weeks later."

"So it *was* Ima Jean's Buchanan's husband," I said, turning to Neely Kate. Dora had also explicitly mentioned Henry in the journal. We were definitely on the right track.

Neely Kate shot me an *I told you so* look, but I wasn't willing to let her gloat. I was pretty sure Miss Opal could have told us the same thing.

Miss Mildred glanced around the neighborhood. "Mitsy Johnson is peering out her picture windows. I can't talk to you out here."

"You want to go inside?" Neely Kate asked.

Miss Mildred looked offended. "What kind of sleuth are you? If I invite you inside, it's gonna look suspicious. I'll meet you somewhere."

"This is getting ridiculous," I muttered.

But Neely Kate's head bobbed. "You're right. Where do you want to meet?"

"I was gonna suggest the produce aisle of the Piggly Wiggly, but that one can't go back there without causing a commotion. She caused enough trouble yesterday." Miss Mildred's eyes filled with disgust and she flicked a finger toward me. "In fact, I'm not sure I want to work with her."

I half expected Neely Kate to tell her I was off our nonexistent team, but instead she squared her shoulders. "Rose stays or it's no deal."

The elderly woman's jaw set.

"Rose is one of the sweetest people I know, but for some reason you're just too pigheaded to see it."

The elderly woman pointed a gnarled finger at me. "That girl is possessed by demons. I can't risk her demons jumping out and taking over my own soul."

Neely Kate put her hand on her hip. "Are you *sure* you don't watch *Supernatural?*"

Miss Mildred gave her a blank stare. "I gave up trying to save her soul years ago."

"Saving Rose's soul isn't part of the bargain." Neely Kate shrugged her shoulder, tossing her hair. "We'll make do without you. We're a pretty good team on our own. We only came to you because it makes sense to go to the best potential source of information first." She turned around. "Come on, Rose. Let's go talk to Miss Opal."

"Fine," Miss Mildred said. "I'll do it, but only because I owe this town my expertise. And I want that trophy."

"Certificate," Neely Kate corrected.

I rolled my eyes. "So where do you want to meet?"

Miss Mildred gave me a sideways glance. "The one place I think my soul will be safe. Church."

Chapter Twelve

A half hour later, I parked my truck in the parking lot of Jonah's church. I'd texted Joe to let him know I'd survived another cryptic encounter with his sister. I slipped my phone into my coat pocket, then turned to Neely Kate. "Tell me again why we're lettin' her think she's in charge?"

Neely Kate gave me an exasperated look. "I told you a half dozen times already. I think she knows things that will help us. And need I remind you that you were the one who suggested we talk to her in the first place?"

"Yeah, talk to her, not cater to her every persnickety demand. Heck, she probably doesn't have any more information than what I already found in Dora's journal."

"I'm not so sure. If you were involved in criminal activity would *you* write it down?"

"We don't *know* that Dora was involved in criminal activity. It's just as likely she stumbled upon it and quit. Maybe she thought she'd get in trouble for not forking over important information."

"We can't go into this with any preconceived notions, Rose. Just because she was your birth mother doesn't mean she couldn't do something bad."

I knew she was right, but I still couldn't believe Dora had extorted anyone. In my opinion, the guilt she'd felt wasn't proof of her active involvement in a crime. But then again, if someone told me three months ago I'd be sniffing out information for Fenton County's crime boss, I would have asked if they'd had a recent head trauma. Desperate people did desperate things. My own situation was proof enough of that. "Fine. We'll find out what Mildred knows and be done with her."

Neely Kate reached for the door handle. "Maybe I should do the talking since she'd not too fond of you."

"Fine."

We walked inside the front doors of the church and I peeked around to look for Miss Mildred. I hadn't seen her old Cadillac in the parking lot, but given her secret agent suggestion of meeting here, it wouldn't surprise me a bit if she'd decided to hide her car. "She's not here yet."

Neely Kate sat in a chair in the foyer. "I'm gonna rest here for a moment."

She looked pale and worn out, which gave me second thoughts about this whole caper. "Maybe we should postpone talking to Miss Mildred for tomorrow. This mystery's been sitting around for twenty-five years. One more day's not gonna matter a hill of beans. I'm sure you could use some rest."

"We're already here, so we might as well see this part through." She grimaced. "Although maybe you could just drop me off at the doctor's office instead of taking me home to get my car. Ronnie's coming, so he can take me home."

"Ronnie's coming to your doctor's appointment?" I was shocked. He usually wanted nothing to do with anything medical. "Is everything okay?"

She shrugged. "It's no big deal. But this way, I can go home and take a nap afterward. My granny is makin' me take her to Bingo tonight."

"You're kidding."

"I wish I was. She says no good ever came from sittin' around and mopin'."

"Is that what she thinks you've been doin'?" I asked in shock. "Because even if you were, there'd be nothin' wrong with that."

She shook her head, tears filling her eyes. "She's right. I wasn't even showin'. It's not like I had a real baby and it died."

I gasped. "*Did she say that?*"

"She didn't have to." A tear rolled down her cheek. "But it's true. I never got to hold them." More tears rolled down her cheeks. "I never even got to see them."

"I know, honey, and I'm so sorry. But that doesn't make them any less real. They were your babies and you have every right to feel sad about it."

The front door opened and Neely Kate sat up, wiping her tears. "Miss Mildred's here."

"She can wait. This is more important."

"No." She stood and lifted her chin. "I don't want to talk about it anymore." She got up out of her chair and passed me to meet Miss Mildred.

Miss Mildred shot a glare in my direction. "I'm surprised you haven't burst into flames."

I scowled. "I come here all the time to talk to Jonah. He's a good friend of mine. Besides," I added, "you've seen me in church before. I'm sure you remember our encounter in the ladies' room."

Miss Mildred didn't look too happy about the reminder.

Neely Kate motioned toward the sanctuary doors. "Why don't we sit in there and talk? I doubt anyone will see us." When Miss Mildred gave her a blank stare, Neely Kate added, "So no one sees us together? That's why we're here, right?" Her voice ended an octave higher, as if she were talking to someone who was senile. Miss Mildred was a lot of things, but senile wasn't one of them. Or at least I hoped as much. Otherwise, this whole ordeal was for nothing.

"Oh. Yeah."

I rolled my eyes as we followed Miss Mildred through the sanctuary door.

Neely Kate leaned close to me and whispered, "Your eyeballs are liable to fall out if you keep doin' that."

Miss Mildred picked a pew in the middle of the sanctuary. It felt strange to see the room so empty. Jonah's televised services had started drawing so many church-goers, especially from neighboring counties, he'd expanded to two services.

Neely Kate sat next to her and I perched in the pew in front of them, turning my body sideways so I could look at them as I pulled my notebook out of my purse.

"So," Neely Kate drawled. "Henry Buchanan owned Atchison Manufacturing?"

Miss Mildred looked around to see if anyone was within earshot—of course there wasn't—before leaning forward and whispering, "He inherited it from his maternal grandparents. They started it before World War II. They made rivets or some such nonsense."

"Rivets?" Neely Kate asked.

Miss Mildred waved. "They used 'em for plane and car parts. But then the fire wiped the whole plum thing out. It was so big you could see the glow all over town."

"Did they ever say what started the fire?" Neely Kate asked as I took down notes.

"They said it was accidental. Some chemicals got too close to a shorted-out electric fire, but my Kennie was an electrical engineer in the navy, and he said he couldn't imagine that fire gettin' started from an electrical short. He said it looked like it was set by explosives."

Neely Kate's eyes widened. "And no one questioned it? Didn't the police and the fire department do an investigation?"

Miss Mildred waved off Neely Kate's question. "The police were as incompetent back then as they are now, just like the DA's office." She shot me a glare. "And it looks like you've used your devil ways to get your boyfriends to ignore my neighborhood watch tips."

I gave her a pointed stare. "You mean like the Contorvas' dog pooping on your lawn? Or me kissing my boyfriend on my own front porch?"

"I might be old, but I can still make a stand for public decency," she said with a self-righteous humph.

We were gonna have to filter everything that came out of her mouth. Her own interpretation of what was right and wrong and what constituted justice was totally skewed. I couldn't forget that she had spearheaded the petition to ban the annual Henryetta Easter egg hunt. Her reasoning was that it mirrored a pagan fertility ritual and the devil was using it to encourage fornication in the town. But she'd abandoned the cause like a virgin in a whorehouse when she couldn't—try as she might—get any more than six hundred and sixty-six signatures.

Neely Kate shook her head. "Back to the warehouse."

Miss Mildred pinched her lips and turned back to my friend.

"Do you know anything else about the warehouse or the fire?"

She leaned toward Neely Kate, lowering her voice to a whisper again. "Everyone suspected he was havin' an affair with his bookkeeper."

I suppressed a cringe.

"Do you know who his bookkeeper was?"

She grimaced. "No, I never caught her name."

I had a pretty good idea who it was.

"We know the factory burned down 1986. You said it happened in November?"

"Right after Thanksgiving."

"Do you know why Henry Buchanan never rebuilt the factory?"

"No. That was a mystery too. It was doing quite well. We'd heard he'd gotten a government contract for his rivets. And it ended up goin' to someone else after the fire."

"Who?" Neely Kate asked.

I could see why she was asking. Maybe a rival company had committed sabotage to land the job.

She shook her head. "I'm not sure, but Petunia Picklebie's husband Dirk would probably know. God rest her soul. He was a ne'er-do-well after the fire. He wore her down with all his gambling." Her mouth pursed in disapproval.

Now we were really getting somewhere. Dirk had been in Dora's journal. "Do you know what he did there?" I asked.

She glared at me, as though this whole mess that had unfurled before my birth was my fault. "He was a foreman. Agnes's husband worked there too."

I scribbled down the name Picklebie before I processed what she'd said. "Agnes? You mean Momma? My daddy worked there?"

She frowned at me. "Up until the fire."

I stifled a gasp of relief. So Daddy *had* worked there.

"And does this Dirk Picklebie still live here in Henryetta?" Neely Kate shifted in her seat. "Do you happen to have a phone number or address?"

Miss Mildred shook her head. "No, but last I heard he was living in the Forest Ridge neighborhood."

"What about Ima Jean?" I asked. "Were you friends with her?"

Miss Mildred's eyes hardened. "We were acquaintances." She squirmed in her seat. "I frequent her shop."

"Did she suspect Henry was havin' an affair?"

"I have no idea. But I never heard rumors of it until after the fire and right before he killed himself."

Neely Kate studied her for a moment. "Do you remember anything else that might be helpful?"

"That's about all I know." Miss Mildred dug around in her purse and pulled out a rectangular black box and handed it to Neely Kate. "Here."

Neely Kate's mouth dropped open as she took it.

She pulled out another one and pushed a button. Static came out of the box. "You suggested walkie-talkies, so I picked these up at Walmart."

"Oh, yeah." Neely Kate sucked in her bottom lip, trying to keep from laughing. "Good idea."

Miss Mildred's head bobbed. "I've been thinking about code names and I want to be White Tiger."

I held back a snort.

To her credit, Neely Kate kept a straight face. "I think that's great. We'll come up with names for us."

"I've already figured yours out for you." The elderly woman pulled a paper out of her purse. "You can be Red Robin and that one there—" she flicked her finger toward me, "—she can be Yellow Lizard."

"Why am *I* Yellow Lizard?" I asked.

Neely Kate covered her mouth to hide a chuckle.

"I think that part's obvious." Miss Mildred stood and used her cane to push Neely Kate's legs out of the way. "I gotta stop by Reverend Pruitt's office and turn in my petition demanding that he take the rock music out of his services." She started hobbling up the aisle toward the doors. "You can report back to me tomorrow after you visit Dirk Picklebie."

We watched her push open the door and she looked over her shoulder. "And don't forget to keep your walkie-talkie on."

Neely Kate let out a low whistle. "This is gonna be interesting."

That wasn't the word I had in mind.

Chapter Thirteen

We waited in the sanctuary for a good five minutes, waiting to stop by Jonah's office to say hello until after Miss Mildred's shouting stopped. We passed her in the hallway as she emerged from the office, muttering, "Why's the bathroom so far? Those brownies kicked in sooner than usual."

Neely Kate chuckled and leaned toward me. "So her gift was a good idea after all."

I shuddered as we walked into Jonah's office.

He stood in the main office, running one hand through his uncharacteristically tousled hair while holding a paper in the other with a paragraph and three signatures.

"You look like you just got run over by a bulldozer," I said.

He shook his head and chuckled. "I think I just did."

"I'm so sorry, Jonah." Jessica, his secretary and now girlfriend, stood behind her desk wringing her hands, her cheeks flushed. "I tried to stop her."

He walked over and took her hands in his. "It's okay, Jessica. We all know Mildred is a force to be reckoned with." His gaze landed on my friend. "It's good to see you out and about, Neely Kate."

"Well," she said softly. "I've been helpin' Rose with a project. We just wanted to say hello because we were in the neighborhood."

His brow lifted. "You two keep out of trouble now, you hear?"

She flashed a smile, but it didn't reach her eyes. "We'll try." She walked out the door, and I started to follow her when Jonah called after me.

"Rose."

I stopped and turned to look him.

"You got her to leave the house," he said softly. "That's wonderful."

"Like she said, we're working on a project." When I saw the worry in his eyes, I held up a hand. "Don't worry. We're lookin' into where Dora worked before she died, which—I might remind you—happened a full twenty-five years ago."

His lips pressed together.

"Jonah, as you can see, Neely Kate isn't herself, but a few times today she's kind of forgotten what she's been through, if only for a few minutes. We're looking into an accidental factory fire a quarter of a century ago. How could that be dangerous?"

"A factory fire here in Henryetta?" Jessica asked, her eyebrows rose. "Atchison?"

I blinked. "Yeah."

"My mom used to work there. She was a secretary."

"Really? Do you think she'd talk to us about it?"

She laughed. "If you're willing to risk it. She'll talk your ear off about that and everything else under the sun."

"I'm willing." This was turning out to be easier than I'd expected.

"I'll call her to set it up." She winced. "She'll insist on meeting for breakfast. She likes to combine pork products with gossip."

"Gossip?" I asked, taken aback. Is that what this was?

She shrugged. "That's how my mom will see it. Still interested?"

Any little piece of information we could gather would only help. "Yeah."

"How about the four of us meet for breakfast at Merilee's? Say eight-thirty tomorrow? I'm sure Mom will agree, but if she can't make it, I'll call you."

I gave her a warm smile. "Thanks, Jessica."

She shifted her weight, then looked down at her feet. "It's the least I could do after you helped Jonah and me get together."

I shook my head. "Jonah was just too blind to see what was right in front of him."

"Hey!" he protested. "First Mildred, then you. I might as well head on over to the Baptist church and let both of the other women who signed this petition—" he waved the paper in his hand "—flog me."

"Save your dramatic flair for the camera, Jonah," I teased, then headed for the door. "I need to catch up to Neely Kate."

Jonah's smile faded. "Keep me updated on how she's doin', okay? I'm still worried about her."

"Me too." I looked over my shoulder as I walked out the door. "Thanks again, Jessica."

Neely Kate was in the same folding chair she'd sat in while we were waiting for Miss Mildred. She was quiet for the entire drive to the Henryetta Family Clinic. I turned to look at her when I pulled into the parking lot. "Neely Kate, maybe you should stay home tonight. I think I made you overdo it today."

"No. I want to go." She gave me a weak smile. "You should come with us. You owe me a night at the Bingo hall."

I grimaced. "I have an...appointment, remember?" Then I realized I was in trouble. "And I don't have an excuse for bein' gone tonight."

She studied me for a moment, then took my hand. "You know I don't want you doin' this, but seein' as how you're good and stuck, what kind of friend would I be if I didn't help?"

"Really?" I asked in amazement.

"Yeah. You're supposed to meet him at eight, right?"

"Yeah."

"Tell Mason you're goin' to Bingo with Granny and me."

A sick feeling settled in my stomach. "I hate lyin' to him, Neely Kate."

"I know, honey. So you meet us at the Bingo hall for a little bit, then you leave and meet Jed. That way you're not lyin'."

I threw my arms around her and pulled her into a sideways hug. "You're the best, Neely Kate. I only wish I could help you too."

She pulled back with tears in her eyes. "You have no idea how much today helped. Thanks for puttin' up with my sulkin'."

I shook my head. "Enough of *that* nonsense. Take a nap after you get home, you hear?"

She smiled. "Yes, ma'am. I'll see you around six-fifty."

I watched her go into the clinic before driving home. Muffy was overjoyed to see me, so I decided to take her on a long walk to make up for being gone most of the day. After pulling on a pair of work boots, I decided to give in to curiosity and head south, toward Joe's new rental house.

The last time Muffy and I had been this way, we'd found poor Mr. Sullivan in a ditch. The loan officer at the bank had been part of a robbery scheme to outbid Skeeter in an auction for the previous crime lord's territory, but after he had a change of heart, one of his partners killed him and dumped his body on the very property Joe was now renting. But if Muffy was traumatized by the experience, she'd overcome it enough to romp around as if she hadn't a care in the world.

When we made it to the gravel road leading up to the house, I had second thoughts. I wasn't even sure Joe was home—in fact, I suspected he wasn't—but I was curious to see what he'd done with his rental. I'd come this far. I might as well keep going.

To my disappointment, the fainting goats that had been kept here were gone. Muffy must have remembered them, though, because she ran up to the fence and peered through the slats, sniffing the ground frantically before releasing a cloud of stench that the breeze blew directly into my face.

I pulled my knit scarf up to cover my face as I gagged. "Muffy! You've got to start giving me a warning!"

She looked over her shoulder, giving me a look that said "good luck with that," then took off running toward the house.

She made the decision for me.

The house wasn't as large as mine. A one-story bungalow with a front porch that ran the length of the house. It reminded me of the house I'd grown up in, but it was older and in worse shape. The blue paint was peeling and faded and there was obvious wood rot around the windows on the west side. Joe had rented the house with some sort of barter with the owner— renovations for reduced rent. The owner had obviously gotten the better end of the deal. Joe's car was parked on the side of the house, but he usually drove his sheriff's car now, so I knew he wasn't home.

I walked up to the porch and peered into the curtain-less windows. The front room had a brick fireplace flanked with bookcases. Tarps covered the floor and the plaster had been stripped off one of the walls, revealing lath boards instead of studs. I couldn't help wondering what project he was doing. But more importantly, I hoped it made him happy.

I was so intent on checking the inside of the house, I didn't hear the car approaching until Muffy began to bark.

Oh great, Joe's going to catch me snooping. However, as I looked closer, I realized it wasn't a sheriff's car. I wasn't sure getting caught snooping by someone else was much better. But when the car stopped and I saw who was getting out of it, I wanted to run off into the fields and hide.

Hilary didn't look any happier to see me than I was to see her. She climbed out of the car wearing brown tweed dress pants and brown pumps. A cute ivory wool coat covered her top half and made her striking auburn hair stand out even more than usual. Her makeup looked like it had been done by a professional. When I compared her attire to my work boots, jeans, and work jacket, it was apparent, once again, that she was many leagues above me in terms of class and sophistication.

"Rose." Her voice was tight. "What are you doing sneaking around Joe's house?"

Muffy sat back on her haunches and released a slow growl. My little dog was obviously a good judge of character, but she'd also given me an alibi.

"I took Muffy for a walk, and she took off running for Joe's house."

Hilary stood at the bottom of the steps, a foil-covered square casserole dish in her hand, a leather handbag slung from the crook of her elbow. "Have you never heard of a *leash?*"

I started toward the steps. "She usually sticks close to me, but she must have realized this was Joe's house." When Hilary's eyes narrowed with disapproval, I couldn't help adding, "She's still very fond of Joe. When we were together, he treated her like she was his dog too."

"Then maybe Joe should petition for joint custody."

"Like he's going to do with you for your baby?" The words were out of my mouth before I even considered them. But the hurt in her eyes made me instantly contrite. I walked down a couple of steps. "Look, Hilary. I'm sorry. That was a terrible thing to say."

She lifted her chin, not even acknowledging my apology. "What are you doing here, Rose Gardner?"

"I told you."

"That's a lie and we both know it."

I was sick to death of lying, so I didn't bother to contradict her.

"You have Mason Deveraux. He's a good man. Why can't he be enough?" The pleading in her voice wrenched at something inside me. "You aren't with Joe. Why can't you leave him alone?"

"We're just friends."

Hate filled her eyes. "He will never be *just friends* with you."

I wasn't sure how to answer that. Though I hoped it wasn't true, I knew there was a chance it might be.

"You need to leave him alone so he can move on."

"With you?" I asked. "I'm not having this conversation again." I tried to move off the steps to the ground, but she blocked my path.

Her eyes narrowed. "Don't mess with me, Rose Gardner. If you think I'm a bitch now, you'll wither like a hothouse rose before I'm done with you." Her glare hardened. "Pun intended."

I put my hands on my hips. "Are you threatenin' me?"

"I'm sorry." She put a hand on her chest. "Did I not make my threat clear enough?"

I shook my head. "I'm not afraid of you."

"You should be. I'm ruthless."

"Are you done now? For someone who wants me to leave, you sure are doin' your darnedest to keep me here."

"I just want to make sure I've gotten my point across."

"Perfectly."

Hilary took a step to the side. "You be careful walking home. I sure would hate for you to twist your ankle all alone out in those fields."

Muffy released another low growl, followed by a cloud of noxious fumes. Hilary frantically waved her hand in front of her face, and for once, I was thankful for my dog's quirk.

"Good God!" Hilary mumbled, blinking rapidly. "What is *wrong* with your *dog?*"

"There's *nothing* wrong with Muffy," I said with more sass than was usual for me. "She's just an excellent judge of character." I strode past Hilary, heading home.

I resisted the urge to look back at her, ruminating over our conversation instead. Did she have it in her to make good on her threat?

I wasn't sure I wanted to find out, but now that I'd found my backbone, I wasn't about to back down. If Hilary wanted a war, it was time to prepare myself for battle.

Chapter Fourteen

I pulled into a parking spot on the side of the Veterans Hall at 6:51. Neely Kate's car was already in the lot and I wondered if I'd get in trouble for being late. It had taken me a while to gather my Lady in Black clothes.

I walked into the hall and spotted Neely Kate right away. Her granny was next to her and now sported pale blue hair. I wondered if she and Miss Mildred frequented the same hairdresser.

As I approached, Neely Kate and her grandmother were starting to set up miniature stuffed animal key chains around their Bingo cards. My friend glanced up and gave me a soft smile. She was still wearing the jeans and flannel shirt she'd worn earlier today, but her red and puffy eyes told me she'd done some major crying after I dropped her off at the doctor's office. "Granny saved you a seat." She pointed to the chair on the other side of her grandmother.

I waved to her grandmother. "Hi, Mrs. Rivers. Thanks for letting me play with you." Neely Kate had told me that her grandmother was particular about who sat close to her. She firmly believed bad luck could seep from someone nearby and mess up her Bingo juju.

She obviously didn't know about my usual misfortunes, or she would have banned me from the hall, let alone the table.

Mrs. Rivers waved her hand and resumed her task as Neely Kate walked around the table to greet me.

"How'd your doctor's appointment go?" I asked, worried. "Is everything okay?"

"It was a routine appointment. You know how those things are." She waved her hand to dismiss any further discussion, but I could tell something was off. "Granny says she has to sit between us. That the strength of our friendship will mess with her luck. She has to separate us."

I grinned. "Okay."

"We got your cards for you, but Granny says you have to set up your own charms if you want 'em to work." She leaned closer and whispered, "Just a heads-up so Granny doesn't yell at you: they have to be no less than one inch from each other but no more than two inches. And if you get one accidently off, you have to start all over again."

I knew her granny was superstitious, but this was crazy. "Okay."

"That's part of the reason we get here so early." She winked. "But don't worry. I made sure you only have a few to set out."

I glanced over her shoulder at her granny. She must have had over thirty trinkets spread out around her cards.

"Did you have any trouble with Mason?"

I sighed, my guilt building anew. "No. When I told him I was coming to Bingo with you, he encouraged me to spend time with you."

Pain flickered through her eyes. "Because he feels sorry for me."

I shook my head. "No, because he cares about you."

She closed her eyes and released a heavy breath before looking at me and giving me a smile. I knew her well enough to recognize it was fake.

"Besides," I added, "he seemed eager to stay at the office and work. This way he doesn't have to feel guilty about it." I was fairly certain he was working on non-Fenton County projects, but whether that was J.R. or Dora was something I didn't care to speculate.

"Well, at least you told him the truth. You *did* meet me at Bingo."

But it was only a partial truth. There was no way around it, so my guilt was useless. "How long does this thing last?" I whispered. "I have no idea how long I'm gonna be at my…meeting."

"Probably not long enough. Just tell Mason you and I talked afterward. He'll believe that."

I nodded. "Good idea."

A muffled musical trill came from the direction of Neely Kate's seat.

She rolled her eyes in response to my questioning look. "It's Miss Mildred and that doggone walkie-talkie."

"She's been calling you?"

"Every dang fifteen minutes or so." She stomped over to her purse—a pink bag covered in rhinestones—and pulled out the two-way radio.

"Red Robin. Red Robin," the box squawked. "Are you there? Over." Then static replaced the words.

Neely Kate rolled her eyes and pressed the button. "Not now, Miss Mildred. I'm at Bingo."

"Use the code names!"

Neely Kate winked at me. "Sorry, White Worm." She released the button before breaking out into giggles.

I laughed right along with her when Miss Mildred barked back, "That's White Tiger!"

Neely Kate got control of her giggles, then said, "Sorry, White Tiger. I'll be sure to let you know as soon as we know something. Now I really have to go." She turned down the sound and tossed the box into her purse.

She noticed me looking at her bag and put her hands on her hips. "Yes, I have my purse. So what?"

I didn't try to hide my smile.

Neely Kate's grandmother banged her hand on the table, causing several of the animal key chains to fall over. "Quit yer yammerin' and get to settin' up."

Oh, crappy doodles. Was she gonna have to start all over again? "You did tell her I was leaving early, right?" I whispered.

"Yeah, but she says you'll still have plenty of time to get in a few rounds."

"Girls! You need to set up before they call the first number or it's bad luck."

I shot Neely Kate a grin and hurried around the table. "How are you tonight, Mrs. Rivers? Ready for Bingo?"

"I was born ready for Bingo. When I popped out of my momma's womb, I had a Bingo card in one hand and a dauber in the other."

There was an image I could live without.

She patted my shoulder. "And I thought I told you to call me Granny Rivers, just like everyone else does."

I grinned. "Okay, Granny Rivers."

"Now get your skinny backside in yer chair and set up yer charms."

I laughed and did as she'd ordered. I was ready with my dauber in hand when the guy pulled the first ball and called out the number.

"Oh, my stars and garters," Neely Kate groaned.

I leaned forward and glanced at her. Something in her voice caught me off guard. "What?"

"Mason's mother is here."

"*What?*"

She pointed across the room, and sure enough, Maeve was setting her papers and dauber on the table.

"Do you think she saw me?" I asked, trying to settle my panic.

Neely Kate shook her head. "No. She's late, so she seems intent on setting up."

I held my hand up to my cheek and let my hair fall down over the other side of my face.

"Yer not payin' attention," Granny barked. "They called B9 and you got one right there!" She pointed to the square on one of my cards, then stamped my sheet.

I tried to hide my smirk, but my amusement quickly faded when I realized Maeve had finished setting up. If she paid attention to the tables across from her, she'd have a good view of the three of us.

Double crap.

I spent the next half hour doing my level best to hide from her, so when the clock on the wall hit 7:40 and I started to get up, Granny Rivers grabbed my arm and pulled me back down into my seat.

"Where do you think yer going?"

"I…" I shot Neely Kate a questioning look. "Neely Kate said she told you I'd need to leave early."

"You can't leave in the middle of a round. It's bad luck."

"But I really have to go."

"You just wait until it's done."

I considered protesting, but I was downright certain Granny Rivers wasn't going to let me leave without a fuss, and I couldn't risk Maeve noticing me. So I sat there, every muscle in my body tense, for five more minutes until Granny Rivers let me loose.

"Go out the back," Neely Kate whispered. "Then Maeve won't see you."

"Oh, good idea."

I didn't have any problem getting out the back of hall, but by the time I got into my truck and pulled out of the parking lot, I realized two things. I was gonna be late meeting Jed and I was still dressed in my jeans and sweater.

I had two choices: Stop at a gas station and change, which would make me even more late, or show up only slightly late in my normal clothes. I decided to just get there and work out the rest later.

Jed was waiting for me when I pulled around the back of the Sinclair station. I hopped out, bag in hand, as he got out of the car.

His eyes widened at the sight of me. "You're not dressed."

"I got hung up."

"Skeeter won't give a shit about excuses."

He wasn't telling me anything I didn't already know. "Turn around."

His eyes widened. "What?"

"*Turn around*," I said as I slipped off my coat. He just kept looking at me, but when I reached for the hem of my sweater and started to lift it up, Jed spun around as quickly as if he'd turned into a top.

"What are you doin', Rose? It's forty degrees outside. You're gonna freeze."

I was perfectly aware of the temperature, but I didn't see any other option. Goosebumps broke out across my skin as I tossed my sweater into my bag. "I have to change and this is the fastest way."

He didn't answer as I continued to disrobe. I kicked off my shoes and shimmied out of my jeans, shivering as I stood in the cold night air in my bra and panties. Then I pulled out my dress and stepped into it. The dress had been purchased in New Orleans and it was much tighter than the ones I normally wore.

I reached around and zipped the dress up to the middle of my back. I started to contort my arms to get it the rest of the way up when I decided to utilize my companion. "Jed, zip me up." Turning sideways, I presented my back to him.

Thankfully he turned to me and reached for my zipper without complaint. When he finished, he opened the back door. "Let's get goin' or we're both gonna be in trouble."

I slid onto the backseat, thankful for the warm interior. "Where are we goin' tonight?" I asked after Jed had gotten back in and pulled onto the county road.

"The tire plant." Back in December, I'd found out that Skeeter secretly owned the plant and kept a secret office inside.

"Who's gonna be there?" I asked as I pulled my heels out of the bag and slipped them on.

"Skeeter and three business associates, all men. You met one of them at the last meeting. Seth Moore. But the other two have moved up in the ranks after a couple of recent vacancies."

I suspected the vacancies were from the two men who had betrayed Skeeter. I'd detected their underhanded activities with visions I'd purposely had for Skeeter as part of our arrangement.

Jed looked into the rearview mirror and caught my eyes in the reflection. "These men are hard and don't mess around. Be on your toes."

"I was on my toes the last time he used me."

"This is different."

I didn't want to be cocky, but I'd handled myself pretty well at his last meeting. I wasn't about to go in thinking I had the world by the tail, but I wasn't as terrified as I'd been last time. Yet I'd also learned that I couldn't let these men know I was afraid. I had to show confidence if I hoped to gain their respect. And I needed their respect if I was going to get answers from them.

"I won't let my guard down."

"Good."

"You'll be there, won't you, Jed?"

He grinned slightly. "Yeah, I'll be there as your bodyguard again."

"And who's protecting Skeeter?"

He chuckled. "Skeeter's on his own in this meeting. But he can handle himself."

"So what's my purpose tonight?"

"Skeeter says you're supposed to sit back, listen, and then deduce."

"But not force any visions?"

"Skeeter will be the judge of whether anyone is worth the risk of havin' you read them."

I'd had multiple visions at his last business meeting, and while I'd gotten some valuable information, I'd pissed off a couple of guys enough to get a gun pulled on me. Skeeter had told me he considered my "gift" too valuable to put me at unnecessary risk.

By the time Jed arrived at the plant, I had my hair up and my black hat pinned in place.

Jed sent a text as he pulled into the parking lot, so I wasn't surprised to see Skeeter exiting the back of the building as Jed parked parallel to the entrance.

Skeeter opened the back car door and reached for me. I took his hand and stood, leaving my street clothes and coat in the backseat of the car. Skeeter took notice and gave me a questioning glance, then bent down. "Jed, get those things out of sight before you come in."

"Will do, Skeeter."

Skeeter closed the car door and led me to the back entrance. "Let's get you in out of the cold, Lady."

I hurried inside, not needing to be asked twice. When the door shut behind us, Skeeter pressed a hand on my lower back and leaned into my ear. "You're late."

"It couldn't be helped."

"What was so important it kept you from my meeting?"

I considered making up an excuse, but went for the truth instead. "I was playing Bingo."

I expected anger, so I wasn't prepared when he burst out laughing. "You were playing *Bingo?*"

I nodded. "I needed an excuse for coming tonight, so I met Neely Kate and her granny there."

Merriment filled his eyes. "I didn't know you were a gambling woman, Lady."

Bingo didn't seem like gambling, but I supposed he was right. "I'm not usually. I like the safe path."

His eyebrows hitched and he gave me a quizzical look. "Lady, you are anything but safe." Stopping outside the conference room door, he gave me a stern look. "I'll introduce you, but as before, let me do all the talking," he said in an undertone. "I'll probably have you talk to one or more of the guys individually, but we'll figure out the how of it after the meeting."

I pushed out a breath, fighting a rush of anxiety. "Okay."

He leaned into my ear again. "You'll do great, and Jed will join us in a moment to be your bodyguard." He paused. "If things go south, get the hell out. You understand?"

"Do you expect things to go south?"

"No. But it's always good to be prepared."

"Like a boy scout."

He chuckled. "I am the furthest thing from a boy scout."

He pushed the door open, revealing three men arranged around a table. I recognized Seth Moore from before, but the other two men were unfamiliar. "Gentlemen," Skeeter drawled. "I'd like to introduce you to the Lady in Black."

"Good evening, gentlemen," I said as I sat in the chair Skeeter had pulled out for me.

Seth Moore nodded in response, a grin plastered on his face. We'd had our own individual meeting in December and he'd made it perfectly clear he'd like to get to know me better.

Skeeter made a sweeping gesture with one arm. "Lady, you remember Seth Moore. Meet Howey Sommers and Scott Humphrey."

Howey looked like he was in his forties. He was compact in size and shape, with dull black hair and some deep-set wrinkles on his forehead. Scott was younger, brown-haired, and probably in his thirties. A toothpick hung out of his mouth. His eyes were hard and focused on me. I wondered if I should offer them my hand, but they didn't seem like the kind of guys who gave handshakes.

The door opened as Skeeter sat down, and Jed entered and took the chair next to mine.

Skeeter placed his forearms on the table and held out his hands. "Gentlemen, I think you know why I've invited you tonight, so let's get to the heart of the matter. Gentry is still runnin' loose and the sheriff's department seems to be chasing their tails. It's no secret he's got it out for me. Gems was just one of his multiple attempts to chip away at my empire."

Howey Sommers leaned back in his chair, taking a casual stance, but I noticed his jaw was tight and his fists were clenching and unclenching at his sides. "Your empire ain't been your empire for all that long, Malcolm. Maybe Gentry thinks he has a legitimate claim to it."

"I paid my dues in blood, sweat, tears, *and* money. I'll take on any man who challenges that." Skeeter's voice came out in a low rumble.

"So you aim to take Gentry on?" Scott Humphrey asked, taking the toothpick out of his mouth and spinning it around in his hand. His gaze turned to me, or more accurately, my cleavage.

Skeeter stood and leaned over, placing his palms on the table now. "I aim to defend what's *mine*."

Howey shifted in his seat. "Gentry's gathering men from Columbia County. They want a stake here, and he intends to give it to them."

"That's a mistake," Skeeter growled. "Once you start selling it all off, it loses its value ten-fold."

I wasn't sure what *it* was, but I could tell every man in the room, with the exception of Jed, wanted *it*.

"What about her?" Humphrey flicked his hand toward me. "She's from Louisiana, ain't she? At least Gentry wants to keep it in state."

Skeeter's arms tensed and I was worried things were about to *go south*. The time to sit here quietly had passed.

I leaned forward. "You're missing a vital difference, gentlemen."

Skeeter gave me a look that wasn't exactly warm and cuddly, but I forged on anyway.

"And what's that, little lady?" Humphrey asked.

"Those boys from Columbia County want all the money to ultimately end up in *their* county. They'll rake y'all over the coals to get a profit. I, on the other hand, plan to leave my investment in Fenton County. I realize it's in my best interest for Mr. Malcolm's business to flourish."

"So what's in it for you?"

"A healthy dividend that doesn't harm Mr. Malcolm's empire, so I can keep making a profit off it for years to come. Consider me a bank."

"Oh, I get it." Humphrey started laughing. "You're screwin' 'im."

I thought Skeeter was gonna have a stroke based on the look of the pounding vein in his temple, but I interjected before he could do something drastic. "It hardly surprises me you would jump to that conclusion. Since I'm a woman, I must be incapable of using my little ol' brain, yes?" I kept my voice calm and controlled even though I was furious. "If I were a man, would you accuse me of sleeping with Skeeter Malcolm? Or would you call me a smart investor?"

His face turned red, but he didn't answer.

"Believe me, Mr. Humphrey, I'm sure the dangling appendage between your legs has addled your brain a hell of a lot more times than my lack of one has affected mine."

Sommers burst out laughing and clapped Humphrey on the back. "Ho, boy, Humphrey! I suspect she's right. Especially after what that Cheryl did to your dangling appendage."

Humphrey's mouth pressed into a tight line.

"I am a *business* woman, Mr. Humphrey," I continued, wanting to settle this matter once and for all. "And I make my business decisions after careful analysis. Not by relyin' on hormones and my crotch."

Skeeter stared the man down before saying in a growl, "Are there any more questions or comments about Lady?"

None of the men said anything, although Sommers was still snickering to himself.

Skeeter took his seat. "Lady's right. Gentry wants to make bank, and he'll sell off every last piece of the empire if it gets him what he wants. Fenton County be damned. Is that what you want?"

Seth Moore and Sommers agreed with Skeeter right away, and though he held out a little longer out of pride, Humphrey finally relented too. They spent the next twenty minutes discussing the three men's roles in the organization, which seemed to involve fenced goods and drug trafficking. I watched Humphrey closely while they talked. After our initial tiff, he seemed to fall in line as a team player, going so far as to convince Sommers to accept Skeeter's decision on how to handle a territory dispute. But although I couldn't put my finger on *what*, something about him didn't sit right with me. When it was clear they were done with their business, I decided it was time for me to act.

"Mr. Malcolm," I said, turning my gaze on him. "I'd like to speak privately with Mr. Humphrey. I hate that we got off on the wrong foot. And since he looks to be a very valuable member of your team, perhaps we can work on letting bygones be bygones. I would hate for our misunderstanding to stand in the way of your future business dealings."

Skeeter turned to face me, a war raging in his eyes before he tipped his head slightly, his way of saying he trusted me, and turned to Humphrey. "If you're amenable..."

He grinned, but there was a glitter in his eyes that made me uneasy. "I'm itching to get a chance to work on those bygones."

I could tell Skeeter sensed the implied threat. He flicked his hand toward the door and said, "Jed, take Lady and Humphrey to the office."

His gaze held Jed's for several seconds, and a world of understanding seemed to pass between them before Jed nodded and stood.

I rose from my seat and walked to the door, but Jed opened it before I could reach for the knob, Humphrey fast on my heels.

As Jed led us down the hall and through the recreation room I'd been in last December, I tried to figure out what to focus on when I read Humphrey. I suspected he worked with Gentry and this was a fact-finding mission for him, although I wasn't sure what basis I had to go on other than gut instinct.

Maybe I could ask some questions first and read him later. Once I was done, Jed could pull him away and I'd talk to Skeeter about what I'd seen. I glanced at the clock on the wall. 9:15. At this rate, I could still get home at a reasonable hour without alarming Mason.

Jed opened the door to the windowless office and allowed me and Humphrey to enter before him. When Jed started to come in and shut the door, Humphrey grunted, "Not you."

Jed's hand tightened on the knob. "I stay with Lady."

"Are you insinuating she's not safe with me?" he asked. "Is that any way to start off our new business relationship?"

Jed's gaze landed on me and I knew he wasn't about to leave me. But it was obvious that Humphrey wasn't going to talk to me unless I did things his way. If he was really in cahoots with Gentry, I suspected he had some ties to the person who'd run me off the road the day before. I tried to control my racing heart. I was scared to death to be alone with this man, but if I could get information to protect Mason, it was worth the risk.

"Jed," I said. "I think Mr. Humphrey and I will be fine on our own for a few minutes."

He stood in the doorway, hesitating. I knew I was putting him in a difficult situation. I was sure Skeeter had made it very clear he was to protect me at all cost. Leaving me alone could get him into trouble.

I moved closer to him and rested my hand on his arm, leaning in toward his ear. "Give me ten minutes," I whispered. "I need to do this."

His gaze shot to Humphrey, anger filling his eyes. "I don't like it and neither will Skeeter."

"Y'all are gonna have to trust me or this is never gonna work."

He took two breaths in and out, his arm tense, before he said, "Five minutes. Then I'm coming in."

"Fine." I'd just have to work fast.

Jed lifted his chin and addressed Humphrey. "I'll be right outside this door."

Humphrey laughed. "What do you think's gonna happen?"

I didn't want to know where either of their imaginations were going. Jed backed out of the room and I shut the door in his face, then turned to face the possible Benedict Arnold.

"How about a drink, Mr. Humphrey?" I asked as I walked over to Skeeter's whiskey stash.

The office was Skeeter's, though it was much more opulently appointed than the bare bones quarters he kept in the pool hall. This room was richly decorated with a sofa, two leather chairs in one corner, and a large mahogany desk in the opposite corner. Next to the desk was a doorway that led to a very nice private bath. But it was the console by the leather chairs where I was headed.

"If you're drinking with me." He sat down in one of the leather chairs, and I almost cursed. The chairs were several feet apart, too far for me to purposely have a vision. I'd have to get up and touch him.

"Of course." I picked up the bottle and poured some into two glass tumblers. After handing one to Humphrey, I sat in a leather chair across from his. I'd already wasted thirty seconds, but I figured I needed to butter him up before diving right into my questions.

We both sipped our drinks, an easier task for me this time than it had been the last. I'd gotten a new hat online as well as a couple of dresses. While it was still black and the veil was heavy enough to make seeing my eyes difficult, it was shorter, coming only to the top of my mouth.

"Why the mystery?" he asked, resting his glass on the arm in his chair. "Why wear a hat with a veil that covers your face?"

"I had an unfortunate accident that left me with a scar. I prefer to keep it covered."

"That ugly, huh?"

There wasn't an answer to that, so I sipped my whiskey. All too conscious of the time ticking down, I decided to take the offensive. "You impressed me tonight."

He leaned back and grinned. "Is that so?"

The way he stretched his legs implied he thought I was impressed with what he might possess under his belt. I planned to clear *that* up straight away. "You're a man who seems to be willing to admit when he's wrong."

His eyes widened slightly and he looked amused. "What makes you say that?"

"I was impressed with how quickly you changed your opinion, especially since I pegged you as someone who's not a team player."

His grin froze. "What are you accusing me of?"

I gave him a half-shrug and took a sip of my whiskey. "Nothing, I'm only confessing my first impression."

He grinned again. "And here I thought we were in here putting our differences to bed." He lifted his drink. "Or we can put other things to bed if you'd prefer."

"After I told you earlier that I don't mix business and...pleasure?" I asked.

Still grinning, he said, "You're the one who told me that I think with my...hormones."

I tilted my head to study him. "You seem like a smart man, Mr. Humphrey, the kind who hedges his bets. What has Gentry offered you?"

"Who says I've negotiated with him?"

"You seem a little too knowledgeable about his plan to bring in the Columbia County men." I paused. "Not to mention comfortable with it."

"It doesn't make a difference to me," he said. "No matter what you say, you're no different than them. Except you're a lot better looking—" he waved to my face, then swept lower, "—at least from the neck down."

"When are you meeting with Gentry?"

"Who says I am?"

"Come now, Mr. Humphrey. I know you're playing both sides, attempting to determine who has the better offer. And since you're so familiar with Mick Gentry's plans, it means you took a meeting with him first. Now you have to contact Gentry and accept or reject allegiance to him."

His mouth twisted into a ghost of a smile. "Aren't you the clever one?"

"Are you going to deny it?" When he didn't answer, I said, "I'd like you to set up a meeting with Mick Gentry myself." It was a somewhat impulsive move, but it made sense. Gentry was probably the one who wanted Mason dead, and if not, he'd likely be able to identify the culprit. Why not go straight to the source? But cold sweat prickled the back of my neck when I thought about actually going through with it.

His surprise was evident in his eyes. "Why? You wantin' to take him to task for wanting a split off the Fenton County crime world?"

I paused, hoping I was taking the right course. "I'd like to discuss a negotiation."

He chortled. "Gentry ain't the negotiatin' type." Then his eyes hardened. "And neither is Skeeter Malcolm. Does he know what you're suggesting?"

It was tricky. To say yes would probably close the door to a meeting. To say no insinuated I was double-crossing Skeeter. "Mr. Malcolm has given me a free hand in strengthening his empire. Animosity with Mr. Gentry is obviously bad for business."

A sly grin curled his lips. "I'll let him know you're interested."

My five minutes were almost up and I was still reeling from my impulsive request, but I needed to have a vision before Jed busted in. I stood and slowly walked behind him, then rested my hand on his shoulder. I considered giving him some excuse, but he didn't pull away from me, so I decided to get right to it.

I closed my eyes and concentrated on Mick Gentry and how Scott Humphrey tied in with him. The tingling in my head started immediately and the vision swept over me. I was sitting at a bar, a beer bottle in my hand. Mick Gentry sat next to me, a ball cap pulled low over his forehead.

"How'd it go?" Gentry asked.

"That woman was there. You're right. She's more involved than I expected."

"What's her end game?"

"She insists she's not screwing Malcolm and I didn't feel any chemistry between them. At least on her end."

"Again, what's her end game?"

"She says it's an investment for her. She wants to meet with you."

His eyebrows rose in surprise. "You don't say." He glanced across the room, then back toward me. "She seems pretty involved for it to be a simple investment."

I shrugged. "Your call. I can't imagine Malcolm would go for it, but she says he's given her free rein. She can do whatever she sees fit to strengthen his empire."

Gentry's mouth pursed and he looked deep in thought for several seconds. "What have you learned about Malcolm's schedule and his men?"

"He had Jed keeping an eye on Lady, but Malcolm was on his own."

"So he might be easy to take out?"

"Time it right, and yeah." I leaned against the bar. "So you gonna meet with her?"

"Timing is everything. Let's deal with Malcolm, then we'll deal with her. And we haven't gotten the green light to snuff him yet."

"Who hired you for the hit?" I asked.

"You don't need to worry about that part. All you need to know is that we take care of Malcolm first…then we move onto the next name on the list."

"You show me the money and I'll wipe out the whole damned town."

The vision ended abruptly. My head cleared and I blurted out, "You'd take out the town."

Humphrey glanced over his shoulder as I pulled my hand away. "What?"

My vision scared the living daylights out of me and left me with a sharp headache. I walked over to Skeeter's desk as though I had a purpose to do so, trying to hide my shaking hands. I had to cover for my post-vision word-vomit. "I asked if you were from out of town."

He turned in his seat to watch me, confusion in his eyes. "No. Born and raised in Fenton County."

Yet he had no qualms about killing its citizens if it turned him a tidy profit. I scratched a fake phone number onto a small notepad on Skeeter's desk. I wasn't about to give my real number. Based on what I'd seen in the vision, Gentry wouldn't meet with me until after Skeeter was dead, and I had no intention of letting that happen. I ripped off the paper and walked toward the door. "This has been enlightening, Mr. Humphrey." I held out the slip of paper. "Tell Mr. Gentry to contact me if he wishes to meet. Thank you for your time."

He stood and approached me, then took the fake number. "We're done?"

"We're done." I opened the door and found myself face to face with Jed. "Could you take Mr. Humphrey back to Mr. Malcolm? I need to see to something."

Jed gave me a quizzical glance. I was sure he was confused by my request, but I wasn't ready to face the other criminals hanging out with Skeeter. The shock of what I'd just seen through Humphrey's eyes had me feeling uneasy and then some.

I shut the door and locked it, then sat on the edge of Skeeter's desk. Maybe I shouldn't have sent Humphrey back to join Skeeter. What if he decided to kill him now instead of waiting? I took in a deep breath. We'd all known Gentry had it in for Skeeter, but apparently that wasn't the extent of his interests. He had a hit list, and the big question was who was on it? Skeeter was first, but there were more. Mason was likely on the list. After what happened at Gems, I was sure of it.

Several minutes passed before the doorknob jiggled, then the door opened seconds later. Skeeter entered, stuffing his keys into his pocket, with a contrite-looking Jed following behind him. "What the hell were you thinking?" Skeeter's voice boomed.

"Are they all gone?"

"Yeah."

Pushing out a sigh of relief, I pulled the pins out of my hair and tossed the hat next to me. "I was trying to do my job."

He stopped in front of me, looming over me. "You were supposed to tell me if something was off and let *me* put things into motion."

I looked up at him and rolled my eyes. "And if I'd said something about him made me suspicious, you would have asked me to bring him in here and question him. Why not just get right to it?"

Anger filled his eyes. "Why the hell would you come in here alone with him? Do you have any idea what Scott Humphrey is capable of?"

"After my vision, I have a fairly good idea."

Some of the anger left his face. "So you got something."

I nodded. "He's definitely working with Mick Gentry, in spite of his little performance out there."

He walked over to his whiskey decanter and poured himself a glass, then saw the two glasses on the table between the chairs. "You gave that snake my good whiskey?"

"I had to." When he started to protest, I said, "Do you want to know what I found out or not?"

He downed the liquor in his glass and slammed it down on the console table. "What did you find out?"

"Gentry has a hit list and you're on the top."

"Who else is on it?"

"I don't know, but I suspect Mason's next. Gentry's not ready to kill you yet. He's waiting for orders to set things in motion. Humphrey's going to carry them out."

Irritation wrinkled his brow. "What the hell's he waiting for?"

"Orders. Someone's hired him to take out the people on the list."

"And you have no idea who's calling the shots?"

I shook my head. "Humphrey asked who it was, and Gentry refused to tell him. He only said he was being paid well."

He started to pace.

"Skeeter, you have to be careful. Part of the reason Humphrey's working with you is to study your security situation. He told Gentry you only had Jed around and it would be an easy job."

"Good."

I sat upright. "*Good?* What part of that is good?"

He shot me a grin. "I wanted him to think I'd be easy to catch off guard."

"So you suspected him? Why didn't you or Jed tell me that?"

"I didn't want you to be influenced. I wanted your totally unbiased opinion."

"He's guilty as hell, but I knew that before I even brought him back here."

He studied me for a moment. "You've got instinct, and while I applaud you for it, you need to follow my orders." Grinning now, he shook his head. "I might have even enjoyed watching you tell Humphrey off if I hadn't been so pissed."

"Well, I'm sorry," I said, sounding miffed even to my own ears. Then I shook my head. "Wait. No, I'm not. You want me to be part of these meetings, but those men are curious about why I'm there. If I continue to sit back and wait for permission to speak, they'll have every reason to believe I'm sleepin' with you."

He held up his hand in surrender. "Okay, okay. Calm down. We'll work on that, but first we need to sort out Gentry. What else did you see?"

"In my vision, Humphrey met Mick in a bar. I suspect he's going to leave here and run right to him. I wouldn't be surprised if it was a vision of something that's gonna happen later tonight."

"You're probably right. Did you recognize the place?"

"No, but I don't frequent bars much."

"You worked at a strip club last month."

I lifted my chin. "I was undercover."

He shrugged. "Give up the good girl act. You've got too much dirt under your nails to call yourself clean."

His words floored me, mostly because he was right. Shame washed over me, as form-fitting as my new dress.

He must have sensed the change in my attitude because he moved closer to me and lowered his voice. "Rose."

I sucked in a breath and looked down at my feet.

"Rose." He was more insistent, so I lifted my gaze to his. "I'm a self-centered son-of-a-bitch, but that's what got me here today. You have to know that you're a natural at this business."

That was what scared me. I was falling into this Lady in Black role like a duck took to water. Maybe it was in my DNA. Evidence was piling up to suggest that my birth parents might have been involved in some sort of criminal activity before I was born. What if the apple didn't fall far from the tree? But I couldn't forget that I was here because I'd made a deal with the devil. And while the devil might don his manners and fool me with his charming ways, he was the devil nonetheless.

His eyes softened. "But while you're a natural, you're not part of this world. For you, this game is about survival, and you happen to be damned good at it. That's no reason for you to feel ashamed, so don't let my asshole behavior convince you otherwise. Got it?"

I nodded, but mostly because I knew it was what he expected of me.

"Tell me what you saw and maybe we can figure out where they are." His tone was still gentle, which caught me off guard. "If he left to go meet Gentry, I can send some men to intercept them."

I wasn't sure that was necessarily a good thing—what if innocent people got caught in the mess?—but it was better than sitting around waiting for Gentry to strike. Especially if Mason was one of the names on his list.

Skeeter pushed on. "How big was the room? What did the tables look like? Could you see the bartender?"

"Um..." I closed my eyes to bring back the memory. "It was dark and they were sitting at the bar. I think the seats were wooden, but I didn't look down at mine. There were bottles of liquor on the shelves behind the counter, but above those were decorations—a Mexican hat, some maracas—"

"That's Pedro's," Jed muttered.

My eyes flew open as Skeeter glanced over his shoulder. "I think you're right. Send Merv and Tig on over, but tell them to be discreet. I want information more than I want blood. We need to know how deep this thing runs."

Jed nodded and pulled out his cell phone.

Skeeter turned back to face me. "Did they say anything else?"

"Gentry wanted to know about me—the Lady in Black. He's wondering about my end game."

"And?"

"Humphrey believes I'm here as an investor."

"Did he say anything else about you?" He seemed on edge. "Think carefully."

"I did something in here that made him suspicious."

"What?"

I swallowed. How was Skeeter going to take this? "I told him I knew that he was playing sides. And I told him to ask Gentry to set up a meeting with me."

"*You did what?*"

I cringed, the boom of his voice hurting my ears. "It was before I had my vision. I needed to know more about Gentry's involvement."

He was beyond furious. "*Now he thinks you're a damned traitor!*"

I squared my shoulders. "No, I told him you'd given me full leeway to do anything to expand your business. I said I wanted to see about a negotiation."

He released two heavy breaths, shaking with anger. "I don't negotiate."

I fought to stay calm. One of us needed to keep a clear mind. "I know that. And so did he. But it's a moot point now. In my vision, Gentry said he wouldn't meet with me until after you were dead." I glared at him. "And that's not gonna happen, so there won't be a meeting."

"You've made it look like I can't control my people!"

"Skeeter." I was proud that my voice didn't shake with fear.

His blazing eyes met mine.

"Everyone knows that a ruler who won't budge is soon toppled by his own arrogance. But a ruler who changes his stance as frequently as he changes his underwear is no better." I swallowed, relieved he was still listening. "A smart ruler has people who do the negotiating for him. He has emissaries who test the waters and work out deals for him so he doesn't lose face." I tilted my head forward, imploring him to listen. "That's *me*."

His chest continued to heave, but the anger in his eyes faded some, so I moved on. Skeeter wasn't the only one at risk. For all I knew, that list could be a mile long. "Humphrey is evil, Skeeter. Just as evil as Gentry, if not more so. Humphrey said he'd take out the town if he was paid enough."

He pursed his lips. "I'm not surprised."

"You have to stop them."

His eyes flew open. "*Me?*"

"Who knows who's on that list, but I don't think Humphrey would hesitate to kill anyone for a profit. Innocent people could die. For all I know, I could be on there too, either as Lady *or* as Rose. And we both know that Mason's probably on there too." While Skeeter didn't give a flip about Mason, he saw me as an investment and I knew he wouldn't risk losing something so valuable.

His jaw set. "And Humphrey had no clue who else was on the list?"

"No. Only Gentry seemed to know. And he wouldn't say a word about who was hiring him. Do *you* have any idea who it is?"

He cast a glance at Jed, who had ended his call, then back at me. "Yeah, but it doesn't make a lick of sense." He shook his head. "You did a good job." He looked pained to admit it.

"So I'm done? I can go home now?"

He was silent for a good five seconds, just staring into space before he said, "No, not yet."

Jed shot Skeeter a look of surprise.

"Do you want me to read someone else?"

"No," he said, still tense. "I want you to have a drink with me."

I shook my head. "I already swiped some of your good whiskey, so there's no need. I should get home."

His eyes narrowed. "We have an agreement and doing what I say is part of it."

I glared at him. "Fine. One drink. Then I'm goin' home."

Skeeter moved toward the console. "Jed, you can leave us."

Jed's mouth dropped open and his gaze turned to me, almost as if he were asking me for permission.

My heart began to race. Why would Skeeter want to be alone with me?

"Jed," Skeeter barked as he grabbed a fresh glass for me and began to pour.

Jed didn't move an inch. "Skeeter, we need to follow up on this Gentry lead. If we can get him now, it'll save us a lot of trouble later."

"Merv and Tig are following up. It can wait. *Leave.*"

Jed moved to the door, casting one last glance at us before closing it behind him. If Jed was nervous, I had every right be terrified.

Skeeter turned around, holding the two glasses. "Come sit." He motioned to the seating area.

Trying to keep my breath even, I sat in the seat Humphrey had vacated.

Skeeter chuckled as he handed me a glass. "Why do you look so nervous? Are you afraid I'll bite?"

I studied him for a long moment. Less than five minutes ago I'd given him just about every reason to whip out his gun and shoot me execution style. Yet here I sat, about to drink whiskey with him. Skeeter Malcolm was many things, but he was no immediate threat to me. "No," I finally said.

He sat in the chair next to me and held up his glass. "To a successful partnership."

I raised my glass and clicked it against his. We both took a sip, his more generous than mine.

"You've surprised me, Rose. When we started this endeavor, I never expected you to be so adept at this business."

Again, I felt a pang of guilt and fear. It wasn't Skeeter who frightened me; it was my own startling aptitude for his business. "I thought we'd already established my feelings about that."

"If you were anyone else, I'd offer you a paid position."

I laughed despite myself. "If my landscaping business goes belly-up, I might take you up on it."

"Rumor has it you need money."

My mouth dropped open. "How do you know that?"

He grinned and took a sip before answering. "Your trip to the Piggly Wiggly has already become Fenton County legend." Then he watched me for a second, turning uncharacteristically serious. "I know we made this arrangement as a barter." He rested an arm on the chair and leaned toward me, lowering his voice. "But if you need money, I would be more than happy to put you on my payroll. You're worth it."

I scowled. "And what would you have me do, Skeeter Malcolm?" There was no way I'd take money from him, but I couldn't help asking.

He laughed. "I'm not offering you money to sleep with me, Lady, if that's where your mind is goin'. I have plenty of women who are more than happy to accept that offer free of charge."

My cheeks burned with embarrassment.

He turned serious again. "Our arrangement only requires you to show up when I call you. But tonight you took initiative I hadn't expected, and while you caught me off-guard, your risk paid off."

"Even though I asked to meet Gentry?"

"*Especially* since you asked to meet Gentry."

"I thought you were furious."

"I was." He paused. "But what you said makes sense." His gaze pinned mine. "Where'd you learn something like that?"

"Watching *Marco Polo*," I said. "On Netflix."

He burst out laughing.

I scowled. "What's so funny about that?"

"You never cease to surprise me." He shook his head, wearing an amused grin.

"I was doin' my job. A deal's a deal."

"No. You could have just sat back and bided your time until Jed took you home."

He was right. So why hadn't I?

Skeeter set his glass on the table and shifted his chair sideways. Leaning over his legs, he clasped his hands together. "Rose, I know this is hard for you. You're working for a criminal." He smiled slightly when I started to speak. "I know what I am. It's not a secret."

"I entered this particular arrangement of my own free will, Skeeter. I gave my word. My feelings have no bearing on the matter."

"I disagree. Your feelings do bear on the matter." He paused. "Rose, there will always be bad guys in the world. There will always be theft and murder. But there are varying levels of evil." He looked into my eyes. "Do you agree?"

Momma always saw the world in black and white, but not me. I realized very early on that most everything in life was some varying shade of gray. "Yes. I think there are."

"Daniel Crocker was a power-hungry maniac. He was insane and this county suffered for it. Mick Gentry is a sadistic bastard. You've met the man, so you've seen that for yourself." He shifted in his seat. "While I might be a criminal, I believe in fairness. No matter what the sheriff does to stop it, there will always be criminal elements in this county. So if the underworld is here to stay, wouldn't it be better to have someone run it who actually has a code of ethics?"

What he said made sense, but we were talking about criminal activity, which made it hard to condone no matter who ran it.

"I think we can both agree that there are two men vying for control of Fenton County right now. Me and Gentry. If you could pick, which one would you choose?"

"Of course, you."

He shook his head. "No, think about. Which of us would you choose to succeed?"

I waited a few moments before answering, but I didn't have to give it more than a millisecond of thought. "You, Skeeter."

He nodded and swallowed, looking nervous. "I need you to help me, Rose. When Crocker ran things, quite a few of us didn't like it, but we had no choice. Crocker knew the men who weren't one hundred percent behind him. Things have changed.

Gentry has infiltrated my organization. I don't know who I can trust anymore. What's worse, there's someone higher up directing him. Someone who wants me dead."

"I already told you that I'll help you, Skeeter."

"But what I need from you isn't just help. I need your loyalty. Tonight you showed me that you're capable of it. But I need *you* to believe in it."

I sighed. "Skeeter..."

"Deveraux and I are enemies, but I wouldn't consider killing the man. Even before I started using you. Gentry wouldn't bat an eye at eliminating him. If he were in control, he'd eliminate him out of sheer principle after that sting operation at Gems."

I knew Skeeter was right, but it still made me light-headed to think of it.

"So by helping me thwart Gentry, you're protecting your boyfriend. And not just him. The citizens of Fenton County. Believe it or not, I meant what I said. I *do* have a code of ethics. No one hurts kids and gets away with it. I don't condone rape. And while I'm responsible for the deaths of more than a few men, it wasn't without just cause. Gentry doesn't give a shit about any of that. You yourself said Humphrey would wipe out the town if his check was big enough."

"So you're your own judge and jury?"

"Are you suggesting I hand them over to the bumbling Henryetta Police Department? And let them spill my secrets while they're at it?"

"Yes." I closed my eyes. "I don't know."

"For argument's sake, let's say Gentry eliminates me and gets caught. Do you think the crime situation is goin' away?"

"No, I'm not that naïve."

"The chances of someone more just than me takin' over are slim to none. That's why I'm having a hard time getting a foothold. Some men see me as weak." He clasped his hands together. "In that meeting tonight, you didn't come across as an investor, Rose. You came across as a partner."

"I'm sorry."

He shook his head and sat up. "I won't deny I was pissed as hell, but after you dressed down Humphrey, those other two men respected you. Together we make a united front. They want to be a part of that."

"What are you suggesting?"

"That I utilize you more. More meetings. More face time."

I shook my head, dread seeping into my bones. "No, Skeeter. I can't."

His eyes hardened. "Why? Because you don't want to help me?"

"No, because I have a business—I have *two* businesses. I have friends and family and a boyfriend. What you're suggesting means I'll be spending a ton of time with you. How can I explain that away?"

"Okay, then answer me this: Do you trust me to be in charge of this county?"

He was asking me to condone his criminal activities, which went against everything I believed. But there was some sense to what he said. And at the auction that snagged him his place as the king of the Fenton County underworld, he would have killed the men who'd robbed the bank if I hadn't coerced him not to use violence. I had a chance to have a positive influence on him, but at what cost?

"Yes, I trust you," I finally said, "but it's not that simple. Mason and the sheriff's department are dyin' with curiosity over the Lady in Black. All that talk was settlin' down, but if I start makin' more appearances, their curiosity will perk up again. You can wander the street a free man, but if I show up in a public place as Lady, someone's bound to question me. I can't risk it."

He was quiet for a moment. "I see your point. If I can make this work with as minimal involvement from you and risk to you as possible, are you on board?"

"According to our bargain, you can request my help whenever and however often you want, Skeeter." I tried to keep the bitterness from my voice.

"Screw the bargain. I need you committed."

"Does that mean you're letting me off the hook?"

He studied me again, his face devoid of emotion. "Do you want to be set free from your agreement?"

It was a tricky question. "A deal's a deal, Skeeter."

He stood and released a loud groan as he moved to the center of the room.

"Doesn't having a woman as a partner make you look weaker?"

"Strangely enough, no. You're strong enough to draw their interest."

I stood and walked over to him. "I realize you have a lot to lose, but so do I. You chose this life. I fell into it by accident. How long would I have to commit to this role?"

"Until Gentry is gone?" But he seemed unsure, which meant he wasn't giving me an end date.

"And what about the man calling the shots? Won't he just take Gentry's place once his stooge disappears?"

"He's hiding for a reason. He wants to stay in the shadows. He won't make himself known."

"I don't know." I turned away from hm. "I'm not saying no, but I'm asking for some time to think about it. It's a big decision."

"I'll give you twenty-four hours. Call me with your answer."

Only twenty-four hours? If I committed to this and got caught, I could face prison time. Not even Mason would be able to save me…that was, assuming he'd still *want* to help. He'd probably leave me and never look back. But I also had the chance to help him and whoever else was on that evil list. Could I really afford to say no? "Fine. Twenty-four hours. So are we done?"

His mouth turned down into a frown. "You're free."

I started for the door, but a sudden thought made me turn around to look at him. "Why didn't you let Jed stay?"

His jaw worked for a moment, then he said, "Jed doesn't know anything about our arrangement."

"But he knows you saved Mason from the fire. He helped you pull him out."

"He thinks I only did it to help you."

I wasn't sure how to answer that. "Why keep it from him? I thought you could trust him."

"I trust him implicitly. But this is between you and me. No one else needs to know."

I nodded. I had a feeling he'd made that decision for my benefit and not his own. The gesture wasn't lost on me. "Thank you."

"Rose." He moved to his desk and opened a drawer. "What you said earlier is true. If Gentry has a hit list, there's a very good chance Deveraux's name is on it."

My stomach cramped. "I know."

"If someone tries to kill him, they might think you're in the way." He pulled out a small handgun and shut the drawer. "I want you to take this."

I shook my head. "I can't carry a gun around."

"You need to protect yourself."

"I don't even know how to use it."

"Then go to a gun range." He shoved it toward me. "Take it."

"That gun isn't in my name. I can't risk Mason finding it and I don't want to lie about where I got it. I'll get my own weapon."

His gaze found mine. "Get it by tomorrow."

"Fine."

He put the gun back in his drawer. "You can tell me that you have it when you call me with your answer."

I nodded. What had I just agreed to? And more importantly, what was I about to get myself into? There was no easy choice here. No black and white. And as I walked out of the room, I couldn't help wondering if Dora had found her own slippery slope of right and wrong. And I couldn't help remembering where it had landed her.

In a grave.

Chapter Fifteen

J ed didn't look happy when I walked out of Skeeter's office. He was pacing in the rec room and his head jerked up as soon as he heard my approach.

"Can you take me back to my truck?"

"Sure thing." He glanced behind me, and I looked back to see Skeeter standing in the doorway.

"Any word from Merv?" Skeeter asked.

"They're at Pedro's, but so far nothing."

Skeeter nodded. "Let me know if it changes."

"Will do."

I shivered from the cold as Jed and I crossed the parking lot in silence. If I continued to do this, I was going to have to get Lady a coat. As Jed opened the back door, I asked, "Can you get my clothes? I'll change in the back. The windows in my truck aren't tinted."

He stumbled and circled around to the trunk. His brow was furrowed when he handed me the bag. "Why are you still outside the car?"

"I need you to unzip me."

"What?"

"The dress is too tight for me to do it on my own."

I presented my back to him and he unzipped me halfway down before climbing into the driver's seat.

I waited until he was on county roads outside of town before I reached around and unzipped my dress the rest of the way. When I got it to my waist, I pulled my sweater over my head, then shimmied the rest of the way out of the dress.

Jed had been quiet the whole way. I could tell he was bothered by my time alone with Skeeter, but I wasn't sure why. Did he not trust Skeeter or did he not trust me?

"Why are you helping Skeeter?" he finally asked while I was trying to tug on my jeans. "The first time you wanted your money. The second you were trying to protect your boyfriend, but why now?"

I wasn't sure how to answer him. If Skeeter wasn't willing to tell anyone the truth about our arrangement, I didn't want to be forthcoming with the information either. "Mason's still in danger. I'm positive his name is on Gentry's list along with Skeeter's. By helping Skeeter, I'm getting information that will benefit Mason."

"But you can't tell Deveraux anything about what goes on while you're Lady."

"I know, but I can still figure out a way to tip him off to Gentry."

He looked in the rearview mirror, catching my gaze. "Skeeter isn't a long-term kind of guy."

"What's that mean?" I asked in confusion.

"It means plenty of women have been hurt by Skeeter Malcolm."

"Oh!" My eyes widened. "You think I want to sleep with him?" I asked in disbelief.

He didn't answer; he only averted his gaze from the mirror.

"No! God no. I'm with Mason. I wouldn't dream of cheating on him. And Skeeter's not interested in me that way."

He didn't respond for several seconds. "Just be careful, Rose."

"What does that mean?"

He pulled into the Sinclair station parking lot. "I'm gonna follow you to your farm."

I slipped my foot into a boot. "Why?"

"Things are unsettled right now. I don't think anyone followed me, but it's better to be safe than sorry." He paused. "You have my number and Skeeter's. If you ever feel unsafe, call us."

Fear prickled the hair on the back of my neck. How had I managed to forget that working with Skeeter was dangerous? But Mason was in more danger than ever, and I'd just found out information that might affect him, not to mention anyone else on Mick Gentry's list. I needed to get home and find a way to tell Mason about my vision without giving away my extracurricular activities.

I pulled on my other boot and opened the car door.

"Rose."

I pulled the door shut and waited.

"You did great tonight. I can tell Skeeter's impressed, and you earned those men's respect."

"That's what Skeeter said."

"Reconsider doin' this." Both hands gripped the steering wheel. "It's a rush in the beginning, but soon you'll grow weary of it. Skeeter would skin me alive for tellin' you so, but you need to get out now, before you get buried too deep. This isn't your world, Rose."

He was right, of course, but it wasn't that simple. "Thanks, Jed. I'll think about what you said." I had lots of pondering to do. Especially over the next twenty-four hours.

I grabbed my bag and climbed into my truck. When I took off, Jed followed an inconspicuous distance behind me. I turned into my driveway a few minutes after ten. Jed drove past and I pulled out my phone to text Neely Kate.

I'm home safe and sound.

I'm just getting home after dropping Granny off. How'd it go?

Good, I texted back. *I'll fill you in tomorrow. xoxo*

I was worried about her. Given how tired she'd looked all day, I didn't like the thought of her being out this late. But I didn't have time to think about it. Muffy's face was pressed to the living room window and she was barking her head off. Mason's car was already parked in front of the house, so he had to know I was home.

I stuffed my bag of Lady in Black clothes on the floorboard of the backseat and headed inside. Mason greeted me at the door, sweeping me into his arms and giving me a sweet kiss that reminded me how much I loved him.

"Did you have fun at Bingo?" he asked.

I forced a laugh and hoped it wasn't too obvious I was faking it. "It was an experience, all right. Neely Kate's granny takes her Bingo seriously."

"Did you win?"

"Apparently, I'm unlucky at Bingo but lucky in love, which is all that matters." I kissed him again to prove the point.

"How's Neely Kate?"

I pressed my cheek to his chest and slid my arms around his back. "It's hard to say. Better, I think, but she gets really tired, and one minute she's fine and the next she's upset. I think it helped her to be out with friends today, but she's still a ways off from being okay."

He kissed my forehead. "You're a good friend."

"I'm trying. I hope I'm doin' enough."

"I'm sure Neely Kate thinks you are."

I looked up at him. I needed to figure out how to tell him about the vision. "How long have you been home?"

"Not long. I took Muffy on a short walk when I got home, so she's ready for bed."

"Good, because I'm exhausted." I paused. Since there was never a good time to bring up your boyfriend's potential murder, now seemed as good a time as any. "Mason?"

He gave me a kiss as his fingers lightly stroked my neck. "Hmm?"

"Has there been any progress in catching Mick Gentry?"

His hand stilled. "Why?"

"I just have a bad feeling about him."

"Just a bad feeling or something more?" When I didn't answer, he lifted his head to look into my face. "Did you have a vision?"

At least I could tell him the partial truth, but I was going to have to fabricate part of it, which gnawed at my gut. "Yeah, on the way home from Bingo. I stopped at the gas station. There were several men around, so I'm not sure which guy prompted it."

"What did you see?"

"I was in a bar, next to another guy sitting at the counter. He had a ball cap pulled low, trying to hide his face. I'm positive it was Mick Gentry."

He straightened. "You saw Mick Gentry in a vision?"

I nodded. "Yeah."

"Why didn't you tell me as soon as you walked through the door?" he asked in alarm.

"Telling you five minutes ago wouldn't matter a hill of beans." I frowned. "And the vision sickened me...I wanted a moment to enjoy your welcome home."

"What did you see?"

"He was telling someone he had a list of people he was supposed to *take care of*, but he was waiting for confirmation. I got the impression it was a hit list."

"Did he say who was on the list?"

This was where things got tricky. I didn't want to lie, but would I be putting Skeeter at risk if I mentioned his name? I decided to do it anyway. Maybe it would help Mason catch Mick, and I wouldn't feel as much pressure to help Skeeter directly. "Skeeter Malcolm."

His face paled. "You're positive?"

I nodded, but his reaction worried me. Why would he be so concerned over Skeeter? "Yes, but Mason, if he has a list, you're sure to be on it after what happened at Gems." I grabbed his shirt with both hands. "What if my accident was related to this list?"

His jaw tightened, but he didn't say anything.

"He was waiting for someone to tell him when to start," I added.

"And you have no idea who?"

"No. I'm sorry."

He gently grabbed my shoulders. "Was there anything else? I know you said he was in a bar, but did you recognize which bar? Was there a sign or something?"

Skeeter had sent his men to the bar, but what difference did it make if Skeeter caught him or the sheriff's department? I may have had the vision at Skeeter's request, but I owed it to Mason to tell him everything I could to save his life. "There were Mexican decorations on the wall—a hat and maracas. And I think saw a sign...Pedro's?"

His eyes lit up and he leaned over and kissed me hard before grabbing his phone out of his pocket. He started to place a call and stopped.

"What's wrong?"

He shook his head and took a step backward. "Nothing. I just better make this call in my office."

"Why?"

"Fenton County business."

"But I gave you the lead!"

He ignored me and headed into the library, closing the door behind him as he held the phone up to his ear. He paced as he talked and lifted a hand to the back of his neck. I wondered if I should head upstairs and get ready for bed so I could give him some privacy, but I was still aggravated he was making his call behind those doors. I wasn't going anywhere.

After a while, his voice rose loud enough for me to hear him. "Are you going to do something about this or not?"

Who was he talking to? Most likely Joe, but why would they be arguing over the lead? Maybe Joe decided not to follow up on it when he heard it came from my vision.

Mason stormed out of the office and into the kitchen.

I ran after him. "Where are you goin'?" I asked when I saw him opening the door to the basement.

"To get my rifle."

I stopped in my tracks in the middle of the kitchen. "Why?"

"To keep us safe."

I heard him stomp down the basement stairs, heading toward the cabinet he'd bought to house his guns. When Daniel Crocker had escaped from jail and come after me, Mason had brought several rifles and handguns to the farm. Had it come to this *again?*

I ran back to the living room and grabbed my own phone to call Joe, who surprised me by actually answering. "Rose?"

"Are you really not gonna follow through on the lead Mason just called in?"

"He's telling you official county business?" he shouted in my ear.

"He didn't have to."

Joe groaned. "Rose, it's a vision."

"Seriously, Joe? You've followed up on my visions before. Do you think I made it up?"

"Of course not."

"Then why won't you do anything?"

"It's not that easy, Rose. There are rules. I have to answer to my boss."

"Those are a whole bunch of poor excuses and you know it." Why would he be dragging his heels on this? "You'd really stand back and let Mason get killed?"

He was silent for several seconds. "You think I would do that?"

Did I? Joe was capable of a lot of things, but I didn't believe he'd resort to that. Especially considering all the changes I'd seen in him. But I'd taken too long to answer.

"You believe I'd knowingly put a man in danger because of *my love life?*"

"Joe—"

"You never knew me at all," he said in disgust.

His statement dredged up more pain than I expected, so I didn't rush to correct him. "And whose fault is that?"

I was greeted with silence, and when I glanced at my phone, I realized he'd hung up. I felt terrible. I knew deep down Joe was a good person who'd never let someone kill Mason. Why had I let him believe otherwise?

Mason came back into the room several minutes later with his gun bag. He took one look at me, and the anger in his eyes shifted to concern. "Rose, I'm sorry. I'm sure I scared you storming off like that."

I shook my head. "I'm a terrible person, Mason."

He put the bag on the floor and sat on the sofa next to me, pulling me into his arms. "What on earth would make you say that?"

"I called Joe."

His arms stiffened slightly before tightening around me and pulling me closer. "I take it that it didn't go well."

"You're not gonna ask me why I called him?"

"You're an intelligent woman. I'm sure you put some of the pieces together. Besides, it was *your* vision."

I rested my head in the crook of his arm. "I had to know why he wasn't following up on it."

"I gather you didn't like the answer any more than I did."

I leaned back to wipe the tears off my cheeks. "I don't understand, Mason. His reason was a crock of cow manure. What's really goin' on?"

Indecision flickered in his eyes. "Joe's under a lot of pressure. I'm sure he thinks he made the right call."

"By letting Mick Gentry get away?"

He sighed, but his arms were tense. "His reasoning is that his men are stretched thin right now, and there was no way of knowing if your vision took place tonight, tomorrow, three days from now, or even at all. Pedro's is close to the Columbia County border. He claims he can't spare the manpower to investigate an unlikely lead."

Anger quickly overcame my guilt. "So he'll leave you as a *sitting duck?*"

He lifted my chin and looked into my eyes. "Rose, he's sending Deputy Miller over to watch the house tonight."

"Oh, Mason." I cringed. "I asked him how he could stand back and let you get killed."

He cupped my cheek. "Oh, sweetheart. It's no secret that Joe Simmons and I have history, and a year ago I might have accused him of the same thing. But we've worked together a lot over these last few months, and I realize now he'd never knowingly let someone get hurt. Even me."

"I know. But I was too slow to tell him that and he assumed I believed it."

Mason sighed.

"I have to call him to apologize. I have to set him straight."

He gave me a soft smile. "Give it a few minutes. I'm sure he's not feeling very charitable at the moment."

Fresh tears filled my eyes.

Mason pulled me close and rubbed my back. "It's going to be okay, sweetheart. I'm sure Joe's feelings were hurt, but he'll get over it."

I shook my head in disbelief. "Why do you care if Joe gets over it? Wouldn't you prefer for him to stay angry with me?"

"Not if it hurts you in the process." He looked into my eyes. "I love you, Rose. I have to trust you and respect your choices, including which friends you choose." When I started to protest, he added, "Do I want you to be Joe Simmons' friend? No. Do I feel threatened by it? Hell, yes. But I trust you." His eyes hardened slightly. "I don't trust him, but I trust you enough to know how to handle it if he gets out of line again."

"Thank you."

He wiped my tears. "Still, if I ever find out he behaves inappropriately, I can't be held responsible for what his face looks like after we have a *chat*." The look in his eyes told me he meant every word.

"I love you."

He gave me a soft kiss. "I love you too." He stood and picked up the bag and set it on the coffee table. "And now I'm going to keep us safe."

I only hoped Jed was keeping Skeeter safe too.

Chapter Sixteen

Mason didn't sleep well. He kept getting out of bed and checking the windows and doors. He'd turned on the alarm system he'd put in after our break-in last December, but he kept checking it to make sure it was still on.

When he came to back to bed for what seemed like the twentieth time, I pulled him close and rested my head in the crook of his arm. "Is Deputy Miller still outside?"

"Yeah."

"You don't trust him to keep watch?"

"I do, but it's just him out there. I'll feel better if I keep an eye on things myself."

"Okay."

"Rose?" he whispered in the dark.

"Hmm?" I asked, already drifting off to sleep.

"Maybe you should go stay with my mom."

That woke me up right quick. I lifted my head. "Are you going too?"

"No."

I settled back down. "Then I'm staying with you."

He was surprisingly quiet.

"No argument?" I asked in surprise.

"I didn't expect you to agree, but I had to try anyway." His fingers began to stroke my back. "I think you should carry some kind of protection."

"What does that mean? A gun?"

"No, not a gun. You're not used to handling one, so you could end up hurting yourself."

"Then what?"

"A Taser."

I bolted upright. "Nuh-uh. Jonah's momma Tased me when she kidnapped me."

"Then you know how incapacitating it is...but it's also not lethal. It could give you the chance to get away without requiring you to use deadly force."

"Get away from what?"

He sat up next to me. "Rose, it's a smart idea for you to have a way to protect yourself no matter where you are or what you're doing. Trouble has a penchant for finding you. Short of keeping you in a padded room, it's the next best thing to make sure you're safe."

I sucked in a deep breath. "And what's to keep me from accidentally Tasing myself or someone else?"

"I'll make sure you know how to use it so you'll feel safe pulling it out if you need it."

I had to admit it was a good idea, and it also took care of my promise to Skeeter, so why was I so reluctant? "Okay."

"Tomorrow morning I'll meet you at Bubba's Gun Shop and I'll help you pick one out."

I lay back down and pulled him with me. "I'll let you have your way. I'm getting a Taser, now get some sleep."

"Say that again," he teased as he settled down next to me and pulled me into his arms.

"Say what again?" I asked through a yawn.

"You'll let me have my way." I heard the grin in his voice.

I softly swatted his chest. "Gloating is not attractive, Mason Deveraux. And besides, I let you have your way with me all the time." My voice was heavy with innuendo.

His hand slid down my back to my behind and I let him have his way with that too. But when Mason's alarm went off the next morning, I was exhausted from lack of sleep.

He kissed my cheek when I stirred. "Do you want to have breakfast together before we go to the gun shop?"

I stretched and remembered I already had breakfast plans. Only Mason didn't know about my research into Dora's background. Just stick to the basics. "I would love to, but I'm having breakfast with Jessica and her mother."

He blinked in surprise. "Who?"

I pushed up on my elbows. "You know, Jonah's girlfriend."

"Oh." He squinted in confusion. "I didn't realize you and Jessica were friends."

"It's nothing really," I said as I slid out of bed. "When Neely Kate and I were at Jonah's church yesterday, Jessica mentioned that she and her momma were having breakfast in the morning and she invited us to come."

"You were at Jonah's church yesterday?" He shook his head as he got out of bed and followed me into the bathroom. "I swear you traipse literally all over this county." He pressed his front to my back as I picked up my toothbrush, and he found my gaze in the mirror. "Just try to stick closer to town for awhile, okay? At least until this Gentry mess is cleared up. Although the Henryetta PD isn't much comfort. All the more reason for you to have some means of defending yourself."

I wasn't sure how much comfort we should take in the Fenton County Sheriff's Department either if Joe wasn't going to follow up on our leads.

After showering in a hurry, I sent Neely Kate a quick text to ask her if she was still up for breakfast.

I'm in, Yellow Lizard. Don't ask any questions until I get there. LOL.

I snickered and walked out of the bathroom just as Mason finished dressing. He pulled out his handgun, and I eyed it nervously, also noticing the holster he'd already strapped over his shoulder.

His eyes caught mine. "It's just a precaution, Rose."

"I know." But my stomach still knotted with worry at the sight of it.

"I know how to handle it. I have permits and Joe's fully aware that I'm carrying it outside the courthouse."

"That's not why I don't like it. It just reminds me that someone out there wants you dead."

He put the gun on the nightstand and pulled me to his chest, searching my eyes. "This isn't the first threat I've received. Everything's going to be fine." He gave me a soft kiss and stepped back. "I'm going to take Muffy outside. Why don't you finish getting ready and I'll follow you into town." He paused. "Do you have any jobs today that would keep you from taking her to work with you?"

"No…"

He winked. "I think she'd be happier with you at the office today."

"What, did you two have a chat while I was in the shower?"

He gave me a mischievous grin. "I can't betray our dog-attorney privilege, but she did petition me to appeal to you on her behalf."

I laughed and wrapped my arms around his neck. "Well…seeing as how she went to the trouble of contacting her attorney, I can hardly say no."

"I'll be sure to tell my client we've reached an agreement." He gave me a slow kiss, then lifted his head, all merriment gone. "Thank you." He broke away and picked up his gun and placed it in his shoulder holster, then headed to the bedroom door. "Come on, Muff. Let's go outside, girl."

She bounded after him with excitement, leaving me alone with my befuddlement. Mason never asked me to take Muffy with me. He left that decision entirely up to me. Then again, he knew she was a good guard dog. I couldn't stop the smile that spread across my face. Just like I had my ways of coercing him, he was figuring out ways to coerce me too.

I headed downstairs and my cell phone began to ring while Mason and Muffy were outside. I was surprised to see it was Violet.

"Hey, Vi."

"Rose, I have a huge favor to ask."

"Okay," I said, hesitantly.

"I'm having a big shipment of potting soil and fertilizer delivered today around ten. Do you think you could spare Bruce Wayne to help move the bags behind the greenhouse? I'm having a weekend sale that starts tomorrow and I need everything straightened up."

Starting the sale on Friday seemed like a good idea. But like I'd told Mason, good ideas had never been her weakness. "I can't speak for Bruce Wayne, but I have no problem with it. How about I call him and I'll let you know."

"Okay. Tell him that I would need him here around the time the bags are dropped off. Thanks, Rose."

I hung up and called Bruce Wayne as I peeked out the window to check on Mason. He was sitting on the porch steps, talking on his phone while rubbing behind Muffy's ears. She looked up at him, her tongue hanging out and her tail wagging.

"Good morning, Rose," Bruce Wayne said when he answered the phone.

"Good morning to you too. Do you have any big plans today?"

"Nothin' I can't set aside for you. What do you need?"

"Don't sound too eager yet," I cautioned. "Violet has asked if you can help her move bags of potting soil and fertilizer. She's getting a shipment at ten and she needs someone to haul the bags behind the greenhouse."

"Oh."

"She's got a new employee," I said, trying to sound cheerful. "I haven't met her yet, so you can get the scoop and report back to me."

He chuckled. "That might work with Neely Kate, but not with me."

"So you can't do it?"

"I didn't say that." I heard the grin in his voice. "I just meant that gossip's more a job for Neely Kate. If it helps the business, just tell me when to show up. I'll be there."

"She says to come around ten. And thank you."

"No problem. I'll talk to you later."

Mason walked through the front door as I hung up. "Everything okay? You look worried."

I waved him off. "It's nothing. Bruce Wayne is going to the nursery today to help Violet with some heavy lifting."

He paused. "I see the reason for your concern."

"I'm sure they'll be fine…as long as Violet minds her manners." I sent her a quick text to let her know to expect him and implored her to treat him kindly. She responded back saying she was insulted I would insinuate she'd treat him any differently.

Mason grabbed his bag out of his office. "Are you ready to go?"

"Yeah." I put on my coat and left the house, Mason following behind me after he turned on the alarm. My gaze drifted to the vacant spot where Deputy Miller had parked his patrol car overnight.

Mason put his arm around my shoulders. "We only have protection at night. But it's less likely for someone to attack in broad daylight."

I cocked my head and looked up at him. "Someone tried to kill you in broad daylight just last month. And I'm still not convinced we know who did it. It could very well be the same person who's trying now."

"Sweetheart, my brake line was cut. Nothing like that is going to happen again. Deputy Miller kept an eye on our vehicles all night and no one's brazen enough to attempt such a thing on the town square."

I wasn't so sure.

"Besides, there's no direct threat. Only suspicions. Joe's pulling strings to get Miller out here. I'm not going to ask him to jeopardize his job any more than he's already done."

I studied him. "You two are getting along a lot more."

He dropped his arm and shrugged. "We're not hanging out to watch Monday night football, but we've reached a place where we can discuss work matters civilly."

I noticed he kept it to work matters, but that was good enough for now. At least it was a start.

Muffy hopped in the truck with me and we rode into town. I kept Mason in my rearview mirror for the entire drive. After we both pulled into parking spots at the town square, Mason walked us to the landscaping office so I could let Muffy in before heading over to Merilee's. I noticed he seemed more on edge than usual.

"Maybe you should get an alarm system for the office," he said as I locked up.

"I can't afford an alarm system. I couldn't afford the alarm system you put in the house." I held up my hand. "And before you comment on the fact that the nursery has one, let me remind you we have thousands of dollars of inventory in there, not to mention a history of intruders. All we have here are several second-hand computers and some thrift store furnishings."

"I'd want it to protect *you*, Rose. And I'd put it in myself, if nothing else than for my own peace of mind."

I sighed. "I'll think about it."

"Good." He gave me a kiss goodbye at the courthouse entrance. "Joe texted while I took Muffy outside. I have a meeting with him in about a half hour, and then I have a few other things to work on. How about I meet you at my car at lunchtime so we can go to Bubba's together?"

I'd almost forgotten about the Taser. "Okay. Meet you then." I gave him a smile and waved as he walked up the stairs and headed inside.

He and Joe were having a meeting. They seemed to have a lot of those lately. I thought about what Mason had said about getting along with Joe, which was enough to send the memory of our misunderstanding the night before rushing back to me.

I pulled out my phone as I crossed the street toward the café. I had to apologize and set things right. "Joe?"

"Have you called to accuse me of kicking puppies too?" he asked, but his tone was defeated rather than angry.

"No," I said softly, with a hint of teasing. "You would never kick a puppy. You're too sweet to Muffy to do such a thing."

"Then why are you calling?"

"To apologize. I never should have insinuated something so terrible. I *do* know you better than that, but my temper got the better of me. I'm sorry."

He was quiet for a moment before he answered. "Thank you."

"But Joe, I'm scared for Mason. I know you had Deputy Miller guarding our house last night, but what about during the day?"

"Anyone going in and out of the courthouse has to go through security. He's safe in there. Probably safer than at the farmhouse."

"And what about when he's not at the courthouse?"

He sighed. "Honestly, Rose. He shouldn't leave the courthouse. Not unless a deputy is with him."

"He's planning on meeting me to run an errand later."

"I'm heading into town for a meeting with him, so I'll talk to him. But you and I both know how bullheaded he can be. I need you to encourage him to stay put in the courthouse. He might actually listen if the advice comes from you."

I wasn't so sure about that. "I'll see what I can do."

"Thanks for the apology, Rose." He cleared his throat. "When I thought you believed I would—"

"I was angry that you wouldn't check out the bar. I still am," I said, adding some sternness to my voice. "But I know you would never knowingly let someone hurt Mason…or anyone else. You could never live with yourself if you did." Savannah's death was proof enough of that. I paused, then lowered my voice. "I've always told you that you're a good person, Joe. You just need to believe it of yourself."

"Thanks." His voice sounded tight. "Listen, I have to go. Be careful. I'd put you under twenty-four-hour surveillance— and don't think Mason hasn't requested it—but I don't have the manpower and I can't justify it based on what few leads I have. But I think you're relatively safe, especially if you're not with Mason." He sighed. "I'd suggest you stay away from him until this is resolved, but seeing how that's not likely, just try to be careful."

"You be careful too, Joe. I have a really bad feeling about Mick Gentry."

"You and me both."

I hung up as Neely Kate approached me on the sidewalk outside the restaurant, her face still pale and devoid of much makeup, her nails free from polish. She wore jeans and cowboy boots with the same canvas jacket from the day before. The only thing about her that looked like my friend was the pink and purple streaks in her long straight, blond hair, which was ironic since they were so new. I definitely wasn't used to seeing her this way.

"How are you feeling today?" I asked. "You look tired."

"I'm fine," she said, forcing a tiny smile. "Let's go get some information."

We found Jessica and her mother sitting at a table for four. Just as Jessica had warned, her mother was a talker. She gushed nonstop about everything, including Neely Kate's hair. Jessica had come to visit Neely Kate when she was in the hospital, so I held my breath as I waited for some comment about the miscarriages. But Jessica must not have told her motor-mouthed mother because she blew right onto discussing the service on Sunday at the Methodist church and how terribly off-key Tina Yonkers had been while singing the hymn "How Great Thou Art."

We were halfway through eating our breakfast and we hadn't even begun to discuss Atchison Manufacturing. "Miss Gloria," I said, trying to be nonchalant as I cut off a piece of my fried egg. "Jessica tells me you used to work for Atchison Manufacturing and would be willing answer some questions for us."

She put down her coffee cup. "She said you were interested in the fire. I haven't thought of that place for years. I was a secretary there."

"I just found out that a friend of my family might have worked there. Dora Middleton. Did you know her?" Only a handful of people knew that Momma wasn't my birth mother and I wanted to keep it that way. If I told Jessica's mother, it would spread over Fenton County like wildfire.

Her eyes widened. "Oh, I knew her." The words were dripping in disdain.

Neely Kate flashed me a look of surprise, then turned back to the woman. "It sounds like you maybe you didn't get along."

She set down her fork, syrup smearing onto the table, and leaned forward, her nose scrunching with disgust. "That woman was a home-wrecker."

My chest squeezed and my whole body went rigid. Jessica squirmed in her seat.

Neely Kate pressed on, feigning ignorance. "What makes you say that, Miss Gloria?"

"She and the owner, Henry Buchanan, had an affair. Right under our noses." She shuddered. "*Shameless.*"

My mind was numb with shock at this revelation that my father might not have been the only married man with whom she'd formed a relationship. I hadn't known Dora Middleton, so why did it bother me so much?

Gloria shook her head in disgust. "Everyone knows she seduced that man with her wicked ways. She must have. He loved his wife until she threw herself at him."

Neely Kate leaned forward. "Why do you think they were having an affair?"

The woman's face reddened. "I caught them!"

"Naked?" Neely Kate asked.

I gasped at Neely Kate's crassness and shot her a look of warning.

"Well, no," Gloria said, taken aback. "But I saw them together when I was at the office one night. I had forgotten my new scarf at my desk, so I used my key to get back into the building. His office door was closed, which wasn't unusual, but the door flung open while I was opening my desk drawer and that floozy walked out with Henry on her heels, pleading with her to come back like they'd had some lover's spat."

"Was she pulling on her clothes?" Neely Kate asked. "Were his pants at his knees?"

"Neely Kate!" I gasped.

Neely Kate shrugged, but Jessica's eyes widened in horror.

Gloria's face reddened with embarrassment. "She was tugging on her sweater and her shirt looked disheveled."

"So how can you be so certain they were having an affair?"

"Why else would they have been in his office at nine o'clock on a Wednesday night? They shoulda been at church." She leaned forward and lowered her voice. "In fact, it's the perfect time to meet to have an affair. Half the town would be at church and the other half would be in the bars. No one would know."

For once, Neely Kate seemed speechless.

"Did you only see them the one time?" I asked.

Gloria turned to me, her face softening. "I'm sorry. You said she was a family friend."

"Distant," I said. I wanted the truth more than I wanted my feelings spared. "Very distant, so don't worry about insulting me. She was a friend of my mother's cousin."

She still looked uncertain, but her desire to gossip apparently overruled her concern about sparing my sensitivities. Jessica studied her plate, probably sorry she'd set up our breakfast meeting.

"Oh, there were other signs. There was only that one time after business hours, but the other girl in the office and I had both noticed them carrying on over the months. Dora'd slip into his office and shut the door. At first it didn't seem all that unusual. She was the bookkeeper and he was the owner. We figured they were going over numbers. But the month before she quit she was going in there more and more and we'd see them whispering together." She gave Neely Kate a smug look. "And then there was her pregnancy."

Neely Kate ignored the dangled carrot. "Do you remember when you saw them in his office at night?"

Gloria looked disappointed. "About a week before Dora resigned. Melody and I figured she insisted he leave his wife because of the baby. When he didn't, she quit and moved on to greener pastures."

Could it be true? Had my birth mother carried on an affair with her boss while she was pregnant with me? Her journal entries never seemed to insinuate she was having an affair with Henry, but many of her entries were vague.

"Did Miss Ima Jean know about it?" Neely Kate asked.

Gloria pursed her lips. "No, not until Dora came back."

"What does that mean?" I asked. "She came back to work for him?" I already suspected she was referring to Dora's visit to see Henry the week before the fire, but Dora had obviously left important things out, like her possible affair with her boss. I had to be sure.

"Good heavens, no. She'd gotten another job and had her baby. She brought the baby in right after Thanksgiving—a cute little girl—and insisted on seeing Henry."

"Why'd she want to see him?" Neely Kate asked, sounding worried.

"We could only speculate. I remember we'd gotten a light snowfall and her tiny baby was bundled up in a pink bunting outfit. I told Dora she couldn't see Mr. Buchanan, but she raised a stink, shouting his name until he opened his door. I tell you, he looked pale as a ghost when his eyes landed on the baby. Then he took her into his office and shut the door. They were in there for a good ten minutes, and when the door opened, Dora was crying and saying, 'What about our baby, Henry?' She ran out with the infant and Mr. Buchanan told me to hold his calls. He sat in his office the rest of the afternoon with the door closed. Miss Ima Jean came in the next day, fit to be tied, and fired the girl who did the filing."

"Why?" Neely Kate asked.

"Because she was young and pretty. Like Dora. We figured word got back to her that Mr. Buchanan had carried on an affair with his bookkeeper and fathered her baby."

I felt like I was gonna be sick, but Neely Kate grabbed my hand under the table and held tight. Jessica noticed my reaction and looked like she wanted to bolt from the restaurant.

Gloria continued, too involved in the story to take much notice of how we were reacting to it. "I'd just married Jessica's father a few months earlier." She fluffed her hair with her hand. "Otherwise I would have been tossed out on my keister too."

Looking at her now, I wasn't so sure about that.

"So Dora didn't come back after that?" Neely Kate asked.

"Shoot no. The factory burned down three days later, and then *none* of us worked there. Henry decided not to reopen. Dora died in a car accident a week later and Henry hung himself a few days after that. We figured he realized he loved her and felt guilty about turning her away."

I tried my best to keep my measly breakfast down, but it was all too much. "Excuse me," I mumbled as I stood, my chair scraping the floor with a loud screech. I ran to the bathroom and locked the door behind me, losing what little I'd eaten in the toilet. Tears burned my eyes, but I fought them back. Mason had warned me that finding out about Dora might destroy my fantasies of her. I just hadn't expected to hear whispers about anything of this magnitude. Did he know this part? Had he been trying to spare me the seedy underbelly of the past until he could gather all the facts?

A few minutes later I heard a knock on the door and Neely Kate's voice. "Rose? Are you okay?"

I wiped my tears and took a deep breath. Neely Kate was going through something ten times worse than me, and here I was hiding in the bathroom like a baby. Besides, all of this had happened twenty-five years ago to people I didn't even know. Water under the bridge. I opened the door and forced a smile. "I'm fine."

She studied me with a frown. "You don't look fine."

"It was just a shock is all." My smile widened. "I'm good now."

Neely Kate didn't look convinced, but she glanced back out into the dining area. "Jessica and her mother left. Gloria said she needed to get to her dentist appointment. She talked so cotton pickin' long, she almost missed it."

"Oh. Okay."

"I've already paid for breakfast. Let's go over to the office and figure out what to do next."

I took another deep breath and pushed it out. "Okay."

We walked across the street, both of us silent. What Gloria had said was tumbling around in my head and sending me into a panic. What if Daddy wasn't my father after all? Then Violet and I weren't even half-sisters. Aunt Bessie and Uncle Earl wouldn't be related to me. It would mean I was truly an orphan.

Neely Kate unlocked the door and led the way into the office. Bruce Wayne had already headed over to the nursery. He'd left a note saying he had to come back later for some paperwork and would take Muffy to the nursery if I didn't have plans for her. I fought my growing anxiety and texted him to say it was fine. As Muffy jumped up on my legs with excitement, I couldn't help thinking he'd be much better company for her than I would be today. "My daddy's not my father."

"Now Rose," Neely Kate said in a firm voice as she unbuttoned her coat. "Don't freak out. Gloria Gunner is the biggest gossip I've ever encountered and that's sayin' something. Besides, your daddy worked at the factory too."

I nodded. "Yeah. You're right."

She pointed to the back table. "Sit."

I did as she said, unfastening my coat on autopilot.

"Get out your notebook and let's sort through what she just said."

"Good idea." I dug out the notebook and journal, then set them on the table. Muffy put her front paws on my legs, desperate for attention, so I absently rubbed her head.

A trill erupted from the brown messenger bag Neely Kate was using as a purse today. She groaned and pulled out her walkie-talkie, then gave me an ornery look as she pressed the button. "Yes, White Gopher?"

"That's White *Tiger*. Over," Miss Mildred boomed. "Have you talked to the suspect?"

"You mean Dick Cumberband?" Neely Kate winked and covered her mouth as her shoulders shook with silent laughter.

"It's Dirk *Picklebie*." Miss Mildred's voice screeched over the two-way radio. "And don't be saying his name over the air. Over."

Neely Kate rolled her eyes and pushed her button. "We were talking to Gloria Gunner. Dirk McGuirk is next on our list." Then, as an afterthought, she added, "Over."

"*Picklebie.* You're a bunch of fumbling incompetents."

My friend burst out laughing, then composed herself enough to say, "You forgot to say *over*. Over."

"Over!" Miss Mildred screeched.

Neely Kate was still grinning when she opened the notebook and turned to the last page I'd used for notes. "Gloria said she and her coworker first started noticing Henry and Dora together months before she quit, which was in late September. Months...that's probably May or June at the earliest."

"Okay."

"Dora had you in early November, so she would have gotten pregnant in January. She wasn't slipping into his office until the summer."

We were talking about pregnancies again, and I searched Neely Kate's face for any sign of distress, surprised when I found none. "They could have just hidden their affair in the beginning. In fact, they probably *would* have been more careful in the beginning."

"True... But wasn't your daddy living with her when you were born? And you have photos of the three of you together."

"Daddy and Dora must have met at Atchison. I guess he didn't know about her affair with Henry."

Neely Kate leaned forward, her forehead wrinkled with irritation. "The only evidence we have that there was an affair between them is the testimony of a gossip. We need more evidence."

"Neely Kate, she walked out of Henry Buchanan's office asking, 'What about our baby, Henry?'"

She let out a sigh. "Well, that does sound bad, but that's just how she remembers it. I wouldn't be surprised if she were embellishing things." We were silent for a moment, then Neely Kate said, "So Dora goes to see Henry. Days later there's a fire. Dora dies a week later and Henry kills himself days after that. The timing of it all is pretty odd."

"Agreed."

She looked up at me. "Rose, I'd bet my Fire Engine Red OPI nail polish that your momma didn't have anything to do with Dora's death."

"You think it was an accident?"

"Shoot, no. I still think she was murdered."

I frowned. "Well, she did have a gun hidden under her bed."

Neely Kate nodded. "Wouldn't you if you thought someone was out to kill you?"

I wasn't so sure. I was resisting carrying a Taser. But while I'd always suspected Dora had been murdered, I'd thought it was a domestic dispute. "You think Ima Jean killed her?"

"No." Her eyes widened. "Think bigger."

"Henry?"

She waved off my answer. "The more I think on it, the more certain I am she wasn't having an affair with Henry Buchanan. Think about it. She was the bookkeeper. She knew about everything to do with the factory's money. What if she saw something funny and went to her boss about it?"

"In her journal she mentioned something about money being missing. But that doesn't explain them meeting at night."

"It might if it was something illegal."

"Maybe she discovered the extortion."

Neely Kate shook her head. "But if Henry was extorting someone, he wouldn't be dumb enough to run it through the company." Her eyes lit up. "It's much more likely that he was being extorted and she's the one who figured it out since she noticed the missing money."

"Miss Mildred said the company was up for a government job. What if it had something to do with that?"

"We really need to talk to that foreman. Dirk Picklebie," Neely Kate said. "And we need to go through Dora's journal together to see if you missed anything."

I wanted to protest that I'd already garnered anything of importance from the diary, but it was obvious I'd missed a ton—whether it was actually in the book or not.

Suddenly the question of my history involved more than what happened to my birth mother. Now I was questioning everything.

Chapter Seventeen

Neely Kate covered my hand with her own. "Are you sure you want to do this? Maybe some things are better left in the dark. What happened twenty-five years ago doesn't have a lick to do with who you are right now."

I shook my head. "My entire life has been a lie, Neely Kate. Maybe if Momma had been kind and loving, I'd be content to let things lie, but we both know she wasn't." I swallowed the lump in my throat. "I just have to know."

She patted my hand. "Then we'll find the truth. Because I'm convinced the two of us can solve any mystery."

"Thank you."

She slid the journal between us and flipped through the pages. "Where do you think we should begin?"

I reached for it and turned the pages. "She started talking about the man she was seeing here." I pointed to the first entry. "See?" I said. "In December, she writes that she started seeing the married man she met at work. And she says they ignored each other as much as possible to avoid suspicion."

Neely Kate groaned. "That doesn't mean she was seeing Henry. She could very well have been talking about your father."

The front door creaked open and I jumped in my seat. I almost jumped again when Joe walked in, looking official. I was struck again by how handsome he was in his uniform, but more noticeable was the change in his demeanor. He seemed so much more at home with himself than he'd been while we were dating...or even back in November when he and Violet sprung the news of his investment on me. But it was there now and it made me happy for him. Maybe he was finding peace.

He grinned as his gaze landed on me. "Do you want to explain why you're wearing a guilty look, Ms. Gardner?" he asked, but there was a teasing glint in his eyes.

I shrugged and grinned back. "Habit."

Muffy raced to him, barking with excitement, and he bent down to rub her head. "Hey, girl. I'm happy to see you too." He glanced at the journal, then back up at my face. "You're not going to hide what you're doin'?"

I gave him a haughty look. "I don't see any reason to. Last I heard there's nothin' illegal about reading your birth mother's journal."

Joe stood, then grabbed the office chair from Neely Kate's desk. He rolled it back over to the table and sat down. "I hope you're finding the answers you're looking for, Rose," he said softly.

I let out a sigh. "More questions than answers, honestly."

"Oh?"

I cast Neely Kate a glance, then turned back to him. I was tired of secrets. Mason had the right to know first, but Joe was sitting in front of me and might be able to offer some advice. "Dora worked at Atchison Manufacturing here in Henryetta as a bookkeeper until about a month before I was born. Then the factory burned down at the beginning of December. Dora died in the car accident a week later and her boss hung himself days later."

Joe sat up straight in his chair, shifting from concerned friend to chief deputy sheriff. "That's a little too coincidental."

"This morning we had breakfast with Jessica Gunner and her mother. Gloria was a secretary at the factory. She knew Dora."

Joe gave me a guarded look. "What does she remember?"

"She painted it to look like Dora was having an affair with the boss," Neely Kate interjected, anger in her voice. "She said she used to go into Henry's office and shut the door...and it happened a lot more often up until the day she quit. But I don't think it means a thing. She could have been talkin' about the books."

I looked into Joe's face. "But there's more. Gloria went into the office one Wednesday night about a week before Dora quit. She saw Dora coming out of her boss's closed office, crying. He followed, calling after her."

"Did this Gloria have anything else to say?" Joe asked.

"After I was born, Dora went back to the office and demanded to see Henry. I guess she raised a fuss, saying she wouldn't leave until he saw her. She had me with her. Henry took her into his office and when she came out she was cryin' again and askin', 'What about our baby, Henry?'" I took a breath. "She said 'our baby', Joe. As in hers and Henry's."

"Gloria Gunner is a gossip," Neely Kate said in disgust. "She'll sensationalize anything to make it more excitin' than it really is."

Joe studied Neely Kate for a moment before turning back to me. "So who else thought they were havin' an affair?"

"The office staff," I said. "I don't know about the factory workers. And I guess Henry's wife thought it was true too. After Dora came in with baby me, Ima Jean steamrolled on into the office and fired the other office worker because she was single and pretty like Dora."

"So Henry's wife could have held a grudge against Dora. Probably would have if she believed it was true." He looked away in thought. "The fact her boss killed himself days after her death could support the affair theory. He might have felt guilty if his wife killed her or maybe he was upset he didn't leave his wife for her."

Neely Kate jumped out of her chair. "Why are you both believin' a flat-out liar?"

Joe's mouth dropped open, but he said softly, "I'm just gatherin' the facts, Neely Kate. That's all."

"Well, I'm not gonna listen to another fool word about any of this." She grabbed her coat and stomped out, leaving me gaping at the front door as it slammed behind her.

I considered going after her, but I'd never seen her like this before. Mason always needed to get away for a bit after we had a fight. If Neely Kate were the same way, I'd only make it worse if I followed her now.

"How's she doin'?" Joe asked quietly.

"I honestly don't know. I thought it was a good idea to get her out of the house and get her mind off her troubles, but now I'm not so sure."

"I'm sure it's not easy for her." Joe's gaze stayed on me. "How are you dealin' with this?" He gestured toward the journal.

I took a breath. "The truth is, I don't know. I was upset at first, but Neely Kate is so insistent Dora didn't have an affair with Henry. Part of the reason is that she doesn't want me to get hurt, but my gut tells me she might be right."

"What if Dora *did* have another affair? If Harrison Gardner isn't your birth father?"

I shrugged. "In the scheme of things, I'm not sure that it matters. It doesn't change a thing." Yet it changed everything.

"Well, I agree with Neely Kate not to jump to conclusions. But if you really want the truth, I encourage you to also keep an open mind."

"So you're okay with us asking questions?" I gave him a leery look.

He grinned. "Don't look so surprised. It sounds like a domestic dispute that turned tragic, but you should always be careful when you're pokin' at a hornet's nest with a stick. This may have happened twenty-five years ago, but you're liable to tick off a few people, especially the man's widow if she's is still alive."

My mouth dropped open. "You're giving me your blessing to investigate this case?"

He leaned forward, resting his forearms on his legs. "Rose, I know you think Dora was murdered, but there's no reason to think that except rumor and speculation. Henry's wife had just as much cause to do Dora harm as your momma did. One suspect is dead and the other is probably walking around with a cane. I think it's safe for you to do a little digging. But let me ask you this." He paused and made sure he had my attention. "Do you ever remember your mother putterin' around with cars?"

"Well...no..."

"And this might be sexist of me to say, but there's a good chance Henry's wife couldn't tell the difference between a radiator hose and a brake line."

He had a point. I was pretty certain I couldn't find the brake line in my truck if my life depended on it.

"Nowadays anyone could look that type of thing up on the Internet, but back then, either one of them would have had to ask someone...and that someone would probably have told the Henryetta police."

I sighed. What he said made sense.

"Rose." He covered my hand with his and said, "I suspect your birth mother died in an unfortunate accident. But from what you just told me, the real question might be who your birth father really is."

I nodded, blinking to ease the burning in my eyes. He was only confirming my own thoughts.

"Are you sure you're ready to face that?"

I stared into the eyes of the man I used to love. Everything we had built together was destroyed because of the things neither one of us were ready to face. I was tired of running from the truth, no matter how difficult it was to face. "Yes."

He nodded, looking serious. "If you need help with anything—unofficially, of course—just let me know."

"Thank you."

He removed his hand and grinned. "But there's actually a purpose to my visit."

"You're not here to harass me?" I teased.

"Oh, that's always fun too, but this time was just a bonus. After I delivered the bad news to Mason that he's sequestered to the courthouse during workin' hours, he asked me to run an errand for him." He reached into his pocket and set a small black plastic box on the table. "This is your new frontline self-defense."

"You got me a Taser?" I asked, staring at it.

"Now don't you go lookin' all surprised." He laughed. "Lord knows you need it with all the trouble you get into, Mick Gentry aside." He reached into his other pocket and pulled out a pink box, which he set beside the other. "I got one for Neely Kate too."

"Pink." I laughed.

He shrugged, still grinning. "Pink seemed to suit her better."

I studied him for a moment. "Why are you so nice to her when she's so mean to you most of the time?"

He hesitated before looking into my eyes. "Because she's probably the best friend a person can have and I'm grateful she's yours." He lifted his shoulder into a half shrug. "She thinks I left you high and dry to run for office. If she's any friend at all, I would hope she'd hold it over my head."

"I'm sorry."

He shook his head. "No. Don't be. I can handle it." He glanced back at the front door. "Besides, I'd take her feisty any day compared to this."

"Me too."

"Let me give you a quick lesson before I go. It won't do you any good if you don't know how to use it." He spent several minutes showing me how to load the barb cartridges, how to recharge it, and most importantly, how to use it to defend myself.

He handed it to me and made me repeat everything he'd said.

"Do you feel ready to use it?"

I took a deep breath, looking at the weapon in my hand. "I guess." I offered him a smile. "Thanks for getting it for me. And for the lesson."

He stood. "Well, I better go." He gestured toward the journal. "And if you need any advice about where to go next with your investigation, let me know."

I shook my head with amazement.

He lowered his gaze to mine. "I'm only givin' you my blessing because it's not an ongoing investigation and you're only talking to people." He reconsidered. "You *are* only talking to people?"

"Of course," I said. "What else would we be doin'?"

He shook his head and headed for the door. "I don't *even* want to know."

"Hey, Joe."

He looked back at me.

"I'm really sorry about last night. I'm just worried…and you've blown off my visions before."

Moving back toward me, he lightly gripped my upper arms. "I'm not blowing it off, Rose. I promise." He hesitated. "There's just a lot you don't know about what's goin' on. A lot Mason and I can't tell you. I need you to trust me. Can you do that?"

I looked into his eyes. "Yes, I trust you." And I found myself surprised to realize that it was true.

The door opened and Neely Kate came back in with a sheepish look that turned to confusion when she saw us.

Joe dropped his arms and headed back toward the door. "I left you a present on the table. All I ask is that you don't go usin' it on any ol' person who irritates you. Use it judiciously."

"What is it?"

"You'll see." He reached for the door, but she put her hand on his arm and stopped him.

"Joe." She looked down at her feet, then up into his face. "About that day."

He shook his head. "You don't have to say another word, Neely Kate."

"But I do." She licked her bottom lip. "Thank you." Tears filled her eyes. "The doctor told me you probably saved my life."

He shook his head again, his cheeks turning pink. "It was nothing."

"No," she insisted. "It was something. You could have waited for the ambulance, but you didn't. And after everything I've said and done—"

He grinned, but his eyes were glistening with tears. "I wouldn't change a thing, Neely Kate. I'm glad you stuck up for Rose. I'm happy you were there for her when I wasn't." He paused. "Besides, I'm not sure how I'd handle you if you suddenly went soft on me. I need you to keep me on my toes."

She threw herself at him and wrapped her arms around his neck.

Joe gave me a look of surprise as he hugged her back. "Now don't you be scarin' us like that again," he said, gruffly. "I need you around to take care of my girl." Then, no doubt realizing what he'd said, he dropped his hold on her and bolted out the door.

Neely Kate kept her gaze on the front door even after he'd gone past the windows. "He's changed."

"I know." I just didn't know what to make of it.

Chapter Eighteen

Neely Kate and I sat down to resume our search through the journal. But as she pulled up her chair, she stopped. "You never told me what happened last night after you left."

I sucked in a breath. I wasn't sure it was a good idea for Neely Kate to know the nitty gritty details. Especially after my private chat with Skeeter. It was probably better if I scaled it down to the essentials. "It was a boring business meeting. Nothing much happened except I had a vision."

"Forced or accidental?"

She knew me too well. "Forced, but before you ask, it was my own decision."

"And?"

I leaned closer and lowered my voice, although I wasn't sure who else was gonna hear. "I had a vision of Mick Gentry. He was in a bar and he was telling the guy I had a vision of that he had a list of names to take out. Skeeter was the first one."

She curled her upper lip. "Good riddance."

Her words caught my breath, and I was surprised at the surge of loyalty I felt toward him. "He's better than Daniel Crocker, and if Mick Gentry got control—" I shuddered, "—God help us all."

"You're defending him?"

"Neely Kate," I said, harsher than I intended. "Gentry has a *list*. We knew all along he had it out for Skeeter, but consider who else is likely on there."

Her eyes widened. "Mason. What are you gonna do?"

"I already told Mason."

"You told him you had a vision of one of Skeeter Malcolm's men?!"

"No! And keep your voice down!"

She looked around. "You think Muffy's gonna tell anyone?"

"*Neely Kate.*"

"Okay," she grumbled. "Sorry."

"I told him I had a vision of some random man at the gas station on the way home from Bingo."

"And he believed you?"

"Yeah. Then he called Joe and they had a fight, but Joe sent Deputy Miller out to watch the house and apparently he's makin' Mason stay in the courthouse during work hours." I pointed to the Tasers, still on the table. "Mason wanted to get me a Taser today, but Joe wouldn't let him out. So Joe got one for both of us; yours is the pink one. He said we probably need them anyway with everything we get into."

Neely Kate picked hers up off the table. "This would have come in handy with Tabitha last month."

"Tell me about it," I groaned, remembering the tussle we'd gotten into with Neely Kate's cousin's best friend. "Joe gave us his blessing to investigate Dora."

"You're kidding?"

I grimaced. "Well, I didn't tell him about the possible extortion scheme."

"A good thing, since you can't rightly tell him why we suspect it."

"Then let's see if I missed anything in Dora's journal. Maybe it'll give us an idea of what to do next."

We bent over the book. Neely Kate flipped through pages, then stopped.

"Look at this." Her voice dripped with satisfaction. "This entry talking about your father telling his wife she wants a divorce is dated October. She mentions Violet by name."

I leaned over. "I remember reading this part while Mason and I were hiding from Daniel Crocker at the farm."

"This proves Dora didn't have an affair with Henry."

I shook my head. "Not necessarily. This was in the fall. She didn't mention Daddy in her journal the previous winter."

Her gaze pinned mine. "Why are you so bound and determined to prove she was involved with Henry?"

"I'm just tryin' to be objective."

She rose from her chair in a huff. "I'm gonna go do some bookkeeping work. But I hope I don't get seen talking to you about the books or someone might think we're *havin' an affair*."

"Neely Kate..." I pleaded, but she ignored me and rolled her desk chair back to its usual place. She had tears in her eyes as she booted up her computer.

For the life of me, I couldn't figure out why she was so upset. I considered trying to talk to her, but decided to give her a little more time.

After I'd scanned more pages, I glanced up at my friend, who was intent on her work. "Neely Kate."

Thankfully she seemed less upset when she turned to look at me.

"Would you come look at this and let me know what you think?"

She walked over and sat in the chair next to me. I opened the journal to the page that had caught my eye and handed it to her, pointing to the top left corner of the page. "Look at this random word."

She leaned over the journal. "Bill." It was scrawled in tiny letters, so small I hadn't noticed it before.

I turned to her in excitement. "She mentioned a Bill earlier. She said he was worried things were going to go bad."

She shook her head. "But why would she write his name at the top of the page like that?"

I flipped several pages ahead and found another word in the top left margin, written in that same tiny scrawl. "The." I pointed to it. "Who randomly writes the word 'the'?"

"I don't know."

I turned several more pages and found another word. "Proof."

She gasped. "Oh, my stars and garters. It's a message."

We continued through the book until we found: *Bill the proof is in the other journal in the room*

Neely Kate jerked the book away from me and frantically searched the book for another hidden word. "What room?"

"I don't know," I murmured. "Maybe she didn't finish her sentence. Or maybe she knew Bill would understand the message."

We were silent for a moment.

I sighed. "She had another journal. I bet that's where we could find all the missing information. The extortion scheme. Who probably killed her. Who my father is."

She shot me a glare. "Your daddy's your father. And that book could be anywhere. I say we focus on talking to people who can help us now."

I thought about it for a moment. "You're right. Finding that journal is gonna be like looking for a needle in a haystack. We should talk to Dirk. We planned to anyway. And maybe he'll be able to tell us who Bill is."

Neely Kate twisted her lips to the side. "Dirk sounds like he might have been involved. She talked about placating him. And Miss Mildred said he was a foreman." She went back to her desk and started typing on her computer. After a few moments, she turned to me. "2345 Crescent Drive. I think we need a field trip." She grabbed her coat and her purse and walked back to the table.

"How are we gonna get him to answer our questions?" I asked as I stood.

She picked up her Taser and put it into her purse. "I've always wanted to use one of these. Maybe we should give them a test drive."

I had a sneaking suspicion I was going to regret Joe giving her that thing.

Chapter Nineteen

W e're only gonna talk to him," I said for what had to be the hundredth time as I pulled my truck up to the curb. But Neely Kate seemed exceptionally bloodthirsty, and truth be told, I didn't trust her all that much to behave. "Let me do the talkin' this time."

"That hardly seems fair," she grumbled.

"It all happened twenty-five years ago, Neely Kate. He's bound to be old and incapacitated. He's probably wheelin' around an oxygen tank." I took the keys out of the ignition. "So just be careful with the elderly gentleman." All we needed was for her to Tase him and give him a heart attack.

"Sure." But she didn't sound like she meant it.

We walked up to the front door of the rundown brick ranch home. I stepped in front of Neely Kate and knocked. When no one answered, I waited a moment and knocked again.

An elderly woman next door poked her head out her front door. "He ain't home."

"Mr. Picklebie?" Neely Kate asked.

"Mr. Picklebie," she spat out in disgust. "Ha! He ain't no mister. And if you're lookin' to collect yer money, good luck to ya."

Collect our money? "Do you know where I can find him?"

"He's down at the pool hall, probably bettin' his money away. Again."

Oh, crappy doodles.

Neely Kate stared at me. "Elderly gentleman, huh? We have to go there."

I didn't answer, but my mind was reeling. Did I really want to risk seeing Skeeter? Other than the morning I'd run into Skeeter when I went out to breakfast with Mason, this would be our first public encounter since I started my role as the Lady in Black. How would he react? It was probably the worst idea of all ideas since the beginning of time, but I found myself saying, "Yeah. Let's go."

We headed for the truck and I pulled away from the curb in silence.

"It's a public place, Rose. There's nothin' wrong with you goin' to the pool hall. We'll go find Dirk Picklebie, get our answers and leave. You don't even have to talk to Skeeter. Shoot, he's probably not even there."

I doubted it. I'd learned enough about Skeeter's work habits over the last two months to know he made Mason's workaholic tendencies look like a cute hobby. "I'm still in charge of asking the questions."

"Fine."

My phone vibrated and I found a text from Mason.

I can't get away for lunch. The sheriff's department has confined me to the courthouse. Joe said he'd take care of our errand. Do you feel safe?

I stopped at a stop sign and answered. *I have it now. I'm fine. I'll see you tonight. <3*

Fifteen minutes later I pulled into the parking lot of the pool hall. It was early enough that there weren't many cars there. I figured it would make finding Dirk Picklebie a whole lot easier.

"Do you see Skeeter's car?" Neely Kate asked.

"I don't know what he drives." Which was strange, but true. "I've only seen the car Jed drives, which isn't here, but I think he parks in the back. If I were a betting woman, I'd put my money on them being here."

"What are you gonna do if you see them?"

"Ignore them. I can't let on to anyone that I'm intimately acquainted with them."

Her eyebrows rose and she teased, "Just how intimately acquainted are you?"

"Not how you're suggesting, and you good and well know it," I grumbled as I opened my door and hopped out.

I took a deep breath before opening the door and walking into the place. It took a few seconds for my eyes to adjust to the gloom that seemed to be the pool hall's defining feature. There were a few guys in the place, none of whom I recognized. So far, so good.

Neely Kate pointed toward a table in the back. "I bet that's him."

A man who looked like he was in his late fifties was bent over a table, pool cue in hand. He made a shot, then rose and grabbed a bottle of beer off a tall table. His flannel shirt was faded and his graying hair was in desperate need of a trim. He looked like he'd hit hard times. Two teens huddled around a table in front. They shot us a look of alarm, then relaxed when they realized we weren't truant officers.

I took a deep breath and pushed my anxiety away. What was I so nervous about anyway? Maybe because Skeeter was expecting an answer from me in less than twelve hours and I still didn't know what to tell him. Unfastening my coat, I walked up to the bar and grabbed the bartender's attention. "I'll have two of whatever he's having." I pointed to the back.

The bartender—a college-age-looking kid—shook his head and squinted toward the back. "Him?"

"Yep." I leaned closer. "Do you know who he is?"

He leaned over the bar. "Dirk Picklebie and he's a major loser. You're wasting your time with him." He gave me a cocky smile. "Sit here with me, baby." He looked over my shoulder and his smile widened. "Your friend too."

I glanced back at Neely Kate. "You want a beer?"

She shrugged and gave me a half-smile.

I turned back to the bartender. "Make it three."

He shook his head in confusion. "Okay," he muttered as he walked to the cooler.

I glanced down at my clothes. I was wearing jeans, a scoop-neck peasant-style shirt, and my brown boots with a three-inch heel. I wasn't overly endowed, so the modest neckline left a lot to the imagination and the heels made me look like I wasn't about to muck out a barn. There was a good chance one of us was going to have to do a little flirting, and since Neely Kate was still sporting her grunge look, that probably left me with the job. Great.

The bartender set the bottles on the counter and started popping the tops. "He fancies himself a pool shark. Don't be makin' any bets with him."

"Really?" Neely Kate's eyes lit up.

The bartender handed Neely Kate her beer and winked. "I'll be over here, more than willin' to keep you pretty ladies company."

"Thanks." I grabbed two of the bottles. "We'll keep that in mind."

Neely Kate winked. "Start a tab."

As we moved away from the bar, she said, "I have an idea."

"Does it involve trying out your new Taser?"

"No...well, maybe... If we need to escape."

I stared at her for three full seconds. "Okay, sounds good. What's your plan?"

"Let's play a game with him and pretend to suck. Then let me do the rest."

Fortunately for her, I didn't have to pretend.

"You start talkin' to him after I make the introduction, then I'll jump in," I said.

"Okay."

She followed me back to the pool table. Dirk was leaning over, the pool cue in his hand, as he eyed his next shot, but his gaze shifted to my stomach and slowly rose to my face after taking a slight delay at my bust.

I held out one of the bottles. "Hi. You look thirsty."

He straightened up and lowered the pool cue to the table as his gaze shifted from Neely Kate and back to me.

Neely Kate shifted out her hip. "My friend and I are here 'cause we want to learn how to play pool. We saw you back here, and I said, 'Rose, he looks smart. I bet he can teach us.'" She turned to me. "Ain't that what I said?"

I nodded, then took a sip of my own beer while still holding out the other one out to him. "Sure is."

A shit-eating grin spread over Dirk's face as he grabbed the bottle from me and clinked it against mine. "I think I can manage that."

Neely Kate gave him a smile full of innocence. "Well, ain't you sweet?" She turned to me. "Ain't he sweet, Rose?"

I nodded my agreement, wondering why she was laying it on so thick, but I'd let her butter him up before I swooped in with my questions.

He took a long drag from the bottle. "I'm Dirk."

"Neely Kate," she pointed to herself, then me. "And my friend Rose."

"Well, let's get started." Dirk grabbed a rack and swept the balls over to one end of the table. "How about eight ball?"

Neely Kate's eyes widened in confusion. "Eight ball?"

I pointed to the table. "Isn't it that little black ball in the middle?"

He chuckled. "Don't you girls worry. I'm gonna teach you all about it."

He explained the rules of the game—pretty much the same rules Skeeter had explained to me the first time we met—and we started playing.

We were halfway through the disastrous game when I asked, "What do you do, Dirk?"

"Oh, a little bit of this and a little bit of that." He took his shot, getting his solid colored ball into the pocket. "I'm into investments right now."

"Oh," Neely Kate squealed. "Like a stock broker."

He chuckled. "Something like that."

"Have you always been a stock broker?" I asked.

"Nah," he leaned over the table for another shot. "I've done a bunch of other things."

"Like what?" Neely Kate asked.

"Oh..." He moved around the table, looking for his next shot. "I was a used car salesman. A truck driver. And once upon a time, I was a supervisor at a plant."

Neely Kate's eyes widened with interest. "You got to boss people around?"

He grinned. "Sure did."

She put her hand on her hip. "A plant, you say? Shoot. I bet you're exaggerating. You probably supervised a few employees at an office supply store."

"You've got it wrong, little lady. I bossed around a lot more than that. Back in the day, I was a supervisor at Atchison Manufacturing."

"You don't say?" Neely Kate said. "Ain't that the place that closed down after a big fire years ago?"

He nodded. "Sure was."

"Goodness," I said, feigning fright. "Were you there when the fire broke out?"

He leaned over the table and lined up his cue. "Nope. It happened late at night after everyone had left for the day."

Neely Kate turned to me. "Hey, Rose. Don't you know someone who used to work there?"

"Oh! You're right. I forgot all about it." I leaned against the table. "Dirk, maybe you knew her."

"Well." He took his shot, sinking another ball. "It depends on when she worked there."

"Right up until the fire," I said. "Gloria Gunner."

Neely Kate flashed me a look of surprise over his head, but I had my reasons. If he knew something about Dora, he might clam up if I mentioned her name.

"Yeah, I knew Gloria." He finished off his beer and set it down on the table. "She was a real busybody."

The bartender was openly staring at us, so I motioned for him to bring another bottle over. He rolled his eyes and shook his head as he moved to the cooler.

"She liked to get in everyone's business?" I asked, taking another sip of my beer.

He eyed it longingly.

The bartender walked over with the fresh bottle and handed it to me. I leaned into his ear. "Keep 'em comin'."

"*Really?*" he asked in dismay before grabbing the three empty bottles on the table. Changing tactics, he waved up and down at his chest, beer bottles clutched between the fingers of both hands, and shot me a cocky grin. "Darlin', I'll give you a round on the house if you come sit with me."

Dirk's head jerked up. "Hey!"

Neely Kate stopped mid-shot, then cast an adoring gaze at Dirk. "I found my honey bunny." She waved her hand in a shooing motion. "You can run along now."

The bartender lifted his eyebrows in question as he turned to me.

I gave him an apologetic grin and tilted my head toward the slovenly man on the other side of the pool table. "We're fighting over him."

Dirk looked like a goat let loose in an aluminum recycling lot.

The bartender groaned his disgust as he stomped back to the bar.

I could see his confusion. Not only did he look a whole lot better than Dirk; he smelled better too.

"How do you know Gloria?" Dirk asked after he'd had another drink. Judging from the empty bottles, this was his fourth beer of the day. His second in about fifteen minutes. How high was his alcohol tolerance? The fact he was drinking his fourth beer before one in the afternoon was pretty suggestive.

"She's my friend's mother. All these years later, she still loves to gossip about the bookkeeper there."

"Dora," he chuckled. "She gave people something to talk about."

"Yeah, Gloria says she carried on with several guys while she was there."

"Several, you say?" He took another shot. "I only know about her and Henry. And the guy on my line."

"Henry?" I asked. "Was he her boss?"

I caught movement out of the corner of my eye and saw someone emerging from the back. My chest constricted when I realized it was Jed. He cast his gaze around the room and landed on our party of three. A look of uncertainty crossed his face, but he quickly recovered and ignored me, heading over to take a seat behind the bar.

Just keep going.

Dirk was oblivious to it all. "Yeah, Henry Buchanan. Everyone knew they were doing the horizontal mambo."

I snapped my fingers and pointed at him. "Dirk. You must be Dirk Picklebie, right?"

He tensed and his smile faded. "Why you askin'?"

I grinned and held up my beer. "Gloria talks nonstop about Dirk Picklebie. She had a huge crush on you."

He stood up straighter, grinning from ear to ear. "You don't say."

"She says you were a supervisor at Atchison."

A smug grin lifted his mouth. "I was. I was made supervisor less than a year after I started working on the line. Only a few months before the fire."

"When I asked her what they made, she said she didn't rightly understand all the details, but it was some kind of rivet for tractors."

"Yeah, all kinds of metal pieces. They fit John Deere tractors and such. But the summer before the fire we switched mid-stream to producin' some hush-hush parts."

"Oh really?" I asked. "Do you know what they were?"

"They didn't give us too many details, but I heard Dora telling one of my linemen they were components for airplane parts." He leaned closer and I got a whiff of cigarettes mixed with BO. I fought the urge to wave my hand in front of my face.

"Airplane parts. Who for?"

His smile wavered and a strange look skated across his face. Crappy doodles, I'd gotten to him. He knew. A war waged in his eyes—his desire to impress me versus his self-protective drive to keep it to himself. I decided to switch topics.

"Why'd you have to hear it second-hand from Dora? It seems like someone as important as you would have known about it."

"There were all kinds of hush-hush things goin' on toward the end. She and Buchanan were the only ones who knew about it all. I think she was trying to impress Gardner by telling him. Gloria said Dora and Buchanan had been fighting in his office, so we figured she was on the prowl for her next man before she cut Henry loose. Hell, he was twice her age anyway. Everyone knew what she was after, but Henry would never have left his wife."

My heart sank and I realized that while I'd been telling Neely Kate I was keeping an open mind, I had never for a minute thought it possible Dora had carried on an affair with Henry Buchanan. Despite the suggestive journal entries. But here was a second person who believed it to be true. Yet, I knew from first-hand experience that you couldn't believe everything you heard, no matter how many people agreed on it. I needed more proof.

The smug expression on Dirk Picklebie's face only confirmed that he knew more than he was telling. I just needed to appeal to his conceited side.

"You must have been quite young," I said. "You don't look a day over forty now." I winked. "I thought they had child labor laws back then." I took another sip of my beer and glanced at the bar. Jed was on the phone now, but his gaze was glued on me. The usual friendliness he showed me wasn't there. He looked pissed. Could he really believe I was flirting with Dirk?

Dirk laughed and preened, flexing his biceps. I could practically feel Neely Kate's disgust rolling off her as she took another shot, sending a striped ball just about as far from any of the pockets as was possible on the table.

"I'm a few years older than that, but I was a young supervisor back then and a lot of men resented it." He winked. "But sometimes it helps who and *what* you know, if you catch my drift." He finished his beer and I glanced at the bartender, who threw his hands up in the air before he went to grab another.

"You don't say," I said with interest. This could be the break we needed.

"Your turn," Dirk said, motioning to the table, and I noticed his feet were stumbling a bit. Thank God. We were finally getting somewhere.

The bartender brought over Dirk's new drink and handed it to him. "Can I get you ladies anything else?"

I shook my head, but Neely Kate said, "Yeah, bring me another."

Raising my eyebrows, I gave her a look, but she didn't respond. Neely Kate rarely drank, and I'd never seen her drink this early.

I purposely missed my shot and waited for Dirk to put down his beer. "So why do *you* think the plant changed to producing plane parts mid-stream?"

He shrugged as he circled the table. "The place had started losing profits and ol' Henry was talkin' layoffs, but I heard we got an influx of cash that summer. Because of the new parts."

"Is that common?" I asked. "Would a plant get paid in advance for something like that?"

"The whole thing was fishy from the beginnin' and bein' the smart man I am, I started diggin'." He leered at me and winked.

I gave him a coy smile. "And bein' the smart man you are, I'm sure you got to the bottom of it." I leaned forward. "Out of curiosity, what did you find out?"

He hesitated before turning his attention to the table. "We sure got a nasty wet and cold spell, huh? I hear it might snow this weekend."

The fact that he was resorting to weather talk meant we'd definitely struck a nerve, and a deep one at that.

Neely Kate caught my eye as he leaned over and sank the last ball. He stood and grinned. "And that, ladies, is how it's done. How about another game?"

Jed brought over Neely Kate's beer, but she'd never seen him before, so she didn't give him a second glance. No longer hiding his interest, he took a seat at a nearby high-top table close to the back door.

I was the only one who seemed to notice.

Neely Kate took a sip of her drink and leaned her hip into the table. "Sure. Just you and me. How about a little wager?"

Dirk's eyes lit up and he rubbed his thumb against his fingertip. "A wager, you say? What kind of wager?"

She moved closer to him and lowered her voice. "Dirk, you're such a captivating man. Worldly, mature, a quick thinker. Just the kind of guy I'm interested in. How about if you win, I'll pay you fifty bucks."

Dirk laughed. "Why are you wantin' to throw your money away like that?"

She put her hand on his chest and her fingers crawled up to his neck. "Maybe I'm feelin' lucky." She batted her eyelashes. "And if I win, you'll give me what I want." Her innuendo was pretty doggone clear and the way his eyes lit up told me he was falling for it hook, line, and sinker.

He swallowed. "So I win either way, huh?"

She just gave him a coy grin. Little did he know that Neely Kate's idea of a prize wasn't anywhere near the same as his.

"Fifty bucks, huh?" He took a long drag of his beer and set it on the table before grabbing the rack. "Well, if you're sure... I'll even let you go first."

She fluttered her eyelashes. "You really are a gentleman. Deal."

He set up the table and she moved to the end, cue stick in hand. She lowered over the table and all pretense of being a dumb blonde was gone. She lined up her shot and the balls scattered, two solid colors slamming into pockets. She spun around and flashed him a look of surprise. "Well, would you look at that? Look what I did, Rose!"

I didn't have to fake my surprise. I'd had no idea she could play pool. "Oh, my word! Dirk, you're an amazing teacher!"

Dirk suddenly seemed less confident.

Neely Kate flashed him a smile, then proceeded to sink two more balls before missing a shot. "Your turn, sweetie."

Dirk picked up his cue stick and stumbled around the table to take his shot. He stood up grumbling after just barely missing the pocket. "Something's wrong with the table."

"There's nothin' wrong with the table," Jed said in a low tone from his seat.

Dirk lifted his hands. "Okay, okay. Maybe I had a bit too much to drink." He didn't seem surprised to see Jed. Maybe he sat out here quite a bit.

Neely Kate gave Jed a glance, then turned toward Dirk. "A deal's a deal. Besides, I've had two myself." Sure enough, her bottle was empty. She turned to Jed again. "Could you trouble yourself to get me another, sugar?"

Jed looked at me, catching me by surprise. He must have noticed she was getting sauced. I nodded. I'd tell her no, but I worried she'd raise a fuss. Besides, she was a grown woman capable of making her own decisions, even if this one seemed like a bad one.

Jed headed for the bar as Neely Kate studied the table, lined up her cue, and sunk another ball. By the time he came back to deliver her drink, she had one solid ball on the table compared to Dirk's three striped ones. She put it into the side hole and said, "Eight ball, right corner pocket." Then she proceeded to do just that. "Now I get what I want. Sit down in that chair over there and answer some questions."

"You cheated," Dirk shouted, his face beet red. He clenched his pool stick in his fist and he looked like he was considering using it for something other than shooting pool.

Jed was at the table in seconds. "We take accusations of cheating very seriously, Dirk. Be careful of your words. *And* your actions."

"She played me," he whined.

Jed put his hands on his hips and eyed Neely Kate up and down. "The lady can't help it if you're a fool, Picklebie. Now sit your ass down and pay up."

He shook his head. "Betting on a pool game's illegal in Fenton County."

Jed's eyes darkened. "Like that ever stopped you before. Sit." His voice boomed, drawing the attention of the two teenage boys who had clearly skipped school and were still playing at a table toward the front of the room.

Dirk sat on a stool at a high-top table, bracing himself as he swayed back and forth like a sheet hung to dry in the wind.

There were only two stools at the table, so I pushed Neely Kate onto the other. I was about to go grab a third when Jed dragged one over for me. His eyes searched mine and I knew he was hoping for some sort of explanation. Finally he said, "I'll be sitting over here, makin' sure there's not any trouble."

I nodded, then sat on the stool and turned to Dirk, whose eyes were half closed. "Look, Mr. Picklebie. I promise we're not tryin' to bamboozle you. I only want some answers. That's all."

"Fine," he huffed, obviously still sore at Neely Kate's deception.

"You said you started diggin' into the switchin' parts. What did you find out?"

Uncertainty filled his eyes. "I'm not sure I should be talkin' about it. It was all pretty hush-hush back then, ya know?"

"But it was twenty-five years ago," I said, lowering my voice. "Surely it's no big deal to tell me now."

"Why do you even want to know?" he grumbled.

"I'm just curious."

He took a drink of his beer, refusing to look at me. "Curiosity killed the cat, you know."

"Good thing I'm not a cat."

He grimaced and scratched his head. "I don't know. There was some big shot involved…one who's still got a lot of power today. I don't want him to find out I'm talkin' about it. I don't think he even knows who I am, and I want to keep it that way."

"Who's the big shot?" When he didn't answer, I decided to try another tactic. The last thing I wanted to do was get him to shut down on us.

"You said the bookkeeper, Dora, was friendly with one of the linemen?" I asked. "Where did you overhear them talking?"

"In the break room on my floor. The office girls never came down there, so I wanted to see what was up."

"You mean you were spyin' on 'em," Neely Kate said, but her words were slurred. "Didn't the diary mention something about that?"

I shot her a look that was half worry and half irritation. My goal was to sweet-talk him, not piss him off.

I decided to focus on a name in the journal. "Do you remember a Bill that worked there?" I asked.

"There were several Bills."

"Anyone higher up?"

He thought for a minute. "Nope. Bill Teeter was the janitor. He died of a heart attack a few years back. Bill Oliver worked on the line."

"Do you know if Bill Oliver was a friend of Dora's?"

He snorted. "No. Bill Oliver kept to himself. Never talked to anyone."

"Do you know anything about the fire?" I asked. "How it started?"

He shifted in his seat, keeping his gaze glued to the tabletop. "No."

I bent my head down to look him in the eye. "Come on. I'm sure you know *something* about the fire."

He turned pale and his hands started to shake. "You need to stay out of this, missy. You're stirring up shit that don't need stirring."

Neely Kate glared at him.

"Be that as it may, Mr. Picklebie," I said. "I still want to know."

His gaze darted from Jed to the back door, as if gauging the likelihood he could make a safe getaway. Clearly coming to the conclusion that Jed would be on him like a bloodhound on a rabbit if he so much as tried, he shook his head and sighed. "It was mysterious. The police investigated, but they didn't come up with nothing."

"They've always been a bunch of incompetent fools," Neely Kate muttered.

"They were sharp before the police chief, Bill Niedermier, died."

"Wait," I said. "Bill? When did he die?"

"A couple of days after the fire." He shook his head. "A burglary. If the police chief ain't safe in his own home, who is?"

I suspected Dirk was right about this whole Atchison mess being a big pile of dog doo. And it was turning out to be a whole lot more dangerous than I'd anticipated. But we were already here with a big ol' shovel. I saw no reason to leave the job half done.

I had to take a deep breath to slow my racing heart. "I think you know more about the money and the deal than you're sayin'. And I just love a good story about corporate intrigue." I glanced back at Jed, then lowered my voice. "We'll keep it between just us three."

He looked torn for a moment, but there wasn't a clearer out for him than there'd been a moment before. Jed hadn't budged from his seat by the door.

"You can't be spreading this around," Dirk said, leaning toward me.

"I won't. Promise."

He licked his lips. "It all started in the summer, like I told you. Buchanan had been talkin' layoffs, but next thing we knew, we were changing the line and we all still had jobs. But around August, we were havin' some problems with the rivets. Gardner was helpin' with quality control tests and I heard him tellin' Dora some of the pieces were failing. Henry was fit to be tied when he found out. If we didn't deliver, he was gonna lose it all. But the investor didn't care. He said to keep on makin' 'em. There was too much money on the line for us to stop." He shifted in his seat. "I couldn't stand back and let them bilk the buyer, so I let Dora and Buchanan know I was...aware of the situation."

"What'd they do?" Neely Kate asked.

"They told me to keep my mouth shut."

"And did you?" I asked.

"Well... If anyone found out, a lot of men would have lost their jobs."

I didn't point out that a lot of men had ended up losing their jobs anyway. Or the defective parts could have been built into planes, causing equipment malfunction and potentially plane crashes.

"Well, what were you to do?" Neely Kate asked, sounding sympathetic. "You had to help those poor men."

"Dora quit after that. Said she didn't have the stomach for it, but Gardner wouldn't back down. He kept insistin' someone had to know. Then Dora came back to the office right after Thanksgiving, bringing her brand-new baby with her. She shouted at Henry about not takin' care of their baby, then the next day Gardner told me on the sly that Dora had found someone to help them out of the mess they were in."

"Do you know who it was?"

"No, but the first shipment was due to go out a few days after Dora came in and threw her fit. Maybe that's why she decided to make one last stand. I was gettin' nervous about the whole thing, and when I found out what the parts were for— U.S. military planes—I *freaked out.* We weren't just messin' with some company. It was the dadgum U.S. government. I didn't want to do no jail time. But Gardner said to hold my horses. It was bein' taken care of."

"What did that mean?" I asked.

"Dunno. The fire wiped out everything a few days later, the night before the shipment was to go out. I suspected that's what he was talkin' about."

I grabbed the edge of the table as the blood rushed from my head. "You think Gardner started the fire?"

He looked down at the table. "Could be."

Had my father really torched the factory? The man I'd known could hardly stomach killing a fly. "Dora died in a car accident a week later."

"Yeah."

"And Henry Buchanan hung himself days after that."

"He shot the wad. His mistress was dead and his company had burned down. And the government contract was gone, so he had nothing. At least his wife got his life insurance. A nice fat policy."

I stared at him in silence, too stunned to say anything.

"Just the insurance policy? What about the factory?" Neely Kate asked, emerging from her alcohol-induced stupor. "Surely there was money to be made from it."

He shrugged. "Never sold. It got tied up in probate. Henry had his lawyer create a paper saying there were three heirs, but he didn't provide a name for the third. Since they couldn't find him or her, they couldn't do anything with it."

"So it's just stuck?" I asked.

"Henry's will was pretty strict. The family was fit to be tied. But there's a time limit. Twenty-five years from when it was logged into probate. That limit's up in another couple of weeks."

I squinted at him. He seemed to know a lot about a will that had nothing to do with him. But then again, some people became obsessed with pieces of their past. Maybe this was one of those situations. But I quickly moved onto *couldn't find one of the heirs*. What if I was Henry's daughter and it was me they were looking for? I felt like I was going to throw up.

"You got any more questions?" he asked, looking at the door like he wanted to bolt.

"One more," I said. I wasn't about to let him go until the biggest question of all had been answered. "I need to know the name of the big shot. The man behind it all."

He shook his head, his eyes wide with terror.

"*The name*," I stated with bite behind my words. Neely Kate shot me a surprised look.

Dirk glanced back at Jed, then at me, still terrified. He licked his lips and looked around the room. When he didn't see anyone else paying us any mind, he said, "If y'all ever tell anyone I said it, I'll deny it and call you bald-face liars."

I squared my shoulders. "I can live with that."

"Okay." He licked his lips again. "I heard Dora tell Buchanan a name. I only heard it once, right before she quit.

She told him she was sorry she'd ever introduced the guy to Buchanan in the first place. She said the guy was unhappy, and I'd never seen Buchanan look so scared."

"And what was that name?" I asked.

"J.R. Simmons."

Chapter Twenty

I'd never felt such a volatile mixture of emotions at once—fear, disgust, elation that we'd gotten solid information, but then the aftertaste of utter horror.

If Dora had been the one to introduce J.R. Simmons to Henry Buchanan, how had she met him? And worse, could he be the older married man Dora had carried on with in the December and January before I was born?

"Can I go now?" Dirk asked, looking over at Jed rather than at me. He didn't look too good—he was paler than ever and he seemed pretty close to losing his beers.

I'd scared the bejiggers out of him. But then, if J.R. Simmons was involved in this mess somehow, I could see why. Especially since a lot of people who were connected to the factory had died—whether "accidentally" or otherwise.

I needed more information. I needed to have a vision. The question was how to steer it. I thought about the visions I'd had for Skeeter as the Lady in Black. I usually saw the person telling someone else the information I needed to know. Someone like Dirk was bound to share his secrets with someone, and I'd bet anything he'd contact them after he left. If I could see who it was, maybe I could track them down.

"Just one more thing." I reached out and grabbed his wrist, closing my eyes and concentrating on whom he'd contact about Atchison.

The vision was strong, hitting me with more force than most. I was suddenly in a car, a phone pressed to my ear.

"Beverly, someone knows," I said, my voice rising in panic.

"Knows what?" a woman's voice asked.

"About the fire at the factory. About the parts. About the blackmail. *All of it.* They were talkin' about a diary."

"Okay, calm down," she said, her tone soothing. "*Who* knows?"

"A woman and her friend hustled me in the pool hall and forced me to tell them."

"What are their names?"

"Rose, and I didn't catch the one who did the hustling. Rose was the one askin' most of the questions. She knew things." I swallowed, starting to hyperventilate. "We're gonna go to jail."

"Calm down, Dirk. I've got everything under control. No one's going to jail. They're bluffing."

The vision faded and I was left with a splitting headache and overwhelming nausea. "No one's goin' to jail."

He looked at me like I was a crazy person. And since he already thought I was out of my mind, I might as well go for broke.

"You were blackmailing Henry Buchanan, weren't you?"

Neely Kate gasped.

Dirk's mouth dropped open and terror filled his eyes. "What are you talkin' about?" He tried to jerk out of my grasp, but I held on tight.

"How does Beverly fit in?"

He pulled free with enough force to fall off the stool.

As Dirk recovered and regained his balance, Jed walked over to us, crossing his arms and making a very imposing presence. "Are you done with him?"

I could press the Beverly issue, but that would include getting Jed involved. And while that was tempting, I wasn't ready to blur the line between the Lady-in-Black world and my real world. I'd find another way. "Yeah," I nodded. "He can go."

Dirk ran for the entrance and I looked over my shoulder to watch him. I was surprised to see Skeeter perched on one of the stools at the bar, his arm draped on the edge of the counter, his gaze directly on me. He certainly didn't look happy.

"We need to go," I said to Neely Kate, getting to my feet. "We have to follow him. Maybe we can find Beverly."

"Who's Beverly?" she asked as she tried to get down, but she swayed like a sailor on shore leave. "Why's the room spinning?"

She was in no shape to be chasing after him. I swallowed my disappointment and pushed her back onto the stool. "I'm gonna get you a glass of water. Wait here."

I walked over to the bar, worried about how Skeeter would react to me showing up in the pool hall, but I was too irritated to take any crap. I ignored him as I asked the bartender for two waters. When he walked out of earshot to get them for me, Skeeter leaned his forearms against the counter. "What are you workin' on?"

"Something personal. Nothing that concerns you."

"Anything you do concerns me. Why are you interrogating Dirk Picklebie in my pool hall?"

I turned to face him, putting my hand on my hip. "Because that's where he happened to be." I lowered my voice. "Believe me, I'm not very happy about bein' here either."

Jed walked over, keeping his gaze on the front door. "Skeeter, he mentioned J.R. Simmons."

Skeeter's eyes hardened. "Now it *is* my business."

My mouth dropped open. "You have business with *J.R. Simmons?*"

His eyebrows rose, but the rest of his face was expressionless. "Do *you?*"

There was no way I was going to tell him about my issue with J.R., although part of me wondered if maybe I *should*. But what was Skeeter's association with Joe's father? I knew he'd never offer the information willingly, especially without getting anything in return, so I decided to change tactics. "What do you care about something that happened twenty-five years ago?"

"What happened twenty-five years ago that's piqued your interest?"

"The Atchison Manufacturing fire."

He studied my face. "Why are you diggin' into that old business?"

I took a deep breath and pushed it out in frustration. "I already told you. It's *personal*."

"Her father had something to do with it," Jed murmured.

I shot Jed a look that hopefully said *stay out of this*.

The bartender handed me the waters, clearly confused by all the attention Skeeter and his right-hand man were showing me. First Neely Kate and I had been hitting on a drunken derelict and now I was in an intimate conversation with his bosses. I winked at him. "Thank you." Then I shot Skeeter a dirty look and stomped back over to our table with the glasses.

If I'd thought I could dismiss Skeeter so easily, I was dead wrong. He slid into the seat Dirk had vacated as I set Neely Kate's water on the table. As soon as she realized who was sitting across from her, she froze.

Skeeter's head lowered and his eyes glittered with anger. "I'm not done talkin' to you."

I glared at him in defiance. "Well, I'm done talkin' to *you*. How many times do I have to say this is none of your business? It doesn't concern you, Skeeter Malcolm. Leave it alone."

His face turned red and he shot Jed a glance I couldn't decipher.

Neely Kate picked up her glass of water and took a sip, her hand shaking. Her attention was on Skeeter.

"You're scaring my friend, Skeeter," I added. "Mind your manners."

His jaw worked, then he took a deep breath as though trying to keep his cool. "We can avoid that if you'll just answer my questions."

Jed pulled up a fourth stool between Neely Kate and me. "Rose, you have to know that since you help Skeeter, he's more than happy to help you. I think he's frustrated that you didn't ask." He looked up at his boss and raised his eyebrows. "Isn't that right, Skeeter?"

Skeeter ignored him. "What the hell are you doin' questioning Dirk Picklebie in my pool hall?"

I threw up my hands. "So we're back to that, are we?"

"You didn't answer my question!" he shouted and Neely Kate cringed.

I heard movement behind me, followed by the racket of the front door slamming shut.

Now I was well and truly ticked. I pointed my finger in his face and lowered my voice so the teens playing pool couldn't hear, which was a moot point when I realized they'd run out of the place. "You may own me as the Lady in Black, Skeeter Malcolm, but what I do when I'm not wearing that hat and veil is *my business*. I'll question *whoever I want!*"

Skeeter got up and towered over me, anger radiating from him. "We have an agreement. In fact, you owe me an answer to the offer I made you last night!"

Jed's face showed his confusion. I doubted that Skeeter had told him anything about our conversation.

I climbed off my stool and stood, looking up, face to face with Skeeter. "*At the moment*, all we have is an agreement that you can use me as the Lady in Black for six months. That agreement doesn't say a blessed thing about what I do in my free time."

"Things have changed. Now I have a say in who you talk to, along with the when and where." His jaw tightened, and if I hadn't known him like I did, I would have been scared to death. A smart part of me said I should be scared anyway, but the angry part of me won out. Neely Kate, on the other hand, looked like she was about to pee her pants.

I clenched my fists at my sides, struggling to keep my anger in check. "Those aren't the rules we agreed to and if you continue to act like a tyrant, I won't need to answer your offer, because my decision will be *perfectly clear*."

"Well, I just changed the rules, whether you accept my offer or not!"

I took two deep breaths to calm down, but I was still just as furious when I shouted, "If you think you can go changin' the rules on a whim, then so will I. *I quit!*"

Jed jumped up and grabbed my elbow. "Rose, if we could just talk about this."

I pulled out of his grasp. "I think I should be goin' now. Before I do something I regret." Of course, I'd probably already gone and done that, but it was too late to worry about that now. I helped Neely Kate off her stool.

"Don't you walk away from me, Rose Gardner!" Skeeter's voice boomed through the pool hall, making Neely Kate jump.

"*You can kiss my rear end, Skeeter Malcolm!*" I shouted at him as I kept right on walking.

I half expected him to stop me, but we made it out into the sunshine without incident. Neely Kate looked down at me, fear in her eyes, after I helped her into the truck. "Rose, I don't think you should have pissed him off."

I pursed my lips. "I'm not gonna let him bully me. I'm not scared of him." And I wasn't. I knew Skeeter was capable of a great many things, but hurting me wasn't on that list. Probably.

I got into the truck and pulled out of the parking lot, trying to sort through everything that had just happened. It was a surprisingly packed experience. Had I really just quit my position as the Lady in Black, and if so, why did I have such mixed feelings about it? This was a blessing in disguise, especially if he had some connection to J.R. Simmons.

I needed to pull myself together before I let my imagination run wild about J.R. Simmons and his involvement with Atchison Manufacturing. And my birth mother.

Neely Kate rested her forehead in her hand, her elbow propped on the door. "Everything is spinnin'."

I wanted to discuss everything we'd just discovered, but Neely Kate looked like she was close to losing her three-beer lunch. And while I didn't want to wait before figuring out who Beverly was—it was clear she could be a danger—Neely Kate wasn't in any shape to help. It was also obvious I couldn't leave her alone at her house. But both of us needed time to collect ourselves. It didn't take me long to figure out where to go.

Ten minutes later, we were standing on Maeve's front porch. She looked pleasantly surprised to see us, but worry quickly crept into her eyes as she took in Neely Kate's unfocused gaze and stumbling. "Is Neely Kate okay?"

"She just had a little too much drama mixed in with a lunch consisting of a few beers. Do you mind if we sit here for a bit and maybe get a sandwich and a cup of coffee—or three?"

"Of course." She stepped aside so I could help Neely Kate into the house.

I led her to the kitchen and helped her sit at the table.

"How many times do I have to tell you that I'm *fine*, Rose," she said, sounding grumpy.

"I know you are, but I had a sudden craving for Maeve's cooking." I caught Maeve's gaze and she nodded.

"You girls are in luck. I have some barbeque brisket as well as some leftover spaghetti and meatballs. And of course I can always make you a sandwich if you'd prefer."

I obviously didn't have to worry about fitting into any little black dresses anytime soon, so I decided to take advantage of Maeve's offer. "Spaghetti and meatballs for me."

Neely Kate shook her head with a grin. "Brisket."

Maeve clapped her hands, beaming. "Coming right up."

She heated up our food, making small talk about Mason, her new position volunteering with a local after-school tutoring program, and the weather. As always, being around her was like being wrapped up in a warm blanket. Even without trying, Maeve couldn't help but be a comfort. Before too long she set our food on the table and sat across from us. When Neely Kate glanced at the empty space in front of our hostess, Maeve said, "I ate earlier."

"Miss Maeve, how come you always have so much leftover food?" Neely Kate asked after taking a bite.

She shifted in her seat. "Well... I love to cook and there's always someone to feed." She winked. "Like two hungry girls."

When we were almost done eating—I was surprised I could eat so much in spite of all my anxiety—my cell phone rang. I dug it out of my pocket, hoping it was Mason. Instead it was a number I didn't recognize. "Hello."

I was shocked to hear Jed's voice. "Rose, Skeeter's got Merv out lookin' for you."

My heart stopped for a second, then jump-started into a gallop. "*What?*"

Neely Kate's worried eyes found mine.

"He's fumin', Rose. I haven't seen him this angry in ages."

"Okay…" I glanced at Maeve, then stood and walked into the living room, lowering my voice. "What do you think he's gonna do?"

He hesitated. "He's spouted off a few options, the most recurring of which is dragging you back here and chaining you to his desk. But he's got a temper, so if we can buy you some time, he'll calm down and be more reasonable."

"Why's he so mad? Because I quit or because I told him off?"

"Both. And more." He paused and lowered his voice. "Look, Rose, he doesn't know how to handle you. When he tries to intimidate you, it doesn't work. But now he's started relying on you…and you just bailed on him."

"Because he's buttin' into my personal life."

"He doesn't see it that way." He paused. "You and I both know you're not one to sit around knitting. Your own entanglement with the underworld is what landed you in Skeeter's office last November. But I think he imagines you puttering around in your kitchen bakin' pies when you're not the Lady in Black."

That couldn't be further from the truth, but all the times I'd told him I couldn't meet him because I was cooking dinner had probably encouraged that illusion.

"Skeeter saw you grillin' that guy and he had no idea what you were doin'."

"So he's annoyed that I didn't loop him in?"

"No, he's scared. When you're working for *him*, I'm there to have your back and make sure nothing happens to you. If you're off interrogating people on your own, you're vulnerable. Skeeter doesn't want to lose you."

This made no sense. "Then why did he let me go into that strip club by myself last month?"

"I was waiting in the wings as backup. Plus he knew what you were up to then. And the way I heard it, you didn't leave him much choice."

I put my hand on my hip and shook my head, even though I quickly realized he could see neither. "You were there today. You even stepped in to help."

"I was there because Picklebie just happened to be in the pool hall. You told Skeeter that yourself. What if you'd followed Picklebie or some other lowlife into a dark alley? You could have gotten jumped or worse. Skeeter knows how criminals behave. You're probably stronger than any woman he's ever met, but he still sees you as vulnerable."

"He told you all that?"

"No, but I know the guy. Trust me."

Crappy doodles, he was probably right. "He can't force me to do anything, Jed."

"But he can. And he usually does." He sighed, sounding frustrated. "He treats you differently than anyone. Ever. Almost like an equal. But it's just not like him, and I'm worried he'll turn on you."

The significance of his words washed over me. Skeeter had pretty much said the same thing to me after extending his offer of partnership. It had to burn that I'd not only quit, but declined his offer as well. I had a feeling it was a one-of-a-kind deal.

"Rose, I know I have no right, and it goes against what I told you last night, but I'm asking you to reconsider your decision to bow out. You challenge Skeeter. He's changed over the last month. For the better. I'm not sure what he'll do if you don't change your mind."

"To me?"

"No. I think he'll go back to bein' who he was before. Perhaps worse."

I groaned. "I can't just let him boss me around whenever he feels like it, Jed. I'm not his slave and I refuse to let him treat me like one."

"Just promise you'll talk to him after he cools off."

And here I'd just eaten all those carbs. "Fine. I'll talk to him." Then I added in a firm tone, "But I'm not promising to go back to being *you know what*."

"He's capable of being a reasonable man...when his temper's not flarin'."

"Fine."

"I'll let you know when it's safe to go back out." I thought he was about to hang up when he added, "And I'd appreciate it if we kept this conversation between us. If he finds out I warned you..."

"Your secret is safe with me."

"Rose, one more thing. J.R. Simmons."

The very sound of the man's name made me shiver. "What about him?"

"Are you in some kind of trouble with him?"

I pushed out a sigh. "More trouble than you could possibly know." I hung up before he could ask more questions and stared at my truck through the living room picture window. Maeve's house seemed like the perfect place to sit and wait Skeeter out, but my big vehicle was bound to give me away.

I went back into the kitchen. How was I gonna explain *this*? "I need to move my truck. Do you mind if I park it in the alley?"

Maeve looked confused, but she smiled and nodded. "Go ahead."

Neely Kate stared at me and mouthed behind Maeve's back, *Trouble?*

I gave her a tight smile and grabbed my coat. "I'll be right back." As I hurried out to my truck, I berated myself for coming to Maeve's and putting her in danger. What if Merv showed up at her door? While I trusted Jed, I knew next to nothing about this other man. Besides, it had to say something that Skeeter was sending out Merv and not Jed…and that something couldn't be good.

I drove around the block and parked, resting my hands on the steering wheel for a moment. More than anything, I needed a few quiet moments to think things through. My predicament with Skeeter was a huge problem, but there was something else I needed to ponder: my parents' involvement in the Atchison Manufacturing fire and who Beverly might be. I still couldn't let my mind wander to J.R. Not yet. I could only deal with one freakout at a time.

I needed to talk to someone who had known my birth mother personally. Perhaps Aunt Bessie could shed some light on the matter. I pulled out my phone and called my aunt's beauty salon in Lafayette County.

Her receptionist answered and said Aunt Bessie was elbow-deep in a hair color appointment.

"Will she be done soon?" I asked, anxious to get answers.

The woman groaned. "It could take a while. We've got ourselves a hair 9-1-1. This poor woman decided to color her own hair at home, and with her pale complexion, she's currently a dead ringer for that clown in Stephen King's movie *It*. She's already frightened enough children that the sheriff has threatened to toss her hiney in jail. In fact, he keeps poppin' in, checkin' on Bessie's progress."

It definitely sounded like Aunt Bessie had her hands full. "Just have her call me when she's free."

As I climbed out of the truck, I noticed a piece of paper tucked under the passenger side windshield wiper. When had that gotten there? At the pool hall or in front of Maeve's house? Neither option was good. Of course it could have shown up while my truck was parked on the town square—the preferable choice if I had to choose—and maybe Neely Kate and I just hadn't noticed it. It looked enough like the paper I'd found at the Piggly Wiggly that my stomach knotted as I pulled it loose.

You were warned. All bets are off.

Warned about what? The first note had said to stay out of other people's business.

Oh, my word. Atchison Manufacturing. But that didn't make any sense. I hadn't known a thing about it when I got the first note.

This meant the first note had actually been intended for me, not Mason. And the person who'd put it there had watched me closely enough to know I was in Mason's car that day.

Realization set in. Dena had told me about Miss Ima Jean and her husband's suicide when I was picking up Neely Kate's cupcakes and Mason's pie. Who else had been in the bakery that day? A man and two women, none of them known to me.

One of them could be responsible. It was a stretch, but it was the only lead I had at the moment. I needed to talk to Dena and find out what she remembered, if anything. I closed my eyes and groaned. How was I going to get there? I was still hiding from Skeeter.

What I needed to do was turn this Dora matter over to the authorities. Clearly there was much more to it than anyone had suspected. I picked up my phone and started to call Mason, then stopped. Joe was with the sheriff's department and would actually be part of the investigation. How would he take the news of his father's involvement? At this point it was a bunch of hearsay and a couple of vague notes in Dora's journal. I needed harder facts before I could expect to be taken seriously. Besides, I couldn't find it in me to show my ex-boyfriend Dora's journal entries from late 1985 and early 1986, not when there was even the remotest possibility J.R. had been her mysterious married lover.

I called Mason instead. He had started his own investigation into both Dora and J.R. Maybe we could get answers together if we pooled our information. I'd convinced myself it was a good idea by the time he answered, sounding breathless. "Rose? Are you okay?" There was a lot of commotion in the background.

I considered asking for his definition of okay, but instead said, "Mason, I need to talk to you. Do you have some time this afternoon?"

"I'm on my way to court, sweetheart, and I have no idea how long this will take."

"Okay," I said, trying to hide my disappointment. Considering the many layers of the Atchison mess, I could hardly explain it to him unless we had a good amount of time to talk it out.

"Rose." His tone was firm. "Are you okay?"

"I'm fine. I promise."

He was silent for a moment, then said, "I can try to get a recess."

"Mason, don't be silly. I told you I'm fine. How about we talk about it tonight? I'll even stop by the Peach Orchard grocery store and pick up something to make for dinner."

"I thought you said they regularly failed their health inspections." I heard the grin in his voice.

"I feel like a gambling woman today," I teased. "But to be safe, maybe I'll stick to non-perishable items. How do you feel about canned Chinese food?"

He laughed. "God, I love you."

"I love you too. Be safe." I hung up and took a deep breath, telling myself it was probably for the best. What if Merv had caught me before I could make it into the courthouse? How would I explain *that?*

Next I called Neely Kate and she sounded confused when she answered. "Rose?"

"How are you feelin'?"

"Better... Eating helped."

"Are you up for paying a visit to Dena's?" It was just as risky as going to the courthouse, and if I had any sense at all, I'd wait until Skeeter reined in Merv, but I needed answers now.

"Maeve has brownies."

"Then I'll get a cupcake and you can come along as my partner in crime. Or if you've had enough adventure, you can hang out with Maeve."

It took her less than a second to say, "I'll be right out."

"Tell Maeve we had a landscaping emergency."

"*We have those?*"

"We do now."

But Maeve followed Neely Kate out to the truck. "A landscaping emergency, huh?"

I smiled at her. "It's the darnedest thing."

An ornery grin spread across her face as she held out her car keys.

I blinked. "What's that for?"

"You're hiding your truck for a reason. If you take my car, you'll have a better chance of going undetected."

I took her keys and held them to my chest. "Maeve, I don't know what to say."

"Don't say anything. I don't want to know. Then I can deny any knowledge of your shenanigans."

"You know I'm up to something and you're helpin' me anyway?"

She looked into my eyes. "We both know there's a whole lot of something goin' on. I saw you at the Bingo hall on Tuesday night, and I also saw you slip out the door."

I blushed.

"Mason thinks you were there the entire time, and I covered for you."

I shook my head. "Why? How do you know I'm not doin' something wrong?"

"Because I just have this *feeling*." She pursed her lips and looked away before turning back to me and taking my hand. "Mason and his father saw the world as black and white. Right and wrong. Mason's rigidity has softened since you came into his life last summer, and that's a good thing. You have a positive influence on him and everyone else you touch." She glanced over at my friend. "Neely Kate, dear, would you give us a moment?"

Her mouth parted in surprise. "Yeah." She wandered over to the back of the truck.

My stomach flip-flopped with nerves. What in the world did she have to say that she wanted to keep from Neely Kate?

"I know you have visions."

Now my mouth dropped open. "What? How?"

She shook her head and waved her hand. "That's not important. I just know you have them. And I think you're using them to help people, am I wrong?"

"Well…yeah. I'm tryin' to. At least lately." I was still floored by her revelation.

She looked nervous as she took another deep breath. "Maybe you won't find my own confession strange then. I've never told a soul save my beloved Van."

"Not even Mason?"

"No. He of all people would find it foolish." She forced a smile. "I have feelings, premonitions. Not visions like yours…it's as if I can sense a rightness or wrongness about things. The impressions I get are vague, but they're strong."

I nodded. "Okay."

"You believe me?"

I released a short laugh. "Maeve, I have visions of the future. What you've told me doesn't sound all that strange."

Her grip tightened around my hand and tears filled her eyes. "I have a terrible feeling that something's about to happen to Mason."

Had Mason told her that his life was in danger? I doubted it. My heart leapt into my throat. "I don't—"

"I'm not asking you to confirm or deny it, and it doesn't matter what you say anyway. It only matters what I know."

"What does that have to do with you helping me?"

"You're the only one who can save him."

A shiver ran down my spine. "Me?"

"Just like someone with arthritis can feel a storm coming, I can feel trouble. I knew something was going to happen to Van before his heart attack. I begged him to go to the doctor, but he refused. Then Savannah..." She paused and straightened her shoulders. "Here's what I'm sensing now..." Her eyes burned bright as they stared into mine. "There are lots of things going on in this town right now, and many of them are interconnected. Mason is at the center of it all, but someone else is there with him. Someone with a lot of power."

"Joe?"

She shook her head. "No. Not Joe." She paused. "I don't know who it is, but you're the key to saving them both."

I wasn't sure I wanted to hear this. I didn't want to be responsible for saving anyone, especially Mason. What if I failed him? How could I live with that?

"So why are you givin' me your car?"

"Because you need to do what feels right, even if other people are telling you it's wrong."

"I don't know." I glanced back at Neely Kate before returning my gaze to Maeve.

She cupped my cheek. "Trust your instincts."

I nodded, still not sure what to make of what she'd said.

"You can come back now, Neely Kate," Maeve called out, entering the code to open her garage door. "You girls be careful, and if you need any help, don't hesitate to ask. I'll be here."

I handed her my truck keys and grimaced. "You might not want to drive this for a bit. I'll let you know when I get the all-clear."

She winked. "Okay."

She watched us back out of the garage and waved as we took off.

"What just happened?" Neely Kate asked, looking shell-shocked.

"This day has been nothin' but strange."

Unfortunately, I had a feeling we were just getting started.

Chapter-Twenty-One

W hat did Maeve say?" Neely Kate repeated.

I wasn't about to break Maeve's trust, but I didn't think there'd be any harm in telling her parts of our conversation. "She told me to trust my instincts."

"And?"

I glanced over at her. "She trusts me. She just has a feeling."

She sank back in her seat. "A *feeling?*"

"Yeah."

"So tell me why we're in Maeve's car, why we're goin' to Dena's, and what you saw in your vision back at the pool hall."

"Where do you want me to start?"

"Let's start with the first one."

I grimaced. "Skeeter is furious, so he has one of his guys out lookin' for me."

"Oh, my stars and garters. Is it Jed?"

"No. He sent Merv. Jed called to warn me"

"Won't he get in trouble for that?"

I had to admit I was worried about him. "Yeah. I'll just have to make sure that Skeeter doesn't find out."

"What are you gonna do?"

I let out a sigh. "Jed thinks I'll be able to reason with Skeeter once he cools down."

Neely Kate shook her head. "I knew Skeeter Malcolm was trouble from the start."

"Maybe so, but what's done is done. Merv's probably lookin' for my truck. He'll never suspect I'm in Maeve's car. So as long as we stay away from the office, we should be good. I just need to figure out how to get Muffy from the nursery."

She lifted her eyebrows and gave me a look that suggested she wasn't as confident in my plan as I was. "So what did you see in the vision?"

"Dirk callin' someone after leaving the pool hall."

"And why would you want to see that?"

"I figured he must have confided in someone about the whole Atchison mess. Scared as he was, it made sense to me he'd run to them first thing. And he did. He called some woman named Beverly. He said we knew everything about the fire and the blackmail."

"You really think Henry Buchanan bribed him?"

"Or Dirk was extorting him? Either way, it stands to reason it involves Dirk."

She was quiet for a moment. "Do you think there's really a chance your daddy started that fire?"

"It doesn't seem like something he'd do, but neither does having an affair and fathering an illegitimate daughter. Although there seems to be some question of whether he's my father after all."

"Rose..."

I glanced at her. "Did you hear the part about the factory? They can't find an heir. What if I really am Henry Buchanan's child and they're lookin' for me?"

"Rose." Her tone softened.

I gripped the steering wheel tighter. "I'd prefer Henry Buchanan to..." I couldn't finish the thought.

"This is *ridiculous*." Her voice rose in protest. "Neither one of those men is your father. Least of all J.R. Simmons." She shuddered her disgust.

I wished I could be as certain as she was. "I've called my Aunt Bessie. She might know more about Dora…or if Daddy's not my real father after all."

"You think she'd keep somethin' like that from you?"

"She hid the fact that Momma wasn't my birth mother until after she died." I turned to her. "Yeah. I think she'd do that."

"Wow." She was quiet for a moment. "If J.R. Simmons is—"

"Stop!" I shouted, then said softer, "Just stop. I can't even let my head go there. It's too much. I just want to talk to Aunt Bessie."

"Okay, let's focus on something else. Dirk said the police chief was murdered after the fire. That's really suspicious, particularly on top of Dora dyin' and Henry killing himself."

I was beginning to have second thoughts about waiting to tell Mason. "Maybe we should give this information to Joe."

"So why haven't you called him yet?"

"Because I have to find out who my father is before we talk to Joe about any of it." I couldn't even imagine how he'd handle it. Probably worse than I was.

"So how about we sit tight until you talk to your aunt?"

While her advice was sound, I felt an underlying drive to forge ahead. I wasn't sure what was spurring me on—Maeve's words, my own stubbornness, or some residual feelings from my vision at the pool hall. I only knew I needed to keep digging. "Let's just talk to Dena first. I want to see if she remembers who was in the bakery when she told me about Ima Jean and Atchison."

"Do you think that's really likely?"

"Maybe not, but I have to try anyway."

"Why does it matter who was in the bakery when you were there?"

"It might help explain the threatening notes."

"You found another one?"

"It was on my truck right now. It said I'd been warned and all bets were off." I turned to her. "I guess the first note was left for me after all."

Neely Kate's eyes flew open. "Rose, you have to tell Joe."

"And I will. After I find out my answer. Plus I called Mason, but he was heading to court. I'll tell him tonight."

"I can't believe I'm sayin' this, but you could always tell Skeeter."

I gaped at her. "Have you lost your mind?"

"He's a pretty powerful guy."

And that was exactly what he wanted—if I ran to him and asked for help, I'd be sucked deeper into his world. "We can do this on our own. We're merely goin' to a bakery. How dangerous could that be?"

"Why do you keep askin' things like that? Nothing's ever that easy for us."

We drove around the town square, taking a peek at the empty RBW Landscaping office before we found a parking space at the opposite end, closer to Dena's. I looked around to make sure Merv wasn't lurking nearby. When the coast looked clear, we got out and walked into Dena's.

There were only two other customers in the store and Dena was behind the case, her usual cheerful smile in place. She glanced up at us and smiled even bigger when she saw Neely Kate. After she waited on the other two customers, we made our way to the counter.

Dena leaned her forearms on the case. "Good to see you, Neely Kate."

Neely Kate offered her a soft smile in return. "Hey."

"Dena," I said. "When I was here a couple of days ago, you told me about Ima Jean Buchanan and her husband."

She pursed her mouth and shook her head. "Sad, sad tale."

"It is," I agreed. "I know you get a lot of people in here, but do you maybe happen to remember the other customers who were in here with me? One was a tall, lanky guy, maybe late fifties? He looked really familiar."

She nodded with a smile. "Ed Barlow. He works at the courthouse. He comes over for a cupcake every afternoon on his break."

"I know him," Neely Kate added. "He works in probate."

"There were also two women. A young woman in her twenties."

She shook her head. "I don't remember her." Her eyes narrowed. "Why are you asking?"

I gave her a tight smile. "I'll tell you in a minute." I didn't want to prejudice her recollection. "What about the middle-aged woman? Maybe in her late forties. She sat at one of the tables in the back while you rang me up. I think her name was Marta."

"Marta Gray. She works down at the dry cleaners."

I gave Neely Kate a questioning glance, but she just shook her head. "Don't know her."

I gave her a look of disbelief. Most days it seemed like she knew all twenty-four thousand residents in the county. I turned my attention back to Dena. "She didn't seem very happy that day."

"She's a bit cranky at times," Dena said. "But her husband is good for nothing and her teenage boys aren't much better."

"Do you know if she worked at Atchison Manufacturing?" I asked.

Dena scrunched her nose. "I don't know. She's kind of young, but I guess she could have started there right out of high school."

I turned to Neely Kate and pulled her away from the counter before I whispered, "Didn't Gloria say the other office girl was let go because Ima Jean thought Henry was having an affair with Dora? What if Marta set the fire and then put the note on my truck to scare me off after she heard me askin' about it?"

Neely Kate made a face. "That's a lot of maybes...and where would Beverly fit in?"

"Maybe Beverly's not part of it at all. For all we know, she could just be Dirk's old girlfriend or wife."

Neely Kate looked dubious.

Dena rested her elbows on the case, squinting at me. "What's going on, Rose?"

I walked back over to her. "Someone left a threatening note on my truck the day I was in here. I'm trying to figure out who it was."

Dena shook her head. "There's no way it could be Marta. She doesn't have it in her. Besides, why would she do such a thing?"

"There's only one way to find out." I glanced over at Dena. "What does Marta usually get?"

Neely Kate put her hand on her hip, giving me a disapproving glare. "You're gonna take her cupcakes and then accuse her of arson?"

Dena gasped. "What?"

I rolled my eyes. "I'm gonna be more subtle than that."

Dena made a face. "I don't know, Rose. I don't think I want any part of this."

"I won't outright accuse her. Neely Kate and I will take her cupcakes and introduce ourselves as new business neighbors from the landscaping office. I'll just ask her where she used to work."

"That might actually work." Neely Kate sounded impressed.

Dena grabbed a box. "I'll go along with this as long as you promise not to be mean to her. That poor woman has had a hard life."

"I'm gonna be as sweet as your cupcakes," I said, holding up my hand. "I'm just gonna ask her a few questions."

Dena handed me the box. "Vanilla bean. Two of 'em. She loves them. And if I find out you were mean to her, I'll ban you from gettin' anything from here again."

"I promise we'll be nice. I'm just ruling her out." I paid for the baked goods and Neely Kate and I headed toward the dry cleaners.

"Which one of us should start?" Neely Kate asked.

"How about we just act like we're really introducing ourselves for no reason and wing it." I gave her a grin. "We've done pretty well so far."

She smiled. "We have, haven't we?"

No one was in the dry cleaners when we entered, but the woman I'd seen in the bakery walked up to the counter. "Can I help you?"

Neely Kate gave her a bright smile. "Hi! I'm Neely Kate and this is Rose. We just opened RBW Landscaping." She held out the box. "We brought you some cupcakes from Dena's to say hi."

She took the box and looked down at it before glancing back up at Neely Kate. "I'm not the owner. I just work here."

Neely Kate leaned forward and cupped her hand around her mouth and said in a stage whisper, "It's okay. I'm just an employee too."

She smiled. "I'm Marta."

She looked so grateful, I didn't believe for a minute she'd left those nasty notes on my truck, but we might as well finish what we'd started. "Don't let Neely Kate fool you, I couldn't run the place without her."

Neely Kate gave her a sly grin. "I abandoned the courthouse to run her books. I'm not sure you can get a worse job than working in the personal property department."

"You never worked at the DMV," I said. "That's the worst job ever."

"What about you, Marta?" Neely Kate asked. "You have any previous crummy jobs?"

"Well, I've worked here for a long time. About twelve years. Before that I worked at a nursin' home." She grimaced. "Nothing like wipin' old people's butts and cleaning up their poop all day."

Neely Kate made a face. "You definitely have a point."

"Did you work anywhere before that?" I asked.

"I worked at the Burger Shack when I was in high school." She lowered her voice. "Which is why I don't eat there anymore. The things they did with their hamburger meat…"

She didn't finish and I didn't want her to. As it stood, I wasn't sure I wanted to eat there anymore either.

"That's it?" Neely Kate asked.

"Ain't it enough?" Marta laughed. She opened the box and held it out. "You girls want a cupcake?"

I felt guilty for even considering the possibility she could be capable of something so devious. "You keep 'em. We got them for you."

Tears filled her eyes. "I was havin' the worst day and you girls just made it better."

Neely Kate leaned over and grabbed her hand. "We're just down the street if you ever need someone to talk to, you hear?"

She nodded. "Thank you."

The bell on the door dinged again and a man walked in, his arms stacked with garments.

Neely Kate waved and headed for the door. "We'll see you later, Marta."

We walked out onto the sidewalk. "Now what?" Neely Kate asked. "We're back to square one."

I let out a loud sigh. Other than meeting someone new who looked like she needed a friend, we'd learned nothing.

"Rose," Neely Kate hissed. "Could that be Merv?" She pointed to a man lurking outside the landscaping office.

We were a good fifty feet away, but there was no mistaking his bulky frame and perpetual scowl. "Oh, crap."

She grabbed my arm. "Come on." The she dragged me over to an office space, pushed open the door, and pulled me into the small reception area. I didn't even have time to look at the sign.

"Hey, Ebola girl!" a familiar man's voice exclaimed. "I knew you couldn't stay away from me."

I spun around to see Carter Hale, the attorney who'd helped Neely Kate in the ER waiting room back in December, after she'd insinuated she had Ebola. He was standing in a short hallway, a smug smile on his face. His secretary stared at us from behind her desk like we were Martians.

Neely Kate put her hands on her hips. "Not likely, Carter Hale."

"Then to what do I owe the pleasure of your visit?"

She lifted her chin. "Rose is a co-owner of the landscaping business across the street, and we're makin' the rounds and saying hi to all our new neighbors. We just took cupcakes to Marta at the dry cleaners."

He held out his hands. "So where are mine?"

She made a face, then looked out the window. "I ate them."

He walked over next to her. "Whatcha lookin' at?"

"Nothin'."

"Is 'Nothin'' the name of that beefy guy hanging around outside your office?"

Carter Hale was too perceptive by half.

She scowled at him.

"Do I need to call Henryetta's boys in blue?" he asked, but there was a sparkle in his eye. "Officer Sprout might run over faster if you tried dangling one of those cupcakes you're not offering me."

"There's no need for that," I said. "He's harmless." Or he would be if we kept avoiding him.

Neely Kate stepped back from the window, but Carter kept looking out of it. "So what's your plan?"

"We'll sell you on our services," Neely Kate said, flashing him a cheesy smile. "Then you can write us a big fat check."

"That'd be like selling a fishing pole to a camel in the desert," Carter laughed, still watching out the window. "I live in a condo and my office has no green space."

"Lucky for you, we have a plan for everyone," Neely Kate countered.

He chuckled. "And what exactly do your services entail?"

"Not what you're thinkin' right now, Carter Hale."

These two were gonna be the death of me.

"Your goon just got into a car and drove away." He turned back to face us. "What kind of trouble did you two get into to gain the notice of one of Skeeter Malcolm's henchmen?"

Oh, crappy doodles.

Thankfully Neely Kate didn't miss a beat. "I made a bet on some horses and Skeeter's sent one of his guys to collect."

"Horses, you say?"

Neely Kate shrugged. "I have a terrible gambling problem. Why, walkin' in here is proof enough of that."

Carter laughed. "Fair enough." He walked over to the desk where his secretary was still staring at us in disbelief. He picked up a couple of business cards and gave one to each of us. "I have a feeling you two might be in need of legal services in the near future. Consider this your get out of jail free card."

Neely Kate took the card and stared at it before looking back up at him. "Rose's boyfriend is the assistant district attorney. I think he's our get out of jail free card."

His grin wavered. "One can never be too careful."

What did Carter Hale know?

Chapter Twenty-Two

My cell phone rang and I pulled it out and stared at the screen. "It's my Aunt Bessie. I need to take this." Then I walked out onto the sidewalk, leaving Neely Kate behind with Carter. I took a deep breath. I felt like I was gonna throw up. "Hey, Aunt Bessie."

"Rose, I'm so happy you called! I miss you, girl."

"I miss you too."

"But I suspect you missing me isn't why you called me on a Thursday afternoon at the salon."

I squared my shoulders. "No, ma'am. It's not." Now that I had her on the phone I wondered if I should have driven over to Lafayette County to talk to her face to face. But I didn't have time to do that right yet, and I couldn't wait for the truth any longer. "I need to ask you some questions about Dora and Daddy."

Neely Kate came out of Carter's office and started gesturing to the front of the building while Carter stood in the doorway with an amused grin on his face. I heard her spouting off something about pots with flowers and vines.

Aunt Bessie was silent for a moment. "I was wondering when you'd start askin' questions. Especially now that you're livin' in her house."

"Do you know when Dora and Daddy first started seeing each other?"

"I'm not sure."

"When did Daddy leave Momma?"

"In early October. Right after Dora quit her job."

"Do you know why she quit?"

"I know she had trouble with her boss. They had a disagreement over something."

That just confirmed Dirk's story. And it meant Aunt Bessie wouldn't know if there was a chance I wasn't my daddy's daughter. "When did you find out they were together?"

Aunt Bessie sighed. "Harrison didn't tell me right away. He had a wife and baby daughter. He was ashamed."

"That didn't answer my question, Aunt Bessie."

"The first I heard of it was in October. When he left your momma."

My heart sank. "But did he ever tell you anything about their relationship before he moved out?"

"No, Rose. I'm sorry. I understand your need to put the pieces together, but I only know about the two of them after he moved out."

"Can you tell me that part?"

"Of course." I heard the smile in her voice. And the regret. "Earl and I first met Dora in the middle of October. We went to the farmhouse to see the two of them. Dora was a lovely woman. So warm and full of life. You're a lot like her, Rose. And your daddy was so happy after he moved in with her. Happier than I'd ever seen him."

I sat down on a park bench outside the courthouse and closed my eyes. Neely Kate sat beside me and I glanced up at her in surprise. I didn't realize she'd walked over. "Did Daddy love me back then?" I asked.

"Oh, Rose. He loved you very much."

"Yeah, for a few months. Until Dora died."

"Rose, he loved you after that too. I told you, part of him died with her. He was never the same afterwards."

Suddenly the significance of that hit me full force. Dora's death had changed him, yes, but perhaps his transformation also had something to do with the fire. "Did Daddy ever say anything about his job at Atchison Manufacturing?"

"You found out he worked there?" she asked in surprise. "I brought up the factory once in conversation, and he got angry with me and said he'd never talk about the place again."

"I read about it in Dora's journal. But why would he react that way?" I wasn't sure what to make of his reaction. It sure sounded like the behavior of someone wracked with guilt.

"I only know it was a tense situation. Your daddy was planning on quitting, but there was no need because the fire destroyed the factory and he lost his job. Then a week later Dora died. It was too much for him. Dora had drawn up a will just days after your birth. Your uncle and I were shocked to find out she'd made Earl the executor of the estate. The farm was yours and Earl would obviously have let your daddy live there until you turned eighteen."

"But he brought me to you."

"Like I told you last June, Rose, he was a broken man."

The rest I knew. Momma brought Violet to Aunt Bessie and Uncle Earl's farm and convinced Daddy to get back together with her. She stayed long enough to claim she'd given birth to me, and then the four of us went back to our unhappy home.

Aunt Bessie let out a small gasp. "I'm not sure why I didn't suggest this before, but if you want to know more about Dora, you should talk to her best friend."

"What?"

"She and Hattie were really close. I'm sure she can tell you all kinds of things about Dora."

"*Hattie?* Do you know her last name?"

"No. But I know they went to school together."

"Thank you, Aunt Bessie. That helps more than you can know." I hung up and turned to Neely Kate. "We have to go out to the farm."

"Why?"

"Dora had a best friend, Hattie, but Aunt Bessie doesn't know her last name. They went to school together, so she's bound to be in Dora's yearbooks. And I know exactly where they are. We can also try to look for the second journal."

"I thought you said that would be like looking for a needle in a haystack."

"It will be. I still need to try."

"Okay. But don't we need to get Muffy first?"

"Yeah. I guess it's later than I thought."

Bruce Wayne was working outside when we pulled up to the nursery. He had a large bag of potting soil slung over his shoulder and he looked up at us and waved.

Neely Kate got out of the car and stared at him. "Ding dong. When did Bruce Wayne start getting so buff?"

"Huh." I studied him, thankful he'd turned his back to us. He'd be horrified if he knew what we were discussing. "I guess all the landscaping work has given him a workout."

As I got out of the car, a woman came out of the nursery carrying a paper coffee cup. She wore a threadbare tweed coat and a pair of jeans. Her face was dark-complected, and her hair was jet-black and fell around her head in tight ringlets that stopped at her shoulders. She stopped next to Bruce Wayne as he tossed the bag of soil on top of a pile next to the greenhouse. He gave her a shy smile as he took the cup from her.

"Oh, my stars and garters," Neely Kate murmured. "He likes her. Is that Violet's new employee?"

I studied them for a minute. The woman watched as he took a sip and then handed the cup back to her before bending down to pick up another bag. Then he turned back to her with a dreamy look in his eyes. Neely Kate was right. Even though I'd never met her, I'd seen her working in the shop in a vision. "Yeah, she must be. I think her name is Anna." I thought about going over to introduce myself, but then I decided otherwise. "Let's let them talk for a moment," I said, grabbing Neely Kate's arm and tugging her toward the front door. "I don't want to interrupt them."

She groaned. "But Violet's in there."

"Suck it up and deal with it," I said as I reached over to pull open the door. I wasn't excited about seeing my sister right now either. But then I realized she hadn't been back to the nursery since the day of her miscarriages. "Oh, my word, Neely Kate. I'm so sorry. I wasn't thinkin'."

Anger filled her eyes. "Don't you dare apologize. It's like I told you. I don't *want* you to handle me with kid gloves. I want to pretend that everything is normal."

I closed the door and looked into her eyes. "But it's *not* normal. Nothing's normal. You have every right to be upset or angry or any other emotion you feel."

Her anger burned brighter. "You don't know what I'm going through, Rose Gardner, so don't you dare preach to me about what I should or shouldn't be doin' or feelin'!"

I nodded, properly chastised. "You're right. I'm sorry."

She closed her eyes, and when she opened them again, her anger had been replaced with contrition. "No, I'm sorry for yelling at you."

I gave her a tear-filled smile. "Don't be. That's what makes us work. We're not afraid to tell each other how it is." My chin quivered. "I have no idea what to do or say to make you feel better, but I'm trying."

She wrapped her arms around me and pulled me into a hug. "I know and I love you for it. Don't give up on me, okay?"

I leaned back and searched her face. "Give up on you? What are you talkin' about? Did you whack your head on something when I wasn't lookin'?"

She laughed. "No."

"Neely Kate," I said, turning serious. "I'm not goin' anywhere. If anything, *you* should be runnin' from *me*. You're the one hurtin' right now and my family drama's taking center stage."

"We all have our family secrets, Rose. Some are just buried deeper than others." Something in her voice made me think she wasn't talking in the abstract.

"What's that mean?"

She forced a smile. "Let's go say hi to Violet." She pushed open the door and called out, "Hey, Violet."

Muffy tore out of the back room, barking up a storm as she plowed into my legs. I bent down and picked her up, rubbing the back of her head. "Hey, girl. Did you miss me?"

She answered by licking my open mouth.

I screeched my disapproval and put her back on the floor.

My sister had been watching us through the window from behind the counter. She walked around the end and gave Neely Kate a soft smile. "How are you doin'?"

Neely Kate's smile faded. "I'm gettin' by."

"My offer still stands, okay?" Violet said, holding Neely Kate's gaze.

She nodded.

What in the world were they talking about? Violet and Neely Kate were usually so antagonistic to each other, it was odd watching them be nice. I looked out the side window at Bruce Wayne. "It looks like he's makin' good progress."

Violet nodded. "He is. Thanks for loanin' him to me. Joe was gonna come move the bags, but he's been tied up with sheriff business."

"Well, we're slow, so if you have anything else for him to do, let us know. I'm sure he won't mind. Business is going to be slow for a while at RBW Landscaping, and he gets stir-crazy with nothin' to do."

Neely Kate grinned. "And it looks like he likes the company."

Violet leaned against the counter. "That's Anna, my new help. It's only her second day, but she fits right in. In fact, if she weren't so great at her job, I might be annoyed. But she's only been out there twice and both times when we had nothing to do. And it is cold, so I can't begrudge her takin' him something warm to drink when he's workin' so hard." She grinned. "And I can't believe I'm sayin' this, but they're cute together."

I smiled at Violet and she gave me a strange look. "What?"

"You said two nice things about Bruce Wayne. In a row."

"So?" she asked, sounding defensive. "I can admit it when I'm wrong."

I expected Neely Kate to offer some jab, but she remained surprisingly quiet.

What was goin' on with this day?

I shook my head. "We just came by to get Muffy." My little dog stood at my feet, looking up at me expectantly.

"She can hang out here if you like," Violet said. "Ashley and Mikey have been missing her. I'm sure they'd love to play with her after school."

I seriously considered letting her stay. It had been a couple of weeks since she'd last seen the kids and she loved them, but given the threat on Mason's life, I felt better with her by my side. But I didn't dare tell Violet any of that or she'd get upset. I cocked my head and smiled. "Can we get a rain check on that?

I feel like I've neglected Muffy sorely these last couple of days and I'd like to spend time with her tonight."

"Sure." But Violet looked unconvinced by my explanation. Thankfully, she didn't press the issue. "Don't forget I have a doctor's appointment tomorrow. You said you'd cover for me."

"Uh…yeah." I felt bad. I *had* forgotten, but in my defense, she'd asked the week before. "Ten, right?"

"The appointment's *at* ten. Can you be here by 9:40?"

"Sure. I'll see you tomorrow."

As we headed for the door, Anna was coming back in. She was pretty, but in a non-made up way. She kept her dark brown eyes downcast before she lifted her gaze to me. She was about my height but thinner, and I couldn't help thinking that she needed a good home-cooked meal at Maeve's.

I held out my hand. "You must be Anna. I'm Rose. Violet's sister."

She shook it before quickly dropping it. "Nice to meet you."

"I see you met my partner Bruce Wayne."

Her cheeks turned pink. "Yeah."

As I got back into the car, setting Muffy in the back seat, I found myself hoping that something was really kindling between the two of them. Bruce Wayne deserved all the happiness in the world. And while I was rooting for him, I had more pressing matters to attend to.

I had to verify the identity of my birth father.

Chapter TwentyThree

I parked Maeve's car behind the house, hoping I could give Mason a believable explanation if he came home before I took Neely Kate back to the office. Muffy took off running to the front of the house and dove for the bushes, rooting around underneath. I unlocked the front door.

"Huh," I said, looking around the living room from the threshold. The alarm usually beeped as soon as we opened the door. "I could swear Mason set the alarm before he left."

"Are you sure?" Neely Kate said, walking up the porch steps behind me.

I walked through the living room into the kitchen and studied the keypad. I hated the alarm system and found it confusing, but Mason always got aggravated when I didn't set it, which happened often enough given the number of times I'd accidentally set it off. "It says it's ready. Maybe he didn't."

"What if someone broke in?" Neely Kate said. "Someone *is* after Mason."

I looked around for any sign of a break-in and found none. "How would they know the code? It's not very likely. It's half the length of the *Encyclopedia Britannica*. Which is why I'm always screwing it up."

"Maybe you should call him and check."

I shook my head as I continued to look around. "He's in court. He said he'd call as soon as he's free." I realized Muffy was still outside, so I went to the front door and called her.

I heard her under the bushes, releasing a slow growl.

I moved to the top of the steps and put my hands on my hips. "Muffy! Leave whatever poor creature you've got trapped under there alone and come inside."

She emerged with her head down, still snarling at the bushes.

"Does she ordinarily do that?" Neely Kate asked.

I sighed. "She had a raccoon trapped under there a few weeks ago. It was next to impossible to get her to come in." Muffy was still at the bottom of the steps. "Muffy!"

She reluctantly made her way up, one step at a time, letting the creature under the bushes know that she wasn't one bit happy about leaving it behind.

Once she was inside, I closed and locked the door behind her and turned to Neely Kate. "The yearbooks are in the office."

I pushed open the French doors and walked around the desk to the bookcases. Mason had taken over the office and it totally reflected him now. An empty coffee mug was on a coaster and he had stacks of legal pads and a few books. His sweatshirt was crumpled in his chair. His mother had given me his forensics trophy from when he'd gone to state his senior year in high school, and I'd put it on a shelf to tease him. I was suddenly struck by how integral he had become to my life and the farmhouse. Parts of him were everywhere. If something were to happen to him, I didn't think I could stand coming home and seeing things like his sweatshirt as he'd left them...not with the knowledge he'd never come home to wear it again.

"Rose?" Neely Kate asked, worry in her voice.

I wiped a stray tear. "Someone wants Mason dead." It was one thing knowing that it was true and another considering this his enemies might actually be successful.

"I know, honey."

"I can't lose him, Neely Kate."

She pulled me into a hug. "You're not going to. Joe's going to make sure he's okay."

I took a deep breath and pulled loose. Here I was whining about hypothetically losing Mason when Neely Kate was grieving an actual loss. "You're right." I forced a smile. "He's gonna be just fine."

I turned to face the bookcases and went straight to the section that held school yearbooks. I ran my finger along the spines, looking for the years that would fit Dora's time in high school. I grabbed four books off the shelf and hefted them onto my hip.

Neely Kate studied the books lining the shelves, most of which I hadn't given so much as a glance since moving into the farmhouse. "While we're in here, why don't we see if the other journal's in here?"

"It seems a little too obvious, doesn't it?"

"Sometimes the best place to hide something is in plain sight."

I put the books on Mason's desk, and we spent the next ten minutes searching titles on the spines and pulling out any book that looked like it could be a journal. No luck.

"Well, it was worth a try," I said, picking up the yearbooks. "Back to plan A."

"Let's take them out to the kitchen," Neely Kate said, leading the way. "I'll start a pot of coffee."

Once we reached the kitchen, she started the coffee and I set the books on the table.

"Since we didn't get any cupcakes for ourselves," I said, moving to the refrigerator, "do you want a piece of Maeve's marble cheesecake?"

"I'm gonna gain fifty pounds if I keep eating that woman's food," Neely Kate said with a grin.

I pulled the pan out and carried it over to the table. "So was that a yes or a no?" I asked, reaching for plates in the cabinet.

"Duh. It's a yes."

After I dished up our dessert and Neely Kate poured our coffee, we sat at the table in front of the books.

"For someone so eager for answers," Neely Kate murmured as she picked up her fork, "you sure are stalling."

I grabbed the corner of the first book and took a deep breath. "What if I don't like the answers we find?"

"Since when do you back down from the truth?" She took a bite. "Mmmm... Maeve should open her own restaurant."

"Don't give her any ideas." I laughed half-heartedly. "And I'm not backin' down from the truth. Just delaying it a bit." I opened the top book, realizing I'd shuffled them out of order. I searched for the junior class and sure enough, I found Dora sandwiched between a girl with long blond hair who looked like the popular cheerleader type and a boy with acne and a sad look in his eyes.

"She was pretty," Neely Kate said, as I slid the book more centrally between us. "You look like her."

Neely Kate was right. I'd been struck by the resemblance the first time I'd seen a photo of her holding a tiny me. "There's something about her that seems so...friendly," I said.

"I agree. She looks like she'd be nice to Donnie Hall." She pointed to the sad-looking boy, then looked up at me. "Just like you would be."

It was strange to think that the person I'd thought I was for twenty-four years wasn't the person I was at all. Or more accurately, the parts that made up *me* weren't what I'd thought they were. Who was the woman who'd carried me for nine months, hoping for a life full of love for the both of us? Had she resorted to something illegal to make that happen?

"We need to look for Hattie." I flipped to the beginning of the junior class and started scanning names.

"I can't believe you haven't looked at these before now."

I twist my mouth into a grimace. "I have…a little. Besides, I've been busy."

"Not that busy."

"I think most of us weren't at our best in high school." I gave her a teasing grin. "Not all of us are like you, you know. Some of us were just trying to make it to graduation."

"So what does that have to do with not looking at Dora's yearbooks?"

"I wouldn't want someone to try and figure out who I was by searching through my high school yearbooks. Maybe Dora felt the same way. Maybe she wouldn't want me to think of her this way."

She studied me for a moment. "You're overthinking it. Besides, who you were in high school is still a part of who you are now. Even if you've evolved. Maybe Dora did too, although she didn't look like she was the type of girl who'd be bullied or treated as an outcast."

We continued to scroll through the names, then I flipped the page.

"That's her! Hattie Rush," Neely Kate exclaimed, pointing to her photo. "She looks nice too."

She had dark brown hair and bright friendly eyes to match her smile.

"I suppose we should make sure she's the right Hattie."

"How many Hatties could there be?" But Neely Kate quickly scanned the rest of the junior class all the same. "I suppose she could be in a different grade, but I'm betting that's her."

"But we're not sure."

Neely Kate pulled the yearbook in front of her and flipped to the front pages which were full of notes and signatures. "Your mom was popular," she said. "Look at all these notes." She scrolled through the pages, then flipped to the back, finally saying, "Aha! *Dora, you're the best part of Fenton County High School. Thanks for helping me pass that cooking exam in Mrs. B's class! I'm so glad we became friends last year. Hattie Rush.*"

It wasn't irrefutable proof, but it was good enough. "Next question is how do we find her?"

"Give me a second." She pulled out her phone and typed Hattie's name into an Internet search engine. I wasn't sure anything she'd find anything, but sure enough, several Hattie Rushes popped up.

"How are we gonna know which one is her?" I asked.

"Well, seeing how we've seen her photo in the yearbook, I think it's safe to assume this woman who looks like she's Native American can be ruled out, as well as the African American."

I glanced over her shoulder and teased, "What about the one who is Mrs. Octogenarian Michigan?"

Her gaze lifted to mine, but she glared at me without saying a word.

"So she's not there?" I asked.

"Not necessarily. Sometimes you have to search a few pages. My cousin has the same name as a famous singer. When she Googles herself, she doesn't show up until page five."

Poor Dolly Parton. But then again, I'd never searched for myself. Who knew what page I'd end up on?

Sure enough, Hattie turned up on page three.

"She lives up in Magnolia," Neely Kate said, searching her Facebook page. "She works at the Magnolia hospital as a nurse. She's not married, but it looks like she's divorced and took back her maiden name. No kids."

"You found all of that out from Facebook?" I asked in disbelief.

She gaped at me. "You've seriously never Facebook-investigated someone?"

"No."

"Huh. You should try it sometime. You never know what you'll turn up." Neely Kate continued tapping on her phone.

I sighed. "This is all great, but what do we do? Friend her and hope she accepts?"

"We could...or we could try to find her phone number in the white pages. And when that doesn't show up, we can look for her parents' phone number." She kept typing all while she was speaking, then she finally looked up and grinned at me. "Bingo."

"You're kidding."

"Nope." She dialed the number. "Hello? Mrs. Rush?" Her eyes lit up with excitement. "Yes, my friend's mother was a friend of your daughter Hattie and she would love to talk to her." She listened for a moment. "Her mother was Dora Middleton." Her smile returned. "Yes, Rose. I know! Rose only just found out about her birth mother a few months ago and she's eager to learn as much as she can about Dora. Do you think Hattie would be willing to talk to her?" She grinned as she listened. "Thank you so much! But have her call Rose's number instead of mine." Then she rattled off my cell number and hung up.

I clasped my shaking hands. Why was I so nervous?

"She says she's sure Hattie will want to talk to you. She was devastated when Dora was killed."

I was silent for a moment. "Thank you."

"What are friends for?" A soft smile lit up her face. "Hattie's momma says she works the night shift. She might not call you until tomorrow, but she'll want to talk to you, so don't worry."

I glanced up at the clock and saw it was close to five. It seemed like an awful long time to wait. "We could search more for the other journal, but I think I should probably get you back to your car so you can go home."

"Yeah." But she didn't look too happy about it.

"You don't want to go home?" I asked in surprise.

"I do...but Ronnie will be there."

Fear lodged in my stomach. Neely Kate and Ronnie were perfect together. But I'd thought the same thing about my sister and her husband. They had faked their happiness so well the dissolution of their marriage had shaken me to the core. Was my best friend having marital problems and I'd missed it? I wasn't sure Neely Kate could handle much more loss. "Are you and Ronnie havin' problems?"

"No. Yes. I don't know." She ran her hand over her head. "He's trying so hard to be supportive."

"How is that bad?"

"It's not. I'm just tired of disappointing him."

I gasped. "Disappointing him? Neely Kate, that man loves you more than life itself. You didn't see him in the waiting room when you were in surgery and we weren't even sure you were even gonna make it. He was devastated. Mason had to take him into the hallway to get him to calm down."

"Because I lost our babies?"

"*No.* Because he couldn't live without you. How is that disappointing him?"

"He wants babies, Rose."

I grabbed her hand. "So you'll get pregnant again and have more. I know it doesn't replace the two babies you lost, but you can try again when you're ready."

She shook her head. "No. I can't."

I stiffened in surprise. "Why not?"

"The doctor said it was a miracle I got pregnant in the first place. He said I have endometriosis and my fallopian tubes are scarred. That's why I had an ectopic pregnancy. Now one of my tubes is gone, and if I get pregnant again, there's a good chance the same thing will happen with the other one."

I stared at her in shock. "Why didn't you tell me?"

She shrugged. "I don't know. I just found out yesterday at my doctor's appointment. And I didn't want to admit that I'm a failure."

That explained why she looked so shaken when I saw her at the Bingo hall that evening. "*A failure?* How can you say that?"

"Ronnie wants kids. He's told me that since we started dating. Now I can't give them to him."

"Neely Kate, I swear to you that Ronnie wants *you*. And you can still have kids." She started to protest, but I kept going. "Maybe not the old-fashioned way, but you can try in vitro. Or you can adopt. There are lots of kids out there who need a home."

"I don't think I'm meant to have kids, Rose." She didn't look upset anymore, simply resigned. "Maybe there's a reason God took those poor innocent babies away from me."

I put my hands on my hips. "Now you're talkin' nonsense. Any baby would be lucky to have you as a mother, Neely Kate Colson." I handed her coat to her. "Come on."

"You tired of me now after all my whining?" she asked, but a tiny spark of mischief lit her eyes.

"I think I've had enough crazy nonsense today to last a lifetime. So don't you be adding more to it."

We headed for the back door. Muffy was asleep in her dog bed, so I left her at home, purposely leaving the alarm off.

Neely Kate was quiet on the drive back to town. I could tell she was tired, both physically and emotionally. I knew she needed a little time to wallow, as I'd need exactly the same thing if I were in her position.

I parked next to her car in front of the landscaping office and she turned to face me. "Rose, thanks for listening. And for not judging me."

"What would I have judged you for?"

She gave me a sheepish grimace. "Drinkin' all those beers at the pool hall this afternoon."

I grinned. "Shoot, everyone deserves to drink a few beers every now and then. I had my turn when I got drunk at Skeeter's pool hall last summer when I was trying to find out if he was Frank Mitchell's bookie. Remember? Mason found me—after *you* sent him—and he threatened to have the pool hall closed, and then he threatened to have me arrested for a DUI if I tried to drive home."

"What are you gonna do about Skeeter?"

It was hard to believe the man I'd met last July was now having me hunted down by one of his guys. Then again, maybe it wasn't so hard to believe. "Hope he cools down sooner rather than later. Maybe Jed will call me soon."

"Let me know if you hear anything—from Jed or Hattie."

"I will." As I watched her get into her car and drive away, I wondered what to do next, but my phone rang and I picked it up, nervous about who might be calling. I breathed a sigh of relief when it was Mason.

"Hey, sweetheart. How was your afternoon?"

"Good. You sound exhausted."

"I am, but my day's not done yet. Joe just called about a homicide south of town and I need to head over to the murder scene. I know you want to talk to me, but I'm not sure how long I'll be. How about you hang out at Mom's until I can get away?"

"They're after *you*, Mason. Not me. I'd rather go home to Muffy. I left her all alone."

"Then call Deputy Miller and tell him you're going home so he can check up on you."

I considered arguing with him, but then I thought of the notes and Merv roaming the streets of Henryetta in search of me. I had to admit, I'd feel better knowing Deputy Miller was there keeping an eye on things. "Be careful," I said. "Okay?"

He chuckled. "I'm going to be surrounded by a bunch of sheriff's deputies. I don't think I can get much safer than that. I'll be home as soon as I can. If I'm late, promise you'll set the alarm."

I made a face, but the alarm system was a better idea than ever right now, so I promised I'd do it and then hung up. I stared at the landscaping office, thinking about Merv hanging around earlier. Jed still hadn't contacted me, but I decided I was sick of sitting around and waiting on other people. I was gonna take the bull by the horns and deal with this head on.

I called Skeeter and he answered on the third ring. "Where the hell are you?" he growled.

I didn't waste any time letting loose. "Why did I see Merv hanging around outside my office on the town square? Someone recognized him, Skeeter!"

"*Who* recognized him?"

I wasn't about to throw Carter Hale under the bus. "Never you mind. I dealt with it, so we're good, but what on earth were you thinkin'? You're smarter than that."

He was surprisingly quiet.

"I'm coming to see you to settle this nonsense. Where are you?"

"I'm at the pool hall, but I don't want you comin' back here. I'll meet you at the Sinclair station in twenty minutes."

"Make it thirty. Now that I know I won't be kidnapped on the streets of Henryetta, I need to get my truck back."

"Fine." He hung up without so much as a goodbye, not that I was surprised. Skeeter wasn't so fond of formalities, but the conversation had me stumped. He was acting surprisingly docile.

I drove to Maeve's, calling her on the way to let her know I was coming to get my truck back. Moments after I parked in the alley behind her house, she came out to greet me. I pushed her garage door opener button so I could pull her car in next to my truck.

"I take it the coast is clear," she said as soon as I climbed out of the car. "You no longer have to hide?"

"No, and while I'm not asking you to lie to Mason, I'd prefer for him not to know about this."

She smiled and handed me the keys for my truck. "Your secret is safe with me. I'll help in any way I can."

I grinned. "Well, in that case I may need you to help with our grocery shopping when things settle down. I hate going to the Peach Orchard store."

"I thought Mason got your Piggly Wiggly shopping rights reinstated."

I grimaced. "He did. Until I lost them again." No need to tell her Mason was the one who'd told them off and pledged never to shop there again.

She laughed. "I'm sure there's a story there you can tell at Sunday dinner. And of course I'll help."

"Thanks." I gave her a hug and waved goodbye as I got into my truck.

I was nervous about meeting Skeeter, and I knew I needed a plan, but darned if I had one. I knew I needed to stick to my guns about quitting the Lady in Black business, but it didn't feel right to renege on our deal, even if he was a criminal. Skeeter was right—it didn't take a genius to see that he was a better option than Daniel Crocker or Mick Gentry.

My anxiety over Maeve's pronouncement had mushroomed too. It had taken me a couple of hours, but I'd figured out the other powerful man in her vision. *Of course* it was Skeeter. Maeve had told me I was supposed to save them both. The visions I'd had for Skeeter seemed to support the theory that his life and Mason's were tied together, and I knew both were likely on Mick Gentry's list. What if playing the role of the Lady in Black was the only way I could save them *both?*

A sedan was backed into the space behind the Sinclair station and Skeeter got out of the driver's door as I pulled in next to him. I was surprised he didn't drive a flashier car. Or a truck.

He opened my door. "Lady."

"Just Rose," I said as I slid off the seat.

Rather than answering, he opened the back door of his car and waited for me get in.

I looked up at him, surprisingly not scared. "Do I need to worry about getting into the back of this car?"

He still didn't answer, his expression guarded. I had no idea where he planned to take me, but I had my Taser in my purse, should I need it. But I wouldn't. Skeeter might be a dangerous man, but I knew there was a different side to him— one I had seen but that he usually hid from the rest of world. Maybe that's why Jed wasn't here with him.

I climbed in, surprised when he slid in next to me. After moving over to let him in, I waited for him to speak. I'd asked for this meeting, but he'd made sure it was held on his turf. I was okay with that. That's where the Lady in Black belonged.

He stared straight ahead for several moments, resting his hands on his knees. When he spoke, he didn't budge his gaze from the windshield. "I may have overreacted this afternoon."

"You think?" I let out a laugh before I realized what I was doing.

He shot me an irritated glance. "I'm trying to apologize and it doesn't come naturally, so cut me some slack."

"Sorry. Go on."

"You're more valuable to me than I think you realize. When you interrogate people for me, you're protected. You're no good to me dead," he said, sounding irritated.

"That's the sweetest thing you could ever say," I teased.

His gaze found mine. "I mean it, Rose."

"Skeeter, I realize—"

"Which is why this won't work."

I froze. "What are you talking about?"

He ran a hand over his head. "You were right. What I did today was stupid. I can't afford stupid. Especially not now. This needs to end."

"What does that mean?"

"I can't let you work for me anymore. It's putting you at risk. Hell, Rich Lowry figured it out at Gems. If *he* knew how valuable you are, it won't take long for anyone else to put it together. Once they do, you're a sitting duck." He shook his head. "Shit, you probably already are." His eyes hardened. "Why didn't you tell me someone tried to run you off the road?"

"How did you—" I shook my head. He had ways of finding out anything, so there was no point in focusing on the "how" of it. "I don't think they were trying to kill *me*. I was driving Mason's car. Whoever has his name on that list was probably behind it."

"Maybe, but I'm not so sure. They could have been after you."

"Why would someone want to kill me?"

"To get to me. To get to Deveraux. To get to that damned deputy sheriff." He cocked his head with an ugly smile. "Should I go on?"

"That's nonsense. No one wants me dead. Especially over you. No one knows I'm helpin' you."

"That's not true. Your boy knows."

"*Bruce Wayne?*" I asked, offended. "And he's not my *boy*. He's my *partner* and business associate. He's scared to death for me, and he wouldn't tell a soul. He's sure you'll get tired of me and put a bullet in my head."

"And you're not worried that I will?" he asked, his words laced with menace.

"No."

"Don't underestimate me, Rose," he said with a low growl.

"You've told me that before, but I'm not scared of you, Skeeter Malcolm. I think *you* underestimate *yourself.*"

His eyes were expressionless as they peered into mine. "I could kill you right now and no one would be the wiser. I know you didn't tell anyone you were meeting me and no one knows I'm here with you."

"Not even Jed?"

"Especially not Jed." He moved closer to me. "I know where his loyalty lies."

For the first time since I'd pulled up, I was nervous. Skeeter didn't suffer disloyalty and his justice was harsh. "What in the world are you talkin' about? Jed is loyal to *you*, Skeeter."

"He's loyal to you first."

I shook my head, tasting bile on tongue. "No, he—"

"I know he called you."

His sentence hung in the air and I struggled to regain control of my racing heart.

He released a heavy breath and leaned over his legs, his face in his hands. "I knew takin' over Crocker's role wouldn't be easy. I expected to fight for my foothold, even after I won it. I thought your talent could help me, but it's only brought me more complications. Now I have disloyalty within my ranks."

I grabbed his beefy bicep, choking on my panic. "Skeeter, please don't hurt him."

He turned to me, surprise in his eyes when he saw my tears. "You care for him?" Jealousy slipped into the end, catching me by surprise. Was he jealous I'd usurped his place with Jed?

"How could I not? He's protected me, Skeeter. He's put his life on the line for me more than once—on your orders!"

"*You love him?*"

His words boomed through the car and I cringed and dropped my hold. "Love him? No! I love Mason."

"Then why do you give a damn what happens to him?"

"Because he's my *friend.*"

"Your friend," he spat out in disgust.

"Why is that so hard to believe? *You're* my friend."

He shook his head with a sneer. "I'm no one's friend."

"Not even Jed's?" I asked in disbelief.

"No."

I stared at him in shock. "Why not?"

"I told you. I can't afford to care about anyone or anything."

My heart was heavy with the implications of what he'd said. "Then what are you fightin' for? What's the point of *any* of this?"

He turned to face the front again, leaning over his legs. "Power."

"Skeeter, listen to me." At first he resisted when I grabbed his hand, but then I tugged it between both of mine. "A year ago, I didn't have friends and I was miserable. My mother had convinced me that I was a terrible person and I didn't deserve happiness. But she was wrong. I don't know who's convinced you otherwise, but they were wrong too."

"Happiness?" he scoffed, trying to jerk his hand away. I wouldn't let him.

"Skeeter, you have to care about someone or something or what's the point of any of this?"

He pulled loose and opened the car door and got out. Leaning over, one hand resting at the top of the door, he said, "It's time for you to go."

"No!" I shouted. "You can't just dismiss me like that, Skeeter! I won't let you."

He leaned his face into the open doorway. "I just did. You've done nothing but throw my world into chaos, Rose Gardner, and I'm done. Get out."

I climbed out, my temper surging. "You know I'm right, but you're too scared to admit it."

"Scared?" he shouted. "I'm not scared of *anything*." His hand curled around my throat, but it was all for show. He'd used more pressure the last time he'd tried this tactic.

"Is that your answer?" I shouted back. "You don't like what I say so you're gonna kill me?"

"Are *you* scared yet?"

"No." I said through gritted teeth. "Go ahead and do it."

His fingers curled tighter as he watched my eyes, then he dropped his hand and spun away, cursing a blue streak.

"Are you ready to talk about this like an adult or are you gonna continue to act like a toddler throwing a tantrum?"

He spun back around to face me, his expression full of bewilderment. Then he dropped his hand, leaned over his legs, and burst out laughing.

I put my hands on my hips, still fuming. "What's so funny?"

He swung a hand toward me as he rose. "You."

I shook my head, trying to come up with a retort.

"There's only one other person in my whole life who has gotten away with talkin' to me like that. Do you wanna know who?"

"Who?"

"My great-grandma Idabelle."

"Well, then it's about damn time, don't you think?"

His laughter died down and he turned solemn.

I walked over to him, stopping a couple of feet away from his chest, and looked up into his face. Part of me questioned why I was doing this. I'd gotten my out. I could have walked away, but I was listening to my instincts, just like Maeve had advised me to do. They were telling me that not only did this man need me, but I needed him too. "I'll continue to work for you as the Lady in Black until you and Mason are no longer in danger, but I have a few conditions."

He threw his hands up in exasperation. "I said I'm cutting you loose."

"No you're not. You need me right now, and I help my friends."

"Friends?" He took several steps back and pointed at me. "I'm not your *friend*."

I advanced toward him, hands on my hips again. "Well, I'm *your* friend, so suck it up and deal with it."

He burst out laughing again, a real belly laugh that filled the cold night air and brought a smile to my face.

"What are your conditions?" he asked when he settled down.

"You're not going to punish Jed."

His face hardened. "I can't entertain disloyalty, Rose. If my men catch wind that I didn't reprimand him, I could have a mutiny on my hands."

"I'm not sure how they'd even find out, but if they do, tell them he works for me now."

He shook his head in confusion. "*What?*"

"If he's going to be my bodyguard whenever I'm with you, then I have to have his total loyalty, right? His job is to protect me. In all things. Even when it comes to you."

He studied me while he scratched his chin. "That works."

I breathed out a sigh of relief.

"What else?"

"You don't have any control over me when I'm not the Lady in Black. You can't boss me around. You can't send Merv all over town lookin' for me."

He watched me for a second. "I'll agree, but I have a condition of my own."

"What's that?"

"I know you're stickin' your nose all over the county sniffin' things out, but from now on, you discuss your extracurricular activities with me."

"What? I just told you that my private business is off limits!"

He gave me a smug smile. "Are you done with your own tantrum?"

I crossed my arms over my chest and jutted out my hip out in response.

He laughed, a genuine laugh, then turned serious. "I meant what I said the other day. I want you as a partner, Rose. While I understand your reluctance to accept payment or reward, I can give you something that you could find more valuable than monetary gain: Information. Protection."

The stiffness left my shoulders. This might work. "I'm listening."

He took a step closer. "I know things in this county. Let me use what I know to help you. And if you're looking into something, I can tell you if you're in danger and send Jed as backup."

I squinted. "You're suggesting that I snoop on a regular basis."

His eyebrows rose and he smirked at me. "Don't you?"

Every time I got wrapped up in an investigation, I told myself that it was a unique situation and it would never happen again. Maybe it was time to accept that these predicaments were part of my life now. "And you're not gonna try to stop me?"

He laughed. "I've learned that trying to stop you is like spitting on a forest fire. So the next best thing I can think to do is offer my assistance. Giving you information isn't illegal. Besides, as I already told you, you're good at this. Why would I stand in the way of a God-given talent?"

"I don't know what to say."

"Say yes. But then I need to know why you were questioning Picklebie and what it has to do with J.R. Simmons."

I had no good reason to keep any of it from him, and I suspected he really could help me. If nothing else, it might be good to get the opinion of someone who understood the criminal mind. "I need full disclosure from you too," I said, still in disbelief that we were coming to this understanding.

"I'll tell you what I think is helpful to you and will protect you." When I started to protest, he held up his hands. "For your own protection, you don't want to know everything. Then you can't be arrested as an accomplice. But I'll tell you more than I would have ordinarily."

That meant I had to trust him, and surprisingly, I did. "Okay."

"So you're agreeing to my partnership?"

I studied him for a moment. "I guess I am."

He moved closer, his mouth pressing into a line as his eyes took on a serious expression. Usually there was a hint of threat in his gaze, but tonight I sensed a certain vulnerability there. He held out his hand. "Rose Gardner, I offer you assistance, guidance, and protection."

I shook his hand. "And I offer you the same."

A twinkle sparked in his eyes. "You think *you* can protect *me?*"

My eyes rose in defiance. "Don't I already?"

He laughed and dropped my hand. "Why do I think this has bad idea written all over it?"

I winked. "Because it probably does." And yet I knew it was one of the best decisions of my life.

"Then let's get to work."

Chapter Twenty-Four

S keeter turned off his car and I grabbed a blanket to set on the bed of my truck. We sat on the tailgate, listening to the silence.

"Why were you questioning Dirk Picklebie?" Skeeter's voice held a gentleness I wasn't used to from him.

"That's kind of a long story."

"Good thing I've got time," he said, pulling a flask from his coat pocket. "Are you sure you don't want to sit inside?" He motioned toward his car with his thumb.

"Nah, I like it out here." I turned to him. "Where do your guys think you are?"

"Probably with a woman." He winked. "And they were right." After taking a swig from the flask, he handed it to me.

I hesitantly took it and lifted it to my nose.

"It's my damn twenty-five-year-old whiskey you keep dolin' out to the deviants of Fenton County. Just take a damned drink." His tone was hard, but I knew he was teasing.

I took a swig and handed back to him, surprised that the warmness in my belly held off the bite of the cold air. "Now I see why they have those little whiskey barrels attached to those St. Bernard dogs in the Alps."

He laughed and took another drink. "Don't tell me you're gonna be givin' my whiskey to your ugly ass dog next."

I turned to him, my mouth open.

He grinned. "Hell, yeah. I know about your dog. I know about your sister and your best friend. I even know about your boyfriend. Both of 'em." He waggled his eyebrows. "I suspect I might know a thing or two more about them than *you* do."

He was probably right, but I wasn't ready to start digging into either of their pasts. Decoding my own history was too much on the forefront of my mind. And I wasn't surprised or even offended Skeeter had researched me. I knew Jed had conducted his own investigation of me in the name of protecting Skeeter.

"My dog's not ugly."

"Okay," he snickered. "If you say so."

"She has her own special...charm."

He just grinned at me.

"You think you're so smart, Skeeter Malcolm," I said, giving him a smug glare. "Tell me what you know about me."

He rattled off a bunch of facts, including my birthdate, Momma and Daddy's names, my work history. It made me realize what a wonderful resource he could turn out to be. When he finished, I grabbed his flask out of his pocket. He gave me an amused look as I took a drink.

"You got part of it wrong." Surprise wrinkled his forehead, making me laugh. "My parentage."

"How did I get it wrong?"

"Well." I took another sip of the whiskey. "What I'm about to tell you is one of my deepest darkest secrets. You can't tell a soul."

He held up his fingers in a boy scout pledge and I burst out into laughter. "Who are you trying to fool, Skeeter Malcolm? You already told me you weren't a boy scout."

"I said I'm not a boy scout *now*. You think I was always gunnin' to run the organized crime world of Fenton County?"

"I bet you were placin' bets in elementary school over who brought pudding in their lunch."

He laughed again. "You aren't far off. Now tell me this deep dark secret of yours."

"My momma wasn't my birth mother." And with that, I told him the whole sordid tale, and I was surprised by how relieved I was to share it with him. He listened to it all, showing interest but keeping quiet. It occurred to me that this was how a man like him found out things. By paying attention. He continued to drink from his flask, offering me sips until it was gone and I was fuzzy-headed.

When I finally finished talking, I waited for his reaction. It took him a full five seconds to say, "Damn."

I sighed. "Dora died in a car accident and the police investigated and said it was an accident. But there were rumors her brake lines had been cut, and my Aunt Bessie said her death was suspicious. Joe didn't think much of it, though, and Mason's been too busy with other projects to do much."

"So you decided to your own digging."

"Only after I found out Dora used to work for Atchison Manufacturing. The factory was never reopened after it burned down in a fire, and there might have been an extortion case tied up in the whole mess of it closing."

"So you were trying to clear your mother of a crime that happened twenty-five years ago, one that nobody gives a shit about anymore?"

"No." I took a breath and looked him in the eye. "I'm trying to find out the truth about my mother. Only the deeper I dig, the more complicated it gets," I said, smoothing back stray hairs the wind blew into my face.

"How does J.R. Simmons come into play?"

"Dirk told me he was the investor who gave them money to switch the product line at the factory. He also says Dora was the one to introduce her boss, Henry Buchanan, to J.R." I told him about the parts and how they were faulty. About the suspicious coincidence of the fire breaking out the night before the parts were to be shipped, followed by the death of the police chief, my mother's accident, and Henry Buchanan's suicide. I even considered telling him about my new uncertainty about my birth father, but he didn't need to know that part. "Dirk had some part in it all. I forced a vision before he left the pool hall, and I saw him calling a woman named Beverly after. He admitted to having taken a bribe to keep quiet and he told her about sharing his story with me and Neely Kate. He's scared that I'm digging. Now I need to find out who this Beverly is."

"What if Dora or your father really did start the fire? How's it gonna help for you to know? Maybe you should just let sleepin' dogs lie."

I shook my head. "I've gotten this far. I want to keep goin'."

"Okay," he said, scratching his chin. "Your call. I'll have Jed check into Picklebie and see if he can identify Beverly."

"Thanks."

He nodded.

"So what's *your* interest in J.R. Simmons?" I asked.

A slow grin spread across his face. "Apparently, Old Man Simmons has it out for me."

"What's that mean?"

"It means I'm on his most expendable list."

"He wants you *dead?*"

"So your boyfriend says."

I blinked. "*Mason?*"

"He called me the day after Christmas and offered me full immunity if I dished on why J.R. wanted me dead. To make me a deal like that, he has to be desperate to take the guy down."

My mouth dropped open. Mason had an early morning meeting the day after Christmas that he kept top-secret from me and had instigated a huge fight between us. Had he found out something while he was in Little Rock the week before? "He was desperate...is desperate." I looked into his face. "He's trying to save *me*."

"*You?*"

I gasped. "What if J.R. Simmons is the man behind the list? What if he's telling Gentry what to do?"

"Why would Simmons want your boyfriend dead? And what is Deveraux trying to save you *from?*"

"J.R. Simmons has falsified evidence suggesting I hired Daniel Crocker to kill Momma. He used it to blackmail Joe into running for the Arkansas Senate. Joe ran and lost, but Mason is terrified J.R.'s going to hand over the evidence on a whim. He's determined to do everything in his power to bring J.R. down."

Skeeter stared at me, a hard glint in his eyes. "You won't have to worry about Simmons for long."

"Why not?" Fear clenched my stomach. "What are you doin'?"

He leaned close and patted my cheek. "This is one of those instances where the less you know, the better." He hopped off the truck bed. "I've been gone too long. I need to get back."

I followed after him. "Skeeter!"

He turned back to look at me. "I set this into motion before I knew about the connection between you and J.R., so I'm not doing it for you. But knowing he's trying to hurt you only makes me more determined." He opened my truck door. "Are you safe to drive?"

I waved him off. Maybe I was becoming more tolerant to his whiskey or maybe it was our serious conversation, but I no longer had a buzz. "Skeeter, please don't do anything stupid."

He grinned. "I could say the same to you. If you think you're heading into something dangerous, call Jed." His eyebrows rose. "And let me know if you get any more information."

"Okay."

I drove home, surprised it was already almost eight o'clock. I called Deputy Miller on the way. He was in the northern part of the county, so he pulled into my driveway a minute after I did.

He checked the house inside and out and then walked me to the front porch after Muffy did her business outside. "We're short-handed with the double murder investigation south of town. I can't stick around tonight."

I gave him a smile. "I'm sure I'll be fine."

"Mr. Deveraux said to be sure you turn on your alarm."

I laughed. "He knows I hate that thing, but I made him a promise. Any idea when Mason will be done?"

"No." He looked grim. "It's a gruesome crime scene."

I sure didn't want any details. "You be careful, Deputy Miller."

He grinned. "Will do."

After I turned on the alarm, I heated up some of the leftover noodles from a couple of nights ago and watched TV with Muffy. I considered texting Neely Kate about my heart-to-heart meeting with Skeeter, but I knew she was with Ronnie. I hoped they'd be able to have a real talk about what happened and their feelings about it.

Around ten o'clock Mason called and said he was going to be another hour.

"Are you okay?" he asked. "Do you feel safe?"

I smiled. "I'm *fine*. Deputy Miller checked the house and I set the alarm. I just need to take Muffy out."

"Wait until I come home and I'll take her out."

That seemed counterproductive considering someone wanted Mason dead—not me—but I wasn't going to argue the point. "Come home to me safe, Mason."

"I will." His voice lowered. "This afternoon I found out I have a meeting I can't miss late tomorrow. I'm not sure if going to my uncle's cabin this weekend is going to work out."

He would be even less likely to want to leave town once I told him everything I'd discovered. But I didn't want to get into any of it on the phone. "We can talk about it later. Okay?"

"Sounds good. See you in a bit."

I checked the alarm and made a cup of tea. I figured I could read in bed while I waited for Mason. But I soon dozed off.

I woke up to Mason snuggling against my back, his arm wrapped around my stomach as he nuzzled my neck.

"You're home," I murmured, trying to rouse myself awake.

"I missed you," he whispered, his breath warm against my cheek.

I rolled over and wrapped my arm around his neck, my mouth finding his in the dark.

"I'm exhausted," he murmured against my lips. "But if you continue to kiss me like that, I'm bound to make a recovery."

I could feel the proof of his recovery against my leg. "I *do* love a challenge."

Chapter Twenty-Five

I woke up the next morning to the sound of a door squeaking. Mason stood in front of the open closet, his hair wet, pulling out a shirt. He was already wearing a pair of dress pants.

"You're up," I said lazily. "Why didn't you wake me?"

He slipped his arms into his shirt, his gaze on me. "You were sleeping so soundly. I didn't want to disturb you."

"You have to go in early?"

"Yeah. I have a meeting at the sheriff's office."

I stretched, accidentally pulling the covers to my waist. The cold air hit my bare skin, making me shiver. I was about to reach for the covers when I noticed he was grinning at me.

"I *do* love to see you naked in our bed."

"Come join me." I kicked the covers all the way off and lifted my arms over my head as I faked another stretch.

He abandoned buttoning his dress shirt and pulled a tie out of the closet before he walked to the edge of the bed and sat down. Leaning over, he kissed me passionately and fondled my breasts, then lifted his head to give me an ornery grin.

"What was that?" I asked, coming to my senses.

"I've hardly seen you the last couple of days. I don't want you to forget about me today."

I laughed as I sat up and fastened his last two buttons. "I think you're safe."

He wrapped an arm around my back and pulled me to his chest to kiss me again. I was beginning to have second thoughts about buttoning him up.

He lifted his head, grinning again.

"And what was *that?*" I teased.

"To give me something to think about during my morning meeting."

I took his tie and looped it around his neck. "What's your meeting about?" I asked, expecting him to give me a vague answer about Fenton County business.

"The murders from yesterday."

I started to knot his tie. "Deputy Miller said it was gruesome."

He cringed. "I wish he hadn't told you that. You have enough to worry about without hearing about a horrific double homicide."

"I'm fine." I slipped the knot to the base of his throat and smoothed out a wrinkle on his chest. "He didn't give me any details."

"Good. I'm sure I'll have nightmares for weeks after what I saw."

I shivered and his arms tightened around my back, pulling me to his chest again. "Be careful today. Joe thinks it might be tied to Skeeter Malcolm."

I jerked away as a cold chill washed through me. "What?"

"Scott Humphrey was a known adversary of Malcolm's. It looks like Humphrey and Marcus Tilton, one of his cronies, were tortured in an abandoned barn south of town."

I closed my eyes. I didn't know Marcus Tilton, but I'd questioned Humphrey a few days ago. Had I gotten him killed? Would Skeeter have tortured him to get his answers?

"Rose?" His hand brushed my cheek and I opened my eyes to see worry on his face. "Are you okay? You're as white as our sheets and you're shaking."

I forced a smile. "I'm sorry I'm bein' such a baby. It's just hard to imagine something like that happening in Fenton County."

"Thankfully, it's pretty rare, but Joe is determined to find out who did this and get them off the streets."

I nodded, but I was lightheaded. "Thank goodness."

"Rose, you're more shaken up about this than I expected." Understanding lit up his eyes. "Are you scared because of our encounter with Malcolm back in December?"

I shook my head. "No. Of course not." Mason and I had seen Skeeter while we were out for breakfast. Skeeter had tormented Mason by paying attention to me, which had in turn caused Mason to panic that I was in harm's way. "Why would I be concerned? I'm nothing to Skeeter Malcolm."

His thumb brushed my cheek as he searched my eyes. "I'm not so sure. He has it out for me. He might use you to get to me."

Little did Mason realize how safe I was. "Mason, Skeeter Malcolm has bigger fish to fry than me. I'm fine. I just overreacted."

"Maybe you should stay home today."

I groaned. Why hadn't I hid my shock? Now I was making him worry over nothing. "I can't. I promised Violet that I'd cover for her at the nursery this morning. She has a doctor's appointment."

"Doctor's appointment? Is she sick?"

Now that he mentioned it, I hadn't asked. "I'm sure it's just a check-up, but the new girl can't handle the nursery on her own yet."

He gave me a gentle kiss. "I'm sure *I'm* the one overreacting now. But if anything happened to you—" He gave me an apologetic look. "I'm sorry, but I think we need to cancel our trip to my uncle's cabin."

"Mason, it's okay."

He shook his head, his eyes full of sadness. "No, it's not. Not really. I keep canceling things on you. I'm giving you the message that you're not important to me."

I grabbed both sides of his face. "I assure you, that couldn't be further from the truth." I still hadn't told him about my own discoveries and now he didn't have time to hear them. "I know how much you love me. I'm counting on it."

He kissed me again, giving me a good idea of what he had in mind to help fill our time if we had gone to the cabin. When he leaned back he shifted on the bed and gave me an ornery grin. "I better go before I lose all volition to leave your side."

I gave him a look of mock reprimand. "We can't have you getting in trouble, so get goin' and I'll see you tonight."

He started to get up, then sat back down. "You wanted to talk to me about something."

I wanted to tell him everything, but I didn't want to make him late or give him the thirty-second version. Besides, it wouldn't make much of a difference if he found out now or tonight, would it? I rubbed his chest, staring into his eyes. "It can wait. I'll tell you later."

He looked at his watch, then back at me, clearly torn.

"Mason. I promise. It's okay." I offered him a smile to assure him. "I love you."

He gave me another kiss, then stood, taking in the sight of my naked body. "My mind will definitely not be on my work."

I pulled the covers up to my chin, grinning. "Go."

"I'll take Muffy out before I go."

"Now I really love you."

"Come on, Muff." He headed out the bedroom door, Muffy racing after him. As soon as I heard the door open and close downstairs, I grabbed my phone off the nightstand, intent on sending Skeeter a text. My own investigation paled in comparison to the double murder. I couldn't believe the man I had come to know, the man who'd assured me he was the least dangerous ruler of all the criminals in Fenton County, would do such a thing. So why did I need his reassurance that he hadn't?

But when I pulled out my phone to type a message, I was surprised to see a text from a number I didn't recognize, which had come in at around midnight.

I heard you would like to meet with me to talk about Dora. How about we meet for lunch at Big Bill's Barbecue before I head to the hospital for my shift? Say 1:00? –Hattie

In all the excitement of the morning, I'd forgotten I was waiting to hear back from her. I texted back.

I'll be wearing a black wool coat and a red scarf.

I got out of bed and pulled on my robe, putting my phone in the pocket before I headed downstairs to start a pot of coffee. I was at the base of the stairs when the front door swung open, and Mason's head poked in as Muffy raced toward the kitchen.

"I'm headed out, sweetheart. Lock the door and turn on the alarm after I leave."

I rolled my eyes. "Go already." I gave him a quick kiss, then shut the door behind him and locked it, watching through the window as he climbed into his car and took off. After I started the coffee, I found the courage to text Skeeter, hoping he would understand my message if I kept it vague.

Did you have anything to do with the incident south of town?

About thirty seconds passed before my phone rang, SM showing up on the screen.

"Did you?" I asked without bothering to preface it with a greeting.

"Not my style." He sounded gruff. And offended. "Do you believe me?"

I knew he had his own style of justice, but I didn't believe torture was part of his repertoire. Or maybe I just couldn't connect the man I'd shared my troubles with last night to a man who would condone such a thing. "Yes, I believe you, but the sheriff thinks you did it."

"Shit." He was quiet for a few moments. "Do they have any hard evidence linking me to it?"

My temper flared. "Why would you be asking that if you weren't a part of it?"

"Because someone is probably setting it up to look like I was!" he barked. "Just like that damn knife in your boyfriend's desk drawer."

I pushed out a breath, feeling guilty about accusing him after I'd just finished saying I believed him. And he was right. Back in December, the farmhouse had been broken into and Mason's office had been rifled through. Joe had found a pocketknife that belonged to Skeeter, although neither Joe nor Mason had actually believed he'd left it there. "So who do you think did it?"

"Gentry? The person pulling the strings behind the hit list? Although I can't figure out why anyone would go to the trouble of framing me if they want me dead."

I had to agree. It didn't make a lick of sense. "What are you gonna do?"

"Nothing for now. If you hear anything—"

"I'll let you know." I was surprised I didn't feel more guilt over betraying Mason and Joe, but the way I saw it, Skeeter could possibly be in the exact same situation as Bruce Wayne the summer before, and *he'd* been a total stranger when I helped him. Hopefully, this would all blow over and that would be the last piece of information I'd pass along. But I didn't believe that for a New York minute.

I finished getting ready and thought about the second journal. Dora's message to Bill had been to look for the journal in *the room*. What room would she mention without specifically identifying it? The police chief would have to know where to look. My gaze drifted to the sheer-covered windows that overlooked the nursery that had been set up for me on the sun porch.

Crappy doodles, I was an idiot.

According to her journal, everything she'd done was for me.

I ran through the door and started opening drawers, rummaging around through all the baby clothes. When I didn't see anything, I started pulling the drawers out and dumping their contents onto the floor. Still nothing.

I grunted in frustration. If I didn't leave soon, I was going to be late. Where would Dora have hidden it? Then I remembered the gun tucked under own bed.

Could it really be that easy?

I dropped to the floor and rolled onto my back, scooting under the dusty baby bed. There, taped to the frame in the corner, was a book. I fought with the tape and worked the book loose, then quickly flipped through the pages.

It was filled with numbers and dates and marks that looked like they could be shorthand, marks secretaries used to use when taking dictation. Unfortunately, I had no idea how to read it. I needed more time to look it over, but I was already running late.

I climbed off the floor and tried to brush off the dirt and grime that had accumulated over twenty-five years, but soon realized it was a hopeless case. So I stripped off the sweater and pulled on another. Then, clutching the journal to my chest, I raced down the stairs and into the kitchen to set the alarm.

I stuffed the book into my purse with the other journal and ran out the door. Muffy hung her head with a major pout. Against my better judgment, I had decided to leave her at home. Between covering for Violet and my lunch with Hattie, I would be busy and I didn't want to worry about leaving her at the office or the nursery.

My phone rang as I climbed in the truck, and I answered as I started down the driveway, not surprised to see it was Neely Kate.

"Hey," I answered, focusing on the traffic on the highway as I waited to turn left.

"Rose, I think I'm going to stay home today."

"That's fine," I said, worried by the strange tone of her voice. "Is everything okay?"

"Ronnie's taking off and we're going to spend the day together."

"That's a good thing, right?"

"Yeah." But she didn't sound so sure.

"Neely Kate, Ronnie loves you. *You.* You *have* to believe that."

"I know."

I considered telling her about finding the other journal and my meeting with Hattie, but I had a sneaking suspicion she might desert Ronnie to come join me. Ronnie had to be her first priority right now. "I love you too. Everything's gonna work out. You just *have* to believe it. I'm here for you. Just let me know if you need me."

"I love you too, Rose."

I hung up, more worried about my friend than ever.

I had hoped to stop by the landscaping office and check on Bruce Wayne, but I was barely going to make it to the nursery on time to cover for Violet as it was. Instead, I called him.

"How'd it go at the nursery yesterday?" I asked.

He paused. "Good."

"Violet was thankful you helped her. Was she nice to you?"

"Yeah. If she needs more help, I wouldn't mind goin' over."

I couldn't stop my smile of happiness. "The new girl, Anna, seems nice."

"Yeah," he choked out.

I chuckled. "I'm covering for Violet this morning while she goes to the doctor. I'm excited to get to know Anna better."

He coughed. "Um, I think I found a good deal on some woodchip mulch, but we have to buy it in bulk, and we'll need a place to store it."

"Huh." Obviously he was changing the subject, and I wanted to encourage his potential new relationship, not detour it. "Do you have a place in mind?"

"I do." He cleared his throat. "But I'm scared you'll read more into my answer than you should."

I grinned. "The nursery? That's actually a good idea. The north side of the lot with the new greenhouse would probably work. Since we're working out of an office and there's some empty space on the nursery lot, it seems logical for us to keep a few things there. Besides, Violet can sell some of the mulch too." This splitting off the landscaping business from the nursery was bound to get messy at times.

"Then I'm goin' to order it. And I'll let you tell Violet it's coming."

"Scared?" I chuckled.

"No sense pushing my luck now that she's toleratin' me."

I shook my head even if he couldn't see it. "I can handle Violet." I pulled into the parking lot and parked in a space on the side of the building. "And speaking of my sister, I've gotta get goin'."

When I walked into the nursery, Violet took one look at me, then shot a glance toward the clock.

"I'm on time, Vi," I said, plopping my bag on the counter.

She lifted her eyebrows but didn't comment. Okay, she'd told me to be there at 9:40 and I'd shown up at 9:42. She bent down and pulled out her purse, looping it over her elbow. "At least you remembered."

I would have offered a retort if I hadn't almost forgotten, but Violet read between the lines and shot me a teasing grin.

Anna stood on the other side of the store with a watering pitcher in her hand, eyeing us with interest.

Violet glanced at Anna before returning her gaze to me. "I like this girl, Rose Anne Gardner. So please don't corrupt her." I started to protest, but then she winked. "Bye." She waggled her fingers as she walked out the door.

Who was this woman who claimed to be my sister? She'd told me she was going to change and from all appearances, she was making great strides. I hated being at odds with her, so I only hoped this phase would last. I watched her climb into her car, wondering what had finally pushed her into making the effort. Could the thought of irreparably harming our relationship have been enough of an incentive?

I heard the clink of a knick-knack moving on a glass shelf and turned to look at my sister's new employee. Anna eyed me with a seriousness I hadn't expected. Then I realized she'd taken Violet's words to heart.

"Don't listen to Violet. She was just joking around."

She nodded and gave me a meek look, her shoulders slumped, but I saw a determination in her eyes that belied her body language. There was a story there. I was curious, of course, but I could hardly begrudge someone else for choosing to keep a secret. Especially when I had so many of my own.

"Violet tells me you're new to Henryetta," I said, moving around behind the counter and opening my bag.

"Yeah."

"Where are you from originally?"

"Mississippi."

"Do you have family here?"

"No." The force behind the word told me to back off.

I pursed my lips in surprise. It still struck me as strange that anyone would move to Henryetta without an honest-to-God reason for it, but she was apparently not in the mood to discuss it. "Well, I hope you like it here in Henryetta."

"Thank you," she murmured, going back to her watering task.

We only had a few customers over the next hour, but Anna greeted each one with a bright smile and sunny disposition. It was enough of a contrast to make me question whether she held a grudge against me, although for the life of me, I couldn't figure out why she would. But her helpfulness gave me plenty of time to work on my landscape designs. I considered scouring the recently discovered journal, but I was paranoid enough not to want random strangers to see the book. I had begun to price out the designs when the door tinkled, and I heard a voice that made my shoulders tense.

"Well, hello, Rose," Hilary said, gliding through the door. "I didn't expect to see you here." She lifted her eyebrows as she scrutinized me. "But I have to say the apron doesn't suit you. You seem more at home in the muck and dirt."

Anna was restocking a shelf a few feet away and her mouth parted in worry as she looked at Hilary.

I was going to be nice to her if it killed me. "Good morning, Hilary. I'm surprised to see you here."

"I just got finished with my doctor's appointment. Before I went home, I thought I'd spend a few dollars to help keep your *business*—" she glanced around with disgust, "—afloat." She waved her hand. "Supporting local stores and all that."

"How generous of you," I said with a sweet smile. "If you decide you'd like to get a job like the rest of us, I hear they're hiring at the Stop-N-Go." So much for my resolve to be nice.

She laughed and began to peruse the shelves. "You're so cute." But her tone suggested otherwise. She rubbed her small baby bump. "In any case, my appointment went well. The baby's heartbeat is strong and I'm about to enter my second trimester. Before you know it, Joe and I will know if we're having a boy or a girl." She gave me a dazzling smile, and despite the malicious intent behind her litany, I could see happiness in her eyes. She really did want this baby.

I wasn't sure what she wanted me to say, so I bit my tongue.

"Where's Violet?" she asked, looking around.

"She's at a doctor's appointment."

"Oh?" she asked in surprise. "At the Henryetta Family Clinic? I didn't see her there. She must have been in an exam room." She shrugged. "Isn't that funny? I could have just asked her at the doctor's office."

"Asked her what?"

She beamed. "To decorate the nursery. Since I'll be finding out the baby's sex soon, I'm eager to start planning the room. I hear Violet has a fabulous eye."

"*What?*" Had she lost her mind?

But she'd gotten exactly the reaction she'd hoped for. "I have connections with *Inviting Arkansas* magazine. I'm sure I can get them to do a spread on my nursery and how Violet is an up and coming decorator. Her business will start booming."

Oh my word. She was right. Based on what Violet had told me, *Inviting Arkansas* was *the* high society state magazine and the Simmonses were in it often. The exposure could bring enough money to keep both of our businesses afloat.

An evil glint flashed through Hilary's eyes. "You wouldn't want to get in the way of your sister's success, would you, Rose?" Rather than waiting for an answer, she turned and pretended to look at the merchandise. "Violet picked out all of this, didn't she? She really does have good taste. It's too bad she's wasted here in Fenton County."

Anna had been silently watching our exchange, but when Hilary began to prowl, she moved around a display stand, keeping her distance.

Smart girl.

Hilary turned her attention to Anna and stopped in her tracks, looking puzzled. I wondered if she kept close enough tabs on the nursery's doings to know if we'd hired employees in the past. My back stiffened as I prepared to come to Anna's defense, but Hilary moved on. She walked around the store, looking less purposeful now, as if Anna had somehow thrown her off her game. After she'd made a circuit around the shop, she spun around to face me. "Tell Violet to give me a call. She has my number."

My mouth dropped open as she abruptly left the store. *Violet had her number?*

I looked up and Anna held my gaze for less than a second, then returned her attention to the outdoor thermometers she was shelving. "She seems evil."

"Yeah," I murmured, but part of me wondered. Hilary was scared; I could feel it in her desperation to get Joe back. And while part of me felt sorry for her, part of me had begun to fear her. When a wild animal was scared, it was unpredictable and dangerous. I had a feeling Hilary was no different.

But even more unsettling was the carrot she was going to dangle in front of my sister, and the insinuation that there was already some sort of groundwork between them. I told myself not to jump to conclusions. Hilary loved to create drama and trouble. I needed to talk to my sister.

It was close to twelve-thirty before Violet returned to the store. I'd already sent Anna to lunch. Violet was a lot less perky when she walked through the door, her gaze down. Without saying a word, she walked around the counter and picked up her apron. "Thanks for covering," she finally said as she pulled the loop over her head.

I stared at her for a good three seconds before I snapped out of my surprise. "What did the doctor say?"

"What?" she asked absently while tying the apron.

"The doctor? Didn't you have an appointment at the Henryetta Family Clinic?"

"Oh." She gave me a smile, but I could recognize a fake smile on her even when no one else could. Too many years of both of us trying to placate Momma. "Everything's fine."

"Then what took so long?"

"The waiting room was full. It took me over an hour and a half to get in."

She was lying.

Hilary said she'd been there all morning and hadn't seen my sister. Of course, Hilary was no stranger to lying, but what purpose would it serve in this situation? And I couldn't ignore how oddly Violet was behaving.

"Violet, are you sure everything is okay?"

"Everything is *fine*," she snapped. There was fire in her eyes when she lifted her gaze, but I saw fear there too. What in the world was going on?

"Hilary stopped by to see you."

"Oh?" she murmured, rummaging through a stack of papers.

"She wants you to call her."

"Okay." Then she looked up. "Did she say why?"

She didn't deny having her number. "She wants you to decorate her baby's nursery."

Her head snapped up. "What?"

"She said she thinks she could get *Inviting Arkansas* to do a story on the nursery decor."

Hope lit up her eyes, but resignation replaced it just as quick. "Well, Hilary can take her nursery and shove it up—"

I squared my shoulders. "I think you should do it."

"What?" she asked in disbelief. "Have you lost your mind? That woman tricked Joe into getting her pregnant and she's doin' her level best to not only ruin his life but yours too."

I grabbed her shoulders. "Violet, listen to me. This is huge. It could save both of our businesses."

She shook her head. "We don't need her help."

I gave her a soft smile, then lowered my voice. "We *do*. We're hurting financially. I'm totally living off Mason right now, but for all we know, he could lose his job soon. The district attorney's as crooked as a dog's hind leg. The landscaping business won't start bringing in money for a few months, and even then it's gonna take some time for it to turn a profit. This job could mean the difference between losing everything and flourishing."

She shook her head again. "Joe won't let us lose it all. He'll put in more money."

"Violet, I don't want him to put more money into it. We're friends now, but we can't have him keep dumping money into our business."

"So you want to jump into a partnership with the spawn of Satan?" she asked in horror. "How is that any better?"

She was right. But still... "I saw the look of excitement in your eyes," I said. "You want to do it."

"I won't deny I'm tempted, but you come first, Rose. I won't betray you again. I swear it." The look in her eyes told me she meant every word.

"Violet, I think you should consider the opportunity. Talk to her and hear what she has to say. Then if you like, you and I can talk it over before you make a final decision."

"I won't hurt you again, Rose." Tears filled her eyes. "I don't want to lose you."

I wrapped my arms around her and pulled her close. "Vi, you have no idea how much that means to me. But I'm tellin' you that I want you to hear her out first."

"Okay."

I kissed her cheek and looked into her eyes. "And I promise you that you won't lose me. We'll still be sisters no matter what." Even if it turned out Daddy wasn't my real birth father, it wouldn't change the years we'd clung to each other as little girls. We had a bond that couldn't be broken. It wasn't determined by blood.

She squinted. "What's goin' on?" Just like I could pick out a fake smile, she could read me too.

"I'll tell you about it later." I glanced at the clock and untied my apron, tossing it on the stool. "But now I'm late for an appointment."

"What kind of appointment?" she asked as I grabbed my coat.

"An appointment with the truth."

There were far too many secrets in this town and it was time to clear this one up, no matter how bad it hurt.

Chapter Twenty-Six

I pulled into the parking lot of Big Bill's Barbecue right at one. The lunch crowd had begun to thin a bit, but it was still as packed as a tin of sardines. It didn't seem like the best place to hold a personal conversation, but maybe Hattie wanted plenty of people around. She didn't know anything about me or even if I were telling the truth. For all she knew, I was a serial killer.

There was a chill in the air, so I tightened my red scarf and headed for the door, but before I could even make it to the sidewalk, a car door opened and a middle-aged woman got out. I relaxed when I saw how closely she resembled the photo in Dora's yearbook.

"Rose?"

I smiled, my stomach a bundle of nerves. "Yes."

"I'm Hattie." She was shorter and heavier than me, and her light brown hair was streaked with gray. She looked wary.

"Thank you for meeting me. I know you don't know me."

"I do. Kind of. I kept track."

I sucked in a breath. "You know about me?"

"I was Dora's best friend. Of course I kept track of her baby."

"How?"

The corners of her mouth tipped up and she said softly, "Harrison."

An unexpected surge of anger raced through my veins and tears pricked my eyes. "So you know how horribly my mother treated me?" When she didn't answer, a tear slid down my cheek. "Did you?"

Her eyes hardened. "Agnes Gardner was *not* your mother."

I began to shake. "Agnes Gardner was the only mother I ever knew. Dora Middleton may have wanted my life to be full of love and happiness, but that couldn't have been further from what happened." My temper flared again. "How many people watched me live through that hell and *just stood by to watch it happen?*"

Contrition filled her eyes. "I'm sorry. We wanted to protect you. I did what I thought was best."

"And that's supposed to make everything I went through *better?*"

People were openly staring at us. I was already enough of a spectacle in this town, so I didn't need any more fuel to add to the fire. "Why are we doin' this here?" I asked. Then I realized my previous assumption about her motives were wrong. She'd already admitted that she knew all about me. She knew I was harmless. By meeting someplace so public, she'd hoped to avoid a scene.

I turned around and stomped off to my truck, aggravated with myself for leaving, but not trusting myself to stay either. I wasn't sure I could go through with this.

Hattie slammed her car door shut and hurried after me. "Rose, please don't go. *Please.* I have so much to tell you. Information you need to know." When I kept walking, she said, "Your life may depend on it."

Now she had my attention, but then again, that had been her intent. I fought back my tears and spun around to face her, squaring my shoulders. "What are you talkin' about?"

She moved closer. "Did you find Dora's journals?"

"Yes... Why?"

"*Both* of them?"

I didn't answer, suddenly unsure that I should trust her.

Her eyes looked wild and a little desperate. In my ever-growing experience, that was never a good thing.

"Oh, God. *You did. You found it.*" Tears filled her eyes. "Of course you did. She was your momma. It makes sense you'd have a special bond."

I had no bond to Dora Middleton other than the inheritance she'd left me, which was starting to feel like a double-edged sword.

Hattie sucked in a breath, as though trying to regain her composure. "Did you read them? I'm sure you did. Harrison never told you anything about Dora. You would want to know about your momma."

I still didn't answer.

"There's more to those books than meets the eye." She paused and looked into my eyes. "Go get the coded one and bring it to Atchison Manufacturing."

As she made the suggestion, it suddenly hit me how odd it was that I hadn't thought to go there since this had all begun. But then again, what could I hope to find there now? It was nothing but a burned-up shell of a building. Any clues to the truth would be long gone. Still, I found myself saying, "All right."

She smiled, tears in her eyes. "Thank you."

"I'll meet you there." She didn't know I had them with me and I was still too angry to let her into my truck. I didn't trust her enough to climb into her car.

She hesitated. "You know how to get there?" She looked nervous.

"Yeah." That was a weird question. Everyone in town knew how to get there. My trust in her dropped even more. Something about this situation didn't add up.

"I don't want anyone to see us together. Give me a five-minute head start." She took off for her car and part of me screamed to run to Mason and tell him everything. I decided to listen this time.

Hattie took off and I grabbed my phone, not wanting to waste any time before calling Mason. But his cell phone went straight to voice mail and when I called his office, his secretary answered.

"He got called into an arraignment. Then he said he had a meeting afterward."

Oh, Lordy. Had they arrested Skeeter? "Do you know what it was for?"

"A robbery case," she murmured. "You don't usually ask about those things."

"I'm just trying to be a good girlfriend and find out more about Mason's work. Thanks, Kaylee." I hung up before I could make myself sound even more suspicious.

I called Joe next, no hesitation, but he answered sounding breathless. "Are you in trouble?"

"No." I wasn't. Not technically.

"Can I call you back in about an hour? I'm up to my elbows in shit at the moment." He sounded really pissed.

"Sure. Don't worry."

My stomach rumbled as I stared at the run-down restaurant. I was starving and I had no idea what to do, so I decided to stall and get some lunch. While I stood in line waiting to order, I ran through the whole sorry situation in my head. Something Hattie had said niggled at me. Why did Hattie and Daddy think keepin' my parentage a secret was *protecting* me? Protecting me from what?

Oh crap.

I left the lunch line and called Jed as I ran to my truck.

"Rose?" He sounded surprised to hear from me.

"Skeeter told me that if I ever found myself in a dangerous predicament, I should give you a call."

"Are you?" His voice was tight.

"Not yet, but something doesn't seem right. I'd feel better knowing that you were close by."

"Where are you?"

"I'm headed to the old Atchison Manufacturing building."

"Why?"

"I'm meeting someone who knows secrets about my past. I had intended to tell Mason and Joe, but both of them are busy. Anyway, after I got to thinkin' about it, I realized this seems more like a job for you. I don't think the woman I'm meeting would tell Mason or Joe anything, and then I might never learn what I need to know."

"You think she'll tell me?"

"No, I think she'll tell *me,* especially if she doesn't know you're there."

I expected him to put up an argument. "You said you're headed there now?"

"Yeah."

"The Sinclair station is on the way. Meet me there and I'll get into the backseat of your truck. Otherwise she might see me drive up."

"Hey, that's a good idea," I said in surprise.

He chuckled. "I've done this a time or two."

I hung up and dug a granola bar out of my purse, left over from when Neely Kate had been pregnant and hungry all the time in between waves of nausea. It was the first time a granola bar had ever made me feel guilty. I considered calling her to update her on the situation, but she'd only worry and maybe try to come. I wasn't sure Hattie posed a real danger, but I wasn't willing to take the risk.

When the Sinclair station appeared, I slowed down and was about to turn in when I saw a sheriff car pull out. My stomach dropped to my feet when I recognized Joe. Thankfully, he seemed intent on getting out of there and kept going, but I wasn't so lucky with the next car that pulled out from behind the station.

Mason recognized me straight away and his mouth parted in surprise. He motioned me over and we both parked in front of the building. My heart seemed to be beating out of my chest as I tried to figure out what to tell him.

He got out of his car and walked over, looking more guilty than accusatory. What had he and Joe been up to?

I rolled down my window. "Hey, Mason. What are you doin' all the way out here?"

He cast a glance toward the direction Joe had gone before returning his gaze to me. "You know I love you, right?" The fear in his eyes scared me.

I pushed open the truck door and slid out, standing in front of him. "Mason, what's goin' on?"

He shook his head. "I'm not sure. But we really need to get out of town this weekend. You can still get away, right?"

"But this morning you said you couldn't leave." Fear stole my breath. What was going on? "What happened to change your mind? Is this about someone trying to kill you?"

He paused as though thinking over what he wanted to say. "Joe thinks something big is looming. It might happen as soon as next week."

My anger rose. "Then why doesn't he have someone protecting you?"

He offered me a sad smile. "He's doin' the best he can, Rose. If he ruffles too many feathers, his job might be at risk too."

I felt lightheaded. Mason was a sitting duck.

He grabbed my upper arms and leaned down into my face. "I'm gonna make sure you're protected."

I shook my head. "I'm more worried about *you*, Mason."

He pulled me close and gave me a slow, gentle kiss. "Sweetheart, I'm fine. I promise." He opened the side of his coat to show me a gun holster strapped to his chest.

My eyes widened and rose to his. "Does Joe—"

"Know?" he finished. "He's the one who suggested it."

"Mason, I'm *beggin'* you to tell me what's goin' on." I knew I sounded whiny, but I didn't care. I was scared for him.

He cupped my cheek. "I'm sorry. You have every right to know what's going on. Tonight I'll tell you every last bit of it. I promise."

"Everything?" I wanted to tell him everything too. I considered telling him about the second journal now, but it could wait. It wasn't like we could read it. Besides, it was a twenty-five-year-old mystery. Not much would have changed by nighttime.

"I swear it. Even something I've been meaning to talk to you about for a few weeks now. I wanted more information before I told you more about it." He ran his hand through his hair, looking down in frustration before searching my face. "Dora might have been doing something illegal. But I wanted more proof before I told you about it. You've had enough shitty people in your life, Rose. You deserve someone good."

A lump filled my throat. "I have *you*, Mason. *You're* my someone good."

He kissed me with an intensity that caught me by surprise, pushing me against the side of the truck. My hands tangled in his hair, pulling him closer. His desperation scared me, and worry slithered in my heart.

Suddenly it was all too much. The Lady in Black. Maeve telling me that Mason and someone else was in danger and I was supposed to save them. Hattie waiting for me at the Atchison factory with information that would probably change my life. It was all so overwhelming. All I wanted was to be with Mason without this constant fear looming over us.

I cupped his cheeks and lifted his head to search his eyes. "Mason, let's just go now. Let's run away from it all."

Resignation and regret filled his eyes. "As much as I'd love to climb into this truck with you, pick up Muffy and never look back, I can't. I have to at least finish out today, then I can let the chips fall where they may."

"What happens today?"

"I have a meeting at six."

My breath caught in my throat. "What's gonna happen at this meeting?"

"Rose, you have to promise me that you won't tell a soul. Not even Neely Kate."

"I promise."

"Joe and I are presenting evidence to get the DA indicted for taking bribes and misuse of power." Hope lit up his face. "I've convinced someone from the state capital to come and let us present our case."

Mason had been digging into J.R. while he was in Little Rock, but I had to wonder if he'd been instigating this too. "Then what?" I asked.

"Hopefully, he'll get removed from office and I'll be free to protect you from J.R. Simmons. It seems the best path at the moment—clear out the man who's most likely to overrule me when I dismiss J.R.'s trumped-up evidence."

I shook my head. "Do you think it's gonna work?"

"It's only a short-term fix, but it's a good stop-gap until we can reach a more permanent solution."

"The trouble brewing next week…"

His eyes hardened. "I'll take care of it. One way or the other."

"Mason, don't do anything to get yourself into trouble."

He winked, but his eyes didn't hold their usual sparkle of playfulness. "The only trouble I want to get into is with you this weekend at my uncle's cabin."

I forced a saucy grin. "Then I better pack that little black thing."

His hand slid from my waist to my hip and around to my butt, pulling me flush against him. "I *love* your little black thing."

I pressed my mouth to his. "You've never seen this little black thing."

He grinned against my lips. "Even better."

I kissed him again, my fear mingling with the love I had for this man. He was far from perfect, but he gave me more love and acceptance than anyone else ever had. I knew I wasn't an easy person to live with, but he took everything in stride and accepted the chaos that followed me like hail in a summer storm. I couldn't lose him. "I love you, Mason."

He wiped a tear that trailed down my cheek. "I love you too. Now I better get going." He turned to the road. "What are you doing out here?"

I looked around, surprised but thankful Jed hadn't shown up yet. "I'm going on a consultation."

"*Here?*"

I scrunched my nose. "Not here. I only pulled in when I saw your car."

"I thought you were staying in town today."

"This was a last-minute thing that was too good to pass up."

He studied me for several long seconds. "Do you have the Taser Joe gave you?"

"In my purse."

"Get it out."

"Okay…" I opened the door and grabbed the weapon out of my bag.

"Did he show you how to use it?"

"Yeah."

"Keep it in your coat pocket. You don't want to have to dig it out of your purse when you need it."

"I hope I don't have to use it at all."

"Well, so do I," he said, taking it from my hand. "But I'll feel better if you're prepared." He leaned close and showed it to me. "Put the part that shoots the barbs pointed toward your pocket. Then all you have to do is pull it out to use it." He handed it to me. "Put it in your right pocket and practice pulling it out like that."

"Mason, this is silly."

"I don't care. Do it anyway."

I put it in my pocket and pulled it out.

"That wasn't fast enough."

"Mason," I groaned.

"Rose, trust me. If you're ever in a predicament where you need it, you'll be glad you practiced."

I pulled it out a dozen times before he was satisfied.

"You better go, Mason."

He looked into my face with an expression I couldn't read. Then he smiled and gave me one last kiss. "I'll see you tonight."

My stomach twisted with nerves. "Good luck at your meeting."

He got into his car and started to pull out. He'd wonder why I wasn't leaving too, so I grabbed my phone and held it up to my mouth, pretending to talk. I pointed at it and smiled, grateful that he seemed to accept my excuse.

As soon as he disappeared from sight, I pulled my truck around the corner of the building. A couple of minutes passed before Jed showed up, riding a motorcycle. Once he climbed off and removed his helmet, he opened the back door of the truck and climbed in.

"I saw your boyfriend leaving. Complications?" he asked.

"Maybe." I wasn't sure what to make of what Mason had told me, but I wasn't sharing this detail with Skeeter or Jed. "I'll deal with it."

"So do you have a plan?" he asked.

"Other than find Hattie, get my answers, and get out, no."

"And you just want me there as backup."

"It seems like the best bet. She thinks I'm comin' alone."

"Then we'll create that illusion. Don't worry about her seeing me."

If things went south, as Skeeter said, I wasn't sure how I'd explain Jed's involvement to the sheriff, but I'd deal with that later. With any luck at all, I'd get my information without an incident. Jed was just my insurance policy.

Chapter Twenty-Seven

Just five minutes later, I pulled into the parking lot of the burned-out factory. The outer walls of the brick building were mostly intact except for one section that was blackened and caved in. Weeds had grown thick against the wall.

Hattie's gray sedan was parked in front of a door that led to the factory itself rather than the offices. Jed poked his head up over the top of the seat and looked around. "It looks safe enough. I'd go first to make sure the coast is clear, but she'll probably be watching. Once she sees you go in alone, she'll feel secure enough. After you've been inside for a minute, I'll follow behind."

I swallowed, trying to settle my stomach. "Thanks."

He nodded. "If you need me, just call out my name. I'll be close enough to get to you in seconds."

"Okay." I took the personal journal out of my purse and hid it under the front seat, then climbed out of the truck, patting my right coat pocket to reassure myself that the Taser was still in my pocket. After I slipped my phone into my other coat pocket, I headed for the metal door. There was a single rectangular window set into it, and sure enough, Hattie's face was peering out at me from behind the windowpane.

The door pushed open and I walked through the opening. "Took you long enough," Hattie said. She kept peering out of the window for a moment longer.

I gauged our surroundings—we were in a small foyer, opposite another metal door leading inside the factory. "I had to run by my house to get it."

"Do you have the journal?" she asked. "The coded one?"

"Yes," I said, although her adamance made me uneasy.

"Were you followed?"

"No. Do you have a reason to think someone would follow me?"

She shook her head and turned around and opened the other door.

"Where are we goin'?" I asked.

"You'll see."

I could push the matter, but I'd find out soon enough. Besides, Jed was nearby, so I'd be protected if she tried to pull anything.

The factory reeked of mold and rot. Metal contraptions filled the warehouse-like building. There weren't many windows, but plenty of sunlight spilled in through the partially missing walls and roof on the eastern side of the building.

"Ever come here before?" she asked, leading the way.

I trailed behind, watching where I stepped and clutching my purse tighter. The floor was covered in toppled machine parts and tree limbs that must have blown in from the outside, along with beer cans and bottles. "No."

"Not even as a teenager?"

That explained the beer cans. "No," I murmured, looking around. This place looked like even more of a tetanus trap than the metal pieces in front of Weston's Garage, Daniel Crocker's old base of operations. "Where are we goin'?"

She didn't answer, just continued through the metal maze.

"I take it that *you've* been here before?"

"Yeah, not that it did me any good. I needed the journal."

"For what?"

"I'll tell you when we get there."

This whole situation was beginning to stink worse than a three-day-old dead catfish. "I thought you were gonna tell me about Dora, not lead me on some sort of treasure hunt."

She stopped and turned to look at me. "This is about your mother. I promise. Trust me."

I'd learned not to trust people who were this secretive, particularly when I didn't understand their motives, yet I had no choice but to follow her if I wanted answers. One thing I'd learned as the Lady in Black was not to show your hand. I would still have some leverage as long as Hattie didn't realize how desperate I was for answers. A small part of me realized the very fact that I was following her through this metal jungle tipped my hand, but I chose to ignore it.

Finally we emerged from the junkyard into an open area with metal beams supporting the ceiling. Several large broken windows lined the western wall, spilling light onto the dirty concrete floor. But dark clouds had blown in, obscuring the sun.

Hattie continued walking, but I stopped, holding my purse close to my side. "I think this is far enough."

She turned around and studied me. "I know you don't understand—"

"You're right," I said. "I don't understand *any* of this. Normal people meet for coffee. Or lunch. They don't meet in burned-down factories."

Something in the building creaked and Hattie swung her head around, searching out the source. When she turned back to face me, her eyes were wide with paranoia.

I was having major second thoughts.

"I'm sorry," she said, taking several steps backward. "But I think she knows. We don't have time to dilly-dally around." Then she turned and kept walking.

"Who knows?" I asked, but her answer was silence. It wasn't a leap to put two and two together. Was "she" Beverly? I decided to not to tip Hattie off that I knew about Beverly's existence. Shoot. For all I knew, Hattie was the one who had left the notes on my car. She'd already admitted to keeping track of me. She could be planning on killing me in here, figuring it would take ages for anyone to find me.

That was a comforting thought. Now I really wished I knew where Jed was.

But I had to wonder what purpose it would serve for someone to kill me. Was it for the inheritance? Everyone at the plant had already suspected Henry was my birth father. One only had to follow the path of publicly acknowledged men in Dora's life to figure out who I actually was, even if Momma had passed me off as her own. In fact, why not just announce I was his heir when I was a baby, then arrange for my death and clear the path for probate? Why wait? None of it made any sense.

We reached the end of the building and Hattie finally came to a stop outside a door. Several desks, file cabinets, and chairs were scattered throughout the open space, as though someone had ransacked the offices and pulled everything out. Considering the mass devastation on the opposite end of the building, though, this end—including the furnishings—looked fairly untouched. It was closed off from the open-air area, so it was darker than the rest of the building, but Hattie had come prepared with a flashlight. She pushed the door open and went inside.

I hesitated, glancing around for Jed. There was no sign of him, but I trusted he was out there, which was good since I *didn't* trust Hattie. I knew she expected me to follow her, but the only leverage I had at this point was the journal.

I pulled it out and tucked it under my arm as I moved past one of the catawampus desks. Before following her into the room, I stuffed it into a desk drawer, grateful the metal drawer didn't squeak.

"Give me the journal," she ordered, rummaging around in a closet, the flashlight beam bouncing around as she juggled it.

"No."

She came back out and shined the light into my face. "I thought you wanted answers."

I lifted my arm to block the light from my eyes. "I do. But most of what I want to know I think you can answer easily enough. Then if I think you've told me the truth, I'll help you with whatever it is you're doing in here."

I took a step toward her, my eyes adjusting to the light. Jed was probably having a conniption fit about me being in this room with only one door. I didn't like it much better. "How about we go back out there where I can actually see so you can answer my questions." I didn't give her a choice in the matter; I just turned and walked out into the factory. She wanted the journal and she thought I had it. If nothing else, she'd follow me out to tackle me.

I continued past the office furniture and into the empty space. Sure enough, she followed me out and stopped several feet away at the edge of a desk. I took several steps backward, keeping at least ten feet between us in case she decided to pull something, then put my hand on my hip, tired of her nonsense. She studied me for several seconds, then smiled. "You're a lot like her, you know."

I lifted my chin. "I wouldn't know, seein' as I didn't even know she existed until a few months ago." I did a poor job of keeping the hurt out of my voice.

The wind blew and metal creaked all around us, making an eerie sound that only added to my uneasiness. I really wished I knew where Jed was hiding.

"I told you," her voice softened. "We did it to protect you."

"From what?" When she didn't answer, I pressed on. "Was Harrison Gardner my father?"

"Oh, Rose. He claimed you as his own."

I fought my rising panic. "That doesn't answer my question."

She was silent for several seconds. "People judged her. They didn't understand what a scared little girl she was. She may have been in her twenties, but she took her grandma's death pretty hard. It made her feel so alone. She wanted more than anything to be loved, and men took advantage of that."

I wanted to ask her what she meant, but I suspected. I didn't need the nitty-gritty details spelled out for me. "Did she have an affair with Henry Buchanan?"

"No," she sighed. "She saw him more as a father figure. She'd known him for years. We went to school with his daughter. I'm sure that's part of the reason he hired her when she came back from Shreveport. He felt sorry for her."

I swallowed my fear and pushed on. "Her journal says she was having an affair with an older married man around the time she got pregnant with me. Was that my daddy?"

She groaned and shook her head. "The key to the mystery of what happened here in this factory and to Dora and Henry and even Bill Niedermier is in that journal!" She flung her finger toward me, her voice rising with every word until she was shouting, her words echoing throughout the plant. "And you're focused on finding out who your *biological father is?*"

"Yes!" I shouted, stomping my foot. "I don't care what you think of me for wanting to know, but it's *my* history! It's *my* DNA! I have a right to know!"

Some of her fight bled out of her, and her voice softened. "Just accept that Harrison Gardner is your father and leave it at that."

I shook my head, surprised my eyes were dry. "I'm not giving you a damn thing until you tell me the truth."

"How do you know I'm not gonna lie to you?"

I lowered my voice. "Because I have ways of finding out."

Her eyes widened and I knew she thought I'd resort to something unsavory. I wondered if Jed thought the same thing as he waited in the wings, prepared to do just that if I asked it of him. But it wasn't what I meant. I could always force a vision. Very few people had secrets they kept entirely to themselves, and I suspected Hattie was the same. All I had to do was force a vision while focusing on the question of my paternity, and I knew there was a good chance I'd see her telling someone.

I nearly gasped as I realized how far I'd come since last June when Joe had encouraged me to force a vision for the first time. But my work as the Lady in Black had prompted the most growth. Skeeter was right. I was good at this. I was learning how to read a situation and ask the questions that would get me the answers I needed. Neely Kate was right too. My visions could actually be a gift, not a curse, and I was going to use them to my advantage.

But my pronouncement still hung out there, and apparently Hattie didn't take kindly to being threatened. "You want to know that Dora wasn't sure who your father was?" Her tone was ugly.

At the moment I didn't care, further proof of how much I'd changed. "Yes. I want you to narrow it down. The list can't be *that* big."

She jutted out her hip and held out her hand. "Let's see. It could have been Bill Trousseau, the bank president. Or maybe

Jim Collins. Or—" But I could see the terror in her eyes. She really didn't want to tell me.

I took two steps closer. "You're lying," I said softly. "You said you were trying to protect me."

"Rose," she said quietly. "You don't want to know."

But I did. I *had* to know. At least I had to rule out one man. I took a deep breath, preparing for the worst. "Was it J.R. Simmons?" My voice broke, betraying my fear.

She watched me for three agonizing seconds before a soft smile spread across her face. "No. I promise you it wasn't J.R. Simmons."

I burst into tears of relief. "Are you sure?"

"Yes." She paused as though trying to decide how much to tell me. Finally, she released a sigh. "Dora met J.R. after she was pregnant with you. Henry Buchanan's daughter Bea moved to Little Rock just after her brother and his wife were killed in a horrific car crash. It was lonely for her in Little Rock, so she asked Dora to come up for a weekend. While she was there, Bea took Dora to a dinner at the state capitol, which is where she met J.R. Dora told him all about the plant and he said that he had a business proposition for someone looking for growth. So he came to Henryetta the next week and Dora, Henry, and J.R. went out to dinner. And so their partnership was born. Henry was thrilled. He thought he was being given a final chance to save his business."

"Until it all went bad," I said quietly.

She gave me a sad smile. "It all went bad long before it went bad on the assembly line. Bea desperately wanted her father's approval, but she was a flighty girl and mostly worthless. She was furious that Dora had accomplished what she couldn't, so she seduced Dirk, the line supervisor, and convinced him to make sure the new parts were flawed and worthless."

I couldn't believe she was giving me answers, even if what she was telling me was horrifying.

"Harrison was in charge of quality control, so he was the one who brought the situation to Henry's attention. Henry was in a panic. He'd put his entire life savings into the venture and if he didn't make the deadline, he would be bankrupt."

"So he was going to send them anyway?"

"He wasn't himself after Paul's death. And neither was Ima Jean. It wasn't hard for Bea to convince her mother that Henry was having an affair with Dora. Especially with the office staff backing her claim."

"The fire?" I asked. "Did Dora or Daddy start it?"

She shook her head. "No. They had both gone to the police chief and he was planning to question Henry and Dirk. But Bill died and the new police chief refused to listen."

"I still don't understand," I said, shaking my head. "You said you and Daddy were protecting me by hiding the truth from me. What were you hiding?"

"Rose, two men could be your father. Harrison is one. The other is Paul Buchanan."

"*Henry's son?*"

She nodded. "Dora loved Harrison, but he was wracked with guilt over their affair, and he offered her nothing. Paul was unhappy with his own marriage and he seduced her. When she found out she was pregnant, he told her that he was going to leave his wife for her. He planned to marry her."

"But why is that dangerous?"

"Because that would make you an heir to the Buchanan estate. The insurance from the fire set up the family for life. If it got out that you were Paul's daughter, you would get a third. After everything Bea and Dirk did to sabotage the parts, the three of us decided it would be safer for no one else to know."

I gasped. "The *three* of us?"

"Henry knew. He had his will changed to include you, but he didn't name you. He prepared another document that was supposed to be produced after his death, naming you as an heir. But after he died, the document never materialized. I think it's in his secret safe. I just checked and the safe's still in his office. Dora's the only other person who knew the combination."

"For heaven's sake! Why didn't the family just hire a locksmith to open it? Why go to all this trouble?"

"For one, it's hidden behind a panel. Hardly anyone knew the safe existed, let alone that it holds Henry's papers. I couldn't very well hire a locksmith to open a safe on a property I didn't own."

"Why didn't you just find the journal with the code yourself?"

"I tried. I searched that house high and low and never found it." She took a breath. "Where'd you find it?"

I hesitated. I wasn't sure I should tell her, but what difference did it make? It wasn't like I planned to put it back there. "Under the baby bed. Taped to the frame."

Hattie sighed, a warm smile flooding her face. "Of course. Everything she did was for you."

I wanted to point out that in the end, none of it had helped me. I would have rather had a poor mother who loved me. "Wait." I realized something had slipped by me. "Dirk and Bea? *Beverly?*"

"Yeah." She reached out toward me. "Now hand me the journal and let's open the safe."

A loud pop echoed in the space and Hattie crumpled into a heap on the floor. I stood stunned as a red stain blossomed on her white shirt.

Someone had shot Hattie.

Chapter Twenty-Eight

I screamed and ducked next to a metal support beam, wondering what had just happened even though the evidence was right in front of me.

As shock washed through my head, I tried to figure out the why of it. Did Jed think I'd been threatened? Had he turned on me?

I turned to run, but I came face to face with the woman from Ima Jean's bakery. Hate filled her eyes as she pointed a gun at me.

I nearly passed out when I realized she was Beverly.

I had to keep my wits about me and fainting wasn't going to help. Where was Jed?

Her eyes narrowed. "You don't look anything like him."

"Who?"

"Paul."

I held up my hands. "I don't know what any of this is about, so I think I'll just leave."

She held the gun higher. "I don't think so."

"Drop it." Jed's voice rang out loud and clear as he came into view next to the metal rubble about ten feet to her right side.

She grinned, but it looked menacing. "I think I'll keep it. Dirk?"

Dirk Picklebie stepped out of the shadows next to Beverly, pointing a gun at me.

Beverly cocked her head with a smirk. "You can't shoot both of us before one of us shoots her. Drop the gun."

Jed's jaw worked as he moved closer to me, still holding his weapon.

Dirk scratched his head with his free hand. "What are *you* doin' here, Jed? You screwing this girl?"

No matter what, I couldn't let Dirk link me to Skeeter. "We hooked up after I met him at the pool hall yesterday," I said. "But it turns out he's the jealous type. He must have followed me here."

I took two steps toward him, but Beverly blocked my path. "If you don't want me to shoot your girlfriend, lover boy, *put down the gun.*"

Jed slowly squatted and gently lowered his gun to the ground, then rose with a murderous look on his face. Dirk Picklebie would be lucky to survive this. If Jed didn't take care of him, I had no doubt that Skeeter would.

Beverly reached out her free hand. "Give me the journal."

I put my left hand on my abdomen pretending to protect the book under my coat as I took a step back. "No."

Beverly's eyes narrowed. "I just shot Hattie. I won't hesitate to shoot you too."

"Rose," Jed growled. "Give it to her."

"No!" I looked over my shoulder at the woman lying on the floor. "We have to call an ambulance!"

"Sure thing," Beverly said. "Just as soon as you give me the book."

I shook my head and glanced over at Jed. He looked like he wanted to rip someone's head off. "I don't have it on me." I slowly opened the flaps of my coat to show her I was telling the truth. "I hid it here in the factory. If you shoot me, you'll never find it."

She swung her gun around and pointed it at Jed. "Then I'll shoot him unless you show me where you put it, sweetie," she said in a mocking tone. "Don't tempt me. I killed your mother and I'm very willing to kill you too."

"*You* killed Dora?" I asked in disbelief.

She scrunched her nose in disgust. "Why do you find that so hard to believe?"

"But why?"

"*Why?* Did you not hear one word of motor-mouth's tale?" She momentarily waved her gun toward Hattie and I could see that Jed was considering tackling her, but he didn't have the chance to act before she returned the barrel to me. "Dora was gonna ruin everything. Her and Daddy dearest. J.R. was pissed the parts were screwed up and heads were gonna roll. Daddy was gonna lose everything. Dirk set the fire so we could collect the insurance. I had no idea Dora had run crying to the police chief. He may have ended up dead a few days later, but Dora was talking about going to the state police with her book of evidence. I couldn't let her do that, especially since J.R. had offered to pay me all that money to get the book for him. If only I'd thought it through, I would have made sure Paul's brat was in the car too, and that it burned up in a fiery crash… Just. Like. Paul's." She grinned. "But I didn't have the time to prepare like I did with Paul's accident. Dora was planning to go to the state police the next day. I had to act quick…and obviously it was a bit sloppy."

I took a step backward and bumped into a piece of metal machinery. "You killed your own brother?"

"He was cheating on his wife."

"*That's* why?"

"She was jealous of him," Dirk said, spitting on the floor. "Henry was about to retire and give it all to Paul—the inheritance too—so Beverly offed him." He chuckled. "Only she didn't realize when she did it that her inheritance didn't amount to a hill of beans." He chuckled again. "She killed him for nothing."

Beverly's upper lip curled. "Shut up, Dirk."

I couldn't believe someone could be so cold. How could Dirk laugh over Beverly killing her own brother? But both Paul and Dora had died in car accidents. While it seemed a little coincidental, it wasn't enough to arouse much suspicion. Obviously. "So why have Dirk screw up the parts if it was going to force the factory into bankruptcy? Why wouldn't you want the factory to make more money?"

Beverly gave Hattie a look of contempt. "The stupid bitch got that part wrong. Dirk had nothing to do with screwing up the parts. It just happened. But that didn't mean we couldn't use it to our advantage. I got Dirk to blackmail my father. If he didn't pay him, Dirk would tip off the authorities."

I shook my head in disbelief. "But you were stealing money from your father, which would have been your inheritance!"

"Are you not listening? There *was no* inheritance," she sneered. "The parts were shoddy. The factory was goin' down. I needed to get money where I could." She patted her chest with her free hand. "I had to look out for number one."

I couldn't believe someone could be so selfish. "So you started the fire, then you killed the police chief—"

She held up her free hand. "*Hey!* I had nothin' to do with killin' the police chief."

"Then who did?" I asked. I turned my attention to Dirk.

He shook his head. "Not me."

"But what about your father?" I asked. "Why did he kill himself?"

An evil grin spread across her face. "He did it after I pointed out how much he'd failed Paul and failed Dora. He'd failed the whole town, so he agreed the best thing to do was to end it all. I thought it was fittin' punishment." She winked. "Besides, there was the life insurance to consider. It wasn't much, but it still paid even though he committed suicide."

"So the factory's worth nothing?" I asked.

"We couldn't sell this place if we tried. And Momma spent most of the money on her bakery, and now it's goin' belly-up too."

"If you're not here for the inheritance, then what are you doin' here?" I asked in frustration and fear. "Why did you shoot Hattie?" But as soon as the words left my mouth, I knew. Sick dread washed through me. I'd been carrying around the evidence Mason needed to bring down J.R. Why hadn't I given it to him when I'd seen him at the abandoned service station?

Beverly started laughing. "You're so cute."

I shot Jed a questioning glance, wondering if he was putting it all together too, but he just shook his head, his eyes dark with fury.

She settled down and gave me an impatient glare. "I already suspected you were Paul's brat. I could have taken care of you years ago, but I saw no point. You were no threat. But then you started asking Dirk questions and your friend told him about the journal, so I figured I could make some money off the deal if I kept an eye on you. Hattie's been obsessed with finding the secret journal since Dora died in the car crash. Just like I suspected, she convinced you to find it, which means I can reap the benefits of your hard work."

I gave her a blank look. I couldn't understand how someone could be so calculating. But the vision I'd had of her now made perfect sense.

She rolled her eyes in disgust. "J.R. Simmons was elated to hear I could get the journal for him, and he's willing to pay a hefty sum to get it."

I couldn't let J.R. get the book. I had to figure a way out of this. Jed caught my eye and gave me a slight nod, his eyes hard. He was ready to make a move. I just needed to keep her distracted. "If you wanted me to find the journal for you, why did you leave the notes on my car?'

Her nose scrunched up and she looked at me like I was crazy. "What notes? I didn't leave you any notes."

Jed took advantage of Beverly's distraction and bolted toward her, but Beverly pivoted, pointing her gun at him, and pulled the trigger. Jed dove toward me, landing several feet away.

"*Jed!*" I screamed in horror, nearly dropping to my knees.

Dirk took advantage of her distraction and rushed me. Wrapping one arm around my waist, he used me as a human shield, pointing his gun at Beverly.

Panic raced through my head and I struggled to keep it at bay. Jed lay on the floor, unmoving. I tried to keep from crying, but I was terrified she'd killed him. Hysteria threatened to take over, but if I didn't keep it together, I would never get us out of this alive.

"What are you *doin'*, Dirk?" Beverly snarled.

"I'm tired of taking orders from you, Bea. I want your word that you're gonna split your money with me. I want at least fifty grand."

I could only imagine what was in that coded journal that made it worth so much money to Joe's father. There was no way I was letting them leave with it.

She gave him a look that told him she thought he'd lost his mind. "I ain't payin' you shit."

"You ain't gonna shoot her." He waved his gun toward my head. "You need the journal to collect your money."

She lowered her gun slightly, but her posture softened. "You're right." She studied him for a moment. "I couldn't have done any of this without you, Dirk, baby. I'll give you twenty grand?"

Dirk's hold on me tightened. "Thirty-five."

Beverly hesitated, then gave him a warm smile. "You always knew how to sweet- talk me, baby. Why'd we break up all those years ago?"

His body tensed. "You found someone with more money."

"With all the money Simmons is gonna pay us, we can get back together."

Dirk paused, appearing to consider her offer. "I still want thirty-five."

She lowered her gun. "Done."

Dirk's hold on me loosened and he pushed me toward Jed. I dropped to my knees next to him. Blood seeped through a hole in the sleeve of his leather jacket. "Jed," I whispered, fighting my tears. "Are you okay?"

He didn't answer, but the way his eyes narrowed told me he planned to put up a fight.

Another gunshot went off and Dirk fell to the ground, a bullet hole in his head.

I shrieked and jumped backward. Jed made a move for me to cover me with his body, but I scrambled to my feet. I knew I was the only one left who could stop her, and it was time for me to step up. "I'll show you where it is."

"Rose," Jed moaned.

"It's okay." I had a plan, but I had to get closer to her to execute it. Which meant I would probably have to act after I got the book, just as I was handing it to her. "It's in here." I carefully made my way to the desk and opened the drawer, hoping my plan didn't backfire. She could very well shoot me as soon as I showed the journal to her. But maybe I could work it another way.

"Pull it out." She motioned with her gun.

I reached into the drawer with my left hand and acted like I was trying to pull it out. "It's stuck."

"Pull harder."

I grunted as I pretended to jerk it back.

"Get out of the way," she said, moving closer. She turned her back to me as she reached into the drawer and I knew I had to time this right. I pulled the Taser from my pocket, feeling it with my fingers to make sure it was ready to shoot. Her back was covered with her heavy coat and the barbs had to come into contact with her skin. I'd have to wait until she turned around or aim it at her legs to make sure it worked. But she made the decision for me when she picked up the journal with ease and spun around with it in her hand. "What the hell was that nonsense?"

I aimed for her exposed stomach and pressed the trigger. The barbs landed on her abdomen. Her body went rigid and she began to shake, her gun and the journal falling to the floor moments before her body hit.

"Rose!" Jed shouted. I realized the desk blocked his view.

"I'm okay. I Tased her and it knocked her out." I picked up her gun, but she'd fallen on top of the journal and I had no intention of leaving it underneath her. I tried shoving her body over, but the journal went with her. Cringing, I stuck my hand under her stomach, my fingers fanning out as I searched for the book. I finally found it and pulled it out, heaving and groaning in the process.

"What in the hell are you doin' over there?" Jed barked.

"Bringing J.R. Simmons down, with any luck." I stood, trying to figure out what to do with everything. I stuck the Taser in my pocket and tucked the journal into a pocket inside my coat, then carried the gun around the desk to him.

He was already sitting up, clutching his left arm. "Call Skeeter."

I glanced over at Hattie's still body on the floor. "I have to call 911."

He tried to reach for his pocket and released a grunt. "Then get my phone out of my right coat pocket."

I put Beverly's gun down before I pulled out Jed's phone and handed it to him. My heart raced as I cast another glance at Hattie, torn between helping her and making sure Jed was safe. "Make your call," he said gruffly.

"But if the sheriff deputies find you…"

"I think she's still alive," he said, releasing his arm and punching numbers into his phone. "But she needs help now."

He was right. I grabbed my phone and called 911, telling the operator where we were and explaining that multiple people had been shot before I managed to Tase the shooter.

Jed climbed to his feet as I searched for Hattie's wound. She was splayed on her side and blood seemed to be oozing from her left shoulder. "Hattie?" I asked, looking for something to put on her shoulder.

She'd lost a lot of blood, but her eyes fluttered open and she grimaced.

"Hang on. The paramedics are coming."

Jed picked up his gun off the floor and walked over to Beverly. "I need to go, Rose."

I stared at him in panic. "What?" It made sense. He couldn't be found here—for either of our sakes—but part of me was terrified to be left alone with this mess.

"You know I can't stay. Just say that some mysterious man showed up and helped you."

"But that's not gonna work. Beverly's gonna tell them I know you."

He grunted and glanced at the pile of mechanical equipment we'd climbed through to get where we were before turning back to me. His fingers curled around his gun as his eyes looked deadly. "Don't think for a moment that bitch would have let you walk out of here knowing what you know."

I sucked in a breath, guessing what he would say next.

His jaw tightened. "I can take care of her and I won't lose a wink of sleep over it." He searched my face. "But I know *you would*. So your call, Rose. Do I make it a non-issue or do you come up with a story?"

He was asking my permission to murder Beverly. I shook my head. "But...I..."

His lips turned up into a slight grin. "I already knew your answer before I suggested it, but I had to let you know it was an option." He stuffed his gun into the waistband of his jeans. "And don't worry. You'll figure it out. You always think of something." He took several steps toward one of the broken windows. "Let us know when the dust settles."

I was jealous of his ability to take off and leave all of this behind. "Thanks."

He nodded and took off toward an open window, then climbed out into the field behind the building.

Relief flooded my body when I heard sirens in the distance. I looked down at Hattie, who gave me a quizzical look. "I take it he doesn't want the authorities to know he was here?"

"No." I swallowed. "I know it puts you in a difficult position."

She gave me a soft smile. "I don't know him from Adam. It's easy enough to say a stranger showed up and helped."

Before I could answer, I heard something behind me. I didn't even have the chance to turn around and look. Someone knocked me to the ground and straddled my back, wrapping cold hands around my throat and squeezing tight. "You little bitch!" Beverly snarled. "You ruined everything!"

I bucked, trying to throw her off as I gasped for air. She lost her balance and fell off me. I started to scramble away, but she grabbed my coat and rolled me over so she could sit on my stomach.

I released a loud grunt as she pushed all the air out of my lungs. "You're not going anywhere." The hate in her eyes scared me as her hands wrapped around my neck again.

I reached for them, curling my fingers around hers, trying to pry them off, but she was pretty determined to finish the job and after several seconds I started to see spots.

"Freeze!" someone shouted. I wanted to cry with relief. The sheriff's department had shown up.

Only I was still being strangled.

In fact, Beverly's grip tightened even more. "I'm gonna make you pay for this!"

"Get off her. *Now!*" Joe shouted. The sound of his voice was enough to give me hope, but Beverly seemed more determined than ever to finish me off. My fingers went numb and my grip on her hands loosened. Everything was fading to black when another gunshot rang out. Beverly's fingers went limp and I barely had a chance to suck in a breath before she fell on top of me, putting pressure on my chest and restricting my air intake again.

I struggled to push her off, but she had to outweigh me by fifty pounds.

Seconds later, Joe rolled her off me and I looked up into his terror-stricken eyes, never so happy to see him.

"Are you okay?" he asked.

"Yeah," I said, my voice sounding raspy.

He closed his eyes and his chest rose as he sucked in a deep breath. "You just scared the shit out of me," he said when he opened his eyes again.

I started to sit up, but he grabbed my arm and helped me up, putting his arm around my back for support. "I'm gonna have a paramedic look at you."

"Hattie…" I glanced behind me, grimacing from the pain in my neck.

"If Hattie is the woman who *wasn't* strangling you, then she's being taken care of by the paramedics right now. And if she *was*, then *she's* waiting for the coroner."

I cringed. "Did you…"

"Shoot her? Yes." His words were harsh. I glanced up at him and I could see his initial concern was quickly turning to anger.

He helped me back onto my feet and kept his arm around me, making sure I was steady, as he surveyed the bodies and guns on the floor.

His mouth pressed into a tight line and a vein in his temple throbbed when he turned back to me. "*What in the hell happened here?*"

"I found Dora's murderer."

Chapter Twenty-Nine

If I thought my announcement was going to calm him down, I had another thing coming.

"*What?*" he shouted.

The other first responders turned toward us in surprise.

"You told me I could investigate, Joe! You gave me your blessing!" I shouted back.

"I gave you my blessing to find out *who your father was!* I gave you my blessing to *talk* to people! Not shoot them!"

"I didn't shoot anyone!" I protested. "Beverly shot Hattie and Dirk, then you shot Beverly. I only Tased her." When he didn't respond, I forged on. "And I came here to talk to Hattie. She told me who my birth father really was. So I was doing exactly what you told me I could do."

Only I still couldn't believe that Daddy wasn't my father. It didn't seem real.

Joe took several deep breaths, his vein still pounding. He pointed to Beverly's body. His voice was low and tight when he spoke. "You know damn good and well this is not what I meant when I told you that you could to *look into it*."

"How the cotton-pickin' hell was I supposed to know that Beverly was gonna show up and start shooting everybody?!" I shouted.

He flung his arms from his sides. "Maybe the suggestion to meet in an abandoned factory could have been *your first clue!*"

I shook my head, wincing from the pain, and put my hands on my hips. "I'm not gonna talk to you if you're gonna be like this."

"You'll damn well talk to me if I tell you to! You need to give me a statement!"

My chest heaved as I struggled to reel in my temper. "Well, *Chief Deputy* Simmons," I forced out, trying my best to retain control. "When you can talk to me without shouting at me, I'll be more than happy to give you my statement."

His face turned red, but his next words came out calmer. "I can haul you to the sheriff's office for questioning if you'd like."

I crossed my arms. "I think I need to call my attorney."

My words sobered him and he ran his hands though his hair before he answered. "Rose, I'm sorry. I'm being an ass. There's no need to call Mason."

I stared at him in shock. "Did you just apologize? *And* call yourself an ass?"

A ghost of a grin crossed his face. "I'm not repeating it."

I pulled out my phone. "I need to call Mason anyway. He's going to be upset if I don't call him."

I started to pull up his number, but Joe covered my hand. "Rose, wait."

I squinted at him in confusion.

He grabbed my arm and tugged me to the edge of the open area, away from the other three deputies, who were openly gawking at us as they went about their duties. "Don't call him. It's only gonna upset him and he's preparing for...something big."

Joe had to be talking about his and Mason's meeting at six, but I wasn't sure if I was supposed to know or not. "Joe, I have to call him. He's going to be furious with me if I don't. And justifiably so."

"Then I'll take full responsibility for it. *Please.* He needs to be on his game tonight. Knowing you were almost strangled to death will distract him."

I could see his point.

I heaved out a sigh, and against my better judgment, stuffed my phone back into my pocket. "Okay, but this feels wrong."

Joe looked relieved. "Thank you. Now how about I take your statement?"

My eyebrows rose in mock surprise. "Isn't that the job of someone with a lower rank?"

He grinned. "I'll slum it for you."

He led me outside to his sheriff's patrol car and I gave him a statement, holding nothing back except for my involvement with Skeeter and Jed. I saw no point in mentioning Jed at all now that Beverly wasn't around to tell stories. When I told Joe that his father was involved and I had in my possession a journal that was likely filled with evidence implicating J.R., I expected some kind of reaction from him. I wasn't prepared to get absolutely nothing.

Joe continued to write down his notes. "And where is this journal now?"

I pulled the book out of my inner coat pocket, but kept it in my hands. "Here. But I can't make heads or tails of what's inside it. It's just numbers that look like dates and times, along with what looks like shorthand. Beverly was convinced it contains evidence against your father."

Joe reached for the journal, but I held onto it. "I think I should give it to Mason myself."

His gaze remained on the book in my hands. "I'll give it to him. It needs to go through the proper channels."

"I still—" I started to say, but without saying a word, he snatched it, stuffing the book inside his coat without even looking at it. "That's mine!" I protested, leaning over and reaching for him.

"Rose," he said, turning to me with guarded eyes. "It's evidence and an important part of this crime scene. I have to take it into custody."

"This isn't right, Joe!" I shouted, my anger flaring. "You can't just take my property! I have to give it to Mason."

He shook his head in exasperation. "And who do you think *I'm* gonna give it to? This way it's more official."

I wasn't so sure going the official route was the best way to handle this.

He was silent for several moments, his eyes staring out the windshield. "I'll make sure he gets it, but I can't give it back to you. I'm sorry."

I told myself to calm down. Joe would give it to Mason, but I couldn't ignore the niggle of doubt in the back of my head. The journal supposedly contained information that could get Joe's father in trouble. Was it safe to trust him with it? In the end, I didn't have a choice. Besides, it was Joe. Of course, I could trust him.

Joe closed his notebook. "I need to wrap up a few things up here before I head back to town." He paused. "You're free to go, but again, I'm asking you to not call Mason. And if he calls you before tonight, please don't tell him about any of this. Especially not the journal."

I stared at him for several seconds. "But you'll tell him? And be sure to explain that you asked me not to say anything."

He nodded and offered me a weak smile. "I'll take care of it."

The sun was low on the horizon when I pulled out of the parking lot. Mason would soon be home and I was going to tell him everything I knew about Dora, whether Joe had had a chance to tell him or not. I had only promised Joe that I'd wait until they had their big meeting. After that, everything was fair game.

As I drove home, I tried to wrap my head around the fact that half of my genetics might belong to Paul Buchanan, a man I knew nothing about. While Hattie clearly believed I was Paul's biological daughter, I decided it didn't matter. Who I was now had nothing to with the genes in my cells. Besides, when I *really* thought about it, I was pretty positive I wasn't Paul's daughter. My visions were telling proof. They came from Daddy's mother, the oracle of Lafayette County. What were the chances I'd have the same gift without being related to her?

My phone rang when I was almost home and I saw a number I didn't recognize on the screen. "Hello?" I answered, sounding guarded.

"Rose," Kate said in a chipper tone that sounded forced, even to my ears. "I heard you had an eventful afternoon."

I tensed with confusion. How had she heard? Kate didn't seem the type to sit around listening to police scanners. "Just another day in Fenton County," I said with more sarcasm than I'd intended, but she rubbed me the wrong way and I was done tolerating bad behavior.

"You need to watch your P's and Q's, Rose Gardner," she said. "Consider this fair warning."

What on earth did that mean? Then I gasped. She knew about the journal. When I started to answer her, I realized she'd hung up.

Now I *really* needed to talk to Mason. I had no idea what Kate's visit to Henryetta was all about, but I couldn't be sure it wasn't part of her father's nefarious plan.

When I opened the front door, Muffy greeted me with her usual gusto. I let her wander around outside, feeling more than slightly unsettled. I half considered calling Mason anyway, but all of this was bound to upset him. Joe was right—he needed to give the meeting his full concentration.

I had a strong urge to check in with Skeeter, so I called him instead after I brought Muffy back into the house. "How's Jed?"

"He'll pull through."

"Is he still at the hospital?"

He chuckled. "He can't go to the hospital. They'd have to report a gunshot wound. I have someone who looked at it."

"But he has—"

"And before you go worryin', he's in great shape. He'll be back to work in a day or two."

"*Skeeter.*"

"His choice. Rose." He was quiet for a moment. "He blames himself for what happened."

"What on earth for? If he hadn't been there, I'd probably be dead. Thanks for loaning him to me."

"He wants to help you again if you'll have him."

"Hopefully, there will be no need."

He laughed. "Keep him in your speed dial."

"Very funny."

"Since Jed's out of commission for a few days, call me if you get into trouble."

"*You're* gonna come get me out of trouble?"

"I'll send Merv to take care of it." He paused. "Do you have any more information about the double homicide?"

"No. I haven't heard any more about it. Have they said anything to you?"

"No, and that's what worries me. Ordinarily, they'd come straight away to ask their questions."

"Then that's a good thing, right?"

"No, I think it's bad. It means they're probably building their case before they come callin'."

Crap. That *did* sound bad. "Have you come up with any idea who might be settin' you up?" I asked.

"No." But the way he answered made me question his truthfulness.

"I have a journal that has information tying J.R. Simmons to Atchison Manufacturing, but I have no idea what it contains. It was all in shorthand and I couldn't read it. If J.R. is behind this, hopefully it will help us bring him down and take care of the situation you and Mason are in."

"Jed told me. I guess you gave it to your boyfriend?"

"No. Joe took it from the crime scene."

He didn't say anything for a moment, but when he spoke next, his voice was tight. "J.R. Simmons' son? You really think that was a good idea?"

"It wasn't like I had much choice in the matter. He just confiscated it and called it evidence. But he promised to give it to Mason."

Skeeter didn't reply.

I thought about J.R.'s involvement with the factory and how he had been willing to pay Beverly a lot of money to hand the book over to him. What could be in that book that was so important? Back in December, both Joe and Mason had shrugged off my suggestion that J.R. might be behind the attempt on Mason's life, saying it wasn't his style.

J.R. Simmons liked to bring people down and make them suffer. The thought set off a chain reaction of other thoughts, all of which led to an inescapable conclusion.

Why hadn't I realized that before?

I gasped. "Oh, mercy! It's not a kill list, even if Mick Gentry and Scott Humphrey thought it was. Skeeter! It's a list of people J.R. intends to make suffer."

"That sounds like a whole lot of work when it would just be easier to kill me. Who would go to so much trouble?"

"J.R. Simmons would. Mason says he thrives on causing people misery."

He released a low whistle. "Well, I'll be damned."

"It's him. I'd bet money on it."

"You might be on to something. What better way to get rid of me than settin' me up for a double homicide? Then I'd be forced to sit in prison watchin' that rat bastard Gentry run my territory."

I sank down into a kitchen chair. "What are you gonna do?"

"I don't know yet. The question is who else is on the list?"

I had a pretty good idea. And now I was really scared for Mason.

I hung up and checked the time. It was six-thirty and I had no idea when Mason would be home. I was on edge, wondering how his meeting was going, wondering what would happen to him if it didn't go well. To kill some time, I scoured the cabinets to look for something to make for dinner. I would feel bad about taking Maeve up on her offer to do some grocery shopping for us, but it might become necessary if Mason intended to uphold our ban of the Piggly Wiggly. In an attempt to occupy my frazzled mind, I started making a list, figuring I could go shopping when we came back from Mason's uncle's cabin, but quit after I listed peanut butter three times.

At seven-fifteen I started to get really nervous. I hadn't heard anything and I wondered if that was a good sign or a bad one. I decided to try to watch some TV with Muffy. We had just settled onto the sofa when I heard a car pull up in front of the house. Less than half a minute later, the front door was flung open. Mason stood in the threshold, his face pale.

I jumped to my feet. "Mason? How'd it go?" But the look on his face pretty much said it all.

He shut the door behind him. "I got fired."

I stumbled toward him as my stomach fell to my feet. "*What?*"

He shook his head, looking bewildered. "It was an ambush, Rose. The DA showed up and it turned into an inquisition of *me* instead of the other way around."

"But what about Joe?"

His hands shook and his face turned red. "He didn't do a goddamn thing. He just sat there and let them pummel me."

I gasped. "I can't believe it."

"I can." He grabbed my hand and pulled me up the stairs. "We have to go."

I let him drag me, but I shook my head in confusion. "What are you talkin' about?"

"We have to get out of Fenton County tonight. Hell, we need to get out of Arkansas."

"Why?"

He stopped in the middle of our bedroom. "Rose. There's absolutely nothing to keep Simmons from releasing his false evidence against you now. I'm not in the Fenton County court system to stop it." He ran his hand through his hair and turned to face the windows. "I just can't understand what got this rolling so quickly. I must have hit a nerve, but for the life of me, I can't figure out how."

"I can," I whispered. "Oh, God. It was me."

He turned around and his eyes widened. "You? How could it be you?"

I covered my mouth with my hand, feeling lightheaded. "Mason, I discovered what happened to Dora."

His mouth parted and confusion flickered in his eyes. "What are you talking about?"

I clasped both hands together in front of me. "Neely Kate and I have been investigating the case over the last few days."

He sat on the edge of the bed. "You're kidding me."

I wrung my hands. "No."

He ran his hand over his head again, then looked up at me. "What did you find out?"

"It's a long complicated story, but the bottom line is that Beverly Buchanan murdered Dora Middleton because my birth mother was trying to tell the world that something bad was goin' on at Atchison Manufacturing. And Dora had a journal full of information to implicate J.R. Simmons."

He shook his head as though trying to clear it. "Wait. I thought you already went through her journal. It didn't sound like there was anything like that in there."

I walked over to the bed and sat down next to him. "There was a *second* journal. I found it this morning taped to the frame of the baby bed in the nursery."

He looked shell-shocked. "Why didn't you *tell me?*"

"Mason." I started to cry. "I swear to you, I didn't know what it was. It was just figures and dates and words written in shorthand. I found it after you left, and I didn't want to bother you with it when I saw you at the abandoned gas station. I figured I'd tell you everything tonight when there was more time. I've been trying to talk to you about it since yesterday."

"*Dammit!*" He jumped to his feet and his gaze spun around the room. "Where is it now?" He sounded panicked.

I wrung my hands, overcome with a feeling of dread. "Joe took it."

He went stock-still. "What?"

I stood and grabbed his arm. "He was one of the sheriff deputies who came to the Atchison factory after I called 911."

He stared at me like a deer caught in headlights.

"Joe didn't tell you *anything?*"

His jaw worked and his eyes darkened. "Joe didn't say a goddamned thing to me."

"He told me he'd tell you." Now I was really scared and my voice shook. "I met Hattie—Dora's best friend—at the factory with the coded journal. She was supposed to tell me who my real birth father was, but Beverly Buchanan and her old boyfriend Dirk Picklebie showed up. Beverly shot Hattie and Dirk and wanted the journal. She said J.R. Simmons was going to pay her money for it."

His eyes widened with terror. "You're sure she said she'd talked to him?"

Oh, God. This was going from bad to worse. "Yes."

"Did Joe take Beverly into custody?"

I hesitated. This next part was bound to upset him. "No. Joe shot her when she wouldn't stop strangling me."

He grabbed my arms. "*What?*"

"I'm fine. My neck is sore, but—"

"Rose." He pulled me to his chest, his arms shaking. "Why didn't you call me? Why am I just hearing about this *now?*"

"Joe begged me not to. He said it would distract you from your meeting. He told me he'd tell you. He really didn't *say anything?*" Hysteria crept into my voice.

His arms stiffened. "No, he was too busy letting the investigator fry my ass." He sucked in a deep breath. "*Shit!*" He dropped his hold and grabbed two suitcases out of the closet and tossed them on the bed. "Start packing. *Now.*"

"Why?"

"We have to leave; the sooner, the better." He grabbed a handful of T-shirts from his drawer and tossed them into the bag.

I followed suit, snatching up clothes and toiletries and tossing them into a suitcase.

When we were completely packed, Mason picked up the bags and sent me downstairs. "Pack food for Muffy and anything else you need for her. I have no idea how long we'll be gone."

"Where are we goin'?"

His eyes filled with fury. "Somewhere J.R. Simmons can't reach you until I can figure out how to take him down."

I hurried to the kitchen and was almost finished when Mason walked in, his gun strapped to his holster again. He sought out my eyes when he noticed me staring at it. "Precaution."

I tried to get control of my fear.

"Tomorrow I'll clean out my bank account." He took several deep breaths. "Maybe we'll head down to Shreveport tonight."

I didn't know what to say. I couldn't believe this was happening.

"Are you sure we need to run?" I asked, my stomach churning, as he led me to the front door where our bags waited.

He turned to me and put his hands on my shoulders, searching my face. "If I thought there was a better way, I'd go that route. But I'm not sure there is one right now. I've already started building a case against Simmons. I just need to keep going." He offered me a tight smile. "Rose, this isn't hopeless. Okay? We're getting close, if he's this desperate."

I nodded. "I trust you, Mason."

He gave me a kiss, but we both jumped when we heard a knock on the front door. He peered out the window. "Dammit." He grabbed the bags and stuffed them into the hall closet.

"Who's out there?"

He pushed me next to the closet. "It's a sheriff's deputy. Let me handle it."

"Okay," I said, numb with shock and fear.

Mason squared his shoulders and opened the door. "Hello, Deputy Abbie Lee Hoffstetter. What can I do for you?"

Crap. She hated my guts. This couldn't be good.

"Good evening, Mr. Deveraux," she said, acting all superior to him. "I'm here on official business."

"Okay."

"Is Rose Gardner here?"

"And why are you asking?"

"Like I said. Official business, sir." I heard the gloating in her voice and knew I was in deep shit.

"And what exactly *is* that official business?"

"With all due respect, *sir*, I hear you're no longer with the DA's office. As you're now merely a citizen of the county, this is none of your business." Her voice turned harsh. "Now where's Rose Gardner?"

He didn't respond. He just hung onto the door with one hand, blocking the partially opened doorway with his body.

"Sir, if you could step aside so we can search the premises for Ms. Gardner."

We? Who was with her?

His back was ramrod stiff, his voice tight. "Deputy, I suggest you come back with a warrant if you want to check out my house."

I heard the rustle of paper. "Then I guess it's a good thing I have one."

Oh crap. If they searched the house they'd probably find my Lady in Black hats.

I ducked under Mason's arm—I couldn't let him get into any more trouble on my account, and things would only be worse if they combed through our house. He tried to pull me away from the doorway, but Deputy Hoffstetter grinned ear to ear with a *gotcha* look.

"Rose Gardner, you're under arrest for the murder of your mother, Agnes Gardner." She grabbed my arm and dragged me onto the front porch.

The blood rushed from my head and I felt my knees weaken, making me stumble. I glanced back at Mason, who looked just as terrified as I felt.

"You have the right to remain silent. Everything you say can and will be used against you in a court of law." Deputy Hoffstetter led me down the stairs. She couldn't have sounded any happier if someone had told her she'd won the Powerball lottery.

I gave her my attention, then gasped when I saw Joe standing at the bottom of my porch steps with his arms crossed over his chest, flanked by two other deputies, one of them being Deputy Miller. The feeling of utter betrayal brought tears to my eyes.

"You have the right to an attorney. If you cannot afford an attorney, one will be appointed for you."

"*Really, Joe?*" I demanded as I passed him. "You're letting her do this?"

He turned his back on me and walked toward one of three sheriff's cars. I'd wondered what it would be like if he ever really turned his back on me, but I'd never expected it to be this literal.

Mason caught up to us and grabbed my shoulders, spinning me around to face him. "Rose, don't say anything. Do you hear me? Not one goddamn word until I get you an attorney."

"But—"

He clapped his hand over my mouth. "Not one word." Tears filled his eyes. "*Promise me.*"

I nodded, fighting my growing panic. I was even more scared now than I'd been when I was dragged away last June on suspicion of murdering my mother. This time they really might put me away for life.

Mason pulled his hand away and kissed me before Deputy Hoffstetter slapped a pair of handcuffs on my wrists, securing them behind my back, and jerked me across the yard.

Mason followed, getting angrier by the second as a deputy I didn't recognize blocked his path.

Mason tried to get around him, pointing his finger at Deputy Hoffstetter. "If you're not more careful, *Deputy*, I'll have you brought up on abuse of power charges."

She dropped her hold on me and hooked her thumbs into her belt, flashing him a big toothy grin. "That's a mighty big threat for a mere citizen." To prove her point, she grabbed my arm and jerked me harder, shoving me toward a sheriff's car. Joe stood beside the open back door, his face rigid and emotionless.

"You condone this?" Mason shouted, getting around the deputy in his path. He rushed Joe and slammed him against the car. "*You're doing his dirty work now?*" He grabbed handfuls of Joe's coat and shoved him again. Deputy Miller and the other deputy grabbed Mason's arms and dragged him back, Mason fighting them with every step.

I started to sob. "Mason! Stop!" I couldn't let him get hurt or arrested.

Deputy Hoffstetter put her hand on my head with more force than necessary to push me into the car. Once I was inside, she leaned into the opening and laughed. "Not so high and mighty now, are you?"

"*Simmons!*" Mason shouted in disbelief. "Are you really going stand back and let your deputies use excessive force on her?" He lunged for me, but the deputies held onto him with a tight grip.

Joe stepped away from the car, rolling back his shoulders, and his eyes narrowed with contempt. "Keep it up, Deveraux, and you'll get your own cell in the county jail." Then he walked over to shut my door, refusing to look at me.

Deputy Hoffstetter slipped in behind the steering wheel and looked at me in the rearview mirror, hate glittering in her eyes. "I'm gonna have a whole lotta *fun* with you."

Things had just gotten a whole lot worse.

Thirty-Five and a Half Conspiracies
Coming November 2015

Acknowledgments

A s always, this book wouldn't be half as good as it is now if not for Angela Polidoro. She reads my first drafts and yet she still works with me. What more can I say? She's taught me so much in the nearly two years and countless books, novellas, and stories we've worked on together. I'm grateful she's still with me after dealing with my frantic and neurotic emails about plots, readers, and my protectiveness of my characters. I emailed her back in the summer of 2014—when I was working on *Picking up the Pieces*—and told her I was thinking about having Neely Kate miscarry. She understood my profound sadness over the decision and grieved for her too.

It's a real bonus when the professional working on your books doesn't just see them as a job, but loves them too. Then when you add a fantastic copy editor, it's pure magic. I'm so grateful to have found Shannon Page.

My children have become accustomed to my crazy life and crazy schedule, yet sometimes I miss things in their lives when I travel. I'm sorry, my babies. I'm sorry for the sacrifices you sometimes make so Mommy can follow her dream. I hope you know how much I love you, even when I'm not always with you. I hope one day you follow your own dreams even when other people tell you how crazy they are. I promise not to be one of those people. I'll be the one helping you figure out how to make it happen.

And finally, to my readers. You're the reason there's a seventh book in this series. A year and a half ago, I released the third book in this series with lackluster sales, and I stood at a crossroads. Did I continue or let the Rose Gardner books die? But you found Rose and you loved her nearly as much as I do, and together, we helped her live on. Thank you.

About the Author

New York Times and *USA Today* bestselling author Denise Grover Swank was born in Kansas City, Missouri and lived in the area until she was nineteen. Then she became a nomadic gypsy, living in five cities, four states and ten houses over the course of ten years before she moved back to her roots. She speaks English and smattering of Spanish and Chinese which she learned through an intensive Nick Jr. immersion period. Her hobbies include witty Facebook comments (in her own mind) and dancing in her kitchen with her children. (Quite badly if you believe her offspring.) Hidden talents include the gift of justification and the ability to drink massive amounts of caffeine and still fall asleep within two minutes. Her lack of the sense of smell allows her to perform many unspeakable tasks. She has six children and hasn't lost her sanity. Or so she leads you to believe.

You can find out more about Denise and her other books at www.denisegroverswank.com or you can email her at denisegroverswank@gmail.com

Don't miss out on Denise's newest releases! Join her mailing list: http://denisegroverswank.com/mailing-list/

19426027R00213

Made in the USA
Middletown, DE
19 April 2015